FICTION WITHOUT BORDERS

JONATHAN CAR

WHITE APPLES

0-765-30388-4 • $24.94/$34.95 Can.

"Carroll has the magic. He'll len
and you'll never see the world i
same way ever again." —Neil Gaiman

TED CHIANG

STORIES OF YOUR LIFE AND OTHERS

0-765-30418-X • $24.95/$34.95 Can.

★"Here is the first must-read SF book of the year .... Chiang's stories are audacious, challenging and moving." —*Publishers Weekly*

JOHN CLUTE

APPLESEED

0-765-30378-7 • $25.95/$35.95 Can.

"*Appleseed* thoroughly engages the intellect and imagination. Clute keeps bursting through the confines of space opera, heading someplace different." —*Locus*

LISA GOLDSTEIN

THE ALCHEMIST'S DOOR

0-765-30150-4 • $23.95/$33.95 Can.

"*The Alchemist's Door* gives [Goldstein] the opportunity to play with both history and myth, and the result is an exciting and wise novel." —*San Francisco Chronicle*

PATRICK O'LEARY

THE IMPOSSIBLE BIRD

0-765-30337-X • $25.95/$35.95 Can.

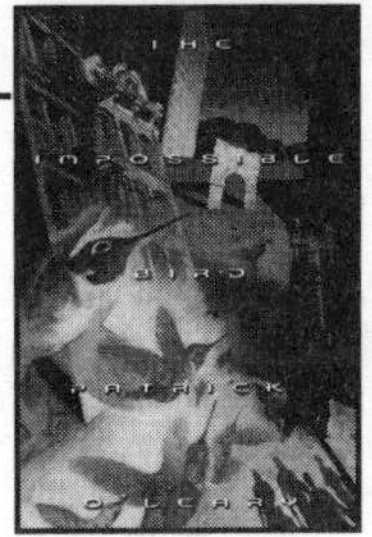

"Should appeal to fans of Vonnegut, Neil Gaiman, and Philip K. Dick .... O'Leary continues to develop as a remarkable writer." —Sfrevu.com

COMING UP IN THE SPRING

Conjunctions:40

40x40

Edited by Bradford Morrow

To celebrate *Conjunctions'* fortieth issue, we're gathering fiction, poetry, plays, and creative essays by forty of our favorite contemporary writers. This volume will feature excerpts of novels-in-progress from authors including Richard Powers, Howard Norman, Paul Auster, and Lois-Ann Yamanaka. Also featured will be China's foremost innovative fiction writer, Can Xue, who contributes a surreal novella, "Heli," in which a boy falls in love with a girl who lives entrapped in a glass cabinet from which he must free her. Short fiction by writers such as Rikki Ducornet, William T. Vollmann, and Diane Williams appears, in addition to a harrowing story by Christopher Sorrentino called "Condition," based on historical events from the 1970s, in which he charts the psychological disintegration of a female newscaster who, on her last day alive, methodically plots her suicide on live TV. The issue will also feature creative nonfiction by David Shields and Eliot Weinberger, and poetry by Cole Swensen, Martine Bellen, John Ashbery, Lyn Hejinian, Brenda Coultas, and a visual poem by Tan Lin. Rounding out this diverse celebration of contemporary work will be a previously unpublished play by Joyce Carol Oates specially commissioned for the issue, and a color narrative portfolio of new work by Russian émigré artist Ilya Kabakov.

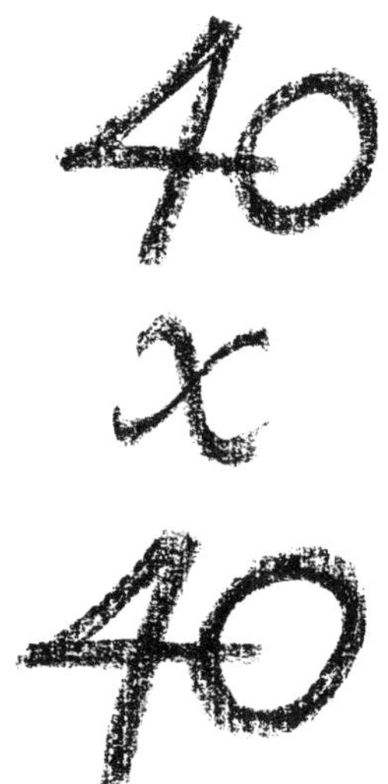

CONJUNCTIONS

Bi-Annual Volumes of New Writing

Edited by
Bradford Morrow

published by Bard College

CONJUNCTIONS is published in the Spring and Fall of each year by Bard College, Annandale-on-Hudson, NY 12504. This issue is made possible in part with the generous funding of the National Endowment for the Arts, and with public funds from the New York State Council on the Arts, a State Agency.

SUBSCRIPTIONS: Send subscription orders to CONJUNCTIONS, Bard College, Annandale-on-Hudson, NY 12504. Single year (two volumes): $18.00 for individuals; $25.00 for institutions and overseas. Two years (four volumes): $32.00 for individuals; $45.00 for institutions and overseas. Patron subscription (lifetime): $500.00. Overseas subscribers please make payment by International Money Order. For information about subscriptions, back issues, and advertising, call Michael Bergstein at (845) 758-1539 or fax (845) 758-2660.

All editorial communications should be sent to Bradford Morrow, *Conjunctions,* 21 East 10th Street, New York, NY 10003. Unsolicited manuscripts cannot be returned unless accompanied by a stamped, self-addressed envelope.

Conjunctions is listed and indexed in the American Humanities Index.

Visit the *Conjunctions* Web site at www.conjunctions.com.

Original cover art by Gahan Wilson. Cover design by Jerry Kelly.

Available through D.A.P./Distributed Art Publishers, Inc., 155 Sixth Avenue, New York, NY 10013. Telephone: (212) 627-1999. Fax: (212) 627-9484.

Printers: Edwards Brothers

Typesetter: Bill White, Typeworks

ISSN 0278-2324
ISBN 0-941964-55-8

Manufactured in the United States of America.

TABLE OF CONTENTS

THE NEW WAVE FABULISTS

Guest-Edited by Peter Straub
Illustrated by Gahan Wilson

GUEST EDITOR'S NOTE

WHO ARE THESE PEOPLE, and what are they doing in *Conjunctions?* Jonathan Lethem won the National Book Critic's Circle Award for *Motherless Brooklyn,* and Harold Bloom put John Crowley's *Little, Big* on his list of 100 Best Books of the Twentieth Century, but aren't Gene Wolfe and Joe Haldeman science fiction writers? And didn't Neil Gaiman become well known with a series of, um, graphic novels, the street or gutter phrase for which is *comic books?*

Yes, they are, and he did, and the author of these words is, even worse, a conspicuously popular horror writer. Should you have a reflexive disdain for anything connected to genre fiction, as you very well may, issue number 39 of *Conjunctions* is going to represent, at least initially, something of an unwelcome aberration in the history of an otherwise honorable literary journal. Those who have just nodded in assent should turn immediately to the back of the book and read the critical essays by Gary K. Wolfe and John Clute, which ought to persuade even the faintest of hearts to persevere. Clute and Wolfe know what they are talking about, far better than I, and my conversations with them over the past few years—conversations that began at the 1998 International Conference for the Fantastic in the Arts in Ft. Lauderdale—have helped me understand the phenomenon this collection is designed to illustrate.

It would be easy but misleading to account for this in evolutionary terms. That is, it is not really accurate to say that over the past two decades the genres of science fiction, fantasy, and horror have been, unnoticed by the wider literary culture, transforming themselves generation by generation and through the work of each generation's most adventurous practitioners into something all but unrecognizable, hence barely classifiable at all except as literature. Even evolution doesn't work that way. The above process did take place, and it was completely overlooked by the wider literary culture but it did not happen smoothly, and the kind of posttransformation fictions represented here owe more than half of their DNA and much of their underlying musculature to their original genre sources. Contemporary, more faithful versions of those sources are to be found all over the place, especially in movie theaters and the genre shelves at

Barnes & Noble. Gene Wolfe, who is necessary to this volume, was producing fiction of immense, Nabokovian rigor and complexity thirty years ago, alongside plenty of colleagues who were satisfied to work within the genre's familiar templates. Now, writers like Nalo Hopkinson, John Kessel, and Patrick O'Leary, for all of whom Gene Wolfe is likely to be what Gary K. Wolfe calls a "touchstone," are still publishing shorter fiction in magazines like *Asimov's* and *Fantasy and Science Fiction*, and so is Kelly Link. (Jonathan Carroll, Jonathan Lethem, Elizabeth Hand, John Crowley, and China Miéville seldom write short fiction, and we are fortunate to have stories from them.) Strictly on grounds of artistic achievement, these writers should all along have been welcome in thoughtful literary outlets.

Some who could easily be included here are not, among them Terry Bisson, Ted Chiang, Tom Disch, Geoff Ryman, Ray Vukovich, Jeffrey Ford, Jeff Vandemeer, Graham Joyce, Kit Reed, and Carol Emshwiller. I regret their absence. Had I approached this literary territory from the other side, I would have included Mark Chabon, Dan Chaon, and Stewart O'Nan: the latter two, especially, approach horror from the inside out, with the understanding that it is above all a point of view.

For remarkably mature examples of that particular point of view, which has literally no points in common with the genre's conventional definitions, see M. John Harrison's "Entertaining Angels Unawares" and John Crowley's limpid, devastating "The Girlhood of Shakespeare's Heroines." These two stories give us an Angel of Death and a gracious Lucifer, and in them the world is spun helplessly toward disorder, loss, uncertainty, and grief—horror being the literature that, as if under a sacred charge, most urgently honors the brute fact of these conditions—while the stories themselves both suggest and preserve a profound internal mystery.

I am grateful for Bradford Morrow's suggestion that I guest edit an issue of his journal, of which I have long been a friend and supporter. Brad's trust in this project, never in question, deepened as we went along, as did my appreciation of the dazzlingly efficient *Conjunctions* team, Michael Bergstein, Martine Bellen, Pat Sims, and Bill White. With a crew like that, Roebling could have put up the Brooklyn Bridge in a matter of weeks.

—Peter Straub
August 6, 2002
New York City

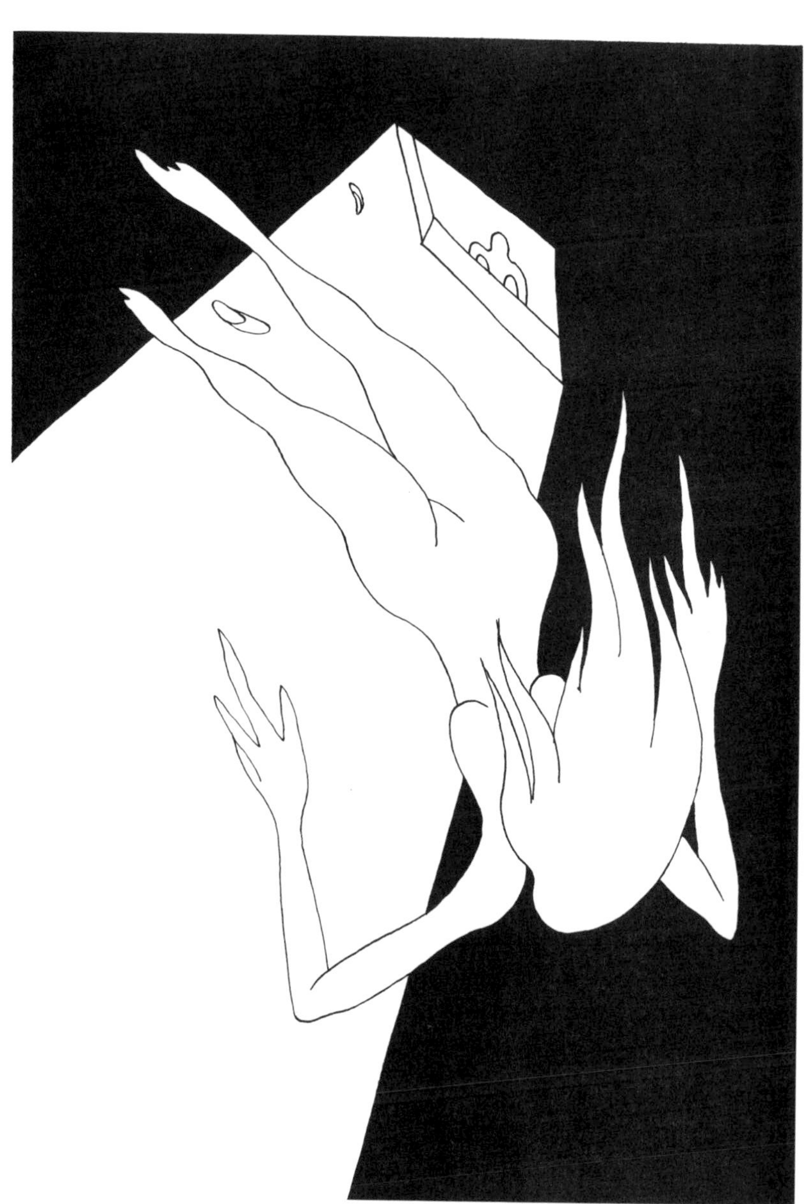

The Girlhood of Shakespeare's Heroines

John Crowley

In the late 1950s the state of Indiana had its own Shakespeare festival, though not much of the world knew about it. Far too little of the world, as it happened, to keep it in existence. But for a few summers it was there, a little Brigadoonish, or like the great Globe itself, that leaves not a trace behind.

That was a time for Shakespeare festivals. One had recently begun in Stratford, Ontario, directed at first by the great impresario Tyrone Guthrie. I used to pore over the pictures in my *Theater Arts* magazine (I was surely one of the few boys my age who had a subscription; who *asked* for a subscription for Christmas). It had begun as simply a big striped tent, then became a tentlike building; it had a clever all-purpose stage set on which Roman and Venetian and English plays could all be accommodated. The man who got the idea for a Shakespeare festival in this little town was a disabled war veteran, who liked the fact that his hometown was named for Shakespeare's. There was a picture of him, shy and good-looking, leaning on his cane.

Stratford, Connecticut, had a Shakespeare festival too, about as far from Indiana, where Harriet Ingram and I both lived, as Stratford, Ontario. On a summer trip to the sea—from which long ago her mother had been taken away by her father to sealess Indiana—Harriet wangled a visit to the Connecticut Stratford. While her family picnicked on the great lawn waiting for the matinee to begin, Harriet walked up and entered the cool dark of the theater, whose smell is one of the few she can recall today from that time; she passed around a velvet rope and down into the empty auditorium. On stage an actor read lines to himself under a single rehearsal light hanging over the stage. Harriet walked down closer and closer, seeing up into the flies and inhaling the charged air, when the floor beneath her vanished and she fell into darkness.

The trap was only six or eight feet deep, and Harriet claimed to be all right, but the actor, who had heard her tumble down, made her lie still till help could be called; they got her out and took her backstage and bound up a nice long gash on her leg with yards of gauze, and she was made to call the theater's doctor on the phone, who put her through a series of movements to find out if any bones were broken. Then the young actor who had rescued her took her all over the theater, into the dressing rooms and the scene shop and the rehearsal rooms. When her mother finally found her, she was talking Shakespeare with her new friend and some others, like Jesus among the doctors, with probably something of a religious glow about her too.

Indiana had no town named Stratford, but there was one named Avon, an almost quaint little Brown County town through which a small river ran, where swans could be induced to reside. Not far from the town, a utopian sect had once owned several hundred acres of farmland, where they began building an ideal community before dying out or moving West; what remained of their community was a cheerless brick dormitory, a wooden meeting house, and a huge limestone and oak-frame circular barn: circular because of the founder's scientific dairying theories, and circular because of his belief in the circle's perfection. The barn was over a hundred feet in diameter, and lit like a church by a clerestory and a central windowed turret; when an ad hoc preservation committee first went in, in 1955, it still smelled faintly of hay and dung. It was as sound as a Greek temple, though the roof was just beginning to leak.

So History wanted the place preserved; and Commerce wanted it to turn a profit and bring custom into the town; and Culture wanted whatever it was used for to be not vulgar or debased. A young man who had grown up in a big house nearby, who had made money in New York and then come home, conceived the festival plan. His money and enthusiasm brought in more, some of it, as we would learn, from unlikely places; and the process began that would turn the great round barn into an Elizabethan theater. Among the methods the organizers used to publicize, and partly to underwrite, the Avon festival was to offer a number of apprentice positions to Indiana high-school students: these were a little more costly to the chosen students than a good summer camp would have been—I think there were scholarships for some—and provided the festival with some enthusiastic labor. When Harriet, that year a junior, heard about the program she felt a tremendous grateful relief, to learn that the world was not after all empty of such a possibility; and at the same time an awful anxiety, that this one would escape from her before she could secure it for herself.

Harriet's mother used to explain Harriet by saying that she was stagestruck, but that wasn't so, and Harriet resented the silliness of the epithet; she connected it with a girlish longing for Broadway and stardom, glamour, her name in lights—Harriet's ambitions were at once more private and more extravagant. When one of her parents' friends asked her what she wanted to be when she grew up—she was about thirteen—Harriet answered that she wanted to be a trage*dee*an.

Harriet and I grew up on different sides of the state. Her parents taught (history and economics) at a little Quaker college in Richmond, in the east; my father was a lawyer in Williamsport. The Williamsport house was a big square Italianate place, almost a mansion, built by my mother's grandfather, who had been lieutenant governor of the state and ambassador to Peru under Grant. A ten-foot ormolu mirror in the front hall came from Peru.

Harriet went to a smelly old public school—Garfield High—and after classes she took dance lessons and on weekends she rode horses; and she read, in that deep and obsessive way, with that high tolerance for boredom, that is (it seems to me) gone from the world: read books about Isadora Duncan and Mae West, read Shaw and Milton's *Comus* and the plays of Byron and Feydeau and Wilde's *Salome.* And Shakespeare: carrying the family's *Complete Works* around with her, its spine cracking and its fore-edge grimy from her fingers. She read the major plays, of course, though to this day she hasn't read *Lear,* but mostly she turned to the odd numbers, *Cymbeline* and *Measure for Measure* and *Troilus and Cressida.* She keeps surprising me with the odd things she read then and still remembers. I went to a little private school my family had an interest in, and spent a year home-schooled (as they call it now) because of my asthma, mostly better now. So we were both smart, sheltered, isolated kids, she isolated by being an only child, I surrounded by four sisters and a brother but miles from anything and dreaming about Theater, or Theatre, as I much preferred to spell it.

Mine was a kind of megalomania not so unusual in a kid with my statistics, so to speak: dreams of dominance and glory. Most of my ambitions, and most of my knowledge, came out of books; just like Harriet, I'd never seen many plays, though I tried to see as many as I could reach. They all seemed comically inadequate to me, shaming even; I bit my nails to the quick and squirmed in my seat till my mother took my shoulder to hush me.

I didn't quite understand then that the theater work I dreamed about mostly dated to a time thirty or forty years before, when the town library acquired the albums and monographs in the Theater section that I pored over. I was studying Max Rheinhardt's vast productions in Weimar Germany, the stage designs of Gordon Craig (he was Isadora Duncan's lover). Once, I found in that library a book about how to build your own Greek theater and put on pageants. I tried to convince my mother that a Greek theater like this would be perfect in our broad backyard, over in front of the tall poplars (the drawings in my books were full of poplars) and look, you could buy these Ionic columns from any building supply house for ten dollars. The book, however (my mother showed me, laughing) had been published in 1912.

Harriet thought that was a sweet story. I told it to her in Avon, that summer we were both apprentices there, the summer that changed everything. We were sitting by the campfire the apprentices made most nights, far enough away not to be grilled, near enough so the smoke discouraged the mosquitoes. She listened and laughed and then told me about falling into the open trap in Stratford, Connecticut. By the end of her story everybody was listening.

It seemed then that Harriet had a better chance than I did of going on the way we were both headed. My visions all needed pots of money to realize, and the cooperation of many others, and the kind of tyrannical will and willingness to be boss that it would turn out I had none of. But everything Harriet needed came right out of Harriet; all she had to do was bring forth more, and there was more—that was clear. I knew it even then.

It's the middle of June in Harriet's thirty-eighth year, a brilliant day of high barometric pressure. Harriet gets up early to take her camera out and make some pictures.

The camera is a huge eight-by-ten plate camera of polished wood, cherry and ebony, with brass fittings and a leather bellows. Harriet thinks it's the most beautiful and affecting object she owns; with its tripod of telescoping legs, also wood and brass, and its great glass eye, it seems to Harriet to be more a relative than a belonging, a gaunt beloved aunt, an invalid but still merry husband. *Did you ever ever ever in your long-legged life* (Harriet sings) *see a three-legged sailor and his four-legged wife.*

Harriet has been using not film in the camera but paper, ordinary panchromatic printing paper. When exposed, the paper becomes a negative, and it can be printed by contact with another sheet. The resulting image is exact and exquisitely detailed but softened and abstracted—both warmed and cooled—by the light's passing through a textured paper negative rather than through a transparent plastic one. The very first photographic negatives were made on paper.

So by the yellow safelight in her bathroom Harriet on this morning removes from their box six sheets of paper, and slips them into her three plate-holders, front and back: six exposures, the most she would ever make on a single trip, even on such a day as this one. She slides each black Bakelite slide back over the face of the paper and locks them up, safe in total darkness till their moment of day has come.

Dismantled and shut up, the camera fits in the back of the Rabbit, though it takes Harriet three trips to bring it and its tripod and the bag of plate-holders out to the car. Harriet goes out of town early, driving up from the river into the old and largely abandoned farmlands above: hillside fields bordered by woods are what she likes to photograph when the slanting sunlight seems to set fire to the tall sedges' heads and the shade is deep; another thing is dirt roads lined with old maples, the sun picking certain masses of leaves to illuminate like stained glass and the sun falling in tigerish stripes over the road's arched back.

Once Harriet and I were talking about what we would most like to have been if we weren't what we are. I said—I forget what I said, but Harriet said she had always thought it would be impossible to be a landscape painter and be unhappy; unhappy in your work anyway. She still believes it's so, but only if you are better at it than she was or could expect ever to be. For a while when she was younger she did paint, and it made her not happy at all to work all day and then next day look at what you had done, which claimed to be what you had seen and felt but wasn't at all. The opposite of happy. But these photographs don't disappoint that way. The happiness they give is a little pale and fleeting—half an hour to set up the camera and make an exposure (hurry, hurry, the earth's turning, the light's changing) and an hour or two to make a true print: but it's real happiness. Since they're made from paper negatives rather than film, they seem to Harriet not to have that look of being stolen from the world rather than made from it that most landscape photographs have; they are shyer and more tentative somehow. Not painting, no, but satisfying in some of the same ways. And she says they are selling pretty well in her shop too.

By nine the sun has stopped making the effects that Harriet likes;

she's made four exposures. She's more weary than she expected to be, getting in and out of the car, dealing with the camera's three legs, and her own four. The tripod lies on the backseat, her two steel crutches (enameled maroon) on top of it.

Coming back into town, Harriet's car pulls up next to mine at a stoplight. She calls over to me:

"Did you hear the news?"

"What news?"

"Somebody killed the pope. I just heard on the radio."

"Yes. I heard that. But he's not dead. He's just hurt."

"Oh." She glances at the red light and scoots over in the seat to see me a little better. "I've been thinking about your question," she says. "I have."

"And?"

"And I have," she calls. "I have."

The month before, heart-turning June, I asked Harriet to marry me. She hasn't answered. The light changes, and we turn in different directions.

Those of us chosen for the Indiana Shakespeare Festival at Avon (it included almost all of those who applied that year, being a summer option unthinkable to most people in that state then or now) received a letter that showed a bust of plump Shakespeare pen in hand—an etching of the monument over his grave in Stratford, I can see now—and instructions on what we were to bring that sounded like any summer camp's: raincoat and sweater, blanket and sneakers and writing materials for letters home. I watched my mother sew tapes with my name on them into every pair of shorts and socks.

We came from around the state by car or bus, pulling into town on the appointed day uncertain where anything was or how to get to the theater or the place we were to go, only to find that the town was so small that it was evident where everyone was gathered, on the little green by the riverside, where a Union soldier stood on a small granite plinth, the names of the town's dead carved on it.

She's almost the only one I can now remember seeing when we arrived, though I know she wasn't the one I looked at most, or took the greatest interest in. No. Harriet had her own way of dressing and looking, and it didn't fit with my received images of what I wanted to look at. The tough girls from northern Indiana, "the Region," favored beehive haircuts, mascara like kohl around their eyes, and pale lipstick; the country girls had blonde flips and wore bobby socks over the stockings they'd put on for the trip. Harriet wore loose peasant blouses, and wide skirts in many colors, and flat shoes or sandals without backs; her haystack hair kept her busy pushing it from her face, and she drew strange orangey eyebrows over her own, above the cat's-eye pink glasses. Her cheeks were flushed; I didn't know if that was makeup or not. She moved with overprecise grace, the studied manner of a dancer, though I didn't recognize that either. She was herself. She was a free spirit.

"Hi."

"Hi."

"Where've you come from?"

"Williamsport."

"Uh . . . ?"

"Near—"

"Oh right. Hi."

"Hi."

Why would she greet me? I didn't think of myself as particularly visible to others then, or possessing anything that would attract their attention; I don't remember my own clothes, but I'm sure they weren't designed to impress, as I wouldn't have known how to do that. I suppose *shy* is the obvious word, though like many shy people I only needed the right signs of acceptance and welcome—however I understood them—to offer myself more completely than the glad-handers.

By afternoon we were all gathered in the center of town, with our clumsy bags and suitcases—backpacks weren't common then; I remember Harriet had a couple of cases with poodles appliquéd on them, one of them round, like a pillbox. The festival director was to put in an appearance, and Robin, who would be directing the plays and managing the apprentices, was to welcome us and give instructions, but no one had seen either of them. Parents who'd brought their kids stood with them by their station wagons, the kids eager to slip away. We were about twenty in all, some of us full-grown, some still children. I don't remember perceiving that but it must be so.

Then—making an entrance, at which he was skilled—Robin was among us, going from one to another with a look on his face as though he had just discovered astonishing and unsuspected treasure. *Oh brave new world, that has such people in it!* He was particularly attentive to the parents. Sandy, his wife, was with him, doing as he did but at the same time watching his performance appreciatively. They were the most beautiful people I'd ever stood near. Sandy with the collar of her soft white shirt up, her hands in the pockets of her capris, looked to me like Kim Novak: the same gray hooded eyes, the same softness; like Novak she would wear, sometimes, no bra. Robin was lean and hawklike with piercing eyes and deeply incised cheeks. They were both remarkably small—not small at all, really, but remarkably so for the persons they were, for the size of the persons they projected.

We apprentices were housed in a nearby summer camp that hadn't been used for a year, the cabins dusty and the mattresses musty; I can still smell them sometimes. An assistant stage manager and his wife were our counselors or chaperones. There was an old bus that each morning drove the twenty of us the five miles to the Swan—that's what they called their theater, their barn-becoming-a-theater—and back again at day's end to the camp, where we were fed huge dinners of children's food, tuna casseroles and spaghetti and Spam. The kitchen help made leftovers into sandwiches and gave them to us in boxes for lunch.

All day we worked in the Swan, cleaning and painting and building seating. That's what we were there for, free labor, but we didn't mind that, there was nothing we wouldn't do, and anyone who complained or refused immediately had his place taken by a volunteer. I'd never played sports unless dragooned into them, as at school; had never made the team or been to camp or done any group task at all—none except the pageants and plays I organized my siblings into—and I had a near-mystical experience being included in this gang. All the same I would often find ways to escape them, sneak out of the horseplay, hide. It wasn't hard. The funny fat little bus that carried us to and fro went through the town center as well, to pick up the actors and others who were staying in tourist homes or with proud citizens, and I would take it into town and sit on the Methodist Church steps, or go into the cool book-odorous little library, or just stand in the street feeling this nameless, wondrous feeling that inhabited me, that was freedom, or something even better. Somehow without my even asking I had been passed through the membrane of common reality into another space, where things were not as they were where I came from; where Shakespeare was important, and everything else less so, and what I knew about mattered, and what I didn't know about was inconsequential, and it was midsummer.

I've always had difficulty associating with actors, and these actors (most of them wanted to be actors) were just embarking on their careers of self-display; there were sullen James Dean and Brando imitators smoking in silence and reading Rimbaud and Kerouac; there were extravagant hearts-on-their-sleeves personalities who had found out that by defining themselves as actors they could pretend to be only pretending to be the people they actually were, and get away with it; there were the narcissists-in-training, both the secret and the patent kind, jealous of their self-assigned centrality. The dramas they improvised all summer were amazing and repellent to me; I saw more tears, male and female, than anywhere else in the whole of that decade. I'm given to nervous laughter, not the best response.

Harriet was different; she seemed at once avid for the blowups and collisions the others created and gently mocking of them—with me, whom she chose to take part in her study of them. I didn't know why.

Harriet was different. Harriet would seek me out at the campfires, take cigarettes from my pack (that was how I was becoming an adult), and let me light them, and then almost immediately discard them into the fire. Harriet called me *dear boy* because an aged, absurdly courtly actor in the company called every male that. Harriet would get up late each morning, sail out past the surly woman handing out the box lunches, skip onto the bus with a smile back at me. Sometimes I caught her looking at me in the rearview mirror of the bus, too. I didn't know why. I don't know why. But I looked frankly back at her in that mirror, and not away; and maybe that was enough.

At the end of a workday soon after we got there, Robin called us together from our jobs and herded us out to the field—it had once been farmyard and was to be the parking lot when the heavy equipment arrived, if it ever did—to the enormous oak that grew all alone there: an oak just like Stratford's, we'd all been told, and warned to carve no initials in it.

By the oak, Robin was hunkered down next to someone we'd never seen before, who sat hands on his knees in a chair that had been brought out for him from the dormitory building where the festival's offices were, or would be. The man wore a seersucker suit and a pale bow tie, the only tie in evidence there, the only jacket too. Beside his chair an old belted leather briefcase sat drooping like a weary dog.

When all of us had gathered (a few late arrivals wandering from faraway parts of the grounds), Robin stood, dusted his hands on the back of his pants, and looked us over. We apprentices were immediately silent. The actors, some at least, immune to his authority or his portrayal of authority, went on talking until Robin at last hushed them with raised hands. Then he paused before he spoke.

"I've asked you to come out and meet a man who has been very important to the progress of this festival theater," he said, "someone without whose help there would very likely be no season this year." He looked down at the man in the chair, who was smiling at once eagerly and apologetically. "It's a great honor to have him here today, he's come a very long way to be here, to see the progress we've made, and he's asked for a little time today to talk to you about something very important, something you may not have thought about."

Then he held out his hand to the man, and said his name, which I have never been able to remember; nor do I recognize it now among the names of those who were of his party, or shared his beliefs, though surely it is there amid all their privately printed publications and pamphlets and books. We applauded politely, and he held up a hand to us but didn't rise. He was an academic-looking man, long-necked and pale, with ginger hair so long and fine it floated in the faint breezes that came and went as he spoke.

"Oh now thank you, Robin," he said, in the warmest and kindest sort of voice, one of those voices so unassuming and good that you almost have to smile in response to it, even before it says anything of consequence. "I won't take up very much of your time at all, I promise, I know how little you have in order to be ready, and I don't want Robin angry at me. But I thought I might bring up something for you to think about in the weeks ahead as you work and study here."

I suppose it was his not standing that made us, or me, study him a little more closely. He wore wing-tip brown shoes that seemed as though they had never been walked in, and around the middle of each, like a stirrup, a band of metal went, and up beneath the cuffs of his wrinkled pants. And in the grass behind his chair a pair of canes. I've thought of those canes, since then, and those braces. I've wished I could ask about them. There are things in your past, preserved in memory almost by chance, that only later on, because of the course your own life takes, come to seem proleptic, or significant, when other things don't.

"All of you," he began, "boys and girls, men and women, are so wonderfully fortunate to be here, in this beautiful place, immersed all day long in the works of the greatest author who ever wrote in

English. I envy you very much. I wonder though how many of you have ever given thought to just who the man was who wrote these wise and witty and passionate works. Who was he? Well, we can look at that picture that accompanied the First Folio, the first complete printing of a number of plays ascribed to this fellow, and try to learn something of him, but we can't learn much, and in fact that picture doesn't actually seem to be a picture of anyone, does it? There's something wholly unreal about it, I think, that gets more unreal the longer you look. In the book a little poem is printed opposite the picture that says it's him to the life, exactly as he lived, but the picture's so odd that you wonder if the poem is a joke, an 'in' joke maybe. And in the end the poem tells us to 'look not on his picture, but his book.' Which takes us back where we started.

"Well, then, we might consult the histories, and look for the contemporary accounts of his life, how he lived, how he struck his friends and admirers, what he said. And of course there is next to nothing. Of the man credited with having written this vast body of deathless writing, we know very, very little. There is not a single letter from him in existence. We know that a man of his name was listed as an actor in the company that produced the plays; we have a few shaky signatures on a few legal documents; we know that the actor retired to Stratford, where he came from, and sued a few people and signed a will and died. That's about it. In his will there is no mention of plays or manuscripts, indeed no mention of books at all; perhaps he had none. He certainly was unconcerned with his own writings."

He pulled a large handkerchief from his pocket and wiped his face. From where I stood beneath the oak, I could see Harriet sitting on the ground near the speaker, elbows on her knees and her cheeks on her fists like a gargoyle, fascinated or seeming to be.

"Very well then," he said. "Suppose we confess that we know just about nothing that we would like to know about the author of these poems and plays, not a thing at all about the mind or opinions of the actor whose name was the same or similar to the author's—I say 'similar' because on none of the documents we have is his name spelled as it's spelled on the First Folio.

"We have to turn around, then, I think, and see if within the works themselves we can learn something of the man who wrote them. Most of them, of course, are plays, and not personal opinions or lyric self-expression, but not all; there's a large body of personal, very personal, writing, the Sonnets, and even in the plays the mind of the man comes through in the allusions he makes, the things he seems to know about and uses for poetic comparison and so on. And what appears when we study the work with this in mind?

"Well, I've made a list," he said, and grinned somewhat self-deprecatingly. "I'm not the first to have made one, and I think that many of you may have a mental list of your own, a list of what you think the man was like." He flapped open the briefcase and after a brief search pulled out some typewritten sheets.

"First of all, he was apparently a man." He looked up, and we laughed dutifully.

"He seems to have had a classical education." He consulted his paper, though it was evident he had no need to. "All his writing is full of allusions to the Greek and Latin classics. He seems to have been very familiar with Italy, with certain other European places, such as Navarre in France. He also read Italian: some of the plays are based on Italian stories that had not been translated when he wrote. What else? Well, the Sonnets picture a man who was at one time poor, in disgrace, in exile. I say exile because Sonnets which complain of his separation from his beloved make it sound so enforced. 'When in disgrace with fortune and men's eyes,' he says, 'I all alone beweep my outcast state.'"

He looked up at us. "He says, not once but several times in the Sonnets, that he's lame," he said. "Interesting. 'I, made lame by Fortune's dearest spite.' Could that be a metaphorical lameness? Well, maybe; but he says it more than once. 'Speak of my lameness, and I straight will halt,' meaning stumble.

"So.

"A few more things. His knowledge of the law is so extensive, and his use of legal terms in all sorts of situations so constant, that it's hard to believe he wasn't trained for the law. And another thing we can guess at, that some critics are more certain of than others. The Sonnets suggest that at least some time in his life he was what the learned of the time described as *paiderastes,* or in our modern language, a sexual invert."

He folded up his paper then and put it away with care, as though to give us time to ponder all this, which we did, I did anyway. I was beginning to feel very odd, as though a trick or a trap were being constructed for me, a *gin* Will would say, and that the man's self-effacement and reasonableness and sweetness were part of it.

"So." He removed his jacket, still without standing, and there were dark sweat-circles under his arms. "What if you were to suppose that you *didn't* know the name of the man who wrote these plays. Suppose you knew *when* they were written, and knew a lot about the people living in England then, and any one of them could have been the author, and not just the one actor fellow with the similar name. Who would you suspect? How would you narrow the search? Where, if you were a detective or a private eye, would you turn your magnifying glass, or your flashlight?

"Well you probably already know, or many of you do, certainly Robin here knows, that this search has in fact been going on for a very long time, ever since people began to suspect that the man Shakespear, or Shaxper, or Shagsberd, made a very poor match with the writings.

"If the author was someone else, he kept his identity secret. That's all we know to start with. He kept his identity secret, and must have had a reason. Well. I can tell you some of the people who have been suspected at one time or another, who various detectives have guessed might fit the particulars we worked out, and other ones, too.

"There are educated poets, like Christopher Marlowe and Edward Dyer. Now Marlowe was certainly a pederast. Of course Marlowe was murdered before the Shakespeare plays began to appear, but, well, maybe he wasn't really. There's the Earl of Oxford, who loved plays and players but maybe wouldn't have wanted to associate himself with the common theater. Unfortunately he died before several of the greatest plays were written. One candidate isn't even a man: someone's claimed that Queen Elizabeth herself was the author."

He paused a moment, waiting for us to join him in marveling at this. Then he wiped his face again. There is nowhere hotter than Indiana on a July afternoon.

"There is one name, though," he said, "that has been consistently proposed by students for nearly a hundred years as the most likely. He was an educated man, a man who was familiar with the courts and the nobility, trained as a lawyer, a major character in the political realm who may well have had reasons for keeping his playwriting a secret. He may have left his signature in the writings, because he was interested in codes and ciphers, and made up his own. He was certainly *paiderastes;* that's well attested. His name was Francis Bacon."

There was a sort of movement among us then, as the name went around, some nodding or crossing their arms or grinning, perhaps because they agreed, or because it was the name they expected to hear, or *not* the one they expected to hear, or simply in acknowledgment that the little speech had reached a climax.

He went on to lay out, I'm sure, the Baconian case that day, and I could recreate it as I've recreated his speech to us; I don't remember it in detail. But I remember what he said at the end.

"I haven't come here to make a convert of anyone," he said. "I'm just fortunate to've been able to help get this wonderful project under way, and these plays produced here, no matter whose name is attached to them. Or why they're here rather than someplace else."

He reached behind him, groping to find the canes in the grass where he had dropped them, and Robin quickly got them and handed them to him. He stood, and we watched him accomplish it.

"Please remember this, though," he said. "Remember that nothing needs to be the way you've always thought it has to be. Even if everyone with the power to say so insists it must. Francis Bacon said *The monuments of wit survive the monuments of power.* Well I think that in his case it's true. The monuments of his wit have survived under another's name, where he hid them himself from the machinations of power. I believe that's so. I don't ask you to do so. I just want to wish you all the very best of luck in this coming season."

He seemed to have moved himself; we were all very quiet, sensing that, and maybe he sensed our stillness. Anyway he laughed, and put out his left hand to Robin, who took it with his right, and we all applauded, rather wildly actually, the whole thing had been so startling and unexpected, and here was the end of it; and then we dispersed.

I knew that this controversy existed, of course; it was the kind of thing I would read about in my mother's *Saturday Review* or see on *Odyssey* on Sunday morning television. I thought Bacon was the old-fashioned choice, and had been passed over in favor of some more convincing others. I didn't really care. I was as interested in these theories as I was in flying saucers, or the guilt of the Rosenbergs, or the miracles at Lourdes. I thought the world was one way, and it was obvious what that way was, and people who struggled to alter it had reasons particular to them, a kind of sublime dissatisfaction that had nothing to do with what is in fact the case. I still think so, most of the time. Between the enthusiasts and the hardheads who dismiss them, I love the enthusiasts and stand with the hardheads. I don't think Harriet likes this about me, all in all. She thinks that nothing needs to be the way that power insists it is. It's part of being a free spirit.

The next day we found screwed into the wood of the Stratford Oak a small and elegant brass plaque.

Placed in Memory of the British Polymath and Genius
Francis Bacon
And in honor of his deathless contributions to our literature & language
July 10, 1959
The Monuments of Wit Survive the Monuments of Power

"But it's ridiculous," Harriet said to me. We walked together from the oak to the theater. "You can't go around talking about *bacon*. 'I've got to study my bacon. So much wisdom can be found in bacon. We can all get smarter by reading bacon. Oops I've misplaced my bacon.' I mean come on."

"'Shakespeare' is a kind of odd name," I said. "It's just that we're used to it."

Harriet looked at me in contempt. "It's a beautiful name," she said. "Maybe the best name ever. The best."

We trudged along, raising dust. In my crowded family the way to go on from here would be to insist on opposition, take a position, tease and deride, all to keep up the connection, maybe even win a victory, of wit or force if not of reason. I knew better not to now. But not what I might do instead, or otherwise.

"What are you doing today?" I asked at last.

"Making armor," she said.

Maybe it was because the company was just beginning, was mostly young and fleet but not so impressive in stature, or maybe it was just that all the available money was going into the theater and the road out to it and the parking lots and offices: but the first production of the Indiana Shakespeare Festival was minimal, radically minimal for the times, and was meant to appear so: that was Robin's conception.

The play was *Henry V.* The company, divided into French and English, were to be dressed only in jeans and sweatshirts, rehearsal clothes; but those of the French were white, and the English dark blue. Their banners were too, just plain rectangles on poles. The play would begin with the Chorus, alone, sitting on the apron of the stage, also in rehearsal clothes of black, with the script in his hands. He was, in effect, the director of the play, and his anxiety about its effectiveness was the director's.

> *But pardon, gentles all,*
> *The flat unraiséd spirits that have dared*
> *On this unworthy scaffold to bring forth*
> *So great an object . . .*

There would be a big wooden box on stage, and from it the actors would take out the "four or five most vile and ragged foils," a mismatched collection of prop sabers and swords, as well as pieces of buckram armor for the nobles. There were four kids recruited from the high school band, two trumpets, a French horn and a kettledrum, who stayed just off the open stage and visible the whole time, playing the alarums and flourishes. Robin himself played the Chorus. I'd wondered why this play had been chosen, certainly not one of the top ten, a patriotic pageant for a country not ours: but in Robin's version it was about theater itself, and making do, and four boards and a passion. In all my grandiose thinking about theater I couldn't have come up with such a gimmick. I think now that he was good; I wonder what became of him.

There were more women in the company than you'd think would be needed, since there are only four female characters in the play (though one gets the best speech). We found out how two older women would be used when they came to rehearsals one day with hair cut short, almost cut off: they were to be the priests who begin the play, who justify Henry's war. And do no fighting themselves.

"That would be hard," Harriet said to me; we watched the women self-consciously touch their gray hair with their hands.

But that wasn't all.

Robin called us all together to see something he'd been working on.

All the plainness, he said, and the bareness, it was all fine, he loved it and it was working, working really well he thought, but it wasn't completely satisfying, was it? Did we think so? I thought whatever he thought, of course, but I nodded with the others and assented that maybe it wasn't enough. Robin said that in Elizabethan theaters they made up for the plain bare stage with brilliant costumes—most of them the cast-off clothes of noble patrons—but we didn't have them here. So he'd developed another idea, and he wanted to show us.

I don't know now if Robin had worked out the new idea long before, if he only wanted to produce in us the same surprise he aimed to achieve in audiences by saying he'd just thought of it. I know it made him seem all the more a magician to me.

He said: "Think, when we talk of horses, that you see them, printing their proud hooves i' the receiving earth." Harriet, next to me, glanced at me for just the briefest second as though it were all the time she could spare me from her attention to what was happening. And Robin lifted his arm and brought forth a horse: from the rear draped chamber it, she, stepped forth.

It was Sandy. She was the horse. She was in a leotard, I suppose, though I probably didn't know that word then; her feet shod in some kind of high shoe, a tall long-nosed mask on her head that seemed to lift her almost to a horse's height. She took slow steps and pawed delicately: printed her proud hoof in the receiving earth. Looked around herself with haughty animal unconcern; tossed her high head as though tugging at her reins.

I felt Harriet stir beside me.

Robin came close to Sandy as though to take her reins, or put his hand on her. "I will not change my horse for any that treads on four pasterns," he said. "When I bestride him I soar, I am a hawk. He trots the air, the earth sings when he touches it."

They were the Dauphin's lines, from the night before the battle of Agincourt. Sandy tossed her head as though the steed heard these compliments.

"It is a beast for Perseus," Robin said. "He is pure air and fire, and the dull elements of earth and water never appear in him but in patient stillness as his rider mounts him."

He took her shoulder. She was still, obedient. We were all still and silent, witnessing what it almost seemed we shouldn't. Then suddenly he dropped the character, laughed, turned Sandy to face us, who lifted off her mask; Robin lifted his hands to say, well that's all.

We applauded.

"There won't be many," Robin said, coming downstage. "Six or eight. If any of you have experience in dance or gymnastics—I know some of you do—I hope you'll come see me and make a time to try out for these parts." He laughed. "Parts. Well. I promise you'll be on stage more than some parts with lines."

"Maybe you should," I said to Harriet, and she turned her head my way as though she had heard a small, unintelligible noise of no interest; then slowly back to the stage, where Sandy was slipping off the high shoes and holding out the mask to the costume people to take away.

Of course she tried out, and was selected. She would be the Duke of Bedford's horse, caparisoned in his arms; the actor playing the Duke was a thick hirsute man with wrestler's wrists and a low, winning voice he seemed to have invented. Steeds and riders practiced together, extra rehearsals with Sandy and the fight captain, as he was called. I could watch, if I wanted.

There's a lot about horses in the play, enough to account for a lot of action. Harriet was one of the exhausted starving English horses the French make fun of:

> *. . . Their poor jades*
> *Lob down their heads, dropping the hides and hips,*
> *The gum down-roping from their pale-dead eyes*
> *And in their pale dull mouths the gimmal bit*
> *Lies foul with chewed grass, still and motionless.*

The Duke rose, weary, sword heavy in his hand; and Harriet his mount arose, in brute pain, her head lobbed down, her shanks trembling, but still willing, still proud, lifting and shaking her high head when the dresser cast her colors over her.

"I learned some more about Bacon," I said to Harriet. She'd come off the stage glistening with sweat, a huge pair of dungarees and a white shirt pulled on over her dance leotard. She laughed that laugh, and I saw what I'd said, and I laughed too. "No. Listen. At the library. I learned a lot."

"Well where else? No, what."

"Do you know who first thought that Bacon might have written Shakespeare?"

"Of course I don't."

"It was a woman. Her name was Delia Bacon."

"Oh no."

"She was no relation though. She said so herself."

"Yeah sure."

"I can show you her book," I said. "If you want. There's a lot of books about this."

"Okay." And her smile of frank complicity.

When the bus came by the theater on its endless round we took it into town, which seemed stunned into motionless silence in the noonday heat, drooping like the grieving Union soldier on his plinth.

"She came from near here," I said. "Western Ohio. A hundred years ago. Her father was a missionary, and they came from Connecticut. She made a living as a teacher, then she wrote books, then she became a public lecturer. She never married."

"Hm."

"She did have an affair, though, or a romance, with this guy in New Haven. She came back to Connecticut to do this lecturing. He was a minister."

"Weren't they all."

"He lived in this hotel where she lived. She sent him a note saying to come visit her, and he told his friends. But he started seeing her."

"Did she tell him about Shakespeare?"

"Yes. He thought she was right."

"How do you know all this?"

"It's in a book." Going into the dim library I shivered dramatically, and Harriet looked at me with interest. Maybe it was the sudden cool air; or a kind of intimacy, as startling as a touch, to take her here.

"There was a scandal," I said. "Delia's family claimed that this guy—his name was McWhorter—had asked Delia to marry him, and now was breaking his promise; but *he* said it was Delia who'd asked him."

"Ha," said Harriet. "She asked him."

"She said."

"Maybe," Harriet said, "she was a free spirit."

I led her down the stacks. "What's that? I mean how do you mean?"

"A free spirit. Is somebody who does what they want. Like a Victorian lady who asks a man to marry her. Or just be lovers."

The stacks were on two levels, green-painted iron, the second level reached by a circular stair. We climbed up.

"My mother says what I want to be is a free spirit," Harriet said. "She says she was one too. So I get it from her."

"Can you want to be one?" I asked. I didn't know what I was talking about. "Isn't wanting to be one the same as being one?"

"No," Harriet said.

The Shakespeare section was three or four shelves, plays in old editions, commentaries, lives, and a dozen books on who else might have been Shakespeare.

"Here," I said. It was *The Philosophy of the Plays of Shakspere*

Unfolded, by Delia Bacon. There was a photograph of her inside: a bonneted dark lady of indeterminate age, smiling a knowing smile, a smile of frankness and good humor.

"I like her." She riffled the pages but read nothing.

"Look at this one," I said. "It's crazy."

A huge volume in moldering leather called *The Great Cryptogram* by Ignatius Donnelly. Thousands of pages of methods for finding the secret words planted in the texts of the plays to reveal the true author. Who was Francis Bacon.

"He liked Delia. He thought she got a bad deal."

We were squatting close together to get at the books on the bottom shelf. I could smell Harriet's perfume and sweat. She drew out a small blue volume from the shelf.

"The Girlhood of Shakespeare's Heroines," she read, and sat to open it, slipping off her laceless sneakers. I pulled out other books: *Bacon Is Shake-speare. Shakespeare, Bacon, and the Great Unknown. "Shakespeare" Identified in Edward De Vere, Seventeenth Earl of Oxford. Shake-speare: The Mystery.*

"Look," I said. "Here's the one that says Queen Elizabeth wrote the plays. Listen: 'The psychic urge that made Elizabeth place Portia, Rosalind, and Viola in men's clothing might explain her disguising her own authorship in masculine raiment. For every strong and mature Shakespeare heroine we have a weak, vacillating, impetuous hero.'"

"Well sure." She was involved in the small book she'd found.

"What is it?"

"It is," she said, "a book about the girlhoods of Shakespeare's heroines. Just as though they were real people who had girlhoods you could tell about." She glanced at the front of the book. "Eighteen ninety-one. Here's one about Beatrice."

"Which one is she?" I hadn't read many of the comedies.

"Much Ado About Nothing," she said, shooting me a schoolmarmish glance. "You know, dear boy. Beatrice and Benedick."

"Oh right. She's a free spirit."

The floor of the level we sat on was of glass: a milky glass that let the light, I guess, fall down to the darker level below. I'd never been anywhere like this cast-iron structure, on this glass floor.

"I want to take this out," Harriet said. "Do you think they'd let me?"

"Sure. I bet."

I don't know how long we sat. Harriet probably looked at her little wristwatch on a gold band and made us leave. I remember that I went down the ringing spiral stair before her, and that she held her hand out to me to be helped: and that afterward I smelled her perfume on that hand. For years after I would catch whiffs of that scent on the street, at parties, and finally I somehow learned its name: Ambush.

Delia Bacon didn't, in fact, at least at first, decide who the real author of the Shakespeare plays was. Her original insight, and it wasn't entirely original with her, though maybe she thought it was, was simply that the lowly mummer from Stratford could never have created so lofty, so vast, so moral a work as the plays seemed to her to be. And she did see them as a single work, growing over time as the Author matured, but enfolding a single unified philosophy, humane, radical, even subversive—a philosophy that she, Delia Bacon, was the first to articulate.

One writer has pointed out that Delia's obsessive denigration of the actor fellow, which appears in her thinking rather suddenly, might be a displacement of her anger at the despicable McWhorter and his falsity, and her replacement of him by a more suitable love object, who had her own name (and her stern beloved father's) to boot: a neat piece of psychologizing, though it doesn't fit with the free spirit conception. A free spirit would never take someone like him so much to heart, or allow herself to be so caught and mishandled. Never.

But there's no doubt she's different from all those who follow her, different in what mattered to her. They all regard the plays with a standard sort of awe, works of genius and so on, couldn't have been written by any lowborn player, but beyond that they have little to say about them: they only search them for clues and codes and secret messages.

Delia's argument was different. The reason she suspected that the true author of the plays—or authors, for she thought it likely that there were several—had hidden behind the Shakespeare name was that the philosophy they enunciated would have been dangerous, even fatal, to espouse. The plays of Shakespeare, she thought, promote a thoroughgoing antiroyalist republicanism, a view of all men as created equal in their needs and desires and sufferings. From the endless, repellent broils of York and Lancaster down to the awful compassion of Lear, the plays show kings as mere men—

flawed, sinful, guilty, overreaching, without claim to divine right or men's allegiance.

And who, she then asked, would have conceived such a philosophy; who would scheme to hide it in a series of popular entertainments, whose secret goal was to educate and uplift and even incite the people who stood to listen, or sat to read? Who would then need to hide his own identity behind the globous face of the faker from Stratford? Bacon, father of science and the new learning, court official, intimate of monarchs, himself ennobled, makes perfect sense to be this person, this fair mind bent on an unimaginable future, the end of kings and nobles and the beginning of equality and a common humanity; of "pity, like a naked new-born babe"; free men and women freely choosing one another in love and fraternity.

What would the queen his mistress have said to that?

Actually Delia conceived an entire cabal within the queen's court, aristocrats risking their heads to reach England's people with their message—which maybe they heard too, since the Englishmen who began in those years to come to America (though admittedly most of them, at least at first, were theater-hating Puritans) eventually *did* found a nation with those ideals; and then the secret of their transmission was uncovered at length by a woman born in that republic, even named for the transmitter, and a free spirit maybe too, certainly with a mind and heart of her own.

Which is why—this just occurs to me—it was right and proper that in the United States we should have sat before his plays, by limelight and lamplight, so persistently; and why it makes perfect sense that in the state of Indiana just a hundred years after Delia Bacon enunciated her, or Shakespeare's, philosophy we democrats should have gathered in a Utopian's barn to read and study and perform his plays. In fact, *Henry V* was one of Delia's examples of Shakespeare (considered collectively) working on the people's souls to show what kings are, and what their wars amount to:

> *I think the king is but a man as I am, the violet smells to him as it does to me; all his senses have but human conditions. His ceremonies laid by, in his nakedness, he appears but a man. . . .*

Of course that's Harry himself speaking, while disguised as a commoner, so the irony is multiple, nearly impenetrable, but Delia knew that; she's actually most sorry for the king—unfitted, as any mere man must be, for the vast responsibilities placed on him; a man who needs as much or more than anyone to be freed.

There was a party at the camp for the actors, the crew, the apprentices, end of a work week, or dress rehearsal, I don't remember. They liked to have parties, they brought in cases of beer and everybody got some: impossible to imagine now.

Harriet in the big dining hall was reading aloud to some kids out of *The Girlhood of Shakespeare's Heroines.* June bugs banged against the screens. I talked to Robin.

"It just can't be true," I said. "You should read some of this stuff I found. These people are nuts."

"Well what's truth?" he said, as though he'd just thought of this big question. "Maybe truth is multiple. I mean how can we ever know? How can we know anything for sure? We don't even know for sure that you and I are here talking, and not just figments."

Considered as a profession, theater people aren't much given to analysis and logic. In the theater somebody who seems to be Lear *is* Lear; maybe it's the same with thought, and to the average actor something that seems like a reasoned argument doesn't differ importantly from an actual one.

Robin looked down at the unopened bottle of Drewry's beer in his lap. He had what we called a church key in his hand. "You know," he said, "I've never been exactly sure he believes this theory." He apparently meant the Bacon advocate who'd talked to us. "He may not be completely convinced the plays were written by Francis Bacon."

He was an actor too in how he "telegraphed"—let you know when a stunner was coming, bad practice in a boxer, skillful in a raconteur.

"Oh?" I said my line.

"No," Robin said. "He thinks maybe it's more likely to have been his smarter brother, Anthony."

He popped off the cap of the bottle, his own rim shot.

"So here little Beatrice gets captured by outlaws," I heard Harriet say. "She's so sharp. 'Corpo di Bellona! A spirited young devil she is! I'll drink your health, young lady!' That's the robber chief. He wants to marry her. 'Fill me a cup, and I'll pledge you all, good gentlemen,' says Beatrice. 'But I have no ambition to be your queen. I should soon be an unpopular monarch among you, for I should begin my rule by reforming your ways.' Oh God."

"I've known him a long time," Robin said. "I know him to be a completely sweet, completely sincere, and very smart man. And. He's nowhere near as mad as his mother."

"'A little gray-eyed red-lipped thing, that looks too bright and fearless to know what tears mean,'" Harriet read. "'She speaks up so open, and looks so straight into your face, that you feel as if she must be right, and you wrong. . . .'"

"His mother," Robin said, with vast seriousness, "has discovered that within the plays of Shakespeare there is a code, or a cipher. There's a difference, but I can't remember what it is. And the code, when you break it, tells a story."

I held my tongue.

"A long story."

I waited.

"It turns out," he said, "that hidden in the plays is the story of how Francis Bacon is actually the son of Queen Elizabeth and Robert of Leicester, her lover."

I started to laugh, that nervous laughter: in too deep, resisting.

"They made a secret marriage," Robin said. Still deadpan. "So Francis Bacon was in fact *rightfully heir to the throne.* Francis I. But if he ever let that be known—" And here Robin drew his hand suddenly across his throat, executing himself. "So he hid the story for this amazing woman to discover, three hundred, three hundred . . ."

Then at last he laughed.

"But," I said, in trouble.

"Listen." He had lost all urgency, dropped the part he'd been playing. I saw that Harriet had come near and stood listening. "It doesn't matter. The fact is that the son has spent most of his life not thinking about Bacon, ha ha, or his mother, but in making money. Quite a lot of it, as I understand. In the commodities market. And whatever else he may have been or is, he is a good son and a generous man. And we wouldn't be here without him. And that's enough. And that's that."

He looked from me to Harriet to me. Harriet, hands behind her back and her finger in the book's pages, looked like an illustration for something. She was smiling with sweet acceptance, and her smile moved from Robin to me. They were both looking at me, both smiling. I felt very odd.

Others came and claimed Robin's attention.

"He's right, dear boy," Harriet said to me.

"But."

"Come on," she said. "I'd like to walk."

Night came on with such solemn slowness those summers, the birds falling silent and the frogs and bugs awaking, the sky turning green and yellow, the trees and low poplars black. Talking nonsense and making dance spins, she led me as though by chance up the way that led from the camp buildings to a knoll where low shrubs grew, and tall grasses; from the little fastness or hideaway they made you could glimpse the road back down to the camp, and look outward over the meadows to the river, an onyx meander in the darkening green.

"You like this?" she said, and she sat, floated with practiced dancer's grace to the soft ground.

Harriet had chosen me. It was as simple as that. Try as I might I can't remember how she let me know this. Maybe she didn't. I only remember being there in the growing dark, already knowing.

"Clipping," she said, and took off her pink-framed glasses. "That's what Shakespeare says. I like that word. Clipping and kissing."

I said nothing.

I was profoundly alarmed. This thing that I had thought so constantly about was before me and I'm sure I looked like an apprehended criminal, like a shy wild thing transfixed by the explorer who's first discovered it. I didn't say anything or do anything of all the many things I could have done, that I knew could and ought now to be done; and Harriet stopped and looked at me cautiously.

"Okay?" she said.

I didn't answer.

"You aren't whatchamacallit, are you?"

"What?"

"That thing Francis Bacon was. Philorumpties."

"*Paiderastes.* No. No no."

"Are you sure?"

"I'm sure."

"Okay then." The only obstacle out of the way. We began. Grass and fields were at any rate my medium; all the little clipping I'd done had been outdoors, like a swain, or a rabbit, though I'd never got even this far anywhere else.

Her peasant blouse was easy to get off, seemed made to come off easily, and then there were the underpinnings, like grappling with a time bomb in the dark, decoupling the wires; she helped out frankly.

"They're liddlies," she said.

Almost all I knew about the act that was to follow, all of it theoretical, I had learned from a book called *Ideal Marriage,* which said that it involves all of the senses, taste, touch, smell, sight, but not hearing, which should, the book said, be notable by its absence. No talking. Harriet talked. It was the strangest thing of all.

There were other features of the act that with delicate care *Ideal Marriage* had described. Those we did or had. One's Shakespearean name I had thought about and said over often to myself, like a charm, or a promise, sometimes with an actual shiver, anticipation mixed with some apprehensive revulsion: *the velvet clasp.*

"Oops you weren't supposed to," she panted in my ear.

As well remind the deer not to start away. Not supposed to: I hardly knew I had.

"I think it's all right," she said. "I think."

It turned out it was all right. God knows what we would have done: I think of that sometimes. And the next time I didn't, nor the next.

I was awed, bewildered, filled with weird guilt—not guilt for any religious reason, I've never had any of that, but because I wasn't in love with Harriet, or she with me; what she had invited me to obviously wasn't the commencement of always-ever-after in my life; I felt like a Shakespearean virgin who's been played the Bed Trick. I couldn't have said any of this then, only felt it. *Dint know whether to shit or go blind* they said then in Indiana. It was part of the free spirit effect, but I didn't know that then either.

I finally got less tongue-tied. My strangulated silence ought to have been outrageously insulting to Harriet, but in fact she didn't change her attitude toward me through the days, only her voice sometimes had a throaty kind of quality when we talked about nothing or about Shakespeare or the work, as though she might start laughing any second from some kind of warmth or pleasure, at my discomfiture only maybe.

"You know something?" she said to me, this time in a counselor's cabin we'd found a way into, a bedstead, a stained mattress. "You know something? You have a nice penis."

Wonderful, wonderful, and most wonderful, wonderful! And yet again wonderful, and after that out of all whooping. In this world into which I had come this happened, this too; everything. Of course I didn't know it happened also in the world I came from, at summer theaters and summer conferences and summer gatherings all over, that it was for this that they foregathered (not entirely or always, no, but still). I sensed, smelled as it were, the hot life all around me, as I never could have done before I became part of it, the clippings and couplings, the satyr-play in the buggy woods and weeds. *Paiderastes* too among them certainly. And she and I. And she and at least one other. She told me later, but I suspected it even then, though "suspected" sounds too cunning; I didn't know what I was supposed to feel or do about that, and so I felt nothing about it in particular, nothing but more.

Henry V opened on the July Fourth weekend. It began just as it had the first day of rehearsals, with Robin in jeans and a sweater dragging the big wooden box of swords and armor out to the middle of the stage. The house lights weren't down, and the audience of course thought he was a stagehand or a stage manager, which he was, and would be. And then the stage lights started to come up, but only a little, and the house darkened, and Robin came and sat on the apron with his script, as he had on the day he began rehearsing. And almost before anyone knew it, he'd begun to speak—not orate, just speak, wistfully almost, about how only a muse of fire and princes to act could bring forth Harry. As he talked the actors playing Harry and the Dauphin and the rest came out of the shadows in their jeans and sweatshirts and chose weapons from the box, and Harry put on his crown. And when he said *Think when we talk of horses that you see them, printing their proud hooves i' the receiving earth,* then a light lit one of the horses, center stage, Henry's, in its bright caparison; she printed her proud hoof, and another horse—Harriet—appeared behind, and another. There was a little gasp or sound from the audience, a titter here and there too, and I felt a sharp deep shudder as though I'd been seized, and tears filled my eyes.

It's good, so good that the play was produced, that she was able to be in it, and that its short run was up.

It was a Sunday. A lot of the actors had gone home, some of them not to return, others to arrive to be in the second play of the year, *The Tempest.* Some of the apprentices too, gone home with bags of dirty laundry and blisters on their hands, to return next week.

I stayed. Harriet stayed too.

That little camp where we'd been put surrounded a small lake, a green torpid body of water reverting to swamp. Some of us swam there sometimes, urging one another in, rowing a foul-bottomed boat to the middle and diving into the duckweed. Harriet wouldn't go in, and neither would I.

But it was hot, insufferably hot. And not far from the town of

Avon, along the little river, was a public beach, a crowded place but clean and sandy. And on Saturday one of the few of us who'd come in his own car took Harriet and me and a couple of others out there.

It too was still, its water brownish and thick. There were crowds of small children, diapers dangling, chased by their mothers; and children older than that, and dogs. No one understands to this day what it was about places like this, public beaches in the summer, if there really was anything about them, or if that was only a kind of leftover medieval fear of plague or cholera. I don't know. We'd been warned so much, every year, threat hanging like the heat over the days.

I see that beach still, I swear, in dreams, every detail the same, only darkened, as though seen through dark glasses, or with sunblind eyes. Soundless. Dreadful. It might not be that place at all I see, of course; and the place itself might be wholly innocent, harmless. I wake up in a sweat.

Next day was Sunday.

The library was open that day. Why open Sunday? Maybe I have something wrong about the days. The library was open. I know it was.

In the library I went to the Shakespeare section, climbed the spiral stair again. I was going to do research. I was going to take some notes, and show them they were wrong, make them admit it. Get this snake out of Paradise: no I didn't think that, surely. But if they had to admit it, then—then what? They'd stop, I suppose. No longer soil the best name in the world.

I don't know what I thought. I was beginning to feel very odd, to feel cluster around me a being, a *soma,* that wasn't my own but that I recognized. I got Ignatius Donnelly and the others in my arms and came down the stairs to sit.

There was a photograph of Donnelly—*Senator* Donnelly—in the front of his book. I realized, looking at it, how old this thing was, how long ago.

> If the reader will turn to page 76 of the *fac-similes,* being page 76 of the original Folio, and the third page of the second part of *King Henry IV.,* and commence to count at the bottom of the scene, to-wit, the scene second, and count upward, he will find that there are just 448 words (exclusive of the bracketed words, and counting the hyphenated

> words as single words) in that fragment of scene second in that column. Now then, if we deduct 448 from 505, the remainder is 57, and if he will count down the next column, forward (second of page 76) the reader will find that the 57th word is the word *her.*

Folded up inside the book was a copy of one of Donnelly's work-sheets, showing his method. I unfolded it. A page of *Henry IV,* the Folio, with red and blue pencil lines, line numbers, arrows drawn to other lines and words, lists of words from other places in black, blue, and red.

> Now let us go a step farther.

My hand was shaking: I lifted it before my eyes and watched the tremors.

There's a sensation that all my life I have hated profoundly, dreaded, even though it hasn't happened to me often (multiplied, though, by my memories of those few times). It's as though all intentionality and will is being drained from the world, all consciousness, a conviction that there is nothing in earthly activity but malign blind indifference; that even the willed behavior of persons, speaking, thinking, doing, is only mechanical ticks and tocks. Finally that they cannot even be heard or seen, because all eyes are blind, all ears are stopped. My own consciousness the only one existent to know this.

I wonder if it's like the onset of schizophrenia: the sense of living in a world of automata. It's often been associated for me with the onset of some illness; I wonder if I didn't first experience it before an asthma attack. Or was that time in the Avon library the first? And is that why I fear it so much?

Donnelly's huge screed, so full of wishing, so human a thing. I looked down at the pages and felt him, the froggy man in the picture at the front, lose his him- or he-ness, sadly wink out into unaliveness, only these endless numbers and words multiplying. I wanted to look away, and couldn't.

Voiceless. And all other books, and Shakespeare too, and all those who thought about him: they lost their voices, couldn't make sound, lost consciousness. The air itself lost mobility. I couldn't move.

The librarian, the only other person there, was looking at me, making the gestures of seeing me, of taking off her glasses, rising from her desk, coming to where I sat. She seemed to say what's wrong, is something wrong.

I think I have a fever, I said without sound.

She touched my head, her cool hand suddenly real and scorching.

Oh my goodness you do.

It's a summer cold.

Where do you belong, she mouthed.

I answered.

She spoke.

I tried to get up from the desk and fell down.

What happened then was that she sent someone—a passing someone in the street—to go out to the offices of the festival and get Robin, out of bed actually, and he drove into town in his Ford convertible; and by the time he got there the librarian had got me outside, and I was sitting on the steps of the library; and then they got me to the office of a doctor, which was just around the corner, and we waited on his step for him. And even before he got there Robin saw that he would have to drive me to the hospital, an hour away, and when the doctor did come that's what they decided.

I didn't know or understand anything of this, and don't remember it now. I was told it all in the days to come, and in a letter from Robin to my parents.

He drove me to the hospital, and I do remember that fact: his car and the smell of its upholstery. I was in back with Sandy, who held me wrapped in a scratchy Army blanket that I also remember. Robin said that all the way there he recited Shakespeare, to keep anxiety down; he said I asked him to, but I don't believe it. He recited most of *The Tempest,* which he was to begin rehearsing the next day:

The cloud-capped towers, the gorgeous palaces,
The solemn temples, the great Globe itself
And all that it inherit, shall dissolve
And like this insubstantial pageant faded
Leave not a rack behind.
We are such stuff as dreams are made on
And our little life is rounded with a sleep.

What I remember is waking in that hospital when the fever broke. I remember the white sheets and a smell of soured milk and disinfectant. And I wondered why I had been strapped down to the bed so that I couldn't move my legs at all. Why had they done that? The nurse came in and pulled the sheet aside and I could see my legs were not strapped down: they just wouldn't move.

Harriet says it was the same for her, strangely. Why have I been strapped to the bed? What good does that do? Why has that been done to me?

They say that in the old days almost everybody got it, but if you were very young when you got infected then it had no lasting effect, it was just like a cold, or like nothing, you didn't even know, and then of course you were immune ever after. The older you were the more likely you were to have damage.

But then they had the vaccine, and somehow it vanished overnight, except that it didn't if you had been missed, if you were at home with asthma when the nurses came to your school, if you didn't go to a school, if your mother was a free spirit and didn't altogether believe in medications and wanted to wait and see a while in spite of what everybody told her. I don't know. I really still don't.

It was the last major national outbreak. There were seven cases in Brown County alone: most of them were kids under twelve, and then me, and Harriet. Over a thousand of us nationwide.

They didn't tell me that Harriet was there, in that hospital, in another ward nearby. She'd been brought by the stage manager and his wife, a couple of hours after me. Why didn't they tell me? Because they didn't tell things then. What they knew might kill you, they thought, if you knew it too.

We lost each other for a long time then, or better say I lost her; I'm not sure how much Harriet thought about me. At first we were in specialized hospitals far apart, and then home. I didn't have her address—we never got to the point of swapping them, or phone numbers; making long-distance calls, even across the state, seemed momentous still in those days. Well that might not have been why it took me so long to call. In any case, when I did at last find her number and talked to her father for a moment, I learned she'd gone to still another hospital, somewhere in the East, for more treatment. It was obvious he didn't want to talk about it, he sounded remote and frightened, as though I'd roused him from a cave.

And that's really what kept us apart: that we had both, each alone, gone off into this disaster, and now were separated, along with our blighted families, from everyone else. It was a secret, what had become of us, but a secret that had to be exposed in every new circumstance you entered, explained, confessed to. *Well he's not as strong as other boys in some ways.* To coaches, teachers, bosses. My family nearly died of shame and bravery.

And I was one of the ones who came back, too. I came back nearly all the way. You can see me now and know right away that something's wrong, but I've walked without aids for most of my life. I was a loner anyway, without much sense that the world was waiting for me to make an entrance on its stage. There were times I was actually relieved—and ashamed, of course, to be relieved—to have a reason, such a profound and unchallengeable one, for nonparticipation.

I can't think Harriet ever felt that way. But I didn't know. I didn't know anything about what had become of her, whether she came back, or not. We were sundered. I got a Christmas card from her that first year. Then nothing.

Harriet calls me at my office in the Liberal Arts Building, the afternoon after we met on the road.

"You were right about the pope," she says. "He's not dead."

"No. Hurt."

"Tough bastard."

When this pope's accession was announced, and it was made known that he'd be taking the name John Paul II after John Paul I, his predecessor, Harriet said No, no, not John Paul again! *George Ringo!*

"I heard them say it was a vulgarian who did it. . . ."

"Not a vulgarian, Harriet."

". . . And I thought that was an odd snap judgment to make."

"A Bulgarian. A spy."

"Yes. I figured it out." I heard her sip tea. "You want to come over tonight?"

"Okay."

"Air-conditioning's still busted."

"Okay."

"Bring a bottle of that wine you think is so good. Brookwood. Woodbridge. Bridgewater."

"Waterbrook. My last class is over at five."

"Good. Okay."

I still have that Christmas card. It isn't different from anyone's—snow, dark pines, star. Inside it says *May your every Christmas wish come true.* And it's signed with her full name, as though I might not remember her. I knew even then, though maybe I couldn't have said, that it wasn't a greeting.

Oh you don't know, you can't: our parents knew it instantly, probably, though my mom with her sense of privilege and being welcome everywhere maybe took longer to understand. The way it was then. You were obliged, for everyone's sake (it seemed) to check out of the world; you found out that after all you had only been a temporary guest there, on sufferance. It was no longer for you, and you were under an obligation not to make others uncomfortable by your presence. Maybe that's why we all shunned one another; two of us at once, outside of a hospital, would have been a shocking solecism. Just think about it: there were a lot of us, and when do you ever remember, if you're old enough to remember, seeing two of us hanging out together? On the street, at the malt shop, the movies? Never.

When I said that once to Harriet she said it was silly: the reason people never saw us was because in those days you couldn't get out of the house, off the front porch, up on the curb, up the stairs. That's all.

"They never saw us together?" Harriet said, and laughed. "*They never saw us at all.* We weren't there to see."

"'Others abide our question; thou art free.' That's what Matthew Arnold says about, or to, Shakespeare." I'm speaking to my summer school class, which is about to read and understand twelve Shakespeare plays in four weeks. "And that question would, I guess, be *What is this guy trying to say?* And Arnold decided that what Shakespeare was trying to say was finally not able to be determined. What did Shakespeare think about things? Was he a propagandist for the Tudor-Stuart monarchy? That's a common opinion. Was he a secret Catholic, secret atheist, secret antiwar activist? I think that whatever opinions the man Shakespeare might have held, there are no opinions at all expressed in the plays: that like all works that occur in time, they are driven by the impetus to complete a certain kind of movement. The things said in a play of Shakespeare's are said because the story told is a story of a certain kind; the characters speak as they do so that the stories can be completed. They are no more the opinions of Shakespeare than the inversions and variations of a fugue are the opinions of Bach. And they touch us in the same way, the same astonishing way, when against all the odds they reach their endings.

"So. Check your syllabus, and for our next meeting we'll look at a play of apparently utter simplicity, and see how a history, supposedly reflecting actual events, is in fact as shaped and typed as a ballad or a fairy tale. How a story that nearly everyone in its original audience knew was to end in disaster and early death could have the shape of a romantic comedy."

By the time I leave school the day has turned dramatically lowering, hot and heavy. I walk across campus with a younger colleague, a woman in American Studies. She's careful to walk slowly to accommodate me, but not quite tactful enough to conceal that she's doing so.

"Tell me something," I ask. "If you heard someone—a woman, say about your age, maybe older—described as a 'free spirit,' what would you think was being said about her?"

"Oh," she says. "That she sleeps around a lot. I knew a lot of them."

"Knew?"

"Well it was kind of a thing to be, wasn't it? A free spirit. Barefoot, living on the earth, sleeping around wherever. You know."

"Don't you mean daisy pickers? Or is there not a difference?"

She shrugs. "Someone without much sense of reality, I guess. About men or life. Some of them got away with it"—and here she makes an airy gesture of escape or detachment—"but not always."

She slows so I can catch up. "Why do you ask?" she says.

"Cultural anthropology," I say.

"I'd worry for her," she says.

I see her logic. But I think that there are—speaking anthropologically—several varieties. There are the ones that anyone could recognize, untrammeled, living in worlds of their own; but then there are the secret ones whom you wouldn't know about unless you know. The librarian and the mailman (curls put up beneath her gray cap) and the dental hygienist. Not soft, not unwise; knowing the costs, and the benefits. Free spirits free even of the label, choosing more carefully than Delia Bacon did.

And Harriet: who's going to guess it about her? Sex is something not expected of us. That's the secret part: and I know it's astonished more than one person. But Harriet's had lovers, dozens of them (*tens*, she says, *not dozens; lovers by the tens*). Maybe she hasn't in her life had all those she wanted; maybe she's been turned down a lot. But being a true free spirit—as I conceive it—means she chose lovers when she wanted them, and didn't when she didn't: could have sex with whoever whenever, but knew when to eschew it too.

"Eschew?" Harriet said to me, in mock wonderment, when I made this case. *"Eschew?"*

That was the night of the first day we met again. The early morning of the following day, actually. In her little apartment here in this New England town on a wide river not named Avon, nowhere either of us would have guessed we'd come to, much less both of us, but have, for altogether different reasons. Mine the mundane one of a job offer; hers something to do with those tens of lovers, though the story's obscure to me still. She loves it here: the shop she's built, the Federal house she owns where both it and she reside, where she has the solitudes she needs as much as she needs company. I've actually wondered if they're entirely different, for her, solitude and company; and if that's sad, or not sad.

"You know something?" she said to me that night or morning. "You have a nice penis." And I remembered, hadn't of course ever forgotten, when she'd said it to me first; wondered too if it was something she said often, just a nice thing to say.

"Yes," I said. "It's a Pendaflex."

"Really. Wow. The rotomatic?"

"No. I'm saving up for one of those."

It was June, June again. She rested her hot face in the crook of my shoulder.

"It'll stand you in good stead," she said. "A nice penis like that."

I thought it ought to be strange to me, even eerie, to have gone so far from where I started and to find her here, and somehow to take up where we were when we parted so completely, but all different: she so altered, in ways I'd long wondered about. Like dreams you might have, dreams I've had. But it didn't seem that way at all. It doesn't now.

Harriet's shop is called As You Like It. Under these words on the painted sign over the door is a sort of scroll or banner that reads *Wonderful wonderful and most wonderful wonderful.* There's a tinkle bell that sounds when the door is opened, though it's hardly needed.

"Hi."

She was waiting on a customer, wrapping something small and precious with wasteless motions, tissue, box, ribbon, label. One of her hands is different from the other, and the work seems to pass from one to the other as needed, as between two friends, one the stronger.

You'd think that the worst thing was how all that physical grace and power was blasted and reft from her, and it's true that that was the loss; but what's just as true is that all Harriet's grace, all her strength and physical precision, lay in a more central part of her than that, a place from which she draws all the time now making her way in the world, and everybody who sees her knows it. I watch her in the absurdly crowded shop turn and move, put out a hand to touch, just touch a wall to keep her balance, reach to take something from a high shelf, turn again and put it before you, without a wasted gesture or effort: she's still that steed.

"I brought you something," I say.

"The wine."

"That too."

I took it from the grocery bag that held the bottle.

"Oh my God."

"It was in the college library."

A small octavo volume, as they used to say, silk-bound, the gold lettering dim but plain. *The Girlhood of Shakespeare's Heroines.*

"You know something?" I say. "All the others are there too."

"Yes?"

"All of them are. Still. Ignatius Donnelly and Delia Bacon and *Shake-speare: The Mystery.* In the same places they always were." As though library time universally stopped that afternoon, at least in that range of Dewey decimals, all those books growing more useless and foolish every year, never changing their minds or hearts.

"Delia Bacon," Harriet says. "The free spirit."

"Well so you thought."

"Did you look in them?"

"I did." I don't say that it took me a long time to open one. Of course I've always known they were there. Volumes that I use in classes and research are nearby them. But I'd never opened one; that's true.

I help Harriet close the shop. Harriet studies *The Girlhood of Shakespeare's Heroines.* White ink numbers on its spine.

"You know," she said. "I never took it back. That one from the library in Avon. I never took it back. It's probably still there, in that cabin, today."

Delia Bacon went to England in 1853, perhaps largely to escape the McWhorter mess, but also because people she knew in Boston and New Haven told her she ought to go and find the facts that would prove her conception. Once there, though, she only went on thinking and studying the plays, growing ever more certain she was right. Bostonian bluestocking that she was, she had letters of introduction from Emerson to Carlyle, who was shocked by her heresies (he shrieked, she says, turned black in the face). She would do no research, though; she wrote essays about her idea, as though all by itself it ought to convince; she ran out of money and was practically destitute when she was taken up by Nathaniel Hawthorne, who was then the American cultural attaché. Hawthorne took her part, generously, and stood by her, and helped her prepare her huge book (*The Philosophy of the Plays of Shakspere Unfolded*) for publication, and paid for it too: but he didn't believe either.

I don't know how she got the idea that the proof she needed—or rather that the world needed—could be found in a grave. First she supposed that it was buried with Bacon at St. Albans, and when she was refused permission to open that tomb, she went to Stratford-on-Avon. Hawthorne says that Delia told him she had "definite and minute instructions" about how to find, beneath Shakespeare's gravestone in Stratford church, the documents that the cabal had caused to be put there.

She got to Stratford sick and shabby, and could find no room at the inn. She wandered the town, and finding a rose-covered cottage whose door stood open (all this is true) she went in, and sat down. And when the ancient woman who lived there alone came in, and saw her there, she couldn't bear to send her away; and there she stayed, looking out at the river Avon and the spire of the church where Shakespeare lay.

You know the doggerel curse that's posted on that grave: *Good friend for Jesus' sake forebear To dig the dust enclosèd here; Blest be the man that spares these stones And curst be he that moves my bones.* It could have been this that kept her away—she wouldn't have been the only one. And of course there was already a huge Stratford Shakespeare industry, and no one was about to let her dig that dust. But she didn't even ask; for months she did nothing at all.

Then one night, she went to the church. Why night? She brought a dark lantern, and some other articles for "the examination I proposed to make," she wrote to Hawthorne: though what they were, or it was, she didn't say. She stayed there for some hours. The bust of Shakespeare on his memorial was above her, but it was too dark to see him; she couldn't see the ceiling at all, it was as though she looked into a midnight sky. After a long time she left, and soon went back to London.

Her book was published the year after that, and she underwent some kind of mental breakdown. She had no money to eat, and so she didn't; she ceased to leave her room. A relative in the Navy happened to be on leave in London, and called on her; he was shocked by her condition, and brought her home with him. She withdrew entirely into silence and inaction. Her relatives committed her to an asylum in New Haven, and she died there two years later. *History rest in me a clue* she wrote not long before her death, but what she meant by that no one knows.

"She died of Shakespeare," Harriet says. She's made omelettes for us with herbs from the pots on her windowsill, and I've opened the wine.

"The Shakespeare curse?"

"Not that. Just Shakespeare. It happens. People like you, sunk in Shakespeare. It's not good."

"I'm sunk in Shakespeare?"

"You make a living from Shakespeare."

"Elizabethan drama," I say. "Not Shakespeare really."

"Look what Shakespeare did to us."

"What?"

"We were so caught up with Shakespeare. Shakespeare, Shakespeare. Just like Delia Bacon."

"Oh Harriet. Come on."

"We got sick from Shakespeare," Harriet says.

"Harriet," I say. "It wasn't Shakespeare."

"Oh no?" she says, with vast conviction. "Oh no? Well."

I say no more. Her challenge, or joke, evanesces. She drinks, looking out at the evening. The flush on her cheeks actually brightens when she gets extravagant that way, like a Victorian heroine's. Still, to this day.

"You should write that story," Harriet says. "In a book."

"What story?"

"Delia Bacon. Killed by Shakespeare."

"Oh I don't know. A whole book?"

"Well aren't you supposed to write books? Publish or perish?"

"The only book I want to write," I say, "is the history of the free spirits."

That draws her eyes to me again. "It's a secret history," she says.

"I know."

"Isn't it already written?"

"Some. Not all."

"Maybe it is, though. Maybe it's all written down someplace. In code."

"Well. If Queen Elizabeth wrote the plays of Shakespeare, maybe it's in there."

"Now she was a free spirit," Harriet says. "Don't you think?"

"Yep. Whatever Delia thought."

"Secret marriages. Illegitimate children."

"'And the imperial votaress passed on / In maiden meditation, fancy-free.'"

She holds out a hand to me, and I get up to help her rise. In her tiny apartment behind the store, she can get around without her braces if she's careful, moving like a gibbon from handhold to handhold to the big low bed. It's where she socializes.

"I'm listing," she says, pausing in the door frame. "Two glasses of wine and I'm listing."

So I take her up, remarkably light, and lay her down on the bed.

Harriet's body isn't like other bodies you're likely to have encountered in this way. Her shoulders are broad and strong and flat, like anvils, and her upper arms look plump and soft till you take hold of them and find them to be iron. Harriet says her orthopedic surgeon could never figure out exactly how Harriet walks; she shouldn't have the muscle strength to do it. However she does it, it's given her washboard abs that any high-school boy would envy, and they look like a boy's, finely cut and tender somehow in spite of being so hard. Her butt is a boy's too: slight and soft and hollowed in the flanks. That's where the nerve damage starts, and goes down her legs.

It's like making love to a marionette, I said to her once, lifting and propping apart her stick-thin legs, and she started laughing and had a hard time stopping and going on. But it had taken her a long time to uncover them when we were in bed, let them be part of our lovemaking.

Two crips like us Harriet says sometimes, but that's only a funny kind of politeness, to include me with her in a commonality, not to make me feel an outsider.

"So you've been thinkng," I say. It's late in the night.

"Yep."

"And?"

"Let me pull this sheet up over me."

"That doesn't sound good."

"Reach me the bottle, will you?" she says. Still a lot of Hoosier in her language. I struggle up to get the bottle and glasses, which leaves me outside the underside of the sheet with her, and posted on the bed's edge.

"So how come you asked me this, by the way?" she says. "Just so I know."

"Because I love you."

"You do?"

"Harriet," I say. "I love you. I've always loved you, even when I didn't know it. I'll love you till the day I die." The wine is sweet and still cold. "That's how come."

She drinks, and thinks; or maybe she already knows what she thinks, but not whether to say it.

"So you're not afraid?"

"Of what?"

"My history. I mean it's not like I've been waiting for Mr. Right. There's reasons I'm alone."

"I know."

"Not lonely. Alone."

"I know. I'm not afraid. Maybe I should be, but I'm not."

"Okay then."

She isn't done. Far off there's a borborygmic rumble of thunder, the uneasy sky heaving.

"So have you heard about this new thing we get?" she says.

"What thing we get?"

"They've just started to discover it. A *syndrome.* Us old polios. My doctor told me about it last week."

"You were at the doctor?"

"I started getting tired," she says. "Or not tired, exactly. More like weaker. I wondered. And he told me. He'd just been reading about it himself. Post-polio syndrome."

"Explain," I say. I say it double-calm. That's a word Harriet invented for how actors say certain things in movies.

She hands me her glass, so she can hike herself up with both hands. "It seems," she says, like a joke's opening, "it seems there's this thing about the nerves you use. I mean everybody. The nerves that get used all the time to do things, in your hands and your arms and so on, they have like redundancies. Backups. As you live your life, the nerves wear out. Their coverings get worn away. Used up. So by late in life you're using the backup ones."

"Ah."

"But in polio, the nerves get damaged. The ones you'd normally use, and even the backups in some places. So you've got nothing. And in the places where you've still got something, you're using the backups, you're using the surplus. Even if it's nerves you think have always been fine: sometimes it's really the backups you're going on. So."

"So you wear them out sooner."

"It's how you come back," she says. "You somehow discover these backup nerves, and how to use them. Or you find other muscles, maybe without so much backup, because they're like minor for most people, and you use them like nobody else. It's how you get better. I got better. Even some of the iron lung kids got way better. Now they're old, and the surplus is gone. So we start to lose."

I wonder if I've noticed any of this, in myself. I can't tell. Maybe I'm more tired, have a harder time with the long walks across campus. Maybe.

"You know what's sad, though," Harriet says. "It's the ones who worked the hardest to come back, get function back, that are going to be losing it soonest. All those exercises, all that grit. The ones who weren't going to be beat."

I put my hand on her leg. She puts her hand on mine.

"So," she says, double-calm. "Get it?"

I get it. I do. It's my answer: Harriet's got a lot less function than I do, and if she knows she's going to start to lose what she has, she can't say yes to me: can't, because it wouldn't seem like a free choice, would seem to have a reason, an urgent reason; it would seem like a way to get the help she knows she's going to need. Would seem, even if it isn't. We'll talk more, talk into the night, and I'll say *Don't fall for that, Harriet, don't fall for that no-pity stuff;* I'll say *Don't believe all they tell you, you didn't believe them when they said you'd never walk;* I'll say *What about me, Harriet, what about the fact that I want to be with you no matter what, for better or for worse.* But it won't matter.

"I think it's rotten," she says.

She's crying now. Only a little.

"I don't usually feel sorry for myself," she says. "Wouldn't you say that's so? Have you seen me being sorry for myself much?"

"Never," I say. And it's so.

"I wish it would rain," Harriet says.

*

It does, toward midnight, wild nearly continuous lightning and hellacious thunder, almost Midwestern in its intensity, and Harriet clings to me whooping and laughing as though on a carnival ride; and when at last it's gone, and quiet, and we've lain a long time listening to the gutters running softly, she sends me home.

The next day she gets up early again, though not quite so early, to go out and make pictures. The day is terribly beautiful, sunshot, raindrop-spattered, mist-hung. She loads her film holders, planning her moves from house to car with all the things needed, hoping she won't miss the light, knowing she can't hurry. Hurry is slow; hurry costs time. *Festina lente.*

By midmorning she reaches the place she set out for, that she imagined in advance. But a vast wind has come up, moving through the leaves of the huge trees, passing amid them, and then going around again. The trees are moving too much for Harriet's slow exposures. She stands by her tall patient camera and watches. The wind stirring the heavy masses of leaves lends the trees one by one a momentary animal life different from their usual vegetable one, a free will, or the illusion of one; and they seem to be glad of it, to delight in it even, raising and shaking their arms and shivering in glee.

On her way back to town she cruises the tag sales. The families have just put out their stacks of mismatched dishes and white elephants and *National Geographics,* the pole lamps and tiered end tables unaccustomed to the outdoor air and looking as though they feel uncomfortably conspicuous on the dewey grass. Harriet is an Early Bird and picks up a few "smalls" for the shop—a set of twelve silver "apostle" spoons and a nice set of wartime tumblers with decals on them of pinup girls in scanty uniforms. At one place she finds a game of Shakespeare, a board game which she has known existed and seen around but never played. The box is shut with a bit of masking tape, and is going for a quarter.

"It's all there," the householder tells her. "Complete."

Harriet gives her a quarter.

Back home again, she unloads her camera and brings in the shoulder bag she carries for purchases. The game of Shakespeare in its box. She thinks a while there, poised on her crutches like Chaplin on his stick. Then she goes to her closets—Harriet has no basement or attic, wouldn't be able to use them, but she has many closets—and after some searching she pulls out a small blue suitcase, one of a matched set that once included a round hatbox; there's a poodle appliquéd on it. She humps the suitcase—it's heavy—to the dining table, which she uses more for laying out and mounting pictures than for dining, and snaps open its clasps. Inside she has yearbooks and photographs and mimeographed programs from long-ago recitals, awards, blue ribbons. Scrapbooks too. She takes out a ragged manila envelope, addressed to her old house in Indiana, and from it the journals she kept and the letters she wrote home that summer, the program of *Henry V,* the eight-by-ten of Robin she took from the bulletin board in the theater.

She has all that piled on her dining table, now in the summer of 1980. She adds the book I brought her, *The Girlhood of Shakespeare's Heroines.* The game of Shakespeare too. She picks that up, hefting it in her hand—heavy, heavier than she expected, or is it some new weakness in that hand, which is not her good hand? Gripping tighter, she picks at the tape holding it shut, and maybe because she's holding it too tight, she loses control of it and the box opens and spills its contents before she can recover. Among the contents are a dozen tiny busts of Shakespeare, the counters in the game, and they go bouncing over the table and onto the floor, rattling into corners and under things in that purposeful way that small dropped things have, as though trying to escape.

Plastic Shakespeares red and white, black and brown. Two or three roll—Harriet catches them in the corner of her eye—under the tall armoire that holds more of her stuff. Now that's a drag. Box still in hand, Harriet stares unmoving. She'll have to get her braces off, lie full length on the floor, grope around in the narrow dark space under there maybe with a broom or some such implement, and knock them out from where they're stuck. And she won't be able to reach them, and she'll have to get someone to shift the wardrobe and reach down the back to extricate them. Someone. Unless she chooses just to leave them there forever.

Lull

Kelly Link

THERE WAS A LULL IN THE conversation. We were down in the basement, sitting around the green felt table. We were holding bottles of warm beer in one hand and our cards in the other. Our cards weren't great. Looking at each other's faces, we could see that clearly.

We were tired. It made us more tired to look at each other when we saw we weren't getting away with anything at all. We didn't have any secrets.

We hadn't seen each other for a while and it was clear that we hadn't changed for the better. We were between jobs or stuck in jobs that we hated. We were having affairs and our wives knew and didn't care. Some of us were sleeping with each other's wives. There were things that had gone wrong, and we weren't sure who to blame.

We had been talking about things that went backwards instead of forwards. Things that managed to do both at the same time. Time travelers. People who weren't stuck like us. There was that new movie that went backwards, and then Jeff put this music on the stereo where all the lyrics were palindromes. It was something his kid had picked up. His kid, Stan, was a lot cooler than we had ever been. He was always bringing things home, Jeff said, saying, *You have got to listen to this. Here, try this. These guys are good.*

Stan was the kid who got drugs for the other kids when there was going to be a party. We had tried not to be bothered by this. We trusted our kids and we hoped that they trusted us, that they weren't too embarrassed by us. We weren't cool. We were willing to be liked. That would have been enough.

Stan was so very cool that he hadn't even minded taking care of some of us, the parents of his friends (the friends of his parents), although sometimes we just went through our kids' drawers, looked under the mattresses. It wasn't that different from taking Halloween candy out of their Halloween bags, which was something we had also done, when they were younger and went to bed before we did.

Stan wasn't into that stuff now, though. None of the kids were. They were into music instead.

You couldn't get this music on CD. That was part of the conceit.

It only came on cassette. You played one side, and then on the other side the songs all played backwards and the lyrics went forwards and backwards all over again in one long endless loop. *La allah ha llal. Do, oh, oh, do you, oh do, oh, wanna?*

Bones was really digging it. "Do you, do you wanna dance, you do, you do," he said and laughed and tipped his chair back. "Snakey canes. Hula boolah."

Someone mentioned the restaurant downtown where you were supposed to order your dessert and then you got your dinner.

"I fold," Ed said. He threw his cards down on the table.

Ed liked to make up games. People paid him to make up games. Back when we had a regular poker night, he was always teaching us a new game and this game would be based on a TV show or some dream he'd had.

"Let's try something new. I'm going to deal out everything, the whole deck, and then we'll have to put it all back. We'll see each other's hands as we put them down. We're going for low. And we'll swap. Yeah, that might work. Something else, like a wild card, but we won't know what the wild card was, until the very end. We'll need to play fast—no stopping to think about it—just do what I tell you to do."

"What'll we call it?" he said, not a question, but as if we'd asked him, although we hadn't. He was shuffling the deck, holding the cards close like we might try to take them away. "DNA Hand. Got it?"

"That's a shitty idea," Jeff said. It was his basement, his poker table, his beer. So he got to say things like that. You could tell that he thought Ed looked happier than he ought to. He was thinking Ed ought to remember his place in the world, or maybe Ed needed to be reminded what his place was. His new place. Most of us were relieved to see that Ed looked okay. If he didn't look okay, that was okay too. We understood. Bad things had happened to all of us.

We were contemplating these things and then the tape flips over and starts again.

It's catchy stuff. We could listen to it all night.

*

"Now we chant along and summon the Devil," Bones says. "Always wanted to do that."

Bones has been drunk for a while now. His hair is standing up and his face is shiny and red. He has a fat stupid smile on his face. We ignore him, which is what he wants. Bones's wife is just the same, loud and useless. The thing that makes the rest of us sick is that their kids are the nicest, smartest, funniest, best kids. We can't figure it out. They don't deserve kids like that.

Brenner asks Ed if he's found a new place to live. He has.

"Off the highway, down by that Texaco, in the orchards. This guy built a road and built the house right on top of the road. Just, plop, right in the middle of the road. Kind of like he came walking up the road with the house on his back, got tired, and just dropped it."

"Not very good feng shui," Pete says.

Pete has read a book. He's got a theory about picking up women that he's always sharing with us. He goes to the Barnes & Noble on his lunch hour and hangs around in front of displays of books about houses and decorating, skimming through architecture books. He says it makes you look smart and just domesticated enough. A man looking at pictures of houses is sexy to women.

We've never asked if it works for him.

Meanwhile, we know, Pete's wife is always after him to go up on the roof and gut the drains, reshingle and patch, paint. Pete isn't really into this. Imaginary houses are sexy. Real ones are work.

He did go buy a mirror at Pottery Barn and hang it up, just inside the front door, because otherwise, he said, evil spirits go rushing up the staircase and into the bedrooms. Getting them out again is tricky.

The way the mirror works is that they start to come in, look in the mirror, and think a devil is already living in the house. So they take off. Devils can look like anyone—salespeople, Latter-day Saints, the people who mow your lawns—even members of your own family. So you have to have a mirror.

Ed says, "Where the house is, is the first weird thing. The second thing is the house. It's like this team of architects went crazy and sawed two different houses in half and then stitched them back together. Casa Del Guggenstein. The front half is really old—a hundred years old—the other half is aluminum siding."

"Must have brought down the asking price," Jeff says.

"Yeah," Ed says. "And the other thing is there are all these doors. One at the front and one at the back and two more on either side, right smack where the aluminum siding starts, these weird, tall, skinny doors, like they're built for basketball players. Or aliens."

"Or palm trees," Bones says.

"Yeah," Ed says. "And then one last door, this vestigial door, up in the master bedroom. Not like a door that you walk through, for a closet, or a bathroom. It opens and there's nothing there. No staircase, no balcony, no point to it. It's a Tarzan door. Up in the trees. You open it and an owl might fly in. Or a bat. The previous tenant left that door locked—apparently he was afraid of sleepwalking."

"Fantastic," Brenner says. "Wake up in the middle of the night and go to the bathroom, you could just pee out the side of your house."

He opens up the last beer and shakes some pepper in it. Brenner has a thing about pepper. He even puts it on ice cream. Pete swears that one time at a party he wandered into Brenner's bedroom and looked in a drawer in a table beside the bed. He says he found a box of condoms and a pepper mill. When we asked what he was doing in Brenner's bedroom, he winked and then put his finger to his mouth and zipped his lip.

Brenner has a little pointed goatee. It might look silly on some people, but not on Brenner. The pepper thing sounds silly, maybe, but not even Jeff teases Brenner about it.

"I remember that house,"Alibi says.

We call him Alibi because his wife is always calling to check up on him. She'll say, so was Alec out shooting pool with you the other night, and we'll say, sure he was, Gloria. The problem is that sometimes Alibi has told her some completely different story and she's just testing us. But that's not our problem and that's not our fault. She never holds it against us and neither does he.

"We used to go up in the orchards at night and have wars. Knock each other down with rotten apples. There were these peacocks. You bought the orchard house?"

"Yeah," Ed says. "I need to do something about the orchard. All the apples are falling off the trees and then they just rot on the ground. The peacocks eat them and get drunk. There are drunk wasps, too. If you go down there you can see the wasps hurtling around in these loopy lines and the peacocks grab them right out of the air. Little pickled wasp hors d'oeuvres. Everything smells like rotting apples. All night long, I'm dreaming about eating wormy apples."

For a second, we're afraid Ed might tell us his dreams. Nothing is worse than someone telling you their dreams.

"So what's the deal with the peacocks?" Bones says.
"Long story," Ed says.

So you know how the road to the house is a private road, you turn off the highway onto it, and it meanders up some until you run into the house. Someday I'll drive home and park the car in the living room.

There's a big sign that says PRIVATE. But people still drive up the turnoff, lost, or maybe looking for a picnic spot, or a place to pull off the road and fuck. Before you hear the car coming, you hear the peacocks. Which was the plan because this guy who built it was a real hermit, a recluse.

People in town said all kinds of stuff about him. Nobody knew. He didn't want anybody to know.

The peacocks were so he would know when anyone was coming up to the house. They start screaming before you ever see a car. So remember, out the back door, the road goes on down through the orchards, there's a gate, and then you're back on the main highway again. And this guy, the hermit, he kept two cars. Back then, nobody had two cars. But he kept one car parked in front of the house and one parked at the back so that whichever way someone was coming, he could go out the other way real fast and drive off before his visitor got up to the house.

He had an arrangement with a grocer. The grocer sent a boy up to the house once every two weeks, and the boy brought the mail, too, but there wasn't ever any mail.

The hermit had painted in the windows of his cars, black, except for these little circles that he could see out of. You couldn't see in. But apparently he used to drive around at night. People said they saw him. Or they didn't see him. That was the point.

The real estate agent said she heard that once this guy had to go to the doctor. He had a growth or something. He showed up in the doctor's office wearing a woman's hat with a long black veil that hung down from the crown, so you couldn't see his face. He took off his clothes in the doctor's office and kept the hat on.

One night half of the house fell down. People all over the town saw lights, like fireworks or lightning, up over the orchard. Some people swore they saw something big, all lit up, go up into the sky, like an explosion, but quiet. Just lights. The next day, people went up to the orchard. The hermit was waiting for them—he had his veil on. From the front, the house looked fine. But you could tell something had caught fire. You could smell it, like ozone.

The hermit said it had been lightning. He rebuilt the house himself. Had lumber and everything delivered. Apparently kids used to go sneak up in the trees in the orchard and watch him while he was working, but he did all the work wearing the hat and the veil.

He died a long time ago. The grocer's boy figured out something was wrong because the peacocks were coming in and out of the windows of the house and screaming.

So now they're still down in the orchards and under the porch, and they still came in the windows and made a mess if Ed forgot and left the windows open too wide. Last week a fox came in after a peacock. You wouldn't think a fox would go after something so big and mean. Peacocks are mean.

Ed had been downstairs watching TV.

"I heard the bird come in," he says, "and then I heard a thump and a slap like a chair going over and when I went to look, there was a streak of blood going up the floor to the window. A fox was going out the window and the peacock was in its mouth, all the feathers dragging across the sill. Like one of Susan's paintings."

Ed's wife, Susan, took an art class for a while. Her teacher said she had a lot of talent. Brenner modeled for her, and so did some of our kids, but most of Susan's paintings were portraits of her brother, Andrew. He'd been living with Susan and Ed for about two years. This was hard on Ed, although he'd never complained about it. He knew Susan loved her brother. He knew her brother had problems.

Andrew couldn't hold down a job. He went in and out of rehab, and when he was out, he hung out with our kids. Our kids thought Andrew was cool. The less we liked him, the more time our kids spent with Andrew. Maybe we were just a little jealous of him.

Jeff's kid, Stan, he and Andrew hung out all the time. Stan was the one who found Andrew and called the hospital. Susan never said anything, but maybe she blamed Stan. Everybody knew Stan had been getting stuff for Andrew.

Another thing that nobody said: what happened to Andrew, it was probably good for the kids in the long run.

Those paintings—Susan's paintings—were weird. None of the people in her paintings ever looked very comfortable, and she couldn't do hands. And there were always these animals in the paintings, looking as if they'd been shot, or gutted, or if they didn't look dead, they were definitely supposed to be rabid. You worried about the people.

She hung them up in their house for a while, but they weren't comfortable paintings. You couldn't watch TV in the same room with them. And Andrew had this habit, he'd sit on the sofa just under one portrait, and there was another one, too, above the TV. Three Andrews was too many.

Once Ed brought Andrew to poker night. Andrew sat a while and didn't say anything, and then he said he was going upstairs to get more beer and he never came back. Three days later, the highway patrol found Ed's car parked under a bridge. Stan and Andrew came home two days after that, and Andrew went back into rehab. Susan used to go visit him and take Stan with her—she'd take her sketchbook. Stan said Andrew would sit there and Susan would draw him and nobody ever said a word.

After the class was over, while Andrew was still in rehab, Susan invited all of us to go to this party at her teacher's studio. What we remember is that Pete got drunk and made a pass at the instructor, this sharp-looking woman with big dangly earrings. We were kind of surprised, not just because he did it in front of his wife, but because we'd all just been looking at her paintings. All these deer and birds and cows draped over dinner tables, and sofas, guts hanging out, eyeballs all shiny and fixed—so that explained Susan's portraits, at least.

We wonder what Susan did with the paintings of Andrew.

"I've been thinking about getting a dog," Ed says.

"Fuck," we say. "A dog's a big responsibility." Which is what we've spent years telling our kids.

The music on the tape loops and looped. It was going round for a second time. We sat and listened to it. We'll be sitting and listening to it for a while longer.

"This guy," Ed says, "the guy who was renting this place before me, he was into some crazy things. There's all these mandalas and pentagrams painted on the floors and walls. Which is also why I got it so cheap. They didn't want to bother stripping the walls and repainting; this guy just took off one day, took a lot of the furniture, too. Loaded up his truck with as much as he could take."

"So no furniture?" Pete says. "Susan get the dining-room table and chairs? The bed? You sleeping in a sleeping bag? Eating beanie weenies out of a can?"

"I got a futon," Ed says. "And I've got my work table set up, the

TV and stuff. I've been going down to the orchard, grilling on the hibachi. You guys should come over. I'm working on a new video game—it'll be a haunted house—those are really big right now. That's why this place is so great for me. I can use everything. Next weekend? I'll fix hamburgers and you guys can sit up in the house, keep cool, drink beer, test the game for me. Find the bugs."

"There are always bugs," Jeff says. He's smiling in a mean way. He isn't so nice when he's been drinking. "That's life. So should we bring the kids? The wives? Is this a family thing? Ellie's been asking about you. You know that retreat she's on, she called from the woods the other day. She went on and on about this past life. Apparently she was a used car salesman. She says that this life is karmic payback, being married to me, right? She gets home day after tomorrow. We get together, maybe Ellie can set you up with someone. Now that you're a free man, you need to take some advantage."

"Sure," Ed says and shrugs. We can see him wishing that Jeff would shut up, but Jeff doesn't shut up.

Jeff says, "I saw Susan in the grocery store the other day. She looked fantastic. It wasn't that she wasn't sad anymore, she wasn't just getting by, she was radiant, you know? That special glow. Like Joan of Arc. Like she knew something. Like she'd won the lottery."

"Well, yeah," Ed says. "That's Susan. She doesn't live in the past. She's got this new job, this research project. They're trying to contact aliens. They're using household appliances: satellite dishes, cell phones, car radios, even refrigerators. I'm not sure how. I'm not sure what they're planning to say. But they've got a lot of grant money. Even hired a speech writer."

"Wonder what you say to aliens," Brenner says. "Hi, honey, I'm home. What's for dinner?"

"Your place or mine?" Pete says. "What's a nice alien like you doing in a galaxy like this?"

"Where you been? I've been worried sick," Alibi says.

Jeff picks up a card, props it sideways against the green felt. Picks up another one, leans it against the first. He says, "You and Susan always looked so good together. Perfect marriage, perfect life. Now look at you: she's talking to aliens, and you're living in a haunted house. You're an example to all of us, Ed. Nice guy like you, bad things happen to you, Susan leaves a swell guy like you, what's the lesson here? I've been thinking about this all year. You and Ellie must have worked at the same car dealership, in that past life."

Nobody says anything. Ed doesn't say anything, but the way we see him look at Jeff, we know that this haunted house game is going to have a character in it who walks and talks a lot like Jeff. This Jeff character is going to panic and run around on the screen of people's TVs and get lost.

It will stumble into booby traps and fall onto knives. Its innards will slop out. Zombies are going to crack open the bones of its legs and suck on the marrow. Little devils with monkey faces are going to stitch its eyes open with tiny stitches and then they are going to piss beautiful ribbons of acid into its eyes.

Beautiful women are going to fuck this cartoon Jeff in the ass with garden shears. And when this character screams, it's going to sound a lot like Jeff screaming. It will scream for a while, which might attract other things. Ed's good at the little details. The kids who buy Ed's games love the details. They buy his games for things like this.

Jeff will probably be flattered.

Jeff starts complaining about Stan's phone bill, this four-hundred-dollar cell-phone charge that Stan ran up. When he asked about it, Stan handed him a stack of twenties just like that. That kid always has money to spare.

Stan also gave Jeff this phone number. He told Jeff that it's like this phone-sex line, but with a twist. You call up and ask for this girl named Starlight, and she tells you sexy stories, only, if you want, they don't have to be sexy. They can be any kind of story you want. You tell her what kind of story you want, and she makes it up. Stan says it's Stephen King and sci-fi and the Arabian Nights and *Penthouse* Letters all at once.

Ed interrupts Jeff. "You got the number?"

"What?" Jeff says.

"I just got paid for the last game," Ed says. "The one with the baby heads and the octopus girlies, the Martian combat hockey. Let's call that number. I'll pay. You put her on speaker and we'll all listen, and it's my treat, okay, because I'm such a swell guy."

Bones says that it sounds like a shit idea to him, which is probably why Jeff went and got the phone bill and another six-pack of beer. We all take another beer.

Jeff turns the stereo down—

Madam I'm Adam Madam I'm Adam

—and puts the phone in the middle of the table. It sits there, in the middle of all that green, like an island or something. Marooned. Jeff switches it on speaker. "Four bucks a minute," he says, and shrugs, and dials the number.

"Here," Ed says. "Pass it over."

The phone rings and we listen to it ring and then a woman's voice, very pleasant, says hello and asks if Ed is over eighteen. He says he is. He gives her his credit card number. She asks if he was calling for anyone in particular.

"Starlight," Ed says.

"One moment," the woman says. We hear a click and then Starlight is on the line. We know this because she says so. She says, "Hi, my name is Starlight. I'm going to tell you a sexy story. Do you want to know what I'm wearing?"

Ed grunts. He shrugs. He grimaces at us. He needs a haircut. Susan used to cut his hair, which we used to think was cute. He and Andrew had these identical lopsided haircuts. It was pretty goofy.

"Can I call you Susan?" Ed says.

Which we think is strange.

Starlight says, "If you really want to, but my name's really Starlight. Don't you think that's sexy?"

She sounds like a kid. A little girl—not even like a girl. Like a kid. She doesn't sound like Susan at all. Since the divorce, we haven't seen much of Susan, although she calls our houses sometimes, to talk to our wives. We're a little worried about what she's been saying to them.

Ed says, "I guess so." We can tell he's only saying that to be polite, but Starlight laughs as if he's told her a joke. It's weird hearing that little-kid laugh down here.

Ed says, "So are you going to tell me a story?"

Starlight says, "That's what I'm here for. But usually the guy wants to know what I'm wearing."

Ed says, "I want to hear a story about a cheerleader and the Devil."

Bones says, "So what's she wearing?"

Pete says, "Make it a story that goes backwards."

Jeff says, "Put something scary in it."

Alibi says, "Sexy."

Brenner says, "I want it to be about good and evil and true love, and it should also be funny. No talking animals. Not too much fooling around with the narrative structure. The ending should be happy but still realistic, believable, you know, and there shouldn't be a moral although we should be able to think back later and have some sort of revelation. No *and suddenly they woke up and discovered that it was all a dream.* Got that?"

Starlight says, "Okay. The Devil and a cheerleader. Got it. Okay."

Kelly Link

The Devil and the Cheerleader

So the Devil is at a party at the cheerleader's house. They've been playing spin the bottle. The cheerleader's boyfriend just came out of the closet with her best friend. Earlier the cheerleader felt like slapping him, and now she knows why. The bottle pointed at her best friend who had just shrugged and smiled at her. Then the bottle was spinning and when the bottle stopped spinning, it was in her boyfriend's hand.

Then all of a sudden an egg timer was going off. Everyone was giggling and they were all standing up to go over by the closet, like they were all going to try to squeeze inside. But the Devil stood up and took the cheerleader's hand and pulled her backwards-forwards.

So she knew what exactly had happened, and was going to happen, and some other things besides.

This is the thing she likes about backwards. You start out with all the answers, and after a while, someone comes along and gives you the questions, but you don't have to answer them. You're already past that part. That was what was so nice about being married. Things got better and better until you hardly even knew each other anymore. And then you said goodnight and went out on a date, and after that you were just friends. It was easier that way—that's the dear, sweet, backwards way of the world.

Just a second, let's go back for a second.

Something happened. Something has happened. But nobody ever talked about it, at least not at these parties. Not anymore.

Everyone's been drinking all night long, except the Devil, who's a teetotaler. He's been pretending to drink vodka out of a hip flask. Everybody at the party is drunk right now and they think he's okay. Later they'll sober up. They'll think he's *pretentious*, an *asshole*, drinking air out of a flask like that.

There are a lot of empty bottles of beer, some empty bottles of whiskey. There's a lot of work still to be done, by the look of it. They're using one of the beer bottles, that's what they're spinning. Later on it will be full and they won't have to play this stupid game.

The cheerleader guesses that she didn't invite the Devil to the party. He isn't the kind of guy that you have to invite. He'll probably show up by himself. But now they're in the closet together for five minutes. The cheerleader's boyfriend isn't too happy about this, but what can he do? It's that kind of party. She's that kind of cheerleader.

They're a lot younger than they used to be. At parties like this, they used to be older, especially the Devil. He remembers all the way back to the end of the world. The cheerleader wasn't a cheerleader then. She was married and had kids and a husband.

Something's going to happen, or maybe it's already happened. Nobody ever talks about it. If they could, what would they say?

But those end-of-the-world parties were crazy. People would drink too much and they wouldn't have any clothes on. There'd be these sad little piles of clothes in the living room, as if something had happened, and the people had disappeared, disappeared right out of their clothes. Meanwhile, the people who belonged to the clothes would be out in the backyard, waiting until it was time to go home. They'd get up on the trampoline and bounce around and cry.

There would be a bottle of extra-virgin olive oil and sooner or later someone was going to have to refill it and go put it back on the pantry shelf. You'd have had these slippery naked middle-aged people sliding around on the trampoline and the oily grass, and then in the end all you'd have would be a bottle of olive oil, some olives on a tree, a tree, an orchard, an empty field.

The Devil would stand around feeling awkward, hoping that it would turn out he'd come late.

The kids would be up in their bedrooms, out of the beds, looking out the windows, remembering when *they* used to be older. Not that they ever got that much older.

But the world is younger now. Things are simpler. Now the cheerleader has parents of her own, and all she has to do is wait for them to get home, and then this party can be over.

Two days ago was the funeral. It was just the way everyone said it would be.

Then there were errands, people to talk to. She was busy.

She hugged her aunt and uncle goodbye and moved into the house where she would live for the rest of her life. She unpacked all her boxes, and the Salvation Army brought her parents' clothes and furniture and pots and pans, and other people, her parents' friends, helped her hang her mother's clothes in her mother's closet. (Not this closet.) She bunched her mother's clothes up in her hand and *sniffed.*

She suspects, remembering the smell of her mother's monogrammed sweaters, that they'll have fights about things. Boys, music, clothes. The cheerleader will learn to let all of these things go.

If her kids were still around, they would say *I told you so.* What they did say was, *Just wait until you have parents of your own. You'll see.*

The cheerleader rubs her stomach. *Are you in there?*

She moved the unfamiliar, worn-down furniture around so that it matched up to old grooves in the floor. Here was the shape of someone's buttocks, printed onto a seat cushion. Maybe it would be her father's favorite chair.

She looked through her father's records. There was a record playing on the phonograph, it wasn't anything she had ever heard before, and she took it off, laid it back in its empty white sleeve. She studied the death certificates. She tried to think what to tell her parents about their grandchildren, what they'd want to know.

Her favorite song had just been on the radio for the very last time. Years and years ago, she'd danced to that song at her wedding. Now it was gone, except for the feeling she'd had when she listened to it. Sometimes she still felt that way, but there wasn't a word for it anymore.

She went up to her room and erased two whole pages in her diary. By Christmas, it will be blank and she can wrap it up and give it back to her parents who will take it back to the store.

She studied family photo albums. She'd been doing that for the past few weeks. What if they showed up and she didn't recognize them?

Tonight, in a few hours, there will be a car wreck and then her parents will be coming home. By then, all her friends will have left, taking away six-packs and boyfriends and newly applied coats of hair spray and lipstick.

She thinks she looks a bit like her mother.

Before everyone showed up, while everything was still a *wreck* downstairs, before the police had arrived to say what they had to say, she was standing in her parents' bathroom. She was looking in the mirror.

She picked a lipstick out of the trash can, an orangey red that will be a favorite because there's just a little half-moon left. But when she looked at herself in the mirror, it didn't fit. It didn't belong to her.

She put her hand on her breastbone, pressed hard, felt her heart beating faster and faster. She couldn't wear her mother's lipstick while her mother lay on a gurney somewhere in a morgue: waiting to be sewn up; to have her clothes sewn back on; to breathe; to wake up; to see the car on the other side of the median, sliding away; to see her husband, the man that she's going to marry someday; to come home to meet her daughter.

The recently dead are always exhausted. There's so much to absorb, so many things that need to be undone. They have their whole lives ahead of them.

The cheerleader's best friend winks at her. The Devil's got a flashlight with two dead batteries. Somebody closes the door after them.

Soon, very soon, already now, the batteries in the Devil's flashlight are old and tired and there's just a thin line of light under the closet door. It's cramped in the closet and it smells like shoes, paint, wool, cigarettes, tennis rackets strung with real catgut, ghosts of perfume and sweat. Outside the closet, the world is getting younger, but in here is where they keep all the old things. The cheerleader put them all in here last week.

She's felt queasy for most of her life. She's a bad time traveler. She gets time-sick. It's as if she's always just a little bit pregnant, *are you in there?* and it's worse in here, with all these old things that don't belong to her, even worse because the Devil is always fooling around with time.

The Devil feels right at home. He and the cheerleader make a nest of coats and sit down on them, facing each other. The Devil turns the bright, constant beam of the flashlight on the cheerleader. She's wearing a little flippy skirt. Her knees are up, making a tent out of her skirt. The tent is full of shadows—so is the closet. The Devil conjures up another Devil, another cheerleader, mouse-sized, both of them, sitting under the cheerleader's skirt. The closet is full of Devils and cheerleaders.

"I just need to hold something," the cheerleader says. If she holds something, maybe she won't throw up.

"Please," the Devil says. "It tickles. I'm tickish."

The cheerleader is leaning forward. She's got the Devil by the tail. Then she's touching the Devil's tail with her pom-poms. He quivers.

"Please don't," he says. He giggles.

The Devil's tail is tucked up under his legs. It isn't hot, but the Devil is sweating. He feels sad. He's not good at being sad. He flicks the flashlight on and off. Here's a knee. Here's a mouth. Here's a sleeve hanging down, all empty. Someone knocks on the closet door.

"Go away," the cheerleader says. "It hasn't been five minutes yet. Not even."

The Devil can feel her smile at him, like they're old friends. "Your tail. Can I touch it?" the cheerleader says.

"Touch what?" the Devil says. He feels a little excited, a little nervous. Old enough to know better, brand-new enough, here in the closet, to be jumpy. He's taking a chance here. Girls—*women*—aren't really domestic animals at the moment, although they're getting tamer, more used to living in houses. Less likely to bite.

"Can I touch your tail now?" the cheerleader says.

"No!" the Devil says.

"I'm shy," he says. "Maybe you could stroke my tail with your pom-pom, in a little bit."

"We could make out," the cheerleader says. "That's what we're supposed to do, right? I need to be distracted because I think I'm about to have this thought. It's going to make me really sad. I'm getting younger, you know? I'm going to keep on getting younger. It isn't fair."

She puts her feet against the closet door. She kicks once, like a mule.

She says, "I mean, you're the Devil. You don't have to worry about this stuff. In a few thousand years, you'll be back at the beginning again and you'll be in good with God again, right?"

The Devil shrugs. Everybody knows the end of that story.

The cheerleader says, "Everyone knows that old story. You're famous. You're like John Wilkes Booth. You're historical—you're going to be really important. You'll be Mr. Bringer-of-Light and you'll get good tables at all the trendy restaurants, choruses of angels and maître d's, et cetera, la, la, la, they'll all be singing hallelujahs forever, please pass the vichyssoise, and then God unmakes the world and he'll put all the bits away in a closet like this."

The Devil smirks. He shrugs. It isn't a bad life, hanging around in closets with cheerleaders. And it gets better.

The cheerleader says, "It isn't fair. I'd tell him so, if he were here.

He'll unhang the stars and pull Leviathan right back out of the deep end of the vasty bathwater, and you'll be having Leviathan tartar for dinner. Where will I be, then? You'll be around. You're always around. But me, I'll get younger and younger and in a handful of years I won't be me at all, and my parents will get younger and so on and so on, whoosh. We'll be gone like a flash of light, and you won't even remember me. Nobody will remember me. Everything that I was, that I did, all the funny things that I said, and the things that my friends said back to me, that will all be gone. But you go all the way backwards. You go backwards and forwards. It isn't fair. You could always remember me. What could I do so that you would remember me?"

"As long as we're in this closet," the Devil says, he's magnanimous, "I'll remember you."

"But in a few minutes," the cheerleader says, "we'll go back out of the closet and the bottle will spin, and then the party will be over, and my parents will come home, and nobody will ever remember me."

"Then tell me a story," the Devil says. He puts his sharp, furry paw on her leg. "Tell me a story so that I'll remember you."

"What kind of story?" says the cheerleader.

"Tell me a scary story," the Devil says. "A funny, scary, sad, happy story. I want everything." He can feel his tail wagging as he says this.

"You can't have everything," the cheerleader says, and she picks up his paw and puts it back on the floor of the closet. "Not even in a story. You can't have all the stories you want."

"I know," the Devil says. He whines. "But I still want it. I want things. That's my job. I even want the things that I already have. I want everything you have. I want the things that don't exist. That's why I'm the Devil." He leers, and it's a shame because she can't see him in the dark. He feels silly.

"Well, what's the scariest thing?" says the cheerleader. "You're the expert, right? Give me a little help here."

"The scariest thing," the Devil says. "Okay, I'll give you two things. Three things. No, just two. The third one is a secret."

The Devil's voice changes. Later on, one day the cheerleader will be listening to a preschool teacher say back the alphabet, with the sun moving across the window, nothing ever stays still, and she'll be reminded of the Devil and the closet and the line of light under the door, the peaceful little circle of light the flashlight makes against the closet door.

The Devil says, "I'm not complaining"—but he is—"but here's the way things used to work. They don't work this way anymore. I don't know if you remember. Your parents are dead and they're coming home in just a few hours. Used to be, that was scary. Not anymore. But try to imagine: finding something that shouldn't be there."

"Like what?" the cheerleader says.

The Devil shrugs. "A child's toy. A ball, or a night-light. Some cheap bit of trash, but it's heavier than it looks, or else light. It shines with a greasy sort of light or else it eats light. When you touch it, it yields. You feel as if you might fall into it. You feel light-headed. It might be inscribed in a language that no one can decipher."

"Wow," the cheerleader says. She seems somewhat cheered up. "So what's the next thing?"

The Devil shines the flashlight in her eyes, flicks it on and off. "Someone disappears. Gone, just like that. They're standing behind you in a line at an amusement park—or they wander away during the intermission of a play—perhaps they go downstairs to get the mail—or to make tea—"

"That's scary?" the cheerleader says.

"Used to be," the Devil says. "It used to be that the worst thing that could happen was, if you had kids, and one of them died or disappeared. Disappeared was the worst. Anything might have happened to them."

"Things are better now," the cheerleader says.

"Yes, well," the Devil says. "Things just get better and better nowadays. But—try to remember how it was. The person who disappeared, only they didn't. You'd see them from time to time, peeking in at you through windows, or down low through the mail slot in your front door. They might pinch your leg or pull your hair when you're asleep. When you talk on the phone, they listen in, you hear them listening."

The cheerleader says, "Like, with my parents—"

"Exactly," says the Devil. "You've had nightmares about them, right?"

"Not really," the cheerleader says. "Everyone says they were probably nice people. I mean, look at this house! But, sometimes, I have this dream that I'm at the mall, and I see my husband. And he's just the same, he's a grownup, and he doesn't recognize me. It turns out that I'm the only one who's going backwards. And then he does recognize me and he wants to know what I've done with the kids."

The last time she'd seen her husband, he was trying to grow a beard. He couldn't even do that right. He hadn't had much to say, but they'd looked at each other for a long time.

"What about your children?" the Devil says. "Do you wonder where they went when the doctor pushed them back up inside you? Do you have dreams about them?"

"Yes," the cheerleader says. "Everything gets smaller. I'm afraid of that."

"Think how men feel!" the Devil says. "It's no wonder men are afraid of women. No wonder sex is so hard on them."

The cheerleader misses sex, that feeling afterwards, that blissful, unsatisfied itch.

"The first time around, things were better," the Devil says. "I don't know if you remember. People died, and no one was sure what happened next. There were all sorts of possibilities. Now everyone knows everything. What's the fun in that?"

Someone is trying to push open the closet door, but the cheerleader puts her feet against it, leaning against the back of the closet. "Oh, I remember!" she says. "I remember when I was dead! There was so much I was looking forward to. I had no idea!"

The Devil shivers. He's never liked dead people much.

"So, okay, what about monsters?" the cheerleader says. "Vampires? Serial killers? People from outer space? Those old movies?"

The Devil shrugs. "Yeah, sure. Boogeymen. Formaldehyde babies in Mason jars. Someday someone is going to have to take them out of the jar, unpickle them. Women with teeth down there. Zombies. Killer robots, killer bees, serial killers, cold spots, werewolves. The dream where you know that you're asleep but you can't wake up. You can hear someone walking around the bedroom picking up your things and putting them down again and you still can't wake up. The end of the world. Spiders. *No one was with her when she died.* Carnivorous plants."

"Oh goody," the cheerleader says. Her eyes shine at him out of the dark. Her pom-poms slide across the floor of the closet. He moves his flashlight so he can see her hands.

"So here's your story," the cheerleader says. (She's a girl who can think on her feet.) "It's not really a scary story. I don't really get scary."

"Weren't you listening?" the Devil says. He taps the flashlight against his big front teeth. "Never mind, it's okay, never mind. Go on."

"This probably isn't a true story," the cheerleader says, "and it doesn't go backwards like we do. I probably won't get all the way to the end, and I'm not going to start at the beginning, either. There isn't enough time."

"That's fine," the Devil says. "I'm all ears." (He is.)

The cheerleader says, "So who's going to tell this story, anyway? Be quiet and listen. We're running out of time."

She says, "A man comes home from a sales conference. He and his wife have been separated for a while, but they've decided to try living together again. They've sold the house that they used to live in. Now they live just outside of town, in an old house in an orchard.

"The man comes home from this business conference, and his wife is sitting in the kitchen and she's talking to another woman, an older woman. They're sitting on the chairs that used to go around the kitchen table, but the table is gone. So is the microwave, and the rack where Susan's copper-bottomed pots hang. The pots are gone, too.

"The husband doesn't notice any of this. He's busy looking at the other woman. Her skin has a greenish tinge. He has this feeling that he knows her. She and the wife both look at the husband, and he suddenly knows what it is. It's his wife. It's his wife, two of her, only one is maybe twenty years older. Otherwise, except that this one's green, they're identical: same eyes, same mouth, same little mole at the corner of her mouth.

"How am I doing so far?"

"So-so," the Devil says. The truth (the truth makes the Devil itchy) is, he only likes stories about himself. Like the story about the Devil's wedding cake. Now that's a story.

The cheerleader says, "It gets better."

It Gets Better

The man's name is Ed. It isn't his real name. I made it up. Ed and Susan have been married for ten years, separated for five months, back together again for three months. They've been sleeping in the same bed for three months, but they don't have sex. Susan cries whenever Ed kisses her. They don't have any kids. Susan used to have a younger brother. Ed is thinking about getting a dog.

While Ed's been at his conference, Susan has been doing some housework. She's done some work up in the attic which we won't talk about. Not yet. Down in the spare bathroom in the basement, she's set up this machine, which we might describe later, and this machine makes Susans. What Susan was hoping for was a machine that would bring back Andrew. (Her brother. But you knew that.) Only it turns out that getting Andrew back requires a different machine, a bigger machine. Susan needs help making that machine, and so the new Susans are probably going to come in handy, after all. Over the course of the next few days, the Susans explain all this to Ed.

Susan doesn't expect Ed will be very helpful.

"Hi, Ed," the older, greenish Susan says. She gets up from her chair and gives him a big hug. Her skin is warm, tacky. She smells yeasty. The original Susan (the Susan Ed thinks is original—I have no idea if he's right about this; later on, he isn't so sure, either) sits in her chair and watches them.

Big green Susan—am I making her sound like Godzilla? She doesn't look like Godzilla, and yet there's something about her that reminds Ed of Godzilla, the way she stomps across the kitchen floor—leads Ed over to a chair and makes him sit down. Now he realizes that the kitchen table is gone. He still hasn't managed to say a word. Susan, both of them, is used to this.

"First of all," Susan says, "the attic is off-limits. There are some people working up there. (I don't mean Susans. I'll explain Susans in a minute.) Some visitors. They're helping me with a project. About the other Susans: there are five of me presently—you'll meet the other three later. They're down in the basement. You're allowed in the basement. You can help down there, if you want."

Godzilla Susan says, "You don't have to worry about who is who, although none of us are exactly alike. You can call us all Susan. We're discovering that some of us may be more temporary than others, or fatter, or younger, or greener. It seems to depend on the batch."

"Are you Susan?" Ed says. He corrects himself. "I mean, are you my wife? The real Susan?"

"We're all your wife," the younger Susan says. She puts her hand on his leg, and pats him like a dog.

"Where did the kitchen table go?" Ed says.

"I put it in the attic," Susan says. "You really don't have to worry about that now. How was your conference?"

Another Susan comes into the kitchen. She's young and the color of green apples or new grass. Even the whites of her eyes are grassy.

She's maybe nineteen, and the color of her skin makes Ed think of a snake. "Ed!" she says. "How was the conference?"

"They're keen on the new game," Ed says. "It tests real well."

"Want a beer?" Susan says. (It doesn't matter which Susan says this.) She picks up a pitcher of green foamy stuff, and pours it into a glass.

"This is beer?" Ed says.

"It's Susan beer," Susan says, and all the Susans laugh.

The beautiful, snake-colored, nineteen-year-old Susan takes Ed on a tour of the house. Mostly Ed just looks at Susan, but he sees that the television is gone, and so are all of his games. All his notebooks. The living-room sofa is still there, but all the seat cushions are missing. Later on, Susan will disassemble the sofa with an axe.

Susan has covered up all the downstairs windows with what looks like sheets of aluminum foil. She shows him the bathtub downstairs where one of the Susans is brewing the Susan beer. Other Susans are hanging long, mossy clots of the Susan beer on laundry racks. Dry, these clots can be shaped into bedding, nests for the new Susans. They are also edible.

Ed is still holding the glass of Susan beer. "Go on," Susan says. "You like beer."

"I don't like green beer," Ed says.

"You like Susan, though," Susan says. She's wearing one of his T-shirts, and a pair of Susan's underwear. No bra. She puts Ed's hand on her breast.

Susan stops stirring the beer. She's taller than Ed, and only a little bit green. "You know Susan loves you," she says.

"Who's up in the attic?" Ed says. "Is it Andrew?"

His hand is still on Susan's breast. He can feel her heart beating. Susan says, "You can't tell Susan I told you. She doesn't think you're ready. It's the aliens." They both stare at him. "She finally got them on the phone. This is going to be huge, Ed. This is going to change the world."

Ed could leave the house. He could leave Susan. He could refuse to drink the beer.

*

The Susan beer doesn't make him drunk. It isn't really beer. You knew that, right?

There are Susans everywhere. Some of them want to talk to Ed about their marriage, or about the aliens, or sometimes they want to talk about Andrew. Some of them are busy working. The Susans are always dragging Ed off to empty rooms, to talk or kiss or make love or gossip about the other Susans. Or they're ignoring him. There's a very young Susan. She looks like she might be six or seven years old. She goes up and down the upstairs hallway, drawing on the walls with a marker. Ed isn't sure whether this is childish vandalism or important Susan work. He feels awkward asking.

Every once in a while, he thinks he sees the real Susan. He wishes he could sit down and talk with her, but she always looks so busy.

By the end of the week, there aren't any mirrors left in the house, and the windows are all covered up. The Susans have hung sheets of the Susan beer over all the light fixtures, so everything is green. Ed isn't sure, but he thinks he might be turning green. He might be getting ripe.

Susan tastes green. She always does.

Once Ed hears someone knocking on the front door. "Ignore that," Susan says, as she walks past him. She's carrying the stacked blades of an old ceiling fan and a string of Christmas lights. "It isn't important."

Ed pulls the plug of aluminum foil out of the eyehole, and peeks out. Stan is standing there, looking patient. They stand there, Ed on one side of the door, and Stan on the other. Ed doesn't open the door, and eventually Stan goes away. All the peacocks are kicking up a fuss.

Ed tries teaching some of the Susans to play poker. It doesn't work so well, because it turns out that the Susans all know what cards the other Susans are holding. So Ed makes up a game where that doesn't matter so much, but in the end, it makes him feel too lonely. There aren't any other Eds.

They decide to play spin the bottle instead. Instead of a bottle, they use a hammer, and the head never ends up pointing at Ed. After a while, it gets too strange watching Susan kiss Susan, and he wanders off to look for a Susan who will kiss him.

Up in the second-story front bedroom, there are always lots of Susans. This is where they go to wait when they start to get ripe. The Susans loll, curled in their nests, getting riper, arguing about the end of some old story. None of them remember it the same way. Some of them don't seem to know anything about it, but they all have opinions.

Ed climbs into a nest and leans back. Susan swings her legs over to make room for him. This Susan is small and round. She tickles the soft part of his arm, and then tucks her face into his side.

Susan passes him a glass of Susan beer.

"That's not it," Susan says. "It turns out that he overdosed. Maybe even did it on purpose. We couldn't talk about it. There weren't enough of us. We were trying to carry all of that sadness all by ourself. You can't do something like that! And then the wife tries to kill him. I tried to kill him. She kicks the fuck out of him. He can't leave the house for a week, won't even come to the door when his friends come over."

"If you can call them friends," Susan says.

"No, there was a gun," Susan says. "And she has an affair. Because she can't get over it. Neither of them can."

"She humiliates him at a dinner party," Susan says. "They both drink too much. They go out in the backyard, after everyone has gone home. He throws up the dirty dinner plates and she shoots them down with a BB gun, and the whole time she just wishes she could shoot him. They're both barefoot and there are plate shards all over. Someone's going to get hurt. They don't have a time machine. We know that they still love each other, but that doesn't matter anymore. Then the police show up."

"Well, that's not the way I remember it," Susan says. "But I guess it could have happened that way."

Ed and Susan used to buy books all the time. They had so many books they used to joke about wanting to be quarantined, or snowed in. Maybe then they'd manage to read all the books. But the books have all gone up to the attic, along with the lamps and the coffee table, and their bicycles, and all Susan's paintings. Ed has watched the Susans carry up paperback books, silverware, old board games, and musical instruments. Even a kazoo. The *Encyclopædia*

Britannica. The goldfish and the goldfish bowl and the little canister of goldfish food.

The Susans have gone through the house, taken everything they could. After all the books were gone, they dismantled the bookshelves. Now they're tearing off the wallpaper in long strips. The aliens seem to like books. They like everything, especially Susan. Eventually, when the Susans are ripe, they go up in the attic, too.

The aliens swap things, the books and the Susans and the coffee mugs, for other things: machines that the Susans are assembling. Ed would like to get his hand on one of those devices, but Susan says no. He isn't even allowed to help, except with the Susan beer.

The thing the Susans are building takes up most of the living room, Ed's office, the kitchen, the laundry room (The Susans don't bother with laundry. The washer and the drier are both gone and the Susans have given up wearing clothes altogether. Ed has managed to keep a pair of shorts and a pair of jeans. He's wearing the shorts right now, and he folds the jeans up into a pillow, and rests his head on top of them so that Susan can't steal them. All his other clothes have been carried up to the attic.), and it's creeping up the stairs, spilling over into the second story. The house is shiny with alien machinery.

Teams of naked Susans are hard at work, all day long, testing instruments, hammering and stitching their machine together, polishing and dusting and stacking alien things on top of each other. If you're wondering what the machine looks like, picture a science-fair project involving a lot of aluminum foil: improvised, homely, makeshift, and just a little dangerous-looking. None of the Susans is quite sure what the machine will eventually do. Right now it grows Susan beer.

When the beer is stirred, left alone, stirred some more, it clots and makes more Susans. Ed likes watching this part. The house is more and more full of shy, loud, quiet, talkative, angry, happy, greenish Susans of all sizes and ages, who work at disassembling the house, piece by piece, and piece by piece, assembling the machine.

It might be a time machine, or a machine to raise the dead, or maybe the house is becoming a spaceship, slowly, one room at a time. Susan says the aliens don't make these kinds of distinctions. It may be an invasion factory, Ed says, or a doomsday machine. Susan says that they aren't that kind of aliens.

Ed's job: stirring the Susan beer with a long, flat plank—a floor board Susan pried up—and skimming the foam, which has a stringy, unpleasantly cheeselike consistency, into buckets. He carries the buckets downstairs and makes Susan beer soufflé and Susan beer casserole. Susan beer surprise. Upside-down Susan cake. It all tastes the same, and he grows to like the taste.

The beer doesn't make him drunk. That isn't what it's for. I can't tell you what's it's for. But when he's drinking it, he isn't sad. He has the beer, and the work in the kitchen, and the ripe, green fuckery. Everything tastes like Susan.

The only thing he misses is poker nights.

Up in the spare bedroom, Ed falls asleep listening to the Susans talk, and when he wakes up, his jeans are gone, and he's naked. The room is empty. All the ripe Susans have gone up to the attic.

When he steps out into the hall, the little Susan is out there, drawing on the walls. She puts her marker down and hands him a pitcher of Susan beer. She pinches his leg and says, "You're getting nice and ripe."

Then she winks at Ed and runs down the hall.

He looks at what she's been drawing: Andrew, scribbly crayon portraits of Andrew, all up and down the walls. He follows the pictures of Andrew down the hall, all the way to the master bedroom where he and the original Susan used to sleep. Now he sleeps anywhere, with any Susan. He hasn't been in their room in a while, although he's noticed the Susans going in and out with boxes full of things. The Susans are always shooing at him when he gets in their way.

The bedroom is full of Andrew. There are Susan's portraits of Andrew on the walls, the ones from her art class. Ed had forgotten how unpleasant and peculiar these paintings are. In one, the largest one, a life-size Andrew has his hands around a small animal, maybe a ferret. He seems to be strangling it. The ferret's mouth is cocked open, showing all its teeth. A picture like that, Ed thinks, you ought to turn it towards the wall at night.

Susan's put Andrew's bed in here, and Andrew's books, and Andrew's desk. Andrew's clothes have been hung up in the closet. There isn't an alien machine in the room, or for that matter, anything that ever belonged to Ed.

Ed puts a pair of Andrew's pants on, and lies down on Andrew's bed, just for a minute, and he closes his eyes.

*

When he wakes up, Susan is sitting on the bed. He can smell her, that ripe green scent. He can smell that smell on himself. Susan says, "If you're ready, I thought we could go up to the attic together."

"What's going on here?" Ed says. "I thought you needed everything. Shouldn't all this stuff go up to the attic?"

"This is Andrew's room, for when he comes back," Susan says. "We thought it would make him feel comfortable, having his own bed to sleep in. He might need his stuff."

"What if the aliens need his stuff?" Ed says. "What if they can't make you a new Andrew yet because they don't know enough about him?"

"That's not how it works," Susan says. "We're getting close now. Can't you feel it?"

"I feel weird," Ed says. "Something's happening to me."

"You're ripe, Ed," Susan says. "Isn't that fantastic? We weren't sure you'd ever get ripe enough."

She takes his hand and pulls him up. Sometimes he forgets how strong she is.

"So what happens now?" Ed says. "Am I going to die? I don't feel sick. I feel good. What happens when we get ripe?"

The dim light makes Susan look older, or maybe she just is older. He likes this part: seeing what Susan looked like as a kid, what she'll look like as an old lady. It's as if they got to spend their whole lives together. "I never know," she says. "Let's go find out. Take off Andrew's pants, and I'll hang them back up in the closet."

They leave the bedroom and walk down the hall. The Andrew drawings, the knobs, the dials, and stacked, shiny machinery, watch them go. There aren't any other Susans around at the moment. They're all busy downstairs. He can hear them hammering away. For a minute, it's the way it used to be, only better. Just Ed and Susan in their own house.

Ed holds on tight to Susan's hand.

When Susan opens the attic door, the attic is full of stars. Stars and stars and stars. (Ed has never seen so many stars.) Susan has taken the roof off. Off in the distance, they can smell the apple trees, way down in the orchard.

Susan sits down cross-legged on the floor and Ed sits down beside her. She says, "I wish you'd tell me a story."

Ed says, "What kind of story?"

Susan says, "When Andrew was a kid, we used to read this book. It had stories about horses, you go for a ride and you stick to their backs like glue, they ride you down into the sea and they either marry you or they drown you. Stories about trolls, people who go under a hill. When they come out, a hundred years have gone by. Do you know how long it's been since Andrew died? I've lost track of time."

"I don't know stories like that," Ed says. He picks at his flaky green skin and wonders what he tastes like. "What do you think the aliens look like? Do you think they look like giraffes? Like marbles? Like Andrew? Do you think they have mouths?"

"Don't be silly," Susan says. "They look like us."

"How do you know?" Ed says. "Have you been up here before?"

"No," Susan says. "But Susan has."

"We could play a card game," Ed says. "Or I Spy."

"You could tell me about the first time I met you," Susan says.

"I don't want to talk about that," Ed says. "That's all gone."

"Okay, fine." Susan sits up straight, arching her back. She wets her green lips with her green tongue and says, "Tell me how beautiful I am."

"You're beautiful," Ed says. "I've always thought you were beautiful. All of you. How about me? Am I beautiful?"

"Don't be sarcastic," Susan says. She slouches back against him. Her skin is warm and greasy. "The aliens are going to get here soon. I don't know what happens after that, but I hate this part. I always hate this part. I don't like waiting. Do you think this is what it was like for Andrew?"

"When you get him back, ask him. Why ask me?"

Susan doesn't say anything for a bit. Then she says, "We think we'll be able to make you, too. We're starting to figure out how it works. Eventually it will be you and me and him, just the way it was before. Only we'll fix him the way we've fixed me. He won't be so sad. Have you noticed how I'm not sad anymore? Don't you want that, not to be sad? And maybe after that we'll try making some more people. We'll start all over again. We'll do everything right this time."

Ed says, "So why are they helping you?"

"I don't know," Susan says. "Either they think we're funny, or else they think we're pathetic, the way we get stuck. We can ask them when they get here."

She pushes Ed back against the wooden floor, and sits on top of him. She reaches down and stuffs his penis, half erect, inside of her. Ed groans.

He says, "Susan."

Susan says, "Tell me a story," and then sits back down, gently. "Any story. I don't care what."

"I can't tell you a story," Ed says. "I don't know any stories when you're doing this."

"I'll stop," Susan says. She stops.

Ed says, "Don't stop. Okay." He puts his hands around her green waist and moves her, as if he's stirring the Susan beer.

He says, "Once upon a time." He's speaking very fast. They're running out of time.

Once, when they were making love, Andrew came into the bedroom. He didn't even knock. He didn't seem to be embarrassed at all. Ed doesn't want to be fucking Susan when the aliens show up. On the other hand, Ed wants to be fucking Susan forever. He doesn't want to stop, not for Andrew, or the aliens, or even for the end of the world.

Ed says, "There was a man and a woman and they fell in love. They were both nice people. They made a good couple. Everyone liked them. This story is about the woman."

This story is about a woman who is in love with somebody who invents a time machine. He's planning to go so far into the future that he'll end up right back at the very beginning. He asks her to come along, but she doesn't want to go. What's back at the beginning of the world? Little blobs of life swimming around in a big blob? Adam and Eve in the Garden of Eden? She doesn't want to play Adam and Eve; she has other things to do. She works for a research company. She calls people on the telephone and asks them all sorts of questions. Back at the beginning, there aren't going to be phones. She doesn't like the sound of it. So her husband says, fine, then here's what we'll do. I'll build you another machine, and if you ever decide that you miss me, or you're tired and you can't go on, climb inside this machine—this box right here—and push this button and go to sleep. And you'll sleep all the way forwards and backwards to me, where I'm waiting for you. I'll keep on waiting for you. I love you. And so they make love and they make love a few more times and then he climbs into his time machine and whoosh, he's gone like that. So fast, it's hard to believe that he was ever there at all.

Meanwhile she lives her life forward, slow, the way he didn't want to. She gets married again and makes love some more and has kids and they have kids and when she's an old woman, she's finally ready: she climbs into the dusty box down in the secret room under the orchard and she pushes the button and falls asleep. And she sleeps all the way back, just like Sleeping Beauty, down in the orchard for years and years, which fly by like seconds, she goes flying back, past the men sitting around the green felt table, now you can see them, now they're gone again, and all the peacocks are screaming, and the Satanist drives up to the house and unloads the truckload of furniture, he unpaints the colored rooms and the pentagrams, soon the old shy man will unbuild his house, carry his secret away on his back, and the apples are back on the orchard trees again, and then the trees are all blooming, and now the woman is getting younger, just a little, the lines around her mouth are smoothing out. She dreams that someone has come down into that underground room and is looking down at her in her time machine. He stands there for a long time. She can't open her eyes, her eyelids are so heavy, she doesn't want to wake up just yet. She dreams she's on a train going down the tracks backwards and behind the train, someone is picking up the beams and the nails and the girders to put in a box and then they'll put the box away. The trees are whizzing past, getting smaller and smaller and then they're all gone too. Now she's a kid again, now she's a baby, now she's much smaller and then she's even smaller than that. She gets her gills back. She doesn't want to wake up just yet, she wants to get right back to the very beginning where it's all new and clean and everything is still and green and flat and sleepy and everybody has crawled back into the sea and they're waiting for her to get back there too and then the party can start. She goes backwards and backwards and backwards and backwards and backwards and backwards and backwards and backwards and backwards and backwards and backwards and backwards—

The cheerleader says to the Devil, "We're out of time. We're holding things up. Don't you hear them banging on the door?"

The Devil says, "You didn't finish the story."

The cheerleader says, "And you never let me touch your tail. Besides, there isn't any ending. I could make up something, but it wouldn't ever satisfy you. You said that yourself! You're never satisfied. And I have to get on with my life. My parents are going to be home soon."

*

Starlight says, "My voice is getting scratchy. It's late. You should call back tomorrow night."

Ed says, "When can I call you?"

Stan and Andrew were friends. Good friends. It was like they were the same person, only of course it turned out that they weren't. Ed hadn't seen Stan for a while, not for a long while, but Stan stopped him, on the way down to the basement. This was earlier. Stan grabbed his arm and said, "I miss him. I keep thinking, if I'd gotten there sooner. If I'd said something. He liked you a lot, you know, he was sorry about what happened to your car—"

Stan stops talking and just stands there looking at Ed. He looks like he's about to cry.

"It's not your fault," Ed said, but then he wondered why he'd said it. Whose fault was it?

Susan says, "You've got to stop calling me, Ed. Okay? It's three in the morning. I was asleep, Ed, I was having the best dream. You're always waking me up in the middle of things. Please just stop, okay?"

Ed doesn't say anything. He could stay there all night and just listen to Susan talk.

What she's saying now is, "But that's never going to happen, and you know it. Something bad happened, and it wasn't anyone's fault, but we're just never going to get past it. It killed us. We can't even talk about it."

Ed says, "I love you."

Susan says, "I love you, but it's not about love, Ed, it's about timing. It's too late, and it's always going to be too late. Maybe if we could go back and do everything differently, and I think about that all the time, but we can't. We don't know anybody with a time machine. How about this, Ed—maybe you and your poker buddies can build one down in Pete's basement. All those stupid games, Ed! Why can't you build a time machine instead? Call me back when you've figured out how we can work this out, because I'm really stuck. Or don't call me back. Goodbye, Ed. I love you. I'm hanging up the phone now."

Susan hangs up the phone.

Ed imagines her, going down to the kitchen to microwave a glass of milk. She'll sit in the kitchen and drink her milk and wait for him to call her back. He lies in bed, up in the orchard house. He's got both bedroom doors open, and a night breeze comes in through that door that doesn't go anywhere. He wishes he could get Susan to come see that door. The breeze smells like apples, which is what time must smell like, Ed thinks.

There's an alarm clock on the floor beside his bed. The hands and numbers glow green in the dark, and he'll wait five minutes and then he'll call Susan. Five minutes. Then he'll call her back. The hands aren't moving, but he can wait.

Entertaining Angels Unawares

M. *John Harrison*

I GOT TWO OR THREE WEEKS' WORK with a firm that specialized in high and difficult access jobs in and around Halifax. They needed a laborer, someone to fetch and carry, clean the site up behind them. The job was on the tower of a church about thirty miles northeast of the town. I wasn't sure what I thought about that. I wondered what I'd say to the vicar if he ever appeared, but he never did.

Generally it was a quiet job. I was there on my own with the supervisor, a man called Sal Meredith.

Meredith picked me up every morning in the firm's van. He drove the van as if he expected it to be a motorcycle, changing lanes at high speed among slow traffic, overtaking on the inside. He made the engine rev and snap so that other motorists stared suddenly over their shoulders. Until I was used to this I didn't have much to say, but we got on well enough, and after a day or two he began to tell me about a recurring dream he had. In it he found himself chasing people through a city.

I asked him what sort of city. Larger than Sheffield, he said, but not as large as London. It was old. "Not right old—not ages and ages ago—but not right modern, either." It was a Victorian city, blackened with soft coal smoke, rotten with industry. In the dream Meredith went up and down the stairwells of factories and tenements, sometimes at a run, sometimes a floaty dreamlike walk, broken glass and iron pipework all around him. "It were the usual thing wi' dreams—corners turn into dead ends just as you get there, even though you've seen people go round them. Anyway, there I were, going along, and I had this absolutely *mega* sword."

I stared at him.

"A sword," I said.

"Biggest fucker you've seen," he said. "Biggest fucker you've ever seen."

His memories of this sword were vivid and exact. It wasn't new. It had been resharpened many times. He could tell from irregularities in the chamfer of the blade. Its hilt—which he called "the handle"—

was built up out of gold rings; and it came in its own long leather scabbard—which he called "the holster"—fastened with a press stud for quick access. "I can just imagine it now in front of me. I feel as I've got one of these somewhere. Anyway, this dream basically consisted of walking around, then going on to tube trains and stuff, and—"

He stared at me, unsure how to proceed.

"—and, well, just basically hacking people's heads off."

"Fucking hell," I said. "Steady away."

"Weird, eh? Isn't that fucking weird?"

I had to say it was. "Do you get it a lot," I said, "this dream?"

He thought.

"Often enough," he admitted.

To get to the job you had to drive through wooded hills on steep, narrow roads. It was beautiful country, even the way Meredith drove. What the fuck, I thought, I might as well sit back and enjoy the ride. The trees were green and lush, oaks and birches. It was rainforest Britain in the first year of Century 21. Then you turned a corner suddenly and the church was in front of you, a blackened square edifice flanked on one side by a farmyard full of wrecked machinery, and on the other by a neat garden in which tame rabbits lolloped stupidly around all morning. Its blue-and-gold clock had stopped at half past five. They had strung the site sign across the tower near the top:

VERTICAL ACCESS.

The church was called for some reason St. John the Baptist in the Wilderness. The story on it was this, Meredith said: when it was built in 1830, the buttresses were an afterthought. They had no real engineering function. Instead of supporting the building they were just leaning against it. By 1900 they were beginning to sag and banana away. A hundred years later, eight-inch gaps had opened up, and the church had been condemned unless it could be fixed. That job was finished now. Meredith's team had gone in and driven thirty-six ten-foot, twelve threads per inch, stainless-steel bolts through the buttresses into the fabric of the tower itself, cementing them in with aerospace resins. You had to hide that, of course, so afterward the restorers came along with something called "gobbo," a kind of grout made from mud and goat hair, and sealed it all up. There were a lot of jokes about gobbo. Not counting assessment and planning it had taken less than a fortnight. All that remained was a bit of repointing. Meredith had also promised he would take the rotten stone louvers out of the bell tower.

"They're all laminated," he told me.

"You mean they're fucked," I said.

"That too."

We decided to do the louvers first. We spent three or four mornings dropping them eighty feet to the floor, where they went off like bombs. It was tiring work getting them out of their slots. We would chuck a few of them down then go up to the top of the tower and have a drink of tea. From up there you could see that St. John's stood at a confluence of valleys, streams, and lanes. You would never have understood that from the ground, Meredith said, because of all the hills and ridges. It would have been impossible to unravel by eye. I drank my tea and said: "That dream of yours. The one with the sword. I mean, what's the point? What's the story on that?"

He shrugged. "I don't know. There's no story. It's more like a video game. Hacking people's heads off, that's the point. And it's not just the odd person. It's doing a lot. That's the tick: getting loads of people all at once. Five or six people are stood round you, and you just sort of start *spinning round* with this thing—*footoof!*—and getting all their heads off." While he was talking two houseflies landed on the parapet and began to copulate on the warm stone. The sun glittered off them blue and green, and off the mica crystals in the stone around them.

"Hey, look at these fuckers," I said. "They're at it."

"Leave them alone," Meredith said. "You wouldn't want people watching you."

I watched the flies a minute more. I could see they were unaware of me, unaware of anything. Every so often they buzzed groggily and lurched into a new position. "I hate flies," I said. "I hate the dirt of them." I crushed them with my thumb, then I wiped my thumb along the parapet to clean it.

"Jesus," Meredith said. "They were only fucking."

"Are you yourself?" I said.

"What?"

"In this dream, are you yourself?"

"I suppose I am," he said. "I never thought about it." Then he said: "I'm taller."

*

We never ate lunch at the top of the tower. It was too hot by then. We could have gone to the Robin Hood in Hebden Bridge, but Meredith wasn't much of a drinker. Anyway, as he said, at lunchtime it was always full of locals playing Fistful of Money. If they weren't doing that they were selling one another shotgun cartridges. So most of the time we took sandwiches down into the back of the church, whatever that's called, which had been converted into a miniature parish hall. It stayed cool there all day. They had a kitchen where we could make tea, chairs and tables, and a piano. It was all separated from the rest of the church by a long glass screen. Pictures and bits of writing by Sunday school kids were displayed on red felt pin boards. Every morning we found a fresh display of leaflets on one of the tables. Someone had arranged them carefully in a fan.

"'Keep Yourself Pure'!" Meredith quoted. He laughed. "What's the difference between perverse and perverted?"

"I don't know."

"You're perverse if you tickle your arse with a feather. If you're perverted you use the whole chicken."

"How do you feel," I said, "in this dream you're having?"

"Weird," he said. "I feel weird." He drank some of his tea. "I'm myself, but I don't feel as if I'm inside myself."

"You're watching yourself," I suggested.

"I suppose I am."

"That's what you're doing."

He was watching himself stalk this gloomy industrial city, getting their heads off. One night adults, the next night children. One moment he was in a huge park with silent blackened monuments, the next following a woman and child along a disused gantry. Suddenly he found himself, hours later, in a tube tunnel. "All these kids came on to the tube-station platform—" Or was it a platform? At its shadowy edges it seemed to him to blend into a kind of courtyard, with a ramp for wheelchairs. "It felt like you were on a platform. But at the same time you could feel you were somewhere else." Anyway, he was with two lads off the hi-tech team, Steve and Paul. He told them to lie down quietly on the ramp out of harm's way. "Then all these kids came running round the corner—you know, eight-, nine-year-old kids, and suddenly it went really dark, and I just remember squatting down to get the right height and—"

"*Footoof!*" I said.

"—all their heads off, five or six heads at one go."

I went and looked at the notice boards where the Sunday school kids had pinned their work up. A recent drawing exercise for the boys had been "My route to church." They had made light work of it, drawing themselves in red Ferraris and adding commentary: "My house." "Whooosh!" "Hinchcliffe Arms." "Screeech!" "Church Bank Lane." "Bang!" The energy of these journeys undercut the cheap parsonical metaphor they were based on. The girls had done paper samplers that read JESUS IS LORD OF LIFE.

Meredith came and looked over my shoulder. "See that?" he said. "One of them's written BORD OF LIFE. Little tinker." He studied his watch. "Hey, time to drop a few more bombs," he said.

"I'm having a piss first."

"You can do that if you want," Sal Meredith said. I went into the lavatory. "Remember, though," he called after me: "More than two shakes is a wank."

The graveyard at St. John's was famous for something, but Meredith couldn't remember what. I ought to go and have a look at it anyway, he told me. It was worth seeing: there were graves out there the size of super tankers. I went round one lunchtime. He was right. The graveyard was also full of fantastic blackened stone obelisks and gesticulating angels. Insects whizzed through the air between them. Brambles, thistles, and fern had sprung up in one corner. Elsewhere it was the kind of grass you only ever see in cemeteries.

There were more children out there than I expected. The ones that died before 1900 were miniature adults full of some earnest churchy future. They got proper graves, serious graves. The modern kids slipped their moorings in the childish boats piled with toys. They buried them close to the church. If the older graves were like super tankers, these new ones went bobbing along in the wake of St. John's like condom packets behind a ferry. I had a look down at them. LOVE NEVER DIES. But we all know it does. Clarence and Katherine lose John, their beloved son. Not much later, Clarence loses Katherine. Two years after that the world loses Clarence, and that's that until Vertical Access arrives. Thrash metal blares from their radio. They hang a yellow plastic bucket out of the belfry, off the end of a hoist made out of scaffolding poles. They bolt everything back together with fucking great bolts. Thinking about this, I went back into the church where Meredith was finishing his tea.

"What do you reckon then?" he said.

"It's disgusting. People are expected to leave monuments to their tragedies, even though that makes them harder to forget."

He stared at me uncertainly.

"Here's that goat's hair you wanted to see," he said.

He threw it onto the table, where it settled next to my cup, a dark brown swatch flecked with gray. It was full of goat dandruff, the biggest dandruff you've ever seen.

"Thanks a lot, Sal."

"You said you were interested," he said. "That's what they bound the gobbo with. Don't ask me how successful it was. In the end they just poured a couple of buckets of it down between the tower and the buttresses. Lo-tech fuckers. Sand and cement, bound up with that stuff. They just call it gobbo to distinguish it from structural concrete." He said: "We could make some up if you like. I mean, if you're that bothered. Apparently the hair needs to be fresh."

I was fascinated by the whole idea.

"So do they have to keep a goat?" I said. "The restorers?"

"Feel it," he said. "It's just like women's hair."

"Fucking hell. What sort of women do you go out with?"

He was right, though. With your eyes closed it felt exactly like human hair.

"We had a chemistry teacher at school called Gobbo," I said. "But that was because he spat a lot when he talked. Really thick spit." We were thirteen, we loved that. We also loved the rubber tubes that fed the Bunsen burners. After six months or so, I told Meredith, we stopped laughing at Gobbo's spit problem and concentrated on setting them on fire instead. "Do they still have Bunsen burners?" I said, but he didn't know what I was talking about. "It was a fair old time ago," I had to admit.

The thing about the graveyard was this: some of the stones had undergone such mechanical erosion you couldn't read what they said. Despite that, the words on them seemed to remain beneath the surface, as if now was just water running over them. "In memory"; "also of three infants"; "a glorious eternity." With the right focus, you thought, you might be able to bring them back. But in the end no meaning swam up into view.

Meredith had done every kind of high-access engineering, from avalanche netting in Gibraltar to cleaning windows in the Barbican; but his fame came from stabilizing the little chalk cliffs at the entrance to Brighton station. The problem was, in that environment explosives couldn't be used to remove the unstable stuff: so he drilled rows of holes one meter apart that he then pumped full of a fast-expanding chemical grout. "Levered it off nicely. Not a bad solution." He'd been on the tower blocks too, everyone in that trade has. He wouldn't go back to it. Gangs of kids wreck your work behind you. The adults steal your equipment: they aren't much more than kids themselves, and they couldn't give a toss about where or how they live.

He'd spent years on that. Even so he was quite a lot younger than me. He had a wife and two kids in Preston or Nelson-and-Colne, some backwater like that. He didn't get on with her anymore, but he saw the kids every weekend. He showed me a photograph of the whole family on some flat northern beach. The tide was out as far as you could see. The wife was nice, a looker if a bit ordinary. One glance at her face and you could understand why they were separated. She didn't trust him, she didn't trust the job with all its risks and its foreign travel opportunities; she didn't trust the tattoos up his arm. Who would? Still, the kids were beautiful—two boys, five and seven, in their England football shirts—and he clearly loved them. In the end that's why I couldn't understand the dream he was having.

"So how do you do with it?" I asked him. "I mean, having these kids of your own? You must feel pretty shit about killing children in a dream."

He thought for a moment.

"I felt like an animal," he said, "the first time I had it."

It always ended the same way, he said, that dream. *Footoof!*—off came the heads of all these kids. One little lad lost only the top of his head, "the top bit like the scalp. I have to give it three or four goes, so it comes off in slices—"

"Christ, Sal!"

"—and eventually I get it. Oh, it doesn't look like you're cutting somebody's head," he said. "It looks more like a cabbage or summat." He paused to consider this. "Coming off in slabs."

After that he always ran for it, in a convulsion of fear and glee—"I can really feel me heart pounding, every step"—and then the dream seemed to jump very quickly and he was out of the city altogether, with a job selling agricultural machinery in some great prairie farming waste, somewhere where the dust boiled off the landscape all summer. "There I am, talking about experimental tractors to some old bloke in a farmhouse but thinking all the time: " 'I'm going to get caught. I'm going to get caught.' "

He wanted to get caught.

"They're never my kiddies," he said. "But I feel like an animal every time I have that dream, and I want to get caught."

The job went well. We pried the rest of the louvers out and replaced them with brand-new stone a rosy color so faint it was almost white. The church people weren't up for sandblasting the rest of the building to match, so we started in on the pointing. Good weather was a requirement for that, and we got it. At the same time we needed shade and cool air. Nine in the morning, we'd already been working three hours. We hung off the abseil ropes, pointing as fast as we could, trying to get a section done before the grout dried up in the bucket. We were working in shorts, drinking four or five liters of water a day, gasping like animals. From up on the tower, the surrounding hills resounded with light. By noon it was so baked and airless the only place you could bear was the inside of the church. About four days of this and the job was finished.

"We'll clear the site tomorrow," Meredith said. "It'll be a late start. "I've got to go to the dentist in the morning."

"Ouch."

"I don't mind it, me," he said.

He had an interesting relationship with his dentist, who had once dared him to have a filling without anesthetic. "It won't take a minute," he promised, staring steadily at Meredith. The challenge was obvious. Meredith looked steadily back at him for fifteen seconds and bought it.

"Did it hurt?" I asked.

He shrugged. "It were bearable. But I love those fucking dental drills! Water cooled, five hundred thousand rpm. Shit hot. You can see this fucking *aerosol* of stuff flying out of your mouth when they're working. Tooth debris, water droplets, saliva, blood, bacteria. The fucking works." Seeing my expression, he laughed. "Anyway we're done here. We'll have a nice short day tomorrow."

He got out his cell phone. "I'll just make arrangements for someone to collect that laminated stone."

He drove me back to Halifax in his usual way, overtaking people on blind bends as if the van were some Kawasaki he'd once owned. I got him to drop me in the center of town, so I could go round Sainsbury's and buy a few things; then I walked home with the stuff in two plastic bags.

It was nine o'clock by then, a Tuesday night in high summer. Something was different about the air: it was filling with humidity. I could see clouds up over the moor outside the town. I cooked. I watched a TV program about a footballer accepting a challenge to be an interior decorator. After that, the news came on, the usual stuff, children without anything to eat enlisted as soldiers in some fucking African war; kids at home suffering all kinds of abuse. It was dark by then. Outside it had just begun to rain, big slow drops, then smaller and faster. I fell asleep in front of the TV and woke up at two o'clock in the morning to find it still on. I went over to satellite to get the adult channels, but after five minutes I couldn't be bothered. I couldn't imagine having sex anymore. The water was more interesting, sluicing down the windows, rushing down the gutters in front. I got up and switched the light on. The house had been a rental when I bought it, a one-up one-down furnished in the seventies with fitted carpets in swirling patterns of purple and green. The bathroom suite and kitchen cupboards were purple too. Nothing got done because I couldn't get the energy up after work. There was grease and dust on top of the cupboards that had been there twenty years.

Looking round, I wished I'd done more. Then I thought if I just went to bed maybe I'd go to sleep again. But I lay awake listening to the rain and thinking about the sword in Sal Meredith's dream. I thought about Meredith himself, and the sense of him I had as feral, full of caution and daring in equal amounts as he went about the city getting their heads off. I thought about him taking the dentist's bet, bracing himself against the vibration in his jaw, trying to bring on anesthesia by staring up and away from the dentist's blank intent face into the spray flying up like fireworks through the tight beam of the overhead lamp.

Why did I like his smile so much? He didn't smile often but when he did it was hard not to respond. All I could think was that it reminded me of my father's smile. It had the same quality of being too young for his age.

"I'm too old for mine," I thought.

I was awake most of the night.

It was still wet the next day, Wednesday, which made it hard to wake up. The light was poor. The air had that gray liquid look it gets in West Yorkshire, where the chemists are still filling prescriptions for seasonal affect disorder in July. Meredith arrived ten minutes late. I was already outside the house waiting for him.

"You're keen," he said.

"Good time at the dentist's?"

That got a grin off him.

"Not bad," he said. "But I had a right epic wi' the van this morning. Smoke coming from under the dash, all sorts. I can see something sparking back there but I just can't get at it with my fingers."

By the time we got to St. John's the sun had come out a bit. A light breeze was helping to dry things out, moving the leaves of the birch and oak above Church Bank Lane. Church Brook, swollen by the night's runoff, rushed along in its narrow defile. The porous old grit-stone they'd built the church from had sucked up the rain; it looked blackened and fucked, like a ruin in the valley. Meredith wouldn't have the radio on, he didn't feel like it. That made us slow. We had trouble getting the VERTICAL ACCESS sign down. Cordless power tools and other tools, locked into the vestry at night, had to be checked into their plastic bins and stacked in the back of the van. Meredith did this on his own, then wandered about the site looking for things he thought he might have missed. He seemed sad the job was finished. "People should look after places like this," he said. If he had his way, he'd always do this kind of work, restoration work. Looking out at the graveyard I wasn't so sure. Eventually we were finished.

"How's that dream of yours?" I said.

"Eh? Oh, that." He rubbed the back of his neck. "Like clockwork these days," he said. "Night after night, getting their heads off."

"I want to be in it," I said.

He grinned.

"What?" he said.

"I'm serious," I said. "I want to be in the dream. I want to share it."

"Come on, Mike," he said. "What's the joke?"

"I mean it, Sal."

He began to look embarrassed.

I said: "There's no joke here."

He laughed.

"Come on, Mike," he repeated. "It's a dream."

I kept looking into his eyes, but he shook his head and walked off. "You're fucking mad," he said.

Two hours later I watched him go round the graveyard looking for me. I was on the tower by then, hidden down behind the parapet. Meredith was calling, "Mike? Mike?" The humidity in the air made his voice sound unpredictable, close by one minute, far away the next. "This is fucking stupid," he said. He looked at his watch. "I'm giving you another five minutes, then I'm going." He waited slightly less than that. "Fuck off then, you stupid fucker," he shouted. I watched him drive the van away, then I went back down into the church. I pulled one of the Sunday school drawings off the pin board and wrote on the back of it: "Places like this reek of death."

I signed that as if it was the visitors' book and put it on one of the tables next to the careful fan of leaflets. As an afterthought I added, "Anyone can see that." Then I went out between the graves with the bucket of gobbo I'd mixed that morning and started smearing it over them at random with a pointing trowel.

Little Red's Tango
Peter Straub

Little Red Perceived as a Mystery

What a mystery is Little Red! How he sustains himself, how he lives, how he gets through his days, what passes through his mind as he endures that extraordinary journey. . . . Is not mystery precisely that which does not yield, does not give access?

Little Red, His Wife, His Parents, His Brothers

Little is known of the woman he married. Little Red seldom speaks of her, except now and then to say, "My wife was half Sicilian," or "All you have to know about my wife is that she was half Sicilian." Some have speculated, though not in the presence of Little Red, that the long-vanished wife was no more than a fictional or mythic character created to lend solidity to his otherwise amorphous history. Years have been lost. Decades have been lost. (In a sense, an entire life has been lost, some might say Little Red's.) The existence of a wife, even an anonymous one, lends a semblance of structure to the lost years.

Half of her was Sicilian; the other half may have been Irish. "People like that you don't mess with," says Little Red. "Even when you mess with them, you don't *mess* with them, know what I mean?"

The parents are likewise anonymous, though no one has ever speculated that they may have been fictional or mythic. Even anonymous parents must be of flesh and blood. Since Little Red has mentioned, in his flat, dry Long Island accent, a term in the Uniondale High School jazz ensemble, we can assume that for a substantial period his family resided in Uniondale, Long Island. There were, apparently, two brothers, both older. The three boys grew up in circumstances modest but otherwise unspecified. A lunch counter, a diner, a small mom-and-pop grocery may have been in the picture.

Some connection with food, with nourishment.

Little Red's long years spent waiting on tables, his decades as a "waiter," continue this nourishment theme, which eventually becomes inseparable from the very conception of Little Red's existence. In at least one important way, *nourishment* lies at the heart of the mystery. Most good mysteries are rooted in the question of nourishment. As concepts, nourishment and sacrifice walk hand in hand, like old friends everywhere. Think of Judy Garland. The wedding at Cana. Think of the fish grilled at night on the Galilean shore. A fire, the fish in the simple pan, the flickeringly illuminated men.

The brothers have not passed through the record entirely unremarked, nor are they anonymous. In the blurry comet trail of Little Red's history, the brothers exist as sparks, embers, brief coruscations. Blind, unknowing, they shared his early life, the life of Uniondale. They were, categorically, brothers, intent on their bellies, their toys, their cars, and their neuroses, all of that, and attuned not at all to the little red-haired boy who stumbled wide-eyed in their wake. Kyle, the recluse; Ernie, the hopeless. These are the names spoken by Little Red. After graduation from high school, the recluse lived one town over with a much older woman until his aging parents bought a trailer and relocated to rural Georgia, whereupon he moved into a smaller trailer on the same lot. When his father died, Kyle sold the little trailer and settled in with his mother. The hopeless brother, Ernie, followed Kyle and parents to Georgia within six weeks of their departure from Nassau County. He soon found both a custodial position in a local middle school and a girlfriend, whom he married before the year was out. Ernie's weight, 285 pounds on his wedding day, ballooned to 350 soon after. No longer capable of fulfilling his custodial duties, he went on welfare. Kyle, though potentially a talented musician, experienced nausea and an abrupt surge in blood pressure at the thought of performing in public, so that source of income was forever closed to him. Fortunately, his only other talent, that of putting elderly women at their ease, served him well—his mother's will left him her trailer and the sum of $40,000, twice the amount bequested to her other two sons.

We should note that, before Kyle's windfall, Little Red periodically mailed him small sums of money—money he could ill afford to give away—and that he did the same for brother Ernie, although Ernie's most useful talent was that of attracting precisely the amount of money he needed at exactly the moment he needed it. While temporarily separated from his spouse, between subsistence-level jobs and cruelly hungry, Ernie waddled a-slouching past an abandoned warehouse, was tempted by the presence of a paper sack placed on the black leather passenger seat of an aubergine Lincoln Town Car, tested the door, found it open, snatched up the sack, and rushed Ernie-style into the cobweb-strewn shelter of the warehouse. An initial search of the bag revealed two foil-wrapped cheeseburgers, still warm. A deeper investigation uncovered an eight-ounce bottle of Poland Spring water and a green Clingfilm-covered brick composed of $2,300 in new fifties and twenties.

Although Ernie described this coup in great detail to his youngest brother, he never considered, not for a moment, sharing the booty.

These people are his immediate family. Witnesses to the trials, joys, despairs, and breakthroughs of his childhood, they noticed nothing. Of the actualities of his life, they knew less than nothing, for what they imagined they knew was either peripheral or inaccurate. Kyle and Ernie mistook the tip for the iceberg. And deep within herself, their mother had chosen, when most she might have considered her youngest son's life, to avert her eyes.

Little Red carries these people in his heart. He grieves for them; he forgives them everything.

What He Has Been

Over many years and in several cities, a waiter and a bartender; a bass player, briefly; a husband, a son, a nephew; a dweller in caves; an adept of certain magisterial substances; a friend most willing and devoted; a reader, chiefly of crime, horror, and science fiction; an investor and day trader; a dedicated watcher of cable television, especially the History, Discovery, and Sci-Fi Channels; an intimate of nightclubs, joints, dives, and after-hour shebeens, also of restaurants, cafes, and diners; a purveyor of secret knowledge; a photographer; a wavering candle flame; a voice of conundrums; a figure of steadfast loyalty; an intermittent beacon; a path beaten through the undergrowth.

Peter Straub

THE BEATITUDES OF LITTLE RED, I

Whatsoever can be repaid, should be repaid with kindness.

Whatsoever can be borrowed, should be borrowed modestly.

Tip extravagantly, for they need the money more than you do.

You can never go wrong by thinking of God as Louis Armstrong.

Those who swing, should swing some more.

Something always comes along. It really does.

Cleanliness is fine, as far as it goes.

Remember—even when you are alone, you're in the middle of a party.

The blues ain't nothin' but a feeling, but *what* a feeling.

What goes up sometimes just keeps right on going.

Try to eat solid food at least once a day.

There is absolutely nothing wrong with television.

Anybody who thinks he sees everything around him isn't looking.

When you get your crib the way you like it, stay there.

Order can be created in even the smallest things, but that doesn't mean you have to create it.

Clothes are for sleeping in, too. The same goes for chairs.

Everyone makes mistakes, including deities and higher powers.

Avoid the powerful, for they will undoubtedly try to hurt you.

Doing one right thing in the course of a day is good enough.

Stick to beer, mainly.

Pay attention to musicians.

Accept your imperfections, for they can bring you to Paradise.

No one should ever feel guilty about fantasies, no matter how shameful they may be, for a thought is not a deed.

Sooner or later, jazz music will tell you everything you need to know.

There is no significant difference between night and day.

Immediately after death, human beings become so beautiful you can hardly bear to look at them.

To one extent or another, all children are telepathic.

If you want to sleep, sleep. Simple as that.

Do your absolute best to avoid saying bad things about people, especially those you dislike.

In the long run, grasshoppers and ants all wind up in the same place.

Little Red, His Appearance

When you meet Little Red for the first time, what do you see?

He will be standing in the doorway of his ground-floor apartment on West Fifty-fifth Street, glancing to one side and backing away to give you entry. The atmosphere, the tone created by these gestures, will be welcoming and gracious in an old-fashioned, even rural, manner.

He will be wearing jeans and an old T-shirt, or a worn gray bathrobe, or a chain-store woolen sweater and black trousers. Black, rubber-soled Chinese slippers purchased from a sidewalk vendor will cover his narrow feet. Very slightly, his high, pale forehead will bulge forward beneath his long red hair, which will have been pulled back from his face and fastened into a ragged ponytail by means of a twisted rubber band. An untrimmed beard, curled at the bottom like a giant ruff, will cover much of his face. When he speaks, the small, discolored pegs of his teeth will flicker beneath the fringe of his mustache.

Little Red will strike you as gaunt, in fact nearly haggard. He will seem detached from the world beyond the entrance of his apartment building. West Fifty-fifth Street and the rest of Manhattan will fade from consciousness as you step through the door and move past your host, who, still gazing to one side, will be gesturing toward the empty chair separated from his recliner by a small, round, marble-topped table or nightstand heaped with paperback books, pads of paper, ballpoint pens upright in a cup.

When first you enter Little Red's domain, and every subsequent time thereafter, he will suggest dignity, solicitude, and pleasure in the fact of your company. Little Red admits only those from whom he can be assured of at least some degree of acknowledgment of that which they will receive from him. People who have proven themselves indifferent to the rewards of Little Red's hospitality are forbidden return, no matter how many times they press his buzzer or rap a quarter against his big, dusty front window. He can tell them by their buzzes, their rings, their raps: he knows the identities of most of his callers well before he glances down the corridor to find them standing before his building's glass entrance. (Of course, nearly all of Little Red's visitors take the precaution of telephoning him before they venture to West Fifty-fifth Street, both for the customary reason of confirming his availability and for one other reason, which shall be disclosed in good time.)

Shortly after your entrance into his domain, his den, his consulting room, his confessional, Little Red will tender the offer of a bottle of Beck's beer from the Stygian depths of his kitchen. On the few occasions when his refrigerator is empty of Beck's beer, he will have requested that you purchase a six-pack on your way, and will reimburse you for the purchase upon your arrival.

His hands will be slim, artistic, and often in motion.

He will sometimes appear to stoop, yet at other times, especially when displeased, will adopt an almost military posture. A mild rash, consisting of a scattering of welts a tad redder than his hair and beard, will now and then constellate the visible areas of his face. From time to time, he will display the symptoms of pain, of an affliction or afflictions not readily diagnosed. These symptoms may endure for weeks. Such is his humanity, Little Red will often depress his buzzer (should the buzzer be operational) and admit his guests, his supplicants, when in great physical discomfort.

He will not remind you of anyone you know. Little Red is not a *type.*

The closest you will come to thinking that someone has reminded you of Little Red will occur in the midst of a movie seen late in a summer afternoon on which you have decided to use a darkened theater to walk away from your troubles for a couple of hours. As you sit surrounded by empty seats in the pleasant murk, watching a scene depicting a lavish party or a crowded restaurant, an unnamed extra will move through the door and depart, and at first you will feel no more than a mild tingle of recognition all the more compelling for having no obvious referent. *Someone is going, someone has gone,* that is all you will know. Then the tilt of the departing head or the negligent gesture of a hand will return to you a quality more closely akin to the emotional context of memory than to memory itself, and with the image of Little Red rising into your mind, you will find yourself pierced by an unexpected sense of loss, longing, and sweetness, as if someone had just spoken the name of a long-vanished, once-dear childhood friend.

Little Red, His Dwelling Place

He came to West Fifty-fifth Street in his early thirties, just at the final cusp of his youth, after the years of wandering. From Long Island he had moved into Manhattan, no one now knows where—Little Red himself may have forgotten the address, so little had he come into his adult estate. To earn his keep, he "waited." Kyle's small collection of jazz records, also Kyle's enthusiasm for Count Basie, Maynard Ferguson, and Ella Fitzgerald, had given direction to his younger brother's yearnings, and it was during this period that Little Red made his initial forays into the world of which he would later become so central an element.

Photographs were taken, and he kept them. Should you be privileged to enter Little Red's inmost circle of acquaintances, he will one night fetch from its hidey-hole an old album of cross-grained fabric and display its treasures: snapshots of the boyish, impossibly youthful, impossibly fresh, Little Red, his hair short and healthy, his face shining, his spirit fragrant, in the company of legendary heroes. The album contains no photographs of other kinds. Its centerpiece is a three-by-five, taken outside a sun-drenched tent during a midsixties Newport Jazz Festival, of a dewy Little Red leaning forward and smiling at the camera as Louis Armstrong, horn tucked beneath his elbow, imparts a never-to-be-forgotten bit of wisdom. On Armstrong's other side, grinning broadly, hovers a bearded man in his midforties. This is John Elder, who has been called "the first Little Red." Little Red was sixteen, already on his way.

From New York he wandered, "waiting," from city to city. A hidden design guided his feet, represented by an elderly, dung-colored Volkswagen Beetle with a retractable sunroof and a minimum of trunk space. Directed by the design, the VW brought him to New Orleans, birthplace of Mighty Pops, and there he began his true instruction in certain sacred mysteries. New Orleans was *instructive,* New Orleans *left a mark.* And his journey through the kitchens and dining rooms of great restaurants, his tutelage under their pitiless taskmasters, insured that henceforth he would never have to go long without remunerative employment.

It was in New Orleans that small groups of people, almost always male, began to visit Little Red at all hours of day or night. Some stayed half an hour; others lingered for days, participating in the simple, modest life of the apartment. John Elder is said to have visited the young couple. In those days, John Elder crisscrossed the country, staying with friends, turning up in jazz clubs to be embraced between sets by the musicians. Sometimes late at night, he spoke in a low voice to those seated on the floor around his chair. During these gatherings, John Elder ofttimes mentioned Little Red, referring to him as his *son.*

Did John Elder precede Little Red to Aspen, Colorado? Although we have no documentation, the evidence suggests he did. An acquaintance of both men can recall Zoot Sims, the late tenor saxophonist, mentioning strolling into the kitchen of the Red Onion, Aspen's best jazz club, late on an afternoon in the spring of 1972 and finding John Elder deep in conversation with the owner over giant bowls of pasta. If this memory is accurate, John Elder was *preparing the way*—six months later, Little Red began working at the Red Onion.

He lived above a garage in a one-bedroom apartment accessible only by an exterior wooden staircase. As in New Orleans, individuals and small groups of men called upon him, in nearly every case having telephoned beforehand, to share his company for an hour or a span of days. Up the staircase they mounted, in all sorts of weather, to press the buzzer and await admittance. Little Red entertained his visitors with records and television programs; he invited them to partake of the Italian meals prepared by his wife, who made herself scarce on these occasions. He produced bottles of Beck's beer from the refrigerator. Late at night, he spoke softly and without notes for an hour or two, no more. It was enough.

But too much for his wife, however, for she vanished from his life midway through his residency in Aspen. Single once more, pulling behind the VW a small U-Haul trailer filled with records, Little Red returned to Manhattan in the summer of 1973 and proceeded directly to the apartment on West Fifty-fifth Street then occupied by his old friend and mentor, John Elder, who unquestioningly turned over to his new guest the large front room of his long, railroad-style apartment.

The dwelling place Little Red has inhabited alone since 1976, when John Elder retired into luxurious seclusion, parses itself as three good-sized rooms laid end to end. Between the front room with its big shielded window and the sitting room lies a demi-warren of two small chambers separated by a door.

These chambers, the first containing a sink and shower stall, the second a toilet, exist in a condition of perpetual chiaroscuro, perhaps to conceal the stains encrusted on the fittings, especially the shower stall and curtain. Those visitors to Little Red's realm who have been compelled to wash their hands after the ritual of defecation generally glance at the shower arrangement, which in the ambient darkness at first resembles a hulking stranger more than it does a structure designed for bodily cleansing, shudder at what they think, what they fear they may have seen there, then execute a one-quarter turn of the entire body before groping for the threadbare towels drooping from a pair of hooks.

Beyond the sitting room and reached via a doorless opening in the wall is the kitchen.

Oh the kitchen, oh me oh my.

The kitchen has devolved into squalor. Empty bottles of Beck's in six-pack configurations piled chest-high dominate three-fourths of the grubby floor. Towers of filthy dishes and smeared glasses loom above the sink. The dirty dishes and beer bottles appear organic, as if they have grown untouched in the gloom over the decades of Little

Red's occupancy, producing bottle after bottle and plate after plate of the same ancient substance.

Heavy shades, the dusty tan of nicotine, conceal the kitchen's two windows, and a single forty-watt bulb dangles from a fraying cord over the landscape of stacked empties.

In the sitting room, a second low-wattage bulb of great antiquity oversees the long shelves, the two chairs, and the accumulation of goods before them. Not the only source of light in this barely illuminated chamber, the bulb has been in place, off and on but for several years mostly off, during the entire term of Little Red's occupancy of the apartment. "John Elder was using that light bulb when I moved in," he says. "When you get that old, you'll need a lot of rest, too." Two ornate table lamps, one beside the command post and the other immediately to the visitor's right, shed a ghostlike yellow pall. Little Red has no intrinsic need of bright light, including that of the sun. Shadow and relative darkness ease the eyes, calm the soul. The images on the rectangular screen burn more sharply in low light, and the low, moving banner charting the moment-by-moment activity of the stock market marches along with perfect clarity, every encoded symbol crisp as a snap bean.

A giant shelving arrangement blankets the wall facing the two chairs, and Little Red's beloved television set occupies one of its open cabinets. Another black shelf, located just to the right of the television, holds his audio equipment—a CD player, a tape recorder, a tuner, a turntable, an amplifier, as well as the machines they have superseded, which are stacked beneath them, as if beneath headstones. A squat black speaker stands at either end of the topmost shelf. A cabinet located beneath the right-hand speaker houses several multivolume discographies, some so worn with use they are held together with rubber bands. All the remaining shelves support ranks of long-playing records. Records also fill the lower half of the freestanding bookshelf in front of the narrow wall leading from the small foyer area into the sitting room. Little Red must strain to reach the LPs located on the highest shelf; cardboard boxes of yet more jazz records stand before the ground-level shelves, their awkwardness and weight blocking access to the LPs arrayed behind them. Sometimes Little Red will wish to play a record hidden behind one of the boxes, then pause to consider the problems involved—the bending, the shoving, the risk to his lower back, the high concentration of dust likely to be disturbed—and will decide to feature another artist, one situated in a more convenient portion of the alphabet.

The records were alphabetized long ago. Two or three years after the accomplishment of the stupendous task, Little Red further refined the system by placing the records in alpha-chronological order, so that they stood not only in relation to the artists' placement in the alphabet, but also by date of recording, running from earliest to latest, oldest to newest, in each individual case. This process took him nearly a year to complete and occupied most of his free time—the time not given to his callers—during that period. For the callers kept coming, so they did, in numbers unceasing.

Actually, the alpha-chronologicalization process has not yet reached completion, nor will it, nor can it, for reasons to be divulged in the next section of this account. Alpha-chronologicalization is an endless labor.

What occupies the territory between the chairs and the bookshelves constitutes the grave, grave problem of this room. The territory in question makes up the central portion of Little Red's sitting room, which under optimum conditions would provide a companionable open space for passage to and from the kitchen, to and from the bathroom and the front door, modest exercise, pacing, and for those so disposed, floor-sitting. Such a space would grant Little Red unimpeded access to the thousands of records packed onto the heavily laden shelves (in some cases so tightly that the withdrawal of a single LP involves pulling out an extra three or four on either side).

Once, a table of eccentric design was installed in the middle of the sitting room. At the time, it would have been a considerable amenity, with its broad, flat top for the temporary disposal of the inner and outer sleeves of the record being played, perhaps as well the sleeves containing those records to be played after that one. A large, square table it was, roughly the size of two steamer trunks placed side by side, and trunklike in its solidity from top to bottom, for its flanks contained a clever nest of drawers for the disposition of magazines, gewgaws, and knick-knacks. It is believed that Little Red found this useful object on the street, the source of a good deal of his household furnishings, but it is possible that John Elder found it on the street, and that the table was already in place when Little Red was welcomed within.

Large as it was, the table offered no obstacle to a gaunt, red-haired individual moving from the command post to the records, or from any particular shelf of records to the cabinetlike space housing the turntable and other sound equipment. The table *cooperated,* it must have done. At one time—shortly after Little Red or John Elder managed to get the unwieldy thing off the sidewalk and into the sitting room—the table must have functioned properly, that is as a literal support system. The table undoubtedly performed this useful function for many months. After that . . . entropy took over, and the literal support system began to disappear beneath the mass and quantity of material it was required literally to support. In time, the table *vanished,* as an old car abandoned in a field gradually vanishes beneath and into the mound of weeds that overtakes it, or as the genial scientist who became ferocious Swamp Thing vanished beneath and into the vegetation that had surrounded, supported, nourished his wounded body. Little Red's is the Swamp Thing of the table family.

From the command post and the guest's chair, the center of the sitting room can be seen to be dominated by a large, unstable mound rising from the floor to a height of something like three and a half feet and comprised in part of old catalogs from Levenger, Sharper Image, and Herrington; copies of *Downbeat, Jazz Times,* and *Biblical Archaeology Review;* record sleeves and CD jewel boxes; take-out menus; flyers distributed on behalf of drugstores; copies of *Life* magazine containing particularly eloquent photographs of Louis Armstrong or Ella Fitzgerald; books about crop circles and alien visitations; books about miracles; concert programs of considerable sentimental value; sheets of notepaper scribbled over with cryptic messages (What in the world does *mogrom* mean? Or *rambichure?*); the innards of old newspapers; photographs of jazz musicians purchased from a man on the corner of West Fifty-seventh Street and Eighth Avenue; posters awaiting reassignment to the walls; and other suchlike objects submerged too deeply to be identified. Like the dishes in the sink, the mound seems to be increasing in size through a version of parthenogenesis.

Leaning against the irregular sides of Swamp Thing are yet more records, perhaps as few as fifty, perhaps as many as a hundred, already alphabetized; and around the listing, accordion-shaped constructions formed by propped-up records sit a varying number of cardboard boxes filled with still *more* records, these newly acquired from a specialist dealer or at a vintage record show. (John Elder, who in his luxurious seclusion possesses eighty to ninety thousand records stored on industrial metal shelves, annually attends a record fair in Newark, New Jersey, where he allows Little Red a corner at his lavish table.)

Long-playing records may be acquired virtually anywhere: in little shops tucked into obscure byways; from remote bins in vast retail outlets; from boxes carelessly arranged on the counters of small-town Woolworth's stores; within the outer circles of urban flea markets located in elementary-school playgrounds; from boxes, marked $1 EACH, displayed by unofficial sidewalk vendors who with their hangers-on lounge behind their wares on lawn furniture, smoking cigars, and muffled up against the cold.

So Little Red gets and he spends, but when it comes to records he gets a lot more than he spends. His friends and followers occasionally give him CDs, and Little Red enjoys the convenience of compact discs; however, as long as they do not skip, he much prefers the sound of LPs, even scratchy ones. They are warmer and more resonant: the atmosphere of *distant places, distant times* inhabits long-playing vinyl records, whereas CDs are always in the here and now.

And what Little Red gets must in time be accommodated within his vast system, and a new old Duke Ellington record will eventually have to find its correct alpha-chronological position.

The word Little Red uses for this placement process is "filing." "Filing" records has become his daily task, his joy, his curse, his primary occupation.

Little Red, His Filing

Should you telephone Little Red and should he answer, you, like numerous others, might ask, with a hopeful lilt in your voice, what he has been up to lately.

"Nothing much," Little Red will answer. "Doing a lot of filing."

"Ah," you say.

"Got started yesterday afternoon around three, right after S___ and G___ G___ left. They were here since about ten o'clock the night before—we played some cards. Between three and six I filed at least two hundred records. Something like that, anyhow. Then I was thinking about going out and having dinner somewhere, but R___ was coming over at eight, and I looked at the boxes on the floor, and I just kept on filing. R___ left an hour ago, and I went right back into it. Got a lot of work done, man. The next time you come over, you'll see a big difference."

This assertion means only that *Little Red* sees a great difference. Nine times out of ten, you won't have a prayer. Swamp Thing will seem no less massive than on your previous visit; the boxes of records and accordion shapes will appear untouched.

Of course, time-lapse photography would prove you wrong, for Little Red's collection, filed and unfiled, is in constant motion. Occasionally, as in the case of the Japanese Gentleman, or during one of Little Red's visits to the record fair, albums are sold, leaving gaps on the shelves. These gaps are soon filled with the new old records from the accordions, which have already been alphabetized, and from the boxes, which have not. The customary progress of an album is from box to accordion, then finally to the shelf, after a consultation of the discographical record has pinned down its chronological moment. (Those discographies are in constant use, and their contents heavily annotated, underlined, and highlighted in a variety of cheerful colors.)

The quantity of rearrangement necessitated by the box-accordion-shelf progression would be daunting, exhausting, unbearable to anyone but Little Red. The insertion onto the proper shelf of four recently acquired Roy Eldridge LPs could easily involve redistributing two or three hundred records over four long shelves, so that a three-inch gap at the beginning of the Monk section might be transferred laterally and up to the middle of the Roys. The transferal of this gap requires twenty minutes of shifting and moving, not counting the time previously spent in chronologicizing the new acquisitions with the aid of the (sometimes warring) discographies. It's surprisingly dirty work, too. After ten or twelve hours of unbroken filing, Little Red resembles a coal miner at shift's end, grubby from head to foot, with grime concentrated on his face and hands, bleary eyed, his hair in wisps and tangles.

At the end of your conversation, Little Red will say, "You can come over tonight, if you feel like it. It doesn't matter how late it is. I'll be up."

None of Little Red's friends, followers, or acquaintances has ever seen him in the act of filing his records. He files only when alone.

Miracles Attributed to Little Red

1. *The Miracle of the Japanese Gentleman*

The Japanese people include a surprising number of record collectors, a good half of whom specialize in jazz. Japanese collectors are famous for the purity of their standards, also for their willingness to expend great sums in pursuit of the prizes they desire. One of these gentlemen, a Kyoto businessman named Mr. Yoshi, learned of Little Red's collection from John Elder, with whom he had done business for many years. By this time, Mr. Yoshi's collection nearly equaled John Elder's in size, though only in the numbers of LP, EP, and 78 records it contained. In memorabilia, Mr. Yoshi lagged far behind his friend: when it comes to items like plaster or ceramic effigies of Louis Armstrong, signed photos of Louis Armstrong, and oversized white handkerchiefs once unfurled onstage by Louis Armstrong, John Elder is and always will be in a class by himself.

Little Red knew that the Japanese Gentleman had a particular interest in Blue Note and Riverside recordings from the 1950s, especially those by Sonny Clark and Kenny Dorham. Mr. Yoshi would accept only records in mint or near mint condition and in their original state—original cover art and record label, as if they had been issued yesterday and were essentially unplayed.

Little Red's monthly rent payment of $980 was coming due, and his bank balance stood at a dismal $205.65. The sale of two mint-condition records to Mr. Yoshi could yield the amount needed, but Little Red faced the insurmountable problem of not owning any mint-condition Sonny Clark or Kenny Dorham records on the Blue Note or Riverside labels. He had, it is true, a dim memory of once seeing *The Sonny Clark Trio,* the pianist's first recording as a leader for Blue Note and an object greatly coveted by Japanese collectors, pass through his hands, but that was the entire content of the memory: the record's shiny sleeve passing into and then out of his hands. He had not been conscious of its value on the collector's market; Sonny Clark had never been one of his favorites. However, he *knew* that he had once purchased a nice copy of Kenny Dorham's *Una Mas,* maybe not in mint condition but Excellent, at least Very Good anyhow, A to A-, worth perhaps $150 to $200 to a fanatical Japanese collector who did not already own one.

Little Red scanned the spines of his Kenny Dorham records without finding a single original 1963 copy of *Una Mas.* He had a Japanese reissue, but imagine offering a Japanese reissue to a Japanese collector!

Yet if he had neither of the most desired records, he did have a good number of consolation prizes, Blue Notes and Riversides maybe not exactly unplayed but certainly eminently playable and with sleeves in Fine to Very Fine condition. These twenty records he coaxed from the shelves and stacked on a folding chair for immediate viewing. With luck, he imagined, they could go for $30 to $40 apiece—he had seen them listed at that price in the catalogs. If he sold them all, he would make about $700, leaving him only a few dollars short of his rent.

Mr. Yoshi appeared at precisely the designated hour and wasted no time before examining the records set aside for him. Five-seven, with a severe face and iron gray hair, he wore a beautiful dark blue pinstriped suit and gleaming black loafers. His English was rudimentary, but his tact was sublime. He had to pick his way around Swamp Thing to reach the folding chair, but the Japanese Gentleman acknowledged its monstrous presence by not as much as a raised eyebrow. For him, Swamp Thing did not exist. All that existed, all that deserved notice, was the stack of records passed to him, two at a time, by Little Red.

"No good," he said. "Not for me."

"That's a shame," said his host, hiding his disappointment. "I hope your trip hasn't been wasted."

Mr. Yoshi ignored this remark and turned to face the crowded shelves. "Many records," he said. "Many, many." Little Red understood it was a show of politeness, and he appreciated the gesture.

"For sale?"

"Some, I guess," said Little Red. "Take a look."

The Japanese Gentleman cautiously made his way around the accordions and through the boxes on Swamp Thing's perimeter. When he stood before the shelves, he clasped his hands behind his back. "You have Blue Note?"

"Sure," said Little Red. "All through there. Riverside, too."

"You have Sonny Clark, Kenny Dorham?"

"Some Kenny, yeah," said Little Red, pointing to a shelf. "Right there."

"Aha," said Mr. Yoshi, moving closer. "I have funny feeling. . . ."

Little Red clasped his own hands behind his back, and the Japanese Gentleman began to brush the tip of his index finger against the spines of the Dorham records. "Here is reason for funny feeling," he said, and extracted a single record. "*Una Mas.* Blue Note, 1963. Excellent condition."

"Yeah, well," said Little Red.

But the record in Mr. Yoshi's right hand was not the Japanese reissue. The Japanese Gentleman was holding, in a state akin to reverence, exactly what he had said it was, the original Blue Note issue from 1963, in immaculate condition.

"Huh!" said Little Red.

"Must look," said Mr. Yoshi, and slid the record from its sleeve. No less than his shoes, the grooved black vinyl shone.

"You try to keep this one for yourself," Mr. Yoshi teased. "Suppose I give you $500, would you sell?"

"Uh, sure," said Little Red.

"What else you hiding here?" asked Mr. Yoshi, more to the intoxicating shelves than to Little Red. He picked his way along, flicking his fingers on the spines. "Uh huh. Uh huh. Not bad. Uh oh, *very* bad. Poor, poor condition. Should throw out, no good anymore to listen."

Little Red said he would think about it.

"I have funny feeling again." Mr. Yoshi stiffened his spine and glared at the spines of the records. "Oh, yes, *very* funny feeling."

Little Red came closer.

"Something here."

The Japanese Gentleman leaned forward and pushed two B- Kenny Clarke Trio records on Savoy as far apart as they would go, about a quarter of an inch. The collector's instincts are not those of an ordinary man. He twitched out the Kenny Clarke Trio records and passed them to Little Red. His hand slid into the widened gap, his head moved nearer. "Aha."

Very gently, Mr. Yoshi pulled out his arm from between the records. A fine layer of dust darkened his elegant cuff. When his hand cleared the shelf, it brought into view two ten-inch LPs which had been shoved into an opening once occupied by John Elder's long-departed reel-to-reel recorder. On the albums' identical covers, staggered red, blue, green, and yellow bars formed keyboard patterns. *The Sonny Clark Trio,* Blue Note, 1957, still in their plastic wrappers.

"You hide, I find," said the Japanese Gentleman. "This the Sonny Clark mother lode!"

"Sure looks like it," said dumbfounded Little Red.

"All three records, I give $2,000. Right now. In cash."

"Talked me into it," said Little Red, and the Japanese Gentleman counted out two months' rent in new, sequentially numbered hundred-dollar bills and pressed them into his host's waiting hand. Little Red threw in a plastic LP carrier that looked a bit like a briefcase, and Mr. Yoshi left beaming.

After the departure of the Japanese Gentleman, Little Red remembered the wad of bills remaining in his guest's wallet after the removal of twenty hundreds and realized that he could have asked for and received another ten.

Don't be greedy, he told himself. *Be grateful.*

2. *The Miracle of the Weeping Child*

Late on a winter night, Little Red emerged from stuporous slumber and observed that he was fully dressed and seated at his command post in the freezing semidarkness. Across the room, the twinkling screen displayed in black and white a flylike Louis Jourdan scaling down the façade of a hideous castle. (He had thought to enjoy the BBC's seventies *Dracula* as a reward for long hours of filing.) By the dim lamplight he saw that the time was 3:25. He had been asleep for about an hour and a half. His arms ached from the evening's labor; the emptiness in his stomach reminded him that he had failed to eat anything during the course of the busy day. Little Red's hands and feet were painfully cold. He reached down for the plaid blanket strewn at the left-hand side of his recliner. Even in his state of mild befuddlement, Little Red wondered what had pulled him so urgently into wakefulness.

How many days had passed without the refreshment of sleep? Two? Three? When deprived so long of sleep, the rebelling body and mind yield to phantoms. Elements of the invisible world take on untrustworthy form and weight, and their shapes speak in profoundly ambiguous voices. Little Red had been in this condition many times before; now he wished only to return to the realm from which he had been torn.

A push on the lever tilted the back of the chair to an angle conducive to slumber. Little Red draped the blanket over his legs and drew its upper portion high upon his chest.

Faintly but clearly, from somewhere in his apartment came the sound of a child weeping in either pain or despair. As soon as Little Red heard the sound, he knew that this was what had awakened him: a dream had rippled and broken beneath its pressure. He had been pulled upward, drawn *up* into the cold.

It came again, this time it seemed from the kitchen: a hiccup of tears, a muffled sob.

"Anybody there?" asked Little Red in a blurry voice. Wearily, he turned his head toward the kitchen and peered at the nothing he had expected to see. Of course no distraught child sat weeping in his kitchen. Little Red supposed that it had been two or three years since he had even *seen* a child.

He dropped his head back into the pillowy comfort of the recliner and heard it again—the cry of a child in misery. This time it seemed to come not from the kitchen but from the opposite end of his apartment, either the bathroom or the front room that served as storage shed and bedroom. Although Little Red understood that the sound was a hallucination and the child did not exist, that the sound should seem to emanate from the bedroom disturbed him greatly. He kept his bedroom to himself. Only in extreme cases had he allowed a visitor entrance to this most private of his chambers.

He closed his eyes, but the sound continued. False, false perception! He refused to be persuaded. There was no child; the misery was his own, and it derived from exhaustion. Little Red nearly arose from his command post to unplug his telephone, but his body declined to cooperate.

The child fell silent. Relieved, Little Red again closed his eyes and folded his hands beneath the rough warmth of the woolen blanket. A delightful rubbery sensation overtook the length of his body, and his mind lurched toward a dream. A series of sharp cries burst like tracers within his skull, startling him back into wakefulness.

Little Red cursed and raised his head. He heard another flaring outcry, then another, and the sound subsided back into pathetic weeping. "Go to sleep!" he yelled, and at that moment realized what had happened: a woman, not a child, was standing distressed on the sidewalk outside his big front window, crying loudly enough to be audible deep within. A woman sobbing on West Fifty-fifth Street at 3:30 in the morning, no remedy existed for a situation like that. He could do nothing but wait for her to leave. An offer of assistance or support would earn only rebuff, vituperation, insults, and the threat of criminal charges. Nothing could be done, Little Red advised himself. Leave well enough alone, stay out. He shut his eyes and waited for quiet. At least he had identified the problem, and sooner or later the problem would take care of itself. Tired as he was, he thought he might fall asleep before the poor creature moved on. He might, yes, for he felt the gravity of approaching unconsciousness slip into his body's empty spaces despite the piteous noises floating through his window.

Then he opened his eyes again and swung his legs from beneath the blanket's embrace and out of the chair, for he was Little Red and could not do otherwise. The woman's misery was intolerable, how could he pretend not to hear it? Thinking to peek around the side of the front window's shade, Little Red pushed himself out of the command center and marched stiff-legged into the toilet.

As if the woman had heard his footsteps, the noise cut off. He paused, took a slow step forward. *Just let me get a look at you,* he thought. *If you don't look completely crazy, I'll give you whatever help you can accept.* In a moment he had passed through the bathroom and was opening the door to his bedroom, the only section of the apartment we have not as yet seen.

The weeping settled into a low, steady, fearful wail. The woman must have heard him, he thought, but was too frightened to leave the window. "Can't be as bad as that," he said, making his slow way down the side of the bed toward the far wall, where an upright piano covered half of the big window. Now the wailing seemed very close at hand. Little Red imagined the woman huddled against his building, her head bent to his window. Her mechanical cries pierced his heart. He almost felt like going outside immediately.

Little Red reached the right edge of the window and touched the stiff, dark material of the shade. Unraised for nearly forty years, it smelled like a sick animal. A pulse of high-pitched keening filled his ears, and a dark shape that huddled beside the piano moved nearer the wall. Little Red dropped his hand from the shade and stepped back, fearing that he had come upon a monstrous rat. His heart pounded, and his breath caught in his throat. Even the most ambitious rat could not grow so large. Little Red quieted his impulse to run from the room and looked down at the being crouching beside the piano.

A small dark head bent over upraised knees tucked under a white stretched-out T-shirt. Two small feet shone pale in the darkness. Little Red stared at the creature before him, which appeared to tighten down into itself, as if trying to disappear. A choked sound of combined misery and terror came from the little being. It was a child after all: he had been right the first time.

"How did you get in here?" Little Red asked.

The child hugged its knees and buried its face. The sound it made went up in pitch and became a fast, repeated *ih ih ih.*

Little Red lowered himself to the floor beside the child. "You don't have to be so afraid," he said. "I'm not going to hurt you."

A single eye peeked at him, then dropped back to the T-shirt and the bent knees. The boy was about five or six, with short brown hair and thin arms and legs. He shivered from the cold. Little Red patted him lightly on the back and was surprised by the relief aroused in him by the solidity of what he touched.

"Do you have a name?"

The boy shook his head.

"No?"

"No." It was the smallest whisper.

"That's too bad. I bet you have a name, really."

No response, except that the shivering child had stopped whimpering *ih ih ih.*

"Can you tell me what you're doing here?"

"I'm *cold,*" the boy whispered.

"Well, sure you are," said Little Red. "Here we are in the middle of winter, and all you have on is a T-shirt. Hold on, I'm going to get you a blanket."

Little Red pushed himself to his feet and went quickly to the sitting room, fearing that the child might vanish before his return. *But why do I want him to stay?* he asked himself, and had no answer.

When he came back, the child was still huddled alongside the piano. Little Red draped the blanket over his shoulders and once again sat beside him.

"Better?"

"A little." His teeth made tiny clicking noises.

Little Red rubbed a hand on the boy's blanket-covered arms and back.

"I want to lie down," the child said.

"Will you tell me your name now?"

"I don't have a name."

"Do you know where you are?"

"Where I am? I'm here."

"Where do you live? What's your address? Or how about your phone number? You're old enough to know your phone number."

"I want to lie down," the boy said. "Put me on the bed. Please." He nodded at Little Red's bed, in the darkness seemingly buried beneath the rounded bodies of many sleeping animals. These were the mounds of T-shirts, underpants, socks, sweatshirts, and jeans Little Red had taken, the previous night, to the 24-hour Laundromat on the corner of Fifty-fifth Street and Ninth Avenue. He had filled five washers, then five dryers with his semiannual wash, taken the refreshed clothing home in black garbage bags, and sorted it all on his bed, where it was likely to remain for the entirety of the coming month, if not longer.

"Whatever you say," said Little Red, and lifted the child in his arms and carried him to the bed. The boy seemed to weigh no more than a handful of kitchen matches. He leaned over the bed and nestled the child between a pile of balled socks and a heap of folded jazz festival T-shirts. "You can't stay here, you know, little boy," he said.

The child said, "I'm not going to stay here. This is just where I *am.*"

"You don't have to be scared anymore."

"I thought you were going to hurt me." For a second his eyes narrowed, and his skin seemed to shrink over his skull. He was actually a very unattractive little boy, thought Little Red. The child looked devious and greedy, like an urchin who had lived too long by its wits. In some ways, he had the face of a sour, bad-tempered old man. Little Red felt as though he had surrendered his bed to a beast like a weasel, a coyote.

But he's only a little boy, Little Red told Little Red, who did not believe him. This was not a child—this was something that had come in from the freezing night. "Do you think you can go to sleep now?"

But the child—the being—had slipped into unconsciousness before Little Red asked the question.

What to *do* with him? The ugly little thing asleep in the midst of Little Red's laundry was never going to produce an address or a telephone number, that was certain. Probably it was telling the truth about not having a name.

But that was crazy—he had gone too long without sleep, and his mind could no longer work right. A wave of deep weariness rolled through him, bringing with it the recognition that his mind could no longer work at all, at least not rationally. If he did not lie down, he was going to fall asleep standing up. So Little Red got his knees up on the mattress, pushed aside some heaps of clothing, stretched out, and watched his eyes close by themselves.

Asleep, he inhaled the scent of clean laundry, which was the most beautiful odor in the world. Clean laundry smelled like sunshine, fresh air, and good health. This lovely smell contained a hint of the celestial, of the better world that heaven is said to be. It would be presumptuous to speak of angels, but if angels wore robes, those robes would smell like the clean, fluffy socks and underwear surrounding Little Red and his nameless guest. The guest's own odor now and then came to Little Red. Mingled with the metallic odor of steam vented from underground regions, the sharp, gamy tang of fox sometimes cut through the fragrance of the laundry, for in his sleep Little Red had shifted nearer to the child.

To sleeping Little Red, the two scents twisted together and became a single thing, an odor of architectural complexity filled with wide plazas and long colonnades, also with certain cramped, secret dens and cells. And from the hidden dens and cells a creature came in pursuit of him, whether for good or ill he did not know. But in pursuit it came: Little Red felt the displacement of the air as it rushed down long corridors, and there were times when he spun around a corner an instant before his pursuer would have caught sight of him. And though he continued to run as if for his life, Little Red still did not know if the creature meant him well or meant to do him harm.

He twisted and squirmed in imitation of the motions of his dream-body, so that eventually he had folded his body around that of his little guest, and the animal smell became paramount.

During what happened next, Little Red could not make out whether he was asleep and dreaming of being half awake, or half awake and still dreaming of being asleep. He seemed to pass back and forth between two states of being with no registration of their boundaries. His hand had fallen on the child's chest—he remembered that, for instantly he had thought to snatch it back from this accidental contact. Yet in pulling back his hand he had somehow succeeded in pulling the child with it, though his hand was empty and his fingers open. The child, the child-*thing,* floated up from the rumpled blanket and the disarranged piles of laundry, clinging to Little Red's hand as metal clings to a magnet. That was how it seemed to Little Red: the boy *adhered* to his raised hand, the boy *followed* the hand to his side, and when the boy-thing came to rest beside him, the boy-thing smiled a wicked smile and bit him in the neck.

The gamy stink of fox streamed into his nostrils, and he cried out in pain and terror . . . and in a moment the child-thing was stroking his head and telling him he had nothing to fear, and the next moment he dropped through the floor of sleep into darkness and knew nothing.

Little Red awakened in late afternoon of the following day. He felt wonderfully rested and restored. A decade might have been subtracted from his age, and he became a lad of forty once again. Two separate mental events took place at virtually the same moment, which occurred as he sat up and stretched out his arms in a tremendous yawn. He remembered the weeping child he had placed in this bed; and he noticed that one of his arms was spattered with drying blood.

He gasped and looked down at his chest, his waist, his legs. Bloodstains covered his clothes like thrown paint. The blanket and the folded clothing littered across the bed were drenched in blood. There were feathery splashes of blood on the dusty floor. Spattered bloodstains mounted the colorless wall.

For a moment, Little Red's heart stopped moving. His breathing was harsh and shallow. Gingerly, he swung his legs to the floor and got out of bed. First he looked at the blanket, which would have to be thrown out, then, still in shock, down at his own body. Red blotches bloomed on his shirt. The bottom of his shirt and the top of his jeans were sodden, too soaked in blood to have dried.

Little Red peeled the shirt off over his head and dropped it to the floor. His chest was irregularly stained with blood but otherwise undamaged. He saw no wounds on his arms. His fingers unbuckled his belt and undid his zipper, and he pushed his jeans down to his ankles. The Chinese slippers fell off his feet when he stepped out of the wet jeans. From midthigh to feet, he was unmarked; from navel to midthigh he was solid red.

Yet he felt no pain. The blood could not be his. Had something terrible happened to the child? Moaning, Little Red scattered the clothing across the bed, looked in the corners of the room, and went as far as the entrance to the sitting room, but saw no trace of his guest. Neither did he see further bloodstains. The child, the *thing,* had disappeared.

When Little Red stood before his bathroom mirror, he remembered the dream, if it had been a dream, and leaned forward to inspect the side of his neck. The skin was pale and unbroken. So it had been a dream, all of it.

Then he remembered the sounds of weeping that had awakened him at his command post, and *ih ih ih,* and he remembered the weight of the child in his arms and his foxy smell. Little Red turned on his shower and stepped into the stall. Blood sluiced down his body, his groin, his legs to the drain. He remembered the blissful fragrance of his clean laundry. That magnificent odor, containing room upon room. Thinking to aid a distressed woman, he had discovered a terrified child, or something that looked like a child, and had given it a night's shelter and a bed of socks and underwear. Standing in the warm spray of the shower, Little Red said, "In faith, a miracle."

3. *The Miracle of C___ M___ and Vic Dickenson*

Late one summer afternoon, C___ M___, a young trombonist of growing reputation, sat in Little Red's guest chair listening to *Very Saxy* and bemoaning the state of his talent.

"I feel stuck," he said. "I'm playing pretty well. . . ."

"You're playing great," said Little Red.

"Thanks, but I feel like there's some direction I ought to go, and I can't figure out what it is. I keep doing the same things over and over. It's like, I don't know, like I have to wash my ears before I'll be able to make any progress."

"Ah," said Little Red. "Let me play something for you." He rose from his chair.

"What?"

"Just listen."

"I don't need this jive bullshit, Little Red."

"I said, just *listen.*"

"Okay, but if you were a musician, you'd know this isn't how it works."

"Fine," said Little Red, and placed on the turntable a record by the Vic Dickenson Trio—trombone, bass, and guitar—made in 1949. "I'm going to my bedroom for a few minutes," he said. "Something screwy happened to my laundry a while ago, and I have to throw about half of it away."

C___ M___ leaned forward to rest his forearms on his knees, the posture in which he listened most carefully.

Little Red disappeared through the door to the toilet and went to his bedroom. Whatever he did there occupied him for approximately twenty minutes, after which he returned to the sitting room.

His face wet with tears, C___ M___ was leaning far back in his chair, looking as though he had just been dropped from a considerable height. "God bless you," he said. "God bless you, Little Red!"

4. *The Miracle of the Blind Beggar-Man*

He had been seeing the man for the better part of the year, seated on a wooden box next to the flowers outside the Korean deli on the corner of Fifty-fifth Street and Eighth Avenue, shaking a white paper cup salted with coins. Tall, heavy, dressed always in a double-breasted dark blue pinstriped suit of wondrous age, his skin a rich chocolate brown, the man was at his post four days every week from about nine in the morning to well past midnight. Whatever the weather, he covered his head with an ancient brown fedora, and he always wore dark glasses with lenses the size of quarters.

He was present on days when it rained and days when it snowed. On sweltering days, he never removed his hat to wipe his forehead, and on days when the temperature dropped into the teens he wore neither gloves nor overcoat. Once he had registered the man's presence, Little Red soon observed that he took in much more money than the other panhandlers who worked Hell's Kitchen. The reason for his success, Little Red surmised, was that his demeanor was as unvarying as his wardrobe.

He was a beggar who did not beg. Instead, he allowed you to give him money. Enthroned on his box, elbows planted on his knees, cup upright in his hand, he offered a steady stream of greetings, compliments, and benedictions to those who walked by.

You're sure looking fine today, Miss . . . God bless you, son . . . You make sure to have a good day today, Sir . . . God bless you, Ma'am . . . Honey, you make me happy every time you come by . . . God bless . . . God bless . . .

And so it happened that one day Little Red dropped a dollar bill into the waiting cup.

"God bless," the man said.

On the following day, Little Red gave him another dollar.

"Thank you and God bless you, son," the man said.

The next day, Little Red put two dollars in the cup.

"Thank you, Little Red, God bless you," said the man.

"How did you learn my name?" asked Little Red. "And how did you know it was me?"

"I hear they come to you, the peoples," the man said. "Night and day, they come. Night *and* day."

"They come, each in his own way," said Little Red. "But how do you know my name?"

"I always knew who you were," said the man. "And now I know what you are."

Little Red placed another dollar in his cup.

"Maybe I come see you myself, one day."

"Maybe you will," said Little Red.

5. *The Miracle of the Greedy Demon (from Book I,* Little Red, His Trials*)*

The greedy demons were everywhere. He saw them in the patrons' eyes—the demons, glaring out, saying *more, more.* While Little Red dressed to go to work, while he laced up his sturdy shoes, while taking the crosstown bus, as he opened the door to the bar and the headwaiter's desk, his stomach tightened at the thought of the waiting demons. Where demons reign, all is hollow, all happiness is pain in disguise, all pleasure merely the product of gratified envy. Daily, as he padded to the back of the restaurant to don his bow tie and white jacket, he feared he would be driven away by the flat, toxic stench of evil.

This occurred in the waning days of Little Red's youth, when he had not as yet entered fully into his adult estate.

The demons gathered here because they enjoyed each other's company. Demons can always recognize other demons, but the human beings they inhabit are ignorant of their possession and don't have a clue what is going on. They suppose they simply enjoy going to certain restaurants, or, say, a particular restaurant, because the food is decent and the atmosphere pleasant. The human beings possessed by demons fail to notice that while the prices have gone up a bit, the food has slipped and the atmosphere grown leaden, sour, stale. The headwaiter notices only that a strange languor has taken hold of the service staff, but he feels too languid himself to get excited about it. Ninety-nine percent of the waiters fail to notice that they seldom wish to look their patrons in the eye and record only that the place seems rather *dimmer* than it once was. Only Little Red sees the frantic demons jigging in the eyes of the torpid diners; only Little Red understands, and what he understands sickens him.

There came a day when a once-handsome gentleman in a blue blazer as taut as a sausage casing waved Little Red to his table and ordered a second sixteen-ounce rib eye steak, rare, and a second order of onion rings, and oh yeah, might as well throw in a second bottle of that Napa Valley Cabernet.

"I won't do that," said Little Red.

"Kid, you gotta be shitting me," said the patron. His face shone a hectic pink. "I ordered another rib eye, more onion rings, and a fresh bottle of wine."

"You don't want any more food," said Little Red. He bent down and gazed into the man's eyes. "Something inside you wants it, but you don't."

The man gripped his wrist and moved his huge head alongside Little Red's. "You act that way with me, kid, and one cold night you could wake up and find me in your room, wearing nothing but a T-shirt."

"Then let it be so," said Little Red.

6. *The Miracle of the Murdered Cat*

Years after he had come into his adult estate, Little Red one day left his apartment to replenish his stock of Beck's beer. It was just before six o'clock on a Saturday morning in early June. Two trumpet players and a petty thief who had dropped in late Thursday night were scattered around the sitting room, basically doing nothing but waiting for him to come back with their breakfasts.

The Koreans who owned the deli on the corner of Fifty-fifth and Eighth lately had been communicating some kind of weirdness, so he turned the corner, intending to walk past the front of their shop and continue north to the deli on the corner of Fifty-sixth Street, where the Koreans were still sane. The blind beggar startled him by stepping out of the entrance and saying, "My man, Little Red Man! Good morning to you, son. Seems to me you ought to be thinkin' about getting more sleep one of these days."

"Morning to you, too," said Little Red. "Early for you to be getting to work, isn't it?"

"Somethin' big's gonna happen today," said the beggar-man. "Wanted to make sure I didn't miss out." He set down his box, placed himself on it, and opened the twelve-ounce bottle of Dr. Pepper he had just purchased.

Only a few taxicabs moved up wide Eighth Avenue, and no one else was on the sidewalk on either side. Iron shutters protected the windows of most of the shops.

As he moved up the block, Little Red looked across the street and saw a small shape leave the shelter of a rank of garbage cans and dart into the avenue. It was a little orange cat, bony with starvation.

The cat had raced to within fifteen feet of the western curb when a taxi rocketing north toward Columbus Circle swerved toward it. The cat froze, eyed the taxi, then gathered itself into a ball and streaked forward.

Little Red stood open-mouthed on the sidewalk. "You worthless little son of a bitch," he said. "Get moving!"

As the cat came nearly within leaping distance of the curb, the cab picked up speed and struck it. Little Red heard a muffled sound, then saw the cat roll across the surface of the road and come to rest in the gutter.

"Damn," he said, and glanced back down the block. The beggarman sat on his box, gripping his bottle of Dr. Pepper and staring straight ahead at nothing. Little Red came up to the lifeless cat and lowered himself to the sidewalk. "You just get on now," he said. "Get going, little cat."

The lump of dead fur in the gutter twitched, twitched again, and struggled to its feet. It turned its head to Little Red and regarded him with opaque, suspicious eyes.

"Git," said Little Red.

The cat wobbled up onto the sidewalk, sat to drag its tongue over an oily patch of fur, and limped off into the shelter of a doorway.

Little Red stood up and glanced sideways. The blind man cupped his hands around his mouth and called out something. Little Red could not quite make out his words, but they sounded approving.

7. *The Miracle of the Kitchen Mouse*

On a warm night last year, Little Red awakened in his command center to a silent apartment. His television set was turned off, and a single red light burned in the control panel of his CD player, which, having come to the end of *The Count on the Coast, Vol. II,* awaited further instructions.

Little Red rubbed his hands over his face and sat up, trying to decide whether or not to put on a new CD before falling back asleep. Before he could make up his mind, a small gray mouse slipped from between two six-packs of Beck's empties and hesitated at the edge of the sitting room. The mouse appeared to be looking at him.

"You go your way, and I'll go mine," said Little Red.

"God bless you, Little Red," said the mouse. Its voice was surprisingly deep.

"Thank you," said Little Red, and lapsed back into easy-breathing slumber.

Peter Straub

THE BEATITUDES OF LITTLE RED, II

Over the long run, staying on good terms with your dentist really pays off.

Bargain up, not down.

When you're thinking about sex, the only person you have to please is yourself.

At least once a day, remember the greatest performance you ever heard.

Every now and then, consider Marilyn Monroe.

Put your garbage in the bin.

When spring comes, *notice* it.

Taste what you eat, dummy.

God pities demons, but He does not love them.

No matter how poor you are, put a little art up on your walls.

Let other people talk first. Your turn will come.

Wealth is measured in books and records.

All leases run out, sorry.

Every human being is beautiful, especially the ugly ones.

Resolution and restitution exist only in fantasy.

Learn to live *broken.* It's the only way.

Dirty dishes are just as sacred as clean ones.

In the midst of death, we are in life.

If some miserable bastard tries to cheat you, you might as well let the sorry piece of shit get away with it.

As soon as possible, move away from home.

Don't buy shoes that hurt your feet.

We are all walking through fire, so keep on walking.

Never tell other people how to raise their children.

The truth not only hurts, it's unbearable. You have to live with it anyway.

Don't reject what you don't understand.

Simplicity works.

Only idiots boast, and only fools believe in "bragging rights."

You are *not* better than anyone else.

Cherish the dents in your armor.

Always look for the *source.*

Rhythm is repetition, repetition, repetition.

Snobbery is a disease of the imagination.

Happiness is primarily for children.

When it's time to go, that's what time it is.

Little Red, His Hobbies and Amusements

Apart from music, books, and television, he has no hobbies or amusements.

*

Peter Straub

EPISTLE OF C___ M___ TO R___ B___, CONCERNING LITTLE RED

Dear R___,
Have you heard of the man, *if he is a man,* called Little Red? Has the word reached you? Okay, I know how that sounds, but don't start getting worried about me, because I haven't flipped out or lost my mind or anything, and I'm not trying to *convert* you to anything. I just want to describe something to you, that's all. You can make up your own mind about it afterward. Whatever you think will be okay with me. I guess I'm still trying to make up my own mind—probably that's one reason why I'm writing you this letter.

I told you that before I left Chicago the last time, I took some lessons from C___ F___, right? What a great player that cat is. Well, you know. The year we got out of high school, we must have listened to *Live in Las Vegas* at least a thousand times. Man, he really opened our eyes, didn't he? And not just about the trombone, as amazing as that was, but about music in general, remember? So he was playing in town, and I went every night and stayed for every set, and before long he noticed I was there all the time, and on the third night I bought him a drink, and we got talking, and he found out I played trombone, and when and where and all that, and he asked me if I would sit in during the second set the next night. So I brought my horn and I sat in, and he was amazing. I guess I did okay, because he said, "That was nice, kid." Which made me feel very, very good, as you can imagine. I asked could he give me some lessons while he was in town. Know what he told me? "I can probably show you some things."

We met four times in his hotel room, besides spending an hour or two together after the gig, most nights. Mainly, he worked on my breathing, but apart from that the real education was just listening to him talk, man. Crazy shit that happened on the road with Kenton and Woody Herman, stories about the guys who could really cut it and the guys who couldn't but got over anyhow, all kinds of great stories. And one day he says to me, When you get to New York, kid, you should look up this guy Little Red, and tell him I said you were okay.

"What is he," I asked, "a trombone player?"

Nah, he said, just a guy he thought I should know. Maybe he could do me some good. "Little Red, he's hard to describe if you haven't met him," he said. "Being with the guy is sort of like doing the tango." Then he laughed.

"The tango?" I asked.

"Yeah," he said. "You might wind up with your head up your ass, but you know you had a hell of a time anyway."

So when I got to New York I asked around about this Little Red, and plenty of people knew him, it turned out, musicians especially, but nobody could tell me exactly what the guy did, or what made him so special. It was like—if you *know,* then there's no point in talking about it, and if you don't, you can't talk about it at all, you can't even begin. Because I met a couple of guys like that. When Little Red's name came up they just shrugged their shoulders and shook their heads. One guy even walked out of the room we were in!

Eventually I decided I had to see for myself, and I called him up. He acted sort of cagey. How did I hear about him, who did I know? "C___ F___ said to tell you I was okay," I said. All right, he said, come on over later, around 10, when he'd be free.

About 10:30, I got to his building—Fifty-fifth off Eighth—an easy walk from my room on Forty-fourth and Ninth. I buzz his apartment, he buzzes me in. And there he is, opening the door to his apartment, this skinny guy with a red beard and long red hair tied back in a ponytail. His face looks sad, and he looks pretty tired, but he gives me a beer right away and sits me down in his incredibly messy room, stuff piled up in front of a wall of about a million records, and asks me what I'd like to hear. I dunno, I say, I'm a trombone player, is it possible he has some good stuff I maybe don't know about? And we're off! The guy has *hundreds* of great things I'd never heard before, some I never heard of at all, and before I know it five or six hours have gone by and I have to get back to my room before I pass out in his chair. He says he'll make me a tape of the best stuff we heard, and I go home. In all that time, I realized, Little Red said maybe a dozen words altogether. I felt like something tremendously important had happened to me, but I couldn't have told you what it was.

The third time I went back to Little Red's, I started complaining about feeling stuck in my playing, and he put on an old Vic Dickenson record that made my head spin around on my shoulders. It was exactly what I needed, and he knew it! He *understood.*

After that, I started spending more and more time at his place. Winter had ended, but spring hadn't come yet. When I walked up Ninth Avenue, the air was bright and cold. Little Red seemed not to notice how frigid his apartment was, and after a while, I forgot all about it. The sunlight burned around the edges of the shades in his kitchen and his living room, and as the time went by it faded away and turned to utter darkness. Sometimes I thought of all the stars filling the sky over Fifty-fifth Street, even though we wouldn't be able to see them if we went outside.

Usually, we were alone. He talked to me—he *spoke.* There were times when other people came in, said a few things, then left us alone again.

Often, he let his words drift away into silence, brought some fresh bread in from his kitchen, and shared it with me. That bread had a wonderful, wonderful taste. I've never managed to find that taste again.

A couple of times he poured out wine for me instead of beer, and that wine seemed extraordinary. It tasted like sunshine, like sunshine on rich farmland.

Once, he asked me if I knew anything about a woman named something like Simone Vey. When I said I'd never heard of her, he said that was all right, he was just asking. Later he wrote her name out for me, and it was spelled W-e-i-l, not V-e-y. Who is this woman? What did she do? I can't find out anything about her.

After a couple of weeks, I got out of the habit of going home when it was time to sleep, and I just stretched out on the floor and slept until I woke up again. Little Red almost always went to sleep in his chair, and when I woke up I would see him, tilted back, his eyes closed, looking like the most peaceful man in the world.

He talked to me, but it wasn't as though he was *teaching* me anything, exactly. We talked back and forth, off and on, during the days and nights, in the way friends do, and to me everything seemed comfortable, familiar, as it should be.

One morning he told me that I had to go, it was time. "You're kidding," I said. "I don't really have to leave, do I?"

I wanted to fall to the floor and beg, I wanted to clutch the cuffs of his trousers and hang on until he changed his mind.

He shoved me out into the hallway and locked the door behind me. I had no choice but to leave. I stumbled down the hall and wandered into the streets, remembering a night when I'd seen a mouse creep out of his kitchen, bless him by name, and receive his blessing in return. When I had staggered three or four blocks south on Eighth Avenue, I realized that I could never again go back.

It was a mistake that I had been there in the first place—he had taken me in by mistake, and my place was not in that crowded apartment. My place might be anywhere, a jail cell, a suburban bedroom with tacky paintings on the wall, a bench in a subway station, anywhere but in that apartment.

I often try to remember the things he said to me. My heart thickens, my throat constricts, a few words come back, but how can I know if they are the right words? He can never tell me if they are.

I think: some kind of love did pass between us. But how could Little Red have loved me? He could not, it is impossible. And yet, R___, a fearful, awkward bit of being, a particle hidden deep within myself, has no choice but to think that maybe, just maybe, in spite of everything, he does after all love me.

So tell me, old friend, have you ever heard of Little Red?

Yours,

C___

The Wisdom of the Skin

James Morrow

EVEN AS I HAULED his shivering body from the river and dragged it onto the pier, examining his ancient face as a numismatist might scrutinize a rare coin, I did not recognize him. He was supposed to be dead, after all—killed along with his wife when their rental Citroën transmuted into a fireball following its collision with a concrete wall in Florence. Not until he'd stopped wheezing, lifted his head, and placed a kiss of gratitude on my cheek did I understand that the newspaper accounts of his incineration were false. This was surely Bruno Pearl. I'd been privileged to rescue the world's greatest sex artist, the genius who'd given his audiences *Sphinx Recumbent, Flowering Judas,* and a dozen other masterpieces of copulation.

Just as musical comedy eclipsed operetta—just as silent movies killed vaudeville, talkies usurped the silents, and television reduced radio drama to a prolix mockery of itself—so did the coming of the Siemanns plasmajector spell the demise of the sex artists, whose achievements today survive largely in the memories of aging aficionados. I shall always regret that I never saw a live concert. How enthralling it must have been to enter a public park during the last century knowing that you might witness a pair of high-wire sensualists, avant-garde couplers, or Viennese orgasmeisters. It was an age of giants. Sara and Jaspar. Quentin and Alessandra. Roger and Dominic. The anonymous Phantoms of Delight. Teresa and Gaston, also known as the Portions of Eternity. Marge and Annette, who styled themselves Enchanted Equinox. You might even find yourself in the legendary presence of Bruno and Mina Pearl.

During my student days at the New England School of Art and Design, I was shrewd enough to take Aesthetics 101, "Metaphysics of the Physical," taught by the benignly fanatical Nikolai Vertankowski. Thanks to Vertankowski's extensive collection of pirated videos and bootleg DVDs, his students experienced tantalizing intimations of the medium that Bruno Pearl and his wife took to such dazzling heights. We learned of the couple's chance meeting at the audition for Trevor Paisley's defiant presentation of *Oedipus Rex* (it began with Antigone's conception), as well as their early struggles on the eros circuit and their eventual celebrity. At the height of the lovers' fame nobody came close to matching their carnal sorcery, their lubricious magic, that bewitchment for which there is no name. Vertankowski also taught us about Bruno and Mina's uncanny and unaccountable decline: the inexplicable fact that, when their Citroën exploded, they had not given a memorable performance in over two years.

Throughout the work week I cross the Hudson twice a day, riding the ferry back and forth between the unfocused city of Hoboken, where I live, and the cavernous reaches of lower Manhattan, where I work. A decade ago my independent film company, Kaleidoscope Productions, received an Oscar nomination for *The Rabble Capitalists,* a feature-length documentary about the unlicensed peddlers of Gotham, those dubious though ambitious folk you see selling fake Rolexes, remaindered books, and sweatshop toys on street corners and in subway stations. Alas, my success was fleeting, and I eventually resigned myself to a career in cranking out instructional videos (tedious and talky shorts intended to galvanize sales forces, inspire stockholders, and educate dentists' captive audiences). One of these days I'm going to sell the business and return to my former life as the SoHo bohemian who signed her oil paintings "Boadicea," though my name is really Susan Fiore.

The night I delivered Bruno Pearl from death, my mood was not far from the syndrome explicated in the Kaleidoscope video called *Coping with Clinical Depression.* At the beginning of the week I'd broken up with Anson, a narcissistic though singularly talented sculptor for whom I'd compliantly aborted a pregnancy one month earlier. As always occurs when I lose a lover, I'd assumed a disproportionate share of the blame, and I was now engaged in a kind of penance, pacing around on the ferry's frigid upper level as the wind cut through my fleece jacket and iced my bones. Despite my melancholy, I took note of the old man, the only other passenger on the weather deck. He was leaning over the stern rail, a skeletal septuagenarian in a tweed overcoat, his face as compacted as a hawk's, his nose supporting a pair of eyeglasses, one lens held in place by a ratty pink Band-Aid. He stared at the Statue of Liberty, an intense gaze, far-reaching, immune to the horizon. My forlorn companion, it seemed, could see all the way to Lisbon.

Glancing north, I fixed on the brightly lit George Washington Bridge, each great sagging cable gleaming like a rope of luminous pearls. Anson believed that our descendants will regard suspension bridges with the same admiration we ourselves accord cathedrals and clipper ships, and tonight I understood what he meant. I turned back to the Statue of Liberty. The gentleman with the broken glasses was gone. In his place—a void: negative space, to use one of Anson's favorite terms.

I peered over the rail. If suicide had been the old man's aim, he'd evidently thought better of the decision; he was thrashing about amid the ferry's widening wake with a desperation indistinguishable from panic. For a fleeting instant the incongruity transfixed me—the lower Hudson, an aquatic wasteland, a place for concrete quays and steel scows but not this fleshy jetsam—and then I tossed aside my rucksack, inhaled sharply, and jumped.

Anyone who has ever studied under Nikolai Vertankowski knows better than to equate performance intercourse with displays of more recent vintage. Today's amateur exhibitionists and open-air stunt fuckers, the professor repeatedly reminded us, are not carrying on a tradition—they are desecrating it. For the true sex artist, all was subtext, all was gesture and grace. In revealing their skin to the world, the classical copulationists achieved not pornographic nudity but pagan nakedness. When Bruno and Mina ruled the eros circuit, they shed each garment so lissomely, planted each kiss so sublimely, and applied each caress so generously that the spectators experienced this tactile cornucopia no less than the lovers themselves.

Then, of course, there was the conversation. Before and after any overt hydraulics, Bruno and Mina always talked to each other, trading astute observations and reciting stanzas of poetry they'd composed especially for the occasion. Sensitive women wept at this linguistic foreplay. Canny men took notes. But the connections themselves remained the sine qua non of each concert. By the time they were famous, Bruno and Mina had perfected over a dozen acts, including not only *Sphinx Recumbent* and *Flowering Judas* but also *Fearful Symmetry, Sylph and Selkie, Chocolate Babylon, Holy Fools, Menses of Venus, Onan in Avalon, Beguiling Serpent, Pan and Syrinx,* and *Fleur de Lis.* When their passions were spent, their skins sated, and their reservoirs of postcoital verse exhausted, Bruno and Mina simply got dressed and watched approvingly as the spectators dropped coins and folding money into their gold-hinged mahogany coffer.

Performance copulators lived by a code, a kind of theatric chivalry whose nuances were known only to themselves. None had an agent or manager. They never published their touring schedules or distributed press kits. Souvenir mongering was forbidden. Videotaping by spectators was tolerated but frowned upon. The artists always arrived unexpectedly, without fanfare, like a goshawk swooping down on a rabbit or a fox materializing in a henhouse. Naturally they favored the major venues, appearing frequently in Golden Gate Park, Brussels Arboretum, Kensington Gardens, and Versailles, but sometimes they brought their brilliance to the humblest of small-town greens and commons. Quixotic tutelaries. Demons of the flesh. Now you saw them, now you didn't.

Although I had never before attempted the maneuvers illustrated in the Kaleidoscope video called *Deep Water Rescue,* my relationship with that particular short was so intimate that, upon entering the Hudson, I spontaneously assumed a backstroke position, placed one hand under the drowning man's chin, bade him relax, and, kicking for motive power, towed him to New Jersey. The instant I levered him onto the derelict wharf, his teeth started chattering, but he nevertheless managed to explain how his eyeglasses had slipped from his face and how in grabbing for them he'd lost his balance and tumbled over the rail. He chastised himself for never learning to swim. Then came the kiss on the cheek—and then the flash of recognition.

"You're Bruno Pearl," I told him.

Instead of responding to my assertion, he patted his pants, front and back, soon determining that his wallet and keys had survived the misadventure.

"Such a wonderfully courageous, a *foolishly* courageous young woman." His teeth continued to vibrate, castanets in the hands of a lunatic. "Tell me your name, dear lady."

"Susan Fiore."

"Call me John."

"You're Bruno Pearl," I informed him again. When you've just saved a person's life, a certain impertinence comes naturally. "You're Bruno Pearl, and the world believes you're dead."

He made no response, but instead rubbed each arm with the opposite hand. "In my experience, lovely Susan," he said at last, "appearances are deceiving."

Whether this was Bruno Pearl or not, my obligation to him clearly had not ended. My beneficiary's most immediate problem was not his lost eyeglasses—though he said he was functionally blind without them—but the threat of hypothermia. When the gentleman revealed that he lived in north Hoboken, near the corner of Willow Avenue and Fourteenth Street, I proposed that we proceed directly to my apartment, a mere two blocks from the wharf.

He readily assented, and so I took him by the hand and led him into the nocturnal city.

By the time we reached my apartment he'd stopped shivering. Supplying him with a dry wardrobe posed no challenge: although my ex-lovers are a heterogeneous bunch, they share a tendency to leave their clothes behind. That night Bruno received Warren's underwear, Jack's socks, Craig's dungarees, and Rich's red polo shirt. I actually had more difficulty replacing my own soggy attire, but eventually I found a clean blouse and presentable khakis.

While Bruno got dressed, I spread the contents of his wallet—money, credit cards, an ancient snapshot of Mina—across the kitchen counter to dry. Next I telephoned the ferry terminal: good news—not only had some admirable soul turned in my abandoned rucksack, the dispatcher was willing to hold it for me. Before Bruno emerged from the bedroom, I managed to feed my cat, Leni, an affectionate calico with a strong sense of protocol, and prepare hot tea for the artist and myself. The instant he appeared in the kitchen, I handed him a steaming mug of oolong, seeking thereby to elevate his spirits and raise his core temperature.

"I had a college professor once, Nikolai Vertankowski, your most devoted fan," I told him as, tea mugs in hand, we moved from my cramped kitchen to my correspondingly minuscule parlor. "We spent most of Aesthetics 101 watching Bruno and Mina tapes, especially the Boston Common concerts."

He settled into my wing chair, fluted his lips, and at long last drew a measure of liquid warmth into his body. He frowned. "Mina and I never authorized any recordings," he muttered, acknowledging his identity for the first time. "Your professor trafficked in contraband."

"He knew that," I replied. "The man was obsessed. Probably still is."

Leni jumped into Bruno's lap, tucked her forelegs beneath her chest, and purred. "Obsessed," he echoed, taking a second swallow of tea. He brushed Leni's spine, his palm smoothing her fur like a spatula spreading frosting on a cake. "Obsession is something I can understand—obsession with Thanatos, obsession with the élan vital.

Speaking of life, I owe you mine. In return, I shall grant you any favor within my capabilities."

"Talk to me."

"A great sex artist is celebrated for his conversation," he said, nodding.

"Talk to me, Bruno Pearl. Tell me the truth about yourself."

"There was a bullet," he said.

There was a bullet. But before the bullet, there was a triumphant performance in Philadelphia. On only two previous occasions had Mina and Bruno succeeded in accomplishing both *Fleur de Lis* and *Holy Fools* in a single afternoon. The Fairmount Park concert had elicited raucous cheers, rapturous sighs, and thunderous applause.

To celebrate their success, the artists treated themselves to a lobster dinner in their hotel room, followed by a stroll along the Delaware. At some undefined moment they crossed an indeterminate boundary, moving beyond the rehabilitated sector of Front Street, with its well-lighted walkways and quaint restaurants, and entering the warehouse district, domain of illegal transactions in flesh and pharmaceuticals. Under normal conditions the artists might have noted their seedy surroundings, spun around in a flurry of self-preservation, and headed south, but they were too intoxicated by their recent success, too high on Aphrodite. *Fleur de Lis* and *Holy Fools*, both in the same concert.

The bullet came from above, flying through a window on the second floor of a gutted factory and subsequently following its evil and inexorable trajectory downward. Bruno would later remember that the shot was actually the first in a series. A heroin deal gone wrong, he later surmised, or possibly a violent altercation between a prostitute and her pimp.

Spiraling toward Mina, the bullet drilled through the left side of her head, drove bits of skull into her cerebral cortex, entered her midbrain, and lodged in her cerebellum.

"Oh my God," I said.

"Those were my exact words," Bruno said. "'Oh my God,' I screamed."

"Did she die?"

Bruno pleasured my cat with his long delicate fingers. "The odds were against her," he replied cryptically.

Mina, delirious, collapsed in Bruno's arms, blood geysering from the wound. He laid her on the asphalt. It was surprisingly warm. Somehow he remained sane enough to administer first aid, tearing off his shirt and bandaging her leaking head. He carried her one block west and hailed a cab. The driver, a Mexican, ten years behind the wheel, had seen worse, much worse, and without a breath of hesitation he drove them to Thomas Jefferson Memorial Hospital. Twenty minutes after her arrival in the emergency room, Mina lay beneath two halogen lamps, hovering on the cusp of oblivion as a surgical team struggled to reassemble her shattered brain.

A soothing and attractive Pakistani nurse directed Bruno down the hall to an ecumenical chapel—a dark place, soft, small, stinking of lilies and candle wax. He was the only patron. Religious music of unknown origin and protean denomination wafted through the air. The artist believed in neither God, Jesus, Allah, nor Krishna. He beseeched them all. He solicited divine intervention more devoutly than when, at age ten, he still knew, absolutely knew, that God always came through for you in the end, that it was just a matter of waiting.

"After I finished praying, I held my hand over a candle flame." Bruno showed me his right palm. The pale, fibrous scar had pulled the skin into a shape resembling a Star of David. "To this day, I'm not sure why I did it. A kind of oblation, I suppose. I felt nothing at first. A tickle. I actually smelled my burning flesh before I apprehended the pain."

Near dawn a bulky man in a white smock waddled into the chapel and introduced himself as Gregor Croom, chief among the surgeons who'd operated on Mina. Dr. Croom was perhaps the most physically unappealing person Bruno had ever met. A great mass of superfluous tissue clung to his upper spine, forcing him into a stoop. Mounds of overlapping flab drooped from the sides of his face, so that his tiny black eyes suggested raisins embedded in a pudding.

The surgeon spoke clinically, phlegmatically. They'd stopped the bleeding, he said, internal and external, and her vital signs were stable—but she'd lost massive quantities of irreplaceable neural matter. It was doubtful that she would ever again move her limbs of her own volition. In all likelihood the bullet had excised her ability to speak.

"I wept," Bruno said, finishing his tea. Leni's errant tail slapped his knee. "I wept like a baby."

"Dear Lord," I said. "My poor Mr. Pearl."

Dr. Croom's demeanor underwent an abrupt transformation. His manner grew gentle, his voice mellifluous. Locking a gnarled hand around Bruno's wrist, he confessed that he was as steadfast an apostle as the sex artists would ever know, proud owner of ninety-eight Bruno and Mina tapes of dubious provenance. His failure to foresee and attend that afternoon's concert in Fairmount Park would haunt him for years to come.

"Please know I shall do all within my power to return Mina to the eros circuit," Dr. Croom told the despairing Bruno. "My expertise lies wholly at your disposal, free of charge."

"Are you saying . . . there's hope?"

"More than hope, Mr. Pearl. A cure."

As the anemic light of dawn washed over Philadelphia, Dr. Croom told Bruno how he had recently perfected a new, audacious, auspicious—and untested—method of rehabilitating victims of neural trauma. He freely revealed that his colleagues had no faith in the technique, and he admitted that it lay outside the bounds of orthodox medical practice. The pioneering experiment would occur in Croom's private laboratory, which he maintained in the basement of his Chestnut Hill mansion.

"The doctor proposed to employ a unique genetic-engineering technology," Bruno told me, massaging Leni with extravagant strokes that began at her nose and continued to the end of her tail. "His desire was to create an embryo bearing Mina's precise genetic heritage. He would then accelerate the fetus's development through hormonal manipulation, so that it would become an infant within seven days, an adolescent within five weeks, and a woman of thirty-six years—Mina's age—in a matter of months. The result, he promised me, would be an exact biological duplicate of my wife."

"But it would *not* be a duplicate," I protested. "It would have none of her experiences, none of her memories."

"You may be sure that I presented this objection to Dr. Croom. His answer astonished me."

The doctor told Bruno about a heuristic computer, the JCN-5000-X. Among the machine's several spectacular functions was an ability to scan a person's cerebrum, encode the totality of its electrochemical contents, and insert these byzantine files into the tabula rasa that is the nervous system of a genetically engineered, hormonally accelerated human replica. In Croom's view, a complete restoration of Mina was entirely feasible, for the bullet had damaged her brain's motor and autonomic areas only—the very motor and autonomic areas that the hypothetical duplicate would boast in full. With the exceptions of certain trivial skills and some useless bits of nostalgia, the facsimile Mina would enjoy a selfhood identical to that possessed by the original before the bullet arrived.

"Look at me, Mr. Pearl," Dr. Croom said. "Contemplate my ugliness. What woman would have this walrus for her lover? And yet, thanks to you and your wife, I have known many a sybaritic satisfaction."

Bruno grew suddenly aware of the pain throbbing in his palm. "This person you're proposing to create . . . would it truly be Mina—Mina restored, Mina reborn—or would it be . . . somebody else?"

"I'm not a philosopher," Dr. Croom replied. "Neither am I a theologian nor a sage. I'm a cyberneurologist with a mission. Sanction this procedure, I beg you. For the sake of art—for the sake of all the world's freaks and Quasimodos—allow me to resurrect your wife."

Bruno requested a second mug of tea. I retired to the kitchen, brewed the oolong, and, upon handing him his replenished mug, voiced my opinion that the duplicate Mina Pearl and the original Mina Pearl would be exactly the same person.

He scowled.

"You disagree?" I said.

"Imagine, sweet Susan, that you have faithfully recorded your every memory, belief, dream, hope, and habit in some massive journal. Call it *The Book of Susan.* Each time you finish making the day's entry, you store the volume on a high shelf in your private library. After your death, the executor of your will—a cousin, let's say—decides to browse among your bookshelves. She spies *The Book of Susan,* stretches for it, dislodges it. Suddenly the volume falls heavily on her head, rendering her unconscious. Five hours later, the executor awakens—as a total amnesiac. She notices the open book in front of her and immediately starts to read it. Her empty mind is like a sponge, absorbing every one of your recorded experiences. Now, dear Susan. Here's the question. At the precise moment when your cousin finishes reading the book and rises from the library floor, have you been reborn?"

"Reborn?"

"Take all the time you want," he said.
"Of *course* I haven't been reborn," I said.
"*Quod erat demonstrandum.*"
"And so you refused to let Dr. Croom carry out his experiment?"
"No," he said.
"No?"

Bruno scratched Leni behind the ears. "I told him he could proceed—proceed with my blessing . . . provided he acceded to one extreme condition. He must also make a duplicate of me, someone to look after the original Mina, nourishing her, cleaning her, caressing her, while my real self again joined the circuit."

"And Croom agreed?"

Bruno nodded. "The man was a romantic."

Like most other Bruno and Mina enthusiasts, I had often wondered about the one-year hiatus in their career. Had they become ill? Grown weary of the circuit? Now the riddle was solved. Thoughout his absence Bruno had occupied a motel on the outskirts of Philadelphia—the first time he had ever settled in one place for more than a week—caring for his frightened, aphasic, and largely paralyzed wife.

He fed her three meals a day, changed her diapers faithfully, and spent many hours reading poetry and fiction aloud in her presence. Despite the lost neurons, Mina retained a modicum of control over her dominant hand, and she managed to compose, at least twice a week, a letter filled with ardor and appreciation. The effort depleted her, and her script bordered on the illegible, but it was obvious from these exchanges that the primal Mina was no zombie. She knew what had happened to her. She understood that her doppelgänger was growing in a Chestnut Hill basement. She realized that a duplicate Bruno would soon replace the loving husband who attended her, so that he might go forth and again practice his art.

"Did Mina approve?" I asked.

"She said she did," Bruno replied. "I was skeptical, naturally, but her letters evinced no feelings of betrayal. Whenever I suggested that she was telling me what I wanted to hear, she became angry and hurt."

Nine months after the bullet ruined Mina's brain, Dr. Croom summoned Bruno to his ramshackle laboratory and presented him not only with a facsimile of the artist's wife but also with his own artificial twin.

"I can't tell you which phenomenon amazed me more"—Bruno finished his second mug of tea—"seeing and speaking with Mina's replica, or interviewing my second self."

"Credible copies?" I asked.

"Perfect copies. And yet I kept wondering: if this was Mina, then who was that person back in my hotel room? I wholly admired the duplicate. You might even say I cherished her. Did I love her? Perhaps. I don't know. My mind was not on love that day."

And so Bruno hit the road once more, coupling with the forged Mina in forty-two parks—famous and obscure, metropolitan and suburban, Old World and New—over the course of a full year. It was one of their most successful tours ever, drawing unqualified accolades from the critics even as audiences presented the artists with vast quantities of applause, adulation, and cash.

"But the new Mina—the Mina duplicate—what did she make of all this?" I asked.

"She didn't like to talk about it. Whenever I broached the subject, she offered the same reply. 'My life is my art,' she said. 'My life is my art.'"

While Bruno and the new Mina pursued the eros circuit, their shadow half—the doppelgänger Bruno and the damaged Mina—journeyed to the south of France, moving into a farmhouse outside of Nîmes. No member of this odd quartet took much joy in the arrangement, but neither did anyone despair. Never before in human history, Bruno speculated, had irreversible brain injury been so cleverly accommodated.

"But cleverness, of course, mere cleverness—it's an ambiguous virtue, no?" Bruno said to me. "After pursuing Dr. Croom's ingenious scheme a mere fourteen months, I felt an overwhelming urge to abandon it."

"Because it was clever?"

"Because it was clever and not beautiful. Everything I knew, everything I held dear, had become false, myself most especially. *The Book of Bruno* had lost its poetry, and instead there was only correct punctuation, and proper spelling, and subjects that agreed with their verbs."

Bruno Pearl, the falsest thing of all, the man with the glass eyes, wooden teeth, crepe hair, putty nose. He could enact his passion for Mina, but he could not experience it. He could enter her body, but not inhabit it. The flawless creature in his arms, this hothouse orchid, this unblemished replica who wore his wife's former face and spoke in her previous voice—nowhere in her flesh did he sense the ten million subtle impressions that had accrued, year by year, decade by decade, to their collective ecstasy.

"The skin is wise," he told me. "Our tissues retain echoes of every kiss and caress, each embrace and climax. Blood is not deceived. Do you understand?"

"No," I said. "Yes," I added. "I'm not sure. Yes. Quite so. I understand, Mr. Pearl."

I did.

Shortly after a particularly stunning concert in Luxembourg Gardens, Bruno and the duplicate Mina drove down to Nîmes, so that the four of them might openly discuss their predicament.

The artists gathered in the farmhouse kitchen, the primal Mina resting in her wheelchair.

"Tell me who you are," the primal Bruno asked the counterfeit.

"Who am I?" the forged Bruno said.

"Yes."

"I ponder that question every day."

"Are you I?" the primal Bruno asked.

"Yes," the forged Bruno replied. "In theory, yes—I am you."

"I was not created to be myself," the facsimile Mina noted.

"True," the primal Bruno said.

"I was created to be someone else," the facsimile Mina said.

"Yes," the primal Bruno said.

"If I am in fact you," the forged Bruno asked, "why do I endure a meaningless and uneventful life while the world lays garlands at your feet?"

"I need to be myself," the facsimile Mina said.

"I hate you, Bruno," the forged Bruno said.

The primal Mina took up a red crayon and scrawled a tortured note. SET THEM FREE, she instructed her husband.

"The right and proper course was obvious," Bruno told me. "My twin and I would trade places."

"Of course," I said, nodding.

"I told my doppelgänger and the duplicate Mina that if they wished to continue the tour, I would respect and support their decision. But I would never do *Sphinx Recumbent* or any other act in public again."

Bruno was not surprised when, an hour before their scheduled departure from Nîmes, the replicas came to him and said that they intended to pursue their careers. What *else* were they supposed to do? Performance intercourse was in their bones.

For nearly five years, the duplicates thrived on the circuit, giving pleasure to spectators and winning plaudits from critics. But then the unexpected occurred, mysterious to everyone except Mina and Bruno and their doubles—and perhaps Dr. Croom comprehended the disaster as well. The ersatz copulators lost their art. Their talent, their touch, their raison d'être—all of it disintegrated, and soon they suffered a precipitous and inevitable decline. Months before the automobile accident, audiences and aestheticians alike had consigned these former gods to history.

"Naturally one is tempted to theorize that the Citroën crash was not an accident," Bruno said.

"The despair of the fallen idol," I said.

"Or, if an accident, then an accident visited upon two individuals who no longer wished to live."

"I guess we'll never know," I said.

"But if they deliberately ran their car into that concrete wall, I suspect that the reason was not their waning reputation. You see, lovely Susan, they didn't know who they were."

A fat, sallow October moon shone into my apartment. It was nearly ten o'clock. Bruno rose from my wing chair, prompting Leni to bail out, and requested that I lead him home. Naturally I agreed. He shuffled into the kitchen, reassembled his wallet, and slid it into his back pocket.

Gathering up Bruno's clothes, still damp, I dumped them into a plastic garbage bag. I told him he was welcome to keep Craig's dungarees, everything else too. I gave him Anson's sheepskin coat as well, then escorted him to the door.

"How do you feel?" I asked.

"Warm," he said, slinging the plastic bag over his shoulder. Leni pushed against Bruno's left leg, wrapped herself around his calf. "Restored."

Retrieving my motorcycle jacket from the peg, I realized that I still felt protective toward my charge: more protective, even, than when I'd first pulled him from the Hudson. As we ventured across the city, I insisted on stopping before each red traffic light, even if no car was in sight. Noticing an unattended German shepherd on the sidewalk ahead, I led us judiciously across the street. Finally, after a half hour of timid northward progress, we reached 105 Willow Avenue.

Removing his keys from Craig's dungarees, Bruno proceeded to enact a common ritual of modern urban life—a phenomenon fully documented in the Kaleidoscope video called *Safe City Living.* Guided by my fingertips, he ascended the stoop, opened the lock on the iron gate, unlatched the main door, climbed one flight of stairs, and, finally, let himself into his apartment.

"Darling, I want you to meet someone," Bruno said, crossing the living room.

Mina Pearl sat in a pool of moonlight. She wore nothing save a wristwatch and a jade pendant. Her bare, pale skin gleamed like polished marble. A fanback wicker chair held her twisted body as a bamboo cage might enclose a Chinese cricket.

"This is Susan Fiore," Bruno continued. "As unlikely as it sounds, I fell off the ferry tonight, and she rescued me. I lost my glasses."

Mina worked her face into the semblance of a smile. She issued a noise that seemed to amalgamate the screech of an owl with the bleating of a ewe.

"I'm pleased to meet you, Mrs. Pearl," I said.

"Tomorrow I'm going to sign up for swimming lessons," Bruno averred.

As I came toward Mina, she raised her tremulous right hand. I clasped it firmly. Her flesh was warmer than I'd expected, suppler, more robust.

She used this same hand to gesture emphatically toward Bruno—a private signal, I concluded. He opened a desk drawer, removing a sheet of cardboard and a felt-tip marker. He brought the implements to his wife.

THANK YOU, Mina wrote. She held the message before me.

"You're welcome," I replied.

Mina flipped the cardboard over. PAN AND SYRINX, she wrote.

For the second time that evening, Bruno shed all his clothes. Cautiously, reverently, he lifted his naked wife from the wicker chair. She jerked and twitched like a marionette operated by a tipsy puppeteer. As her limbs writhed around one another, I thought of Laocoön succumbing to the serpents. A series of thick, burbling, salivary sounds spilled from her lips.

Against all odds, Mina and Bruno connected. It took them well over an hour, but eventually they brought *Pan and Syrinx* to a credible conclusion. Next came a two-hour recital of *Flowering Judas,* followed by an equally protracted version of *Sphinx Recumbent.*

The lovers, sated, sank into the couch. My applause lasted three minutes. I said my goodbyes, and before I was out the door I understood that no matter how long I lived or how far I traveled, I would never again see anything so beautiful as Bruno and Mina Pearl coupling in their grimy little Willow Avenue apartment, the pigeons gathering atop the window grating, the traffic stirring in the street below, the sun rising over Hoboken.

Shift

Nalo Hopkinson

Down,
Down,
Down,
To the deep and shady,
Pretty mermaidy,
Take me down.

—African-American folk song

"DID YOU SLEEP WELL?" she asks, and you make sure that your face is fixed into a dreamy smile as you open your eyes into the morning after. It had been an awkward third date; a clumsy fumbling in her bed, both of you apologizing and then fleeing gratefully into sleep.

"I dreamt that you kissed me," you say. That line's worked before.

She's lovely as she was the first time you met her, particularly seen through eyes with color vision. "You said you wanted me to be your frog." *Say it, say it,* you think.

She laughs. "Isn't that kind of backward?"

"Well, it'd be a way to start over, right?" You ignore the way that her eyes narrow. "You could kiss me," you tell her, as playfully as you can manage, "and make me your prince again."

She looks thoughtful at that. You reach for her, pull her close. She comes willingly, a fall of little blonde plaits brushing your face like fingers. Her hair's too straight to hold the plaits; they're already feathered all along their lengths. "Will you be my slimy little frog?" she whispers, a gleam of amusement in her eyes, and your heart double-times, but she kisses you on the forehead instead of the mouth. You could scream with frustration.

"I've got morning breath," she says apologetically. She means that you do.

"I'll go and brush my teeth," you tell her. You try not to sound grumpy. You linger in the bathroom, staring at the whimsical shells she keeps in the little woven basket on the counter, flaunting their salty pink cores. You wait for anger and pique to subside.

"You hungry?" she calls from the kitchen. "I thought I'd make some oatmeal porridge."

So much for kissing games. She's decided it's time for breakfast instead. "Yes," you say. "Porridge is fine."

Ban . . . Ban . . . ca-ca-Caliban . . .

You know who the real tempest is, don't it? The real storm? Is our mother Sycorax; his and mine. If you ever see her hair flying around her head when she dash at you in anger; like a whirlwind, like a lightning, like a deadly whirlpool. Wheeling and turning round her scalp like if it ever catch you, it going to drag you in, pull you down, swallow you in pieces. If you ever hear how she gnash her teeth in her head like tiger shark; if you ever hear the crack of her voice or feel the crack of her hand on your backside like a bolt out of thunder, then you would know is where the real storm there.

She tell me say I must call her Scylla, or Charybdis.

Say it don't make no matter which, for she could never remember one different from the other, but she know one of them is her real name. She say never mind the name most people know her by; is a name some Englishman give her by scraping a feather quill on paper.

White people magic.

Her people magic, for all that she will box you if you ever remind her of that, and flash her blue, blue y'eye-them at you. Lightning *braps* from out of blue sky. But me and Brother, when she not there, is that Englishman name we call her by.

When she hold you on her breast, you must take care never to relax, never to close your y'eye, for you might wake up with your nose hole-them filling up with the salt sea. Salt sea rushing into your lungs to drown you with her mother love.

Imagine what is like to be the son of that mother.

Now imagine what is like to be the sister of that son, to be sister to that there brother.

There was a time they called porridge "gruel." A time when you lived in castle moats and fetched beautiful golden balls for beautiful golden girls. When the fetching was a game, and you knew yourself to be lord of the land and the veins of water that ran through it, and you could graciously allow petty kings to build their palaces on the land, in which to raise up their avid young daughters.

Ban . . . ban . . . ca-ca-Caliban . . .

When I was small, I hear that blasted name so plenty I thought it was me own.

In her bathroom, you find a new toothbrush, still in its plastic package. She was thinking of you then, of you staying overnight. You smile, mollified. You crack the plastic open, brush your teeth, looking around at the friendly messiness of her bathroom. Cotton, silk, and polyester panties hanging on the shower-curtain rod to dry, their crotches permanently honey-stained. Three different types of deodorant on the counter, two of them lidless, dried out. A small bottle of perfume oil, lid off so that it weeps its sweetness into the air. A fine dusting of baby powder covers everything, its innocent odor making you sneeze. Someone *lives* here. Your own apartment—the one you found when you came on land—is as crisp and dull as a hotel room, a stop along the way. Everything is tidy there, except for the wastepaper basket in your bedroom, which is crammed with empty pill bottles: marine algae capsules; iodine pills. You remind yourself that you need to buy more, to keep the cravings at bay.

Caliban have a sickness. Is a sickness any of you could get. In him it manifest as a weakness; a weakness for cream. He fancy himself a prince of Africa, a mannish Cleopatra, bathing in mother's milk. Him believe say it would make him pretty. Him never had mirrors to look in, and with the mother we had, the surface of the sea never calm enough that him could see him face in it. Him would never believe me say that him pretty already. Him fancy if cream would only touch him, if him could only submerge himself entirely in it, it would redeem him.

Me woulda try it too, you know, but me have that feature you find amongst so many brown-skin people; cream make me belly gripe.

Truth to tell, Brother have the same problem, but him would gladly suffer the stomach pangs and the belly-running for the chance to drink in cream, to bathe in cream, to have it dripping off him and running into him mouth. Such a different taste from the bitter salt sea milk of Sycorax.

That beautiful woman making breakfast in her kitchen dives better than you do. You've seen her knifing so sharply through waves that you wondered they didn't bleed in her wake.

You fill the sink, wave your hands through the water. It's bliss, the way it resists you. You wonder if you have time for a bath. It's a pity that this isn't one of those apartment buildings with a pool. You miss swimming.

You wash your face. You pull the plug, watch the water spiral down the drain. It looks wild, like a mother's mad hair. Then you remember that you have to be cautious around water now, even the tame, caged water of swimming pools and bathrooms. Quickly, you sink the plug back into the mouth of the drain. You'd forgotten; anywhere there's water, especially rioting water, it can tattle tales to your mother.

Your face feels cool and squeaky now. You mouth is wild cherry–flavored from the toothpaste. You're kissable. You can hear humming from the kitchen, and the scraping of a spoon against a pot. There's a smell of cinnamon and nutmeg. Island smells. You square your shoulders, put on a smile, walk to the kitchen. Your feet are floppy, reluctant. You wish you could pay attention to what they're telling you. When they plash around like this, when they slip and slide and don't want to carry you upright, it's always been a bad sign. The kisses of golden girls are chancy things. Once, after the touch of other pale lips, you looked into the eyes of a golden girl, one Miranda, and saw yourself reflected back in her moist, breathless stare. In her eyes you were tall, handsome, your shoulders powerful and your jaw square. You carried yourself with the arrogance of a prince. You held a spear in one hand. The spotted, tawny pelt of an animal that had never existed was knotted around your waist. You wore something's teeth on a string around your neck and you spoke in grunts, imperious. In her eyes, your bright copper skin was dark and loamy as cocoa. She had sighed and leapt upon you, kissing and biting, begging to be taken. You had let her have what she wanted. When her father stumbled upon the two of you, writhing on the ground, she had leapt to her feet and changed you again; called you monster, attacker. She'd clasped her bodice closed with one hand, carefully leaving bare enough pitiful juddering bosom to spark a father's ire. She'd looked at you regretfully, sobbed crocodile tears, and spoken the lies that had made you her father's slave for an interminable length of years.

You haven't seen yourself in this one's eyes yet. You need her to kiss you, to change you, to hide you from your dam. That's what you've always needed. You are always awed by the ones who can work this magic. You could love one of them forever and a day. You just have to find the right one.

You stay a second in the kitchen doorway. She looks up from where she stands at the little table, briskly setting two different-sized spoons beside two mismatched bowls. She smiles. "Come on in," she says.

You do, on your slippery feet. You sit at the table. She's still standing. "I'm sorry," she says. She quirks a regretful smile at you. "I don't think my cold sore is quite healed yet." She runs a tongue tip over the corner of her lip, where you can no longer see the crusty scab.

You sigh. "It's all right. Forget it."

She goes over to the stove. You don't pay any attention. You're staring at the thready crack in your bowl.

She says, "Brown sugar or white?"

"Brown," you tell her. "And lots of milk." Your gut gripes at the mere thought, but milk will taint the water in which she cooked the oats. It will cloud the whisperings that water carries to your mother.

Nowadays people would say that me and my mooncalf brother, we is "lactose intolerant." But me think say them misname the thing. Me think say is milk can't tolerate we, not we can't tolerate it.

So: he find himself another creamy one. Just watch at the two of them there, in that pretty domestic scene.

I enter, invisible.

Brother eat off most of him porridge already. Him always had a large appetite. The white lady, she only passa-passa-ing with hers, dipping the spoon in, tasting little bit, turning the spoon over and watching at it, dipping it in. She glance at him and say, "Would you like to go to the beach today?"

"No!" You almost shout it. You're not going to the beach, not to any large body of water ever again. Your very cells keen from the loss of it, but She is in the water, looking for you.

"A true. Mummy in the water, and I in the wind, Brother," I whisper to him, so sweet. By my choice, him never hear me yet. Don't want him to know that me find him. Plenty time for that. Plenty time to fly and carry the news to Mama. Maybe I can find a way to be free if I do this one last thing for her. Bring her beloved son back. Is him she want, not me. Never me. "Ban, ban, ca-ca-Caliban!" I scream in him face, silently.

"There's no need to shout," she says with an offended look. "That's where we first saw each other, and you swam so strongly. You were beautiful in the water. So I just thought you might like to go back there."

You had been swimming for your life, but she didn't know that. The surf tossing you crashing against the rocks, the undertow pulling you back in deeper, the waves singing their triumphant song: *She's coming. Sycorax is coming for you. Can you feel the tips of her tentacles now? Can you feel them sticking to your skin, bringing you back? She's coming. We've got you now. We'll hold you for her. Oh, there'll be so much fun when she has you again!*

And you had hit out at the water, stroked through it, kicked through it, fleeing for shore. One desperate pull of your arms had taken you through foaming surf. You crashed into another body, heard a surprised "Oh," and then a wave tumbled you. As you fought in its depths, searching for the air and dry land, you saw her, this woman, slim as an eel, her body parting the water, her hair glowing golden. She'd extended a hand to you, like reaching for a bobbing ball. You took her hand, held on tightly to the warmth of it. She stood, and you stood, and you realized you'd been only feet from shore. "Are you all right?" she'd asked.

The water had tried to suck you back in, but it was only at thigh height now. You ignored it. You kept hold of her hand, started moving with her, your savior, to the land. You felt your heart swelling. She was perfect. "I'm doing just fine," you'd said. "I'm sorry I startled you. What's your name?"

Behind you, you could hear the surf shouting for you to come back. But the sun was warm on your shoulders now, and you knew that you'd stay on land. As you came up out of the water, she glanced at you and smiled, and you could feel the change begin.

She's sitting at her table, still with that hurt look on her face.

"I'm sorry, darling," you say, and she brightens at the endearment, the first you've used with her. Under the table, your feet are trying to paddle away, away. You ignore them. "Why don't we go for a walk?" you ask her. She smiles, nods. The many plaits of her hair sway with the rhythm. You must ask her not to wear her hair like that. Once you know her a little better. They look like tentacles. Besides, her hair's so pale that her pink scalp shows through.

Chuh. *I'm sorry, darling.* Him is sorry, is true. A sorry sight. I follow them out on them little walk, them Sunday perambulation. Down her street and round the corner into the district where the trendy people-them live. Where those cunning little shops are, you know the kind, yes? Wildflowers selling at this one, half your wages for one so-so blossom. Cheese from Greece at that one, and wine from Algiers. (Mama S. say she don't miss Algiers one bit.) Tropical fruit selling at another store, imported from the Indies, from the hot sun places where people work them finger to the bone to pick them and box them and send them, but not to eat them. Brother and him new woman meander through those streets, making sure people look at them good. She turn her moon face to him, give him that fuck-me look, and take him hand. I see him melt. Going to be easy to change him now that she melt him. And then him will be gone from we again. I blow a grieving breeze oo-oo-oo through the leaves of the crab apple trees lining that street.

She looks around, her face bright and open. "Isn't it a lovely day?" she says. "Feel the air on your skin." She releases your hand. The sweat of your mingled touch evaporates and you mourn its passing. She opens her arms to the sun, drinking in light.

Of course, that white man, him only write down part of the story. Him say how our mother was a witch. How she did consort with monsters. But you know the real story? You know why them exile her from Algiers, with a baby in her belly and one at her breast?

She spins and laughs, her print dress opening like a flower above her scuffed army boots. Her strong legs are revealed to midthigh.

Them send my mother from her home because of the monster she consort with. The lord with sable eyes and skin like rich earth. My daddy.

An old man sitting on a bench smiles, indulgent at her joy, but then he sees her reach for your hand again. He scowls at you, spits to one side.

My daddy. A man who went for a swim one day, down, down, down, and when he see the fair maid flowing toward him, her long hair just a-swirl like weeds in the water, her skin like milk, him never 'fraid.

As you both pass the old man, he shakes his head, his face clenched. She doesn't seem to notice. You hold her hand tighter, reach to pull her warmth closer to you. But you're going down, and you know it.

When my mother who wasn't my mother yet approach the man who wasn't my father yet, when she ask him, "Man, you eat salt, or you eat fresh?" him did know what fe say. Of course him did know. After his tutors teach him courtly ways from since he was small. After his father teach him how to woo. After his own mother teach him how to address the Wata Lady with respect. Sycorax ask him, "Man, you eat salt, or you eat fresh?"

And proper proper, him respond, "Me prefer the taste of salt, thank you please."

That was the right answer. For them that does eat fresh, them going to be fresh with your business. But this man show her that he know how fe have respect. For that, she give him breath and take him down, she take him down even farther.

You pass another beautiful golden girl, luxuriantly blonde. She glances at you, casts her eyes down demurely, where they just happen to rest at your crotch. You feel her burgeoning gaze there, your helpless response. Quickly you lean and kiss the shoulder of the woman you're with. The other one's look turns to resentful longing. You hurry on.

She take him down into her own castle, and she feed him the salt foods she keep in there, the fish and oysters and clams, and him eat of them till him belly full, and him talk to her sweet, and him never get fresh with her. Not even one time. Not until she ask him to. Mama wouldn't tell me what happen after that, but true she have two pickney, and both of we shine copper, even though she is alabaster, so me think me know is what went on.

There's a young black woman sitting on a bench, her hair tight peppercorns against her scalp. Her feet are crossed beneath her. She's alone, reading a book. She's pretty, but she looks too much like your sister. She could never be a golden girl. She looks up as you go by, distracted from her reading by the chattering of the woman beside you. She looks at you. Smiles. Nods a greeting. Burning up with guilt, you make your face stone. You move on.

In my mother and father, salt meet with sweet. Milk meet with chocolate. No one could touch her while he was alive and ruler of his lands, but the minute him dead, her family and his get together and exile her to that little island to starve to death. Send her away with two sweet-and-sour, milk chocolate pickney; me in her belly and Caliban at her breast. Is nuh that turn her bitter? When you confine the sea, it don't stagnate? You put milk to stand, and it nuh curdle?

Chuh. Watch at my brother, there, making himself fool-fool. Is time. Time to end this, to take him back down. "Mama," I whisper. I blow one puff of wind, then another. The puffs tear a balloon out from a little girl's hand. The balloon have a fish painted on it. I like that. The little girl cry out and run after her toy. Her father dash after her. I puff and blow, make the little metallic balloon skitter just out of the child reach. As she run, she knock over a case of fancy bottled water, the expensive fizzy kind in blue glass bottles, from a display. The bottles explode when them hit the ground, the water escaping with a shout of glee. The little girl just dance out of the way of broken glass and spilled water and keep running for her balloon, reaching for it. I make it bob like a bubble in the air. Her daddy jump to one side, away from the glass. He try to snatch the back of her dress, but he too big and slow. Caliban step forward and grasp her balloon by the string. He give it back to her. She look at him, her y'eye-them big. She clutch the balloon to her bosom and smile at her daddy as he sweep her up into him arms.

The storekeeper just a-wait outside her shop, to talk to the man about who going to refund her goods.

"Mother," I call. "Him is here. I find him."

The water from out the bottles start to flow together in a spiral.

You hear her first in the dancing breeze that's toying with that little girl's balloon. You fetch the balloon for the child before you deal with what's coming. Her father mumbles a suspicious thanks at you. You step away from them. You narrow your eyes, look around. "You're here, aren't you?" you say to the air.

"Who's here?" asks the woman at your side.

"My sister," you tell her. You say "sister" like you're spitting out spoiled milk.

"I don't see anyone," the woman tells you.

"El!" you call out.

I don't pay him no mind. I summon up one of them hot, gusty winds. I blow over glasses of water on café tables. I grab Popsicles *swips!* out from the hands and mouths of children. The Popsicles fall down and melt, all the bright colors; melt and run like that brother of mine.

Popsicle juice, café table water, spring water that break free from bottles; them all rolling together now, crashing and splashing and calling to our mother. I call up the whirling devils. Them twirl sand into everybody eyes. Hats and baseball caps flying off heads, dancing along with me. An umbrella galloping down the road, end over end, with an old lady chasing it. All the trendy Sunday people squealing and running everywhere.

"Ariel, stop it!" you say.

So I run up his girlfriend skirt, make it fly high in the air. "Oh!" she cry out, trying to hold the frock down. She wearing a panty with a tear in one leg and a knot in the waistband. That make me laugh out loud. "Mama!" I shout, loud so Brother can hear me this time. "You seeing this? Look him here so!" I blow one rassclaat cluster of rain clouds over the scene, them bellies black and heavy with water. "So me see that you get a new master!" I screech at Brother.

The street is empty now, but for the three of you. Everyone else has found shelter. Your girl is cowering down beside the trunk of a tree, hugging her skirt about her knees. Her hair has come loose from most of its plaits, is whipping in a tangled mess about her head. She's shielding her face from blowing sand, but trying to look up at the sky above her, where this attack is coming from. You punch at the air, furious. You know you can't hurt your sister, but you need to lash out anyway. "Fuck you!" you yell. "You always do this! Why can't the two of you leave me alone!"

I chuckle, "Your face favor jackass when him sick. Why you can't leave white woman alone? You don't see what them do to you?

"You are our mother's creature," you hiss at her. In your anger, your speech slips into the same rhythms as hers. "Look at you, trying so hard to be 'island,' talking like you just come off the boat."

"At least me nah try fe chat like something out of some Englishman book." I make the wind howl it back at him. "At least me remember is boat me come off from!" I burst open the clouds overhead and drench the two of them in mother water. She squeals. Good.

"Ariel, Caliban; stop that squabbling or I'll bind you both up in a split tree forever." The voice is a wintry runnel, fast-freezing.

You both turn. It's Sycorax. Your sister has manifested, has pushed a trembling bottom lip out. Dread runs cold along your limbs. "Yes, Mother," you both say, standing sheepishly shoulder to shoulder. "Sorry, Mother."

Sycorax is sitting in a sticky puddle of water and melted Popsicles, but a queen on her throne could not be more regal. She has wrapped an ocean wave about her like a shawl. Her eyes are open-water blue. Her writhing hair foams white over her shoulders and the marble swells of her vast breasts. Her belly is a mounded salt lick, rising from the weedy tangle of her pubic hair, a marine jungle in and out of which flit tiny blennies. The tsunami of Sycorax's hips overflows her watery seat. Her myriad split tails are flicking, the way they do when she's irritated. With one of them, she scratches around her navel. You think you can see the sullen head of a moray eel, lurking in the cave those hydra tails make. You don't want to think about it. You never have.

"Ariel," says Sycorax, "have you been up to your tricks again?"

"But he," splutters your sister, "he . . ."

"*He* never ceases with *his* tricks," your mother pronounces. "Running home to Mama, leaving me with the mess he's made." She looks at you, and your watery legs weaken. "Caliban," she says, "I'm getting too old to play surrogate mother to your spawn. That last school of your offspring all had poisonous stings."

"I know, Mother. I'm sorry."

"How did that happen?" she asks.

You risk a glance at the woman you've dragged into this, the golden girl. She's standing now, a look of interest and curiosity on her face. "It's your fault," you say to her. "If you had kissed me, told me what you wanted me to be, she and Ariel couldn't have found us."

She looks at you, measuring. "First tell me about the poison babies," she says. She's got more iron in her than you'd thought, this one. The last fairy-tale princess who'd met your family hadn't stopped screaming for two days.

Ariel sniggers. "That was from his last ooman," she says. "The two of them always quarreling. For her, Caliban had a poison tongue."

"And spat out biting words, no doubt," Sycorax says. "He became what she saw, and it affected the children they made. Of course she didn't want them, of course she left; so Grannie gets to do the honors. He has brought me frog children and dog children, baby mack daddies and crack babies. Brings his offspring to me, then runs away again. And I'm getting tired of it." Sycorax's shawl whirls itself up into a waterspout. "And I'm more than tired of his sister's tale tattling."

"But Mama . . . !" Ariel says.

"'But Mama' nothing. I want you to stop pestering your brother."

Ariel puffs up till it looks as though she might burst. Her face goes anvil-cloud dark, but she says nothing.

"And you," says Sycorax, pointing at you with a suckered tentacle, "you need to stop bringing me the fallout from your sorry love life."

"I can't help it, Mama," you say. "That's how women see me."

Sycorax towers forward, her voice crashing upon your ears. "Do you want to know how *I* see you?" A cluster of her tentacle tails whips around your shoulders, immobilizes you. That *is* a moray eel under there, its fanged mouth hanging hungrily open. You are frozen in Sycorax's gaze, a hapless, irresponsible little boy. You feel the sickening metamorphosis begin. You are changing, shrinking. The last time Sycorax did this to you, it took you forever to become man enough again to escape. You try to twist in her arms, to look away from her eyes. She pulls you forward, puckering her mouth for the kiss she will give you.

"Well, yeah, I'm beginning to get a picture here," says a voice. It's the golden girl, shivering in her flower-print dress that's plastered to her skinny body. She steps closer. Her boots squelch. She points at Ariel. "You says he's color-struck. You're his sister, you should know. And yeah, I can see that in him. You'd think I was the sun itself, the way he looks at me."

She takes your face in her hands, turns your eyes away from your mother's. Finally, she kisses you full on the mouth. In her eyes, you become a sunflower, helplessly turning wherever she goes. You stand rooted, waiting for her direction.

She looks at your terrible mother. "You get to clean up the messes he makes." And now you're a baby, soiling your diapers and waiting for Mama to come and fix it. Oh, please, end this.

She looks down at you, wriggling and helpless on the ground. "And I guess all those other women saw big, black dick."

So familiar, the change that wreaks on you. You're an adult again, heavy-muscled and horny with a thick, swelling erection. You reach for her. She backs away. "But," she says, "there's one thing I don't see."

You don't care. She smells like vanilla and her skin is smooth and cool as ice cream and you want to push your tongue inside. You grab her thin, unresisting arms. She's shaking, but she looks into your eyes. And hers are empty. You aren't there. Shocked, you let her go. In a trembling voice, she says, "Who do you think you are?"

It could be an accusation: *Who* do you *think* you are? It might be a question: Who do *you* think you are? You search her face for the answer. Nothing. Your mother and your sib both look as shocked as you feel.

"Hey," says the golden girl, opening her hands wide. Her voice is getting less shaky. "Clearly, this is family business, and I know better than to mess with that." She gathers her little picky plaits together, squeezes water out of them. "It's been really . . . interesting, meeting you all." She looks at you, and her eyes are empty, open, friendly. You don't know what to make of them. "Um," she says, "maybe you can give me a call sometime." She starts walking away. Turns back. "It's not a brush-off; I mean it. But only call when you can tell me who you really are. Who you think you're going to become."

And she leaves you standing there. In the silence, there's only a faint sound of whispering water and wind in the trees. You turn to look at your mother and sister. "I," you say.

WELCOME

The Dystopianist, Thinking of His Rival, Is Interrupted by a Knock on the Door

Jonathan Lethem

THE DYSTOPIANIST DESTROYED the world again that morning, before making any phone calls or checking his mail, before even breakfast. He destroyed it by cabbages. The Dystopianist's scribbling fingers pushed notes onto the page: a protagonist, someone, *a tousle-haired, well-intentioned geneticist,* had designed a new kind of cabbage for use as a safety device—the *"air bag cabbage."* The air bag cabbage mimicked those decorative cabbages planted by the sides of roads to spell names of towns, or arranged by color—red, white, and that eerie, iridescent cabbage indigo—to create American flags. It looked like any other cabbage. But underground was a network of gas-bag roots, *vast inflatable roots,* filled with pressurized air. So, *at the slightest tap,* no, more than a tap, or vandals would set them off for fun, right, *given a serious blow such as only a car traveling at thirty miles or more per hour could deliver,* the heads of the air bag cabbages would instantly inflate, drawing air from the root system, to cushion the impact of the crash, saving lives, *preventing costly property loss.* Only—

The Dystopianist pushed away from his desk, and squinted through the blinds at the sun-splashed street below. School buses lined his block every morning, like vast tipped orange juice cartons spilling out the human vitamin of youthful lunacy, that chaos of jeering voices and dancing tangled shadows in the morning light. The Dystopianist was hungry for breakfast. He didn't know yet how the misguided safety cabbages fucked up the world. He couldn't say what *grievous chain of circumstance* led from the *innocuous genetic novelty* to another *crushing totalitarian regime.* He didn't know what light the cabbages shed on the *death urge in human societies.* He'd work it out, though. That was his job. First Monday of each month the Dystopianist came up with his idea, the *green poison fog* or *dehumanizing fractal download* or *alienating architectural fad* which would open the way to another ruined or oppressed reality. Tuesday he began making his extrapolations, and he had the rest of the month to get it right. Today was Monday, so the cabbages were enough.

The Dystopianist moved into the kitchen, poured a second cup of coffee, and pushed slices of bread into the toaster. The *Times* "Metro" section headline spoke of the capture of a celebrated villain, an addict and killer who'd crushed a pedestrian's skull with a cobblestone. The Dystopianist read his paper while scraping his toast with shreds of ginger marmalade, knife rushing a little surf of butter ahead of the crystalline goo. He read intently to the end of the account, taking pleasure in the story.

The Dystopianist hated bullies. He tried to picture himself standing behind darkened glass, fingering perps in a lineup, couldn't. He tried to picture himself standing in the glare, head flinched in arrogant dejection, waiting to be fingered, but this was even more impossible. He stared at the photo of the apprehended man and unexpectedly the Dystopianist found himself thinking vengefully, hatefully, of his rival.

Once the Dystopianist had had the entire Dystopian field to himself. There was just him and the Utopianists. The Dystopianist loved reading the Utopianists' stories, their dim, hopeful scenarios, which were published in magazines like *Expectant* and *Encouraging.* The Dystopianist routinely purchased them newly minted from the newsstands and perverted them the very next day in his own work, plundering the Utopianists' motifs for dark inspiration. Even the garishly sunny illustrated covers of the magazines were fuel. The Dystopianist stripped them from the magazines' spines and pinned them up over his desk, then raised his pen like Death's sickle and plunged those dreamily ineffectual worlds into ruin.

The Utopianists were older men who'd come into the field from the sciences or from academia: Professor this or that, like Dutch Burghers from a cigar box. The Dystopianist had appeared in print like a rat among them, a burrowing animal laying turds on their never-to-be-realized blueprints. He liked his role. Every once in a blue moon the Dystopianist agreed to appear in public alongside the Utopianists, on a panel at a university or conference. They loved to gather, *the fools,* in fluorescent-lit halls behind tables decorated with sweating pitchers of ice water. They were always eager to praise him in public by calling him one of their own. The Dystopianist ignored them, refusing even the water from their pitchers. He played directly to the audience members who'd come to see him, who shared his low opinion of the Utopianists. The Dystopianist could always spot his readers by their black trench coats, their acne, their greasily teased hair, their earphones, resting around their collars, trailing to Walkmans secreted in coat pockets.

The Dystopianist's rival was a Utopianist, but he wasn't like the others.

The Dystopianist had known his rival, the man he privately called *the Dire One,* since they were children like those streaming in the schoolyard below. *Eeny-meeny-miney-moe!* they'd chanted together, each trembling in fear of being permanently *"It,"* of never casting off their permanent case of *cooties.* They weren't quite friends, but the Dystopianist and the Dire One had been bullied together by the older boys, quarantined in their shared nerdishness, forced to pool their resentments. In glum resignation they'd swapped Wacky Packages stickers and algebra homework answers, offered sticks of Juicy Fruit and squares of Now-N-Later, forging a loser's deal of consolation.

Then they were separated after junior high school, and the Dystopianist forgot his uneasy schoolmate.

It was nearly a year now since the Dire Utopianist had first arrived in print. The Dystopianist had trundled home with the latest issue of *Heartening,* expecting the usual laughs, and been blindsided instead by the Dire Utopianist's first story. The Dystopianist didn't recognize his rival by name, but he knew him for a rival instantly.

The Dire Utopianist's trick was to write in a style which was *nominally* Utopian. His fantasies were nearly as credible as everyday experience, but bathed in a radiance of glory. They glowed with wishfulness. The other Utopianists' stories were crude candy floss by comparison. The Dire Utopianist's stories weren't blunt or ideological. He'd invented an *aesthetics* of utopia.

Fair enough. If he'd stopped at this burnished, closely observed dream of human life, the Dire Utopianist would be no threat. Sure, heck, let there be one genius among the Utopianists, all the better. It raised the bar. The Dystopianist took the Dire One's mimetic brilliance as a spur of inspiration: Look closer! Make it real!

But the Dire Utopianist didn't play fair. He didn't stop at utopianism, no. He poached on the Dystopianist's turf, he encroached. By limning a world so subtly transformed, so barely *nudged* into the ideal, the Dire One's fictions cast a shadow back onto the everyday. They induced a despair of inadequacy in the real. Turning the last page of one of the Dire Utopianist's stories, the reader felt a mortal pang at slipping back into his own daily life, which had been proved morbid, crushed, unfair.

This was the Dire One's pitiless art: *his utopias wrote reality itself into the most persuasive dystopia imaginable.* At the Dystopianist's weak moments he knew his stories were by comparison contrived and crotchety, their darkness forced.

It was six weeks ago that *Vivifying* had published the Dire One's photograph, and the Dystopianist had recognized his childhood acquaintance.

The Dire Utopianist never appeared in public. There was no clamor for him to appear. In fact, he wasn't even particularly esteemed among the Utopianists, an irony which rankled the Dystopianist. It was as though the Dire One didn't mind seeing his work buried in the insipid Utopian magazines. He didn't seem to crave recognition of any kind, let alone the hard-won oppositional stance the Dystopianist treasured. It was almost as though the Dire One's stories, posted in public, were really private messages of reproach from one man to the other. Sometimes the Dystopianist wondered if he were in fact the *only* reader the Dire Utopianist had, and the only one he wanted.

The cabbages were hopeless, he saw now.

Gazing out the window over his coffee's last plume of steam at the humming, pencil-colored school buses, he suddenly understood the gross implausibility: a rapidly inflating cabbage could never have the *stopping power* to alter the fatal trajectory of a *careening steel egg carton full of young lives.* A cabbage might halt a Hyundai, maybe a Volvo. Never a school bus. Anyway, the cabbages as an image had no implications, no *reach.* They said nothing about mankind. They were, finally, completely stupid and lame. He gulped the last of his coffee, angrily.

He had to go deeper, find something resonant, something to crawl beneath the skin of reality and render it monstrous from within. He paced to the sink, began rinsing his coffee mug. A tiny pod of silt had settled at the bottom and now, under a jet of cold tap water, the grains rose and spread and danced, a model of Chaos. The Dystopianist retraced his seed of inspiration: *well-intentioned, bumbling geneticist,* good. Good enough. The geneticist needed to stumble onto something better, though.

One day, when the Dystopianist and the Dire Utopianist had been in the sixth grade at Intermediate School 293, cowering together in a corner of the schoolyard to duck sports and fights and girls in one deft multipurpose cower, they had arrived at one safe island of mutual interest: comic books, Marvel brand, which anyone who read them understood weren't comic at all but deadly, breathtakingly serious. Marvel constructed worlds of splendid complexity, full of chilling, ancient villains and tormented heroes, in richly unfinished storylines. There in the schoolyard, wedged for cover behind the girls' lunch hour game of hopscotch, the Dystopianist declared his favorite character: *Doctor Doom,* antagonist of the Fantastic Four. Doctor Doom wore a forest green cloak and hood over a metallic, slitted mask and armor. He was a dark king who from his gnarled castle ruled a city of hapless serfs. An imperial, self-righteous monster. The Dire Utopianist murmured his consent. Indeed, Doctor Doom was awesome, an honorable choice. The Dystopianist waited for the Dire Utopianist to declare his favorite.

"Black Bolt," said the Dire Utopianist.

The Dystopianist was confused. *Black Bolt* wasn't a villain or a hero. Black Bolt was part of an outcast band of mutant characters known as *The Inhumans,* the noblest among them. He was their leader, but he never spoke. His only *demonstrated* power was flight, but the whole point of Black Bolt was the power he restrained himself from using: speech. The sound of his voice was cataclysmic, an unusable weapon, like an Atomic Bomb. If Black Bolt ever uttered a syllable the world would crack in two. Black Bolt was leader *in absentia* much of the time—he had a tendency to exile himself from the scene, to wander distant mountaintops contemplating—what? His curse? The things he would say if he could safely speak?

It was an unsettling choice there, amidst the feral shrieks of the schoolyard. The Dystopianist changed the subject, and never raised the question of Marvel Comics with the Dire Utopianist again. Alone behind the locked door of his bedroom the Dystopianist studied Black Bolt's behavior, seeking hints of the character's appeal to his schoolmate. Perhaps the answer lay in a storyline elsewhere in the Marvel universe, one where Black Bolt shucked off his pensiveness to function as an unrestrained hero or villain. If so, the Dystopianist never found the comic book in question.

Suicide, the Dystopianist concluded now. The geneticist should be studying suicide, seeking to isolate it as a factor in the human genome. *The Sylvia Plath Code,* that might be the title of the story. The geneticist could be trying to *reproduce it in a nonhuman species.* Right, good. To breed for suicide in animals, to produce a creature with the impulse to take its own life. That had the relevance the

Dystopianist was looking for. What animals? Something poignant and pathetic, something pure. Sheep. *The Sylvia Plath Sheep,* that was it.

A variant of sheep had been bred for the study of suicide. The Sylvia Plath Sheep had to be kept on close watch, like a prisoner stripped of sharp implements, shoelaces and belt. And the Plath Sheep escapes, right, of course, *a Frankenstein creature always escapes,* but the twist is that the Plath Sheep is dangerous only to itself. *So what?* What harm if a single sheep quietly, discreetly offs itself? *But the Plath Sheep,* scribbling fingers racing now, the Dystopianist was on fire, *the Plath Sheep turns out to have the gift of communicating its despair.* Like the monkeys on that island, who learned from one another to wash clams, or break them open with coconuts, whatever it was the monkeys had learned, look into it later, *the Plath Sheep evoked suicide in other creatures,* all up and down the food chain. Not humans, but anything else which crossed its path. Cats, dogs, cows, beetles, clams. Each creature would spread suicide to another, to five or six others, before *searching out a promontory from which to plunge to its death.* The human species would be powerless to reverse the craze, the epidemic of suicide among the nonhuman species of the planet.

Okay! Right! Let goddamn Black Bolt open his mouth and sing an aria—he couldn't halt the Plath Sheep in its *deadly spiral of despair!*

The Dystopianist suddenly had a vision of the Plath Sheep wandering its way into the background of one of the Dire One's tales. It would go unremarked at first, a bucolic detail. Unwrapping its bleak gift of *global animal suicide* only after it had been taken entirely for granted, just as the Dire One's own little nuggets of despair were smuggled innocuously into his Utopias. The Plath Sheep was a bullet of pure dystopian intention. The Dystopianist wanted to fire it in the Dire Utopianist's direction. Maybe he'd send this story to *Encouraging.*

Even better, he'd like it if he could send the Plath Sheep itself to the door of the Dire One's writing room. *Here's your tragic mute Black Bolt, you bastard!* Touch its somber muzzle, dry its moist obsidian eyes, runny with sleep-goo. Try to talk it down from the parapet, if you have the courage of your ostensibly rosy convictions. Explain to the Sylvia Plath Sheep why life is worth living. Or, failing that, let the sheep convince you to follow it up to the brink, and go. You and the sheep, pal, take a fall.

There was a knock on the door.

The Dystopianist went to the door and opened it. Standing in the corridor was a sheep. The Dystopianist checked his watch—9:45. He wasn't sure why it mattered to him what time it was, but it did. He found it reassuring. The day still stretched before him; he'd have plenty of time to resume work after this interruption. He still heard the children's voices leaking in through the front window from the street below. The children arriving now were late for school. There were always hundreds who were late. He wondered if the sheep had waited with the children for the crossing guard to wave it on. He wondered if the sheep had crossed at the green, or recklessly dared the traffic to kill it.

He'd persuaded himself that the sheep was voiceless. So it was a shock when it spoke. "May I come in?" said the sheep.

"Yeah, sure," said the Dystopianist, fumbling his words. Should he offer the sheep the couch, or a drink of something? The sheep stepped into the apartment, just far enough to allow the door to be closed behind it, then stood quietly working its nifty little jaw back and forth, and blinking. Its eyes were not watery at all.

"So," said the sheep, nodding its head at the Dystopianist's desk, the mass of yellow legal pads, the sharpened pencils bunched in their holder, the typewriter. "This is where the magic happens." The sheep's tone was wearily sarcastic.

"It isn't usually *magic*," said the Dystopianist, then immediately regretted the remark.

"Oh, I wouldn't say that," said the sheep, apparently unruffled. "You've got a few things to answer for."

"Is that what this is?" said the Dystopianist. "Some kind of reckoning?"

"Reckoning?" The sheep blinked as though confused. "Who said anything about a reckoning?"

"Never mind," said the Dystopianist. He didn't want to put words into the sheep's mouth. Not now. He'd let it represent itself, and try to be patient.

But the sheep didn't speak, only moved in tiny, faltering steps on the carpet, advancing very slightly into the room. The Dystopianist wondered if the sheep might be scouting for sharp corners on the furniture, for chances to do itself harm by butting with great force against his fixtures.

"Are you—very depressed?" asked the Dystopianist.

The sheep considered the question for a moment. "I've had better days, let's put it that way."

Finishing the thought, it stared up at him, eyes still dry. The Dystopianist met its gaze, then broke away. A terrible thought occurred to him: the sheep might be expecting *him* to relieve it of its life.

The silence was ponderous. The Dystopianist considered another possibility. Might his rival have come to him in disguised form?

He cleared his throat before speaking. "You're not, ah, *the Dire One,* by any chance?" The Dystopianist was going to be awfully embarrassed if the sheep didn't know what he was talking about.

The sheep made a solemn, wheezing sound, like *"Hurrrrhh."* Then it said, "I'm *dire* all right. But I'm hardly the only one."

"Who?" blurted the Dystopianist.

"Take a look in the mirror, friend."

"What's your point?" The Dystopianist was sore now. If the sheep thought he was going to be manipulated into suicide it had *another think coming.*

"Just this: how many sheep have to die to assuage your childish resentments?" Now the sheep had assumed an odd false tone, plummy like that of a commercial pitchman: *"They laughed when I sat down at the Dystopiano! But when I began to play—"*

"Very funny."

"We try, we try. Look, could you at least offer me a dish of water or something? I had to take the stairs—couldn't reach the button for the elevator."

Silenced, the Dystopianist hurried into the kitchen and filled a shallow bowl with water from the tap. Then, thinking twice, he poured it back into the sink and replaced it with mineral water from the bottle in the door of his refrigerator. When he set it out the sheep lapped gratefully, steadily, seeming to the Dystopianist an animal at last.

"Okay." It licked its lips. "That's it, Doctor Doom. I'm out of here. Sorry for the intrusion, next time I'll call. I just wanted, you know—a look at you."

The Dystopianist couldn't keep from saying, "You don't want to die?"

"Not today," was the sheep's simple reply. The Dystopianist stepped carefully around the sheep to open the door, and the sheep trotted out. The Dystopianist trailed it into the corridor and summoned the elevator. When the cab arrived and the door opened the Dystopianist leaned in and punched the button for the lobby.

"Thanks," said the sheep. "It's the little things that count."

The Dystopianist tried to think of a proper farewell, but couldn't before the elevator door shut. The sheep was facing the rear of the elevator cab, another instance of its poor grasp of etiquette.

Still, the sheep's visit wasn't the worst the Dystopianist could imagine. It could have attacked him, or tried to gore itself on his kitchen knives. The Dystopianist was still proud of the Plath Sheep, and rather glad to have met it, even if the Plath Sheep wasn't proud of him. Besides, the entire episode had only cost the Dystopianist an hour or so of his time. He was back at work, eagerly scribbling out implications, extrapolations, another illustrious downfall, well before the yelping children reoccupied the schoolyard at lunchtime.

From Guardian
Joe Haldeman

THE WORST STORM of the year piled snow on ice while I taught the last day of class before Christmas. On the way home, I fell several times and arrived at the cabin sore and soaked and freezing.

I bolted the door behind me and crossed the room slowly, groping to the table where I felt candle and matches. With one match I lit the candle and a couple of peg lamps, and then the main kerosene lamp, for its smoky warmth. When I went back to snuff the peg lamps, I saw that I'd trod upon a letter that had been slid under the door.

It was from the Yukon Territory, the address barely legible, a pencil scrawl unlike my son Daniel's schoolboy hand.

With curiosity rather than premonition, I took a paring knife and slit open the worn foolscap and carried its scrawled message back to the lamp. It was from Daniel's friend Chuck. The letter is long since gone, but I think I have the wording set in my memory:

"Mrs. Flammarian both my Pa and your son are murdered. A drunkard fell upon Pa on the street in Dawson City, thinking him someone else, and when Dan went to his aid the drunk shot them both with a pistol. When he seen what he had done he shot his own self, but not to much effect, and he will be hung this week. But my Pa and Dan died right there, shot in the heart and the head, while I was out at the claim, and by the time someone got me the terrible news and I got me into the town, they was both froze solid in back of the corner office. I don't know no way to tell this to make it gentle. It's the worst thing that ever happened."

I didn't burst into tears or scream or rend my garments. I sat there in the sputtering light and read the note again, sure that must be some cruel trick or stupid joke. I had sure knowledge that Chuck could not write much beyond signing his name. But then I turned over the paper and found a note in the same hand:

"Writ this 14th day of December year of our Lord 1898 by Morris Chambers, for the hand of Chuck Coleman, his mark here." And there was Chuck's scrawl with this note appended beneath: "I was not there at the time but here tell that your son was very brave.

My gravest condolences in your loss.   MC."

Then I was blinded by tears and collapsed, striking my head on the pine floor, and then striking it again and again, hard bright sparks in my eyes. I rolled on the floor weeping, and lost my water, beyond care.

I remembered the moment in Skagway when Dan handed me the Pinkerton man's revolver, agreeing with some reluctance that he should never need it.

I needed it now.

I staggered to the dresser by the bed and jerked open the top drawer. There it was in a corner, wrapped in blue muslin. I unwrapped it, sudden oil smell, and verified that it was loaded, and raised it to my temple. Then I thought about the horrible mess that would be made, and lowered the muzzle to where I thought my heart was, beneath my left breast, and a large raven came through the door.

The door didn't open. He walked through it as if it were made of air. "Rosa," he said in a clear voice, "you can't do that. Your God would not approve."

He stalked across the floor in that determined way that ravens have. "One Corinthians, chapter 6: 'know thee not that your body is the temple of the Holy Ghost, which is in you . . . and ye are not your own?' "

With a clatter of feathers, he hopped up onto the dresser. "Chapter 20 of Exodus. Verse 13. You must know that one."

"What are you?"

"A raven, dummy. Exodus 20:13. Give it to me."

"You're the one who kept telling me 'no gold'?"

"Yes. Exodus 20:13?"

" 'Thou shalt not kill.' "

"Let's get that straight. It doesn't say 'thou shalt not kill anybody but yourself.' "

I turned the gun on him. "It does tell us that the Devil quotes scripture."

"Luke. And you're gonna kill the Devil with an eggbeater." The gun was suddenly light in my hand. I looked down and it was an eggbeater. I dropped it and it hit the floor with a loud thump, and formed back into a revolver.

"Not that I'm actually the Devil. I'm not actually even a raven." He hopped to the floor, impossibly slow, and for an instant turned into old Gordon. He had his huge nest of hair let down, all the way to his knees, and was wearing nothing else. He turned back into the raven.

"You're the Tlingit Shaman Gordon, aren't you?"

"No and yes. You know what the Tlingit raven is."

"A shape-changer. But—"

"And a creature who can talk to all animals, including humans. Leave it at that, for the time being."

I picked up the letter and turned it over to the terrible message. "You have something to do with this?"

"I didn't cause it. I'm here because of it, of course."

"To save me . . . from myself?"

"I haven't saved you yet."

I groped for the chair behind me, and sat down. I couldn't speak, couldn't even think. "What do you really look like, if you aren't a bird or Gordon?"

He flickered, like a candle flame, but didn't change.

"In a sense, the question is meaningless; I take whatever form is appropriate. I do have a shape for resting, but I think it would disturb you."

"Demonic?"

"No. Forget demons and gods. It's as plain and natural as changing clothes. Stand up."

I did, and suddenly the room changed. I could see three walls at once, in sharp detail, even though the light was low and flickering. My eyes were only about three feet off the ground. Effortlessly, I turned my head completely around, and saw on the wall behind me the shadow of a large bird.

"What?" came out both as a word and a squawk.

"You're a bald eagle," he said. "Come over to the mirror."

Walking was strange, bobbing talons scraping along the wood. In the full-length mirror by the wardrobe, the image of a magnificent eagle, cocking its head when I cocked mine, raising and lowering its feet. I raised my arm and spread my fingers; it raised a wing and the end-feathers spread out. My mind and body knew exactly how that would change my course of flight, scooping air to slow and drop.

It was a strange mental state, simple and beautiful. I tried to say something about that, but all that came out was another squawk: "I am!"

"You certainly are." The eagle in the mirror stretched impossibly tall and with a little "pop" turned back into me, nude. I covered myself reflexively, as if a crow or demon would care, and clothes appeared on my flesh.

Nothing like normal clothing, though. I looked at my strange image in the mirror: it looked as if I had been dipped in wax, a garment like a second skin, covering everything but my head, hands, and feet. Slippers appeared on my feet.

"That will keep you warm. Follow me." He walked through the door, again without opening it.

"But . . ." I blew out the lights and pushed open the door. It had stopped snowing, and the raven was standing there in the moonlight. It was bitter cold, but the suit of clothes warmed up automatically. It also warmed my face and hands somehow. I touched my face and it felt slippery.

"This way." He hopped and fluttered down the path at the rate of a fast walk. We went away from town, up the hill toward Mount Verstovaia.

I followed him without question, numb and confused. We walked down a game trail for a few hundred yards—I was starting to worry about bears—and then picked our way through undergrowth for a few minutes.

The raven said something in a language neither bird nor human, and a door opened in the middle of the air. I stepped sideways and saw that there was nothing behind it. The door was a rectangle of soft golden light that led into a room that was manifestly *not there.* But the raven walked in, and I cautiously followed him.

The floor of the room was soft, the air warm with a trace of something like cinnamon. As if someone had been baking rolls. The door closed and the raven disappeared. I think I did, too. At least I had no sense of being in any one place—all of the room seemed equally close. Perhaps I became the room, in some sense.

"I want to go a few places," the raven said in my mind, "and show you a few things. You've read *Gulliver's Travels.*"

"Yes, I have."

"Wasn't a question. This is not that. But there may be some aspects of it you will find amusing, or educational."

A rush of anxiety finally caught up with me. "I don't want to go anyplace. I want to go home, and sort things out."

"You'll get home. Right now I want to put some distance between you and that revolver."

"That was a rash impulse. I won't do it." As I said that, I wondered whether it was a lie.

"You'll be home in less than no time. Close your eyes until I tell you to open them."

I obeyed for a couple of minutes, though it was extremely uncomfortable—as if I were being rotated slowly about one axis, like a leisurely figure skater, and revolved about a different one, cartwheeling.

I opened my eyes for one blink and regretted it. Colors I couldn't put a name to, and unearthly shapes that seemed to pass through my body. I started to vomit and choked it back.

"Don't look!" the bird shrieked, and I squeezed my eyes shut, hard, the acid taste burning my throat and soft palate, anxiety rising. "Only a few minutes more. Calm down." Maybe this was hell, I thought. Maybe I did pull the trigger, and this was my punishment—not imps and flames, but an eternity of confusion and nausea.

It was shorter than eternity, though. Eventually the sensation subsided, and the bird told me to open my eyes. Once more I had the sense of "being" the room, and then the raven materialized, and so did I. I sat down on the soft floor, exhausted.

"You've read *Mars as the Abode of Life,*" he said, "by Percival Lowell."

"You know everything I read?"

"That, and more. You also read your namesake's book, of course."

"Have we . . . have you gone all the way to Mars?"

"No. Lowell was wrong. Mars never had anything more interesting than moss. But there are living creatures elsewhere."

"Venus?"

"You know what a Bessemer converter is."

I remembered the flame- and smoke-belching refineries of Pittsburgh. "Venus is like that?"

"Worse. No place in your solar system, other than Earth, has life that's at all interesting. There's some wildlife on satellites of Jupiter and Saturn, but they're less intelligent than a congressman, as Mark Twain would say. Dumber than a snail, actually.

"We've gone farther than that. Ten million times farther." The door opened and a soft reddish glow came in, like the end of sunset.

I stepped to the door. The sun was not setting; it was two hand spans above the horizon. There was enough mist or smoke in the air that I could look at it directly. It was much larger than our sun, and it looked like a piece of coal in a cooling stove, bright red with crusts of black.

Perhaps I *had* gone to hell. The landscape was Dantean, treeless chalk cliffs with precipitous overhangs. We stepped outside and were on such an overhang ourselves, facing a drop of a hundred yards down to a brown trickle of water. The air was hot and chalky, like a schoolroom in summer after the boards are cleaned.

There was vegetation on our side of the gorge, weeds and gnarled bushes that were purple rather than green. They all stuck out of the cliff at the same angle, pointing toward the sun.

"The sun never moves," the raven said. "This planet always keeps one face to it, as often happens given enough time."

"Like the moon, or Mercury," I said.

"Half right," he said. "They're wrong about Mercury." He suddenly became old Gordon, and took my hand in his. "We're going to fly now. Don't be afraid."

"Fly?" Something pressed up under my feet and we rose, slowly at first, and floated out over the precipice. That set my heart to hammering, and I squeezed his hand so hard his knuckles cracked.

"There's no way you could drop. Relax and enjoy the view." We stopped rising and moved forward, faster and faster, with no wind or sense of acceleration.

(Gordon was still wearing only his hair, which came down far enough in back for a semblance of modesty. But only in back.)

On the other side of the canyon, the vegetation was sparse and regularly spaced, not in cultivated rows as such, but rather in that each commanded a certain area of ground, larger for the larger clumps and plants. Some seemed to be the size of trees, though it was hard to estimate, not really knowing how high we were. I studied the plants fiercely; it helped me fight the anxiety of flying.

"I wanted to stop here first partly because it so resembles your Christian concept of Hell. But it's Heaven to the people who live here."

"People?"

"Or 'creatures.' In Tlingit there's a word that encompasses both. There!"

We descended toward what looked like a patch of a different kind of vegetation, a clump of large transparent tubes. Unlike the other plants, though, they were mobile, twining slowly around each other. They looked like something that belonged in the sea, caressed by slow currents.

As we touched ground, he changed back into his avian manifestation. "They know me as Raven," he said, and I heard the capitalization. He fluttered down to the base of the seven tubes. "Take off your shoes."

I did, and the ground was surprisingly pleasant, warm and spongy.

I worked my toes into it, though, and was rewarded by a sharp pinch.

"Don't do that. This is their brain you're standing on—the part they all share, anyhow. Stand still and they'll talk to you through your feet."

That's exactly what they did, and it was amazing. It felt as if they'd asked me a thousand questions over the course of a minute, and my brain responded directly, without translating the answers into speech.

They talked back, in a sense. It wasn't language so much as feeling. There was sympathy for my loss—six of them were children of the central one—but with an admonition to hold on to life, although what they actually meant was both more specific and harder to express. The point of life was, to them, posing problems and solving them, and passing on the solutions.

"These people were old before life appeared on your Earth," Raven said. "This particular seven have been alive for more than a million years."

"Are they immortal? They'll live forever?"

"No. They'll live another million or ten million years. When they agree to die, they produce a spore, which will grow into another family on this spot."

"Another seven?"

"Or eleven, sometimes, or thirteen. One of them volunteers to stay alive for a while and act as parent, as teacher.

"It's not suicide, since their essence is preserved in the parent, as is the essence of the thousand generations that went before."

How ugly and alien they might seem if I hadn't been literally in touch with them. Worms wriggling around, sticky secretions. But they were in a state of perfect love, angels living in Hell. "Why do they have to die?"

"They die when they've learned all they can. You know of Mendel's genetics experiments."

"Yes." Again, it hadn't been a question.

"They need to replace themselves with a genetically different family. A group that can look at all the accumulated knowledge from a different point of view."

"That's all they do?" I said. "They don't have to worry about food, water, shelter?"

"Angels don't strive. They absorb radiant energy through the plants around them. They have a thing like a tap root that extends below the water table. As for shelter, there's no weather on this part of the planet—though it's fierce around the circumference where dark meets light, a never-ending storm."

"But if they don't go anyplace or do anything, how can they find new things to think about?"

"Through people like you and me. They've never met anyone from Earth before, so you gave them lots of new experiences and feelings to consider."

"You said they know you. You're from Earth."

"Not actually. I'm a kind of a visitor. A 'guardian' is the closest human word."

"My guardian?"

"Don't flatter yourself." He hopped around to face the angels. "People like me are especially interesting to them, because we travel around. They want to know where they themselves came from, and how and why they wound up here."

"Couldn't it be like Darwin contends? If they evolved from simpler forms, they wouldn't remember that far back, any more than we remember being infants."

"Very good, Rosa, but that's the point: on this whole planet there's nothing more complicated than a bush. Nothing for them to have evolved *from.*

"Furthermore, on almost every planet there's a particular kind of molecule that every living thing has. That's true of every other species here, but not of them: they have a different molecule."

"So they originally came from another planet?"

"That's the simplest explanation. But their curiosity is not just a matter of genealogy—they wonder whether they were put here for some purpose, and what it might be."

I smiled. "That sounds familiar."

He let out an annoyed squawk, and continued in Gordon's voice. "I'm not trafficking in religion here. These people don't even know whether they're natural, or some sort of artificially contrived biological machine, hidden in this out-of-the-way place to grind away at information for millions of millennia, ultimately to solve some problem that now is still beyond their ken.

"And if they *are* machines to that purpose, will they be switched off once they solve the problem?"

They began singing then. There was no other noise in this still place, except when Raven or I talked, but at first I didn't realize it was coming from them. It was a sweet pure sound, like a glass harmonica, complex chords that became words in English:

Before you go back to Earth
Before you go home
Come here to share what you've learned
Come here to learn what we've thought about you.

"That's unusual," Raven said. "I didn't know they could do that."

"Can I, may I tell them 'yes'?"

"Do."

I told them that I would be glad to help them in their quest, and their response was a jolt of pure sensual pleasure that started in the center of me and radiated out. I curled my toes into their brain and got the warning pinch again. I didn't have a word for it then, orgasm, but I knew the feeling from Doc's tender ministrations. So the most powerful orgasm I'd ever had came through the soles of my feet, through the brain of seven man-sized worms. It was stranger than strange, but it did give me incentive to return.

"They know the workings of your body better than any human physician could. I suspect they've fixed things here and there."

"They have." I moved my arm in a circle, and the shoulder pain was gone. So was the pain in my finger joints. "But I'm the first human being they've met! Human from Earth, I mean."

"They've seen a million varieties of both life and pain."

Including the pain of loss. I still grieved as strongly for Daniel, but it didn't make me want to stop living. I would live for both of us now.

"I could go back now," I said to Raven, "and be out of danger. God bless you for bringing me here."

"You might want to withhold your thanks for a while." The golden room appeared behind him.

"That's right, other places to go." I tried to thank them with my most fervent prayer—praying through my feet!—then followed Raven into the room.

The cinnamon smell was gone, replaced by a soft musk, like the smell of a kitten. I closed my eyes and braced myself for the wrenching disorientation.

It wasn't as bad the second time. I knew what to expect, and knew it wouldn't last forever.

"Open your eyes." Room, raven, door. Outside the door, a steamy fetid jungle. "I'll go out first. They don't much like mammals here, except as food."

He hopped out into the jungle about twenty feet, looking left and right, and then began to change. He grew to the size of an eagle, and then larger, impossibly large for a bird—and as he grew even larger, his shape changed, the wings becoming arms with taloned claws, his head a monstrous dragon's head. He yawned, showing rows of white fangs longer than fingers, and roared, as loud and deep as an ocean liner's foghorn. Steam issued from his horrible mouth; I expected flame.

The raven beckoned with impressive claws and I stepped out, a little apprehensive, feeling like food. But as soon as I was out of the room I started to transform, myself. My viewpoint rose higher off the ground and my vision began to change, as it had done when I was an eagle, eyes on opposite sides of my head. I could feel my body bulking and changing. I leaned back naturally and balanced on a long thick tail. Tilting my head to inspect myself, I saw that I was a smaller version of the raven, with the same pebbly skin, but where he was glossy black, I was a kind of paisley of green and brown.

Ten or twelve feet tall, I probably weighed as much as a small elephant. And I had an elephant-sized hunger. Through the jungle smell of mold and earth, marigold and jasmine, came a clear note of rotting flesh, as mouth-watering to this body and brain as a pot roast to my other.

The raven made a series of grunts and clicks that I understood: "This way." He started crashing through the undergrowth and I followed him, rocking unsteadily from side to side at first, and then gaining confidence in the powerful legs. We came to a clearing where a large creature, twice the size of the creature he had become, lay dead and quickly decomposing in the heat. About half had been eaten, perhaps by whoever killed it. Smaller lizards and things that seemed both lizard and bird were feasting on the carcass. The raven roared at them, and I added my higher-pitched scream. They backed and flapped away, not in total retreat, but just to wait while we had our fill.

"Hurry," the raven grunted and clicked. "Be ready to move fast."

I hesitated, not because the maggoty carcass looked unpalatable—it looked as good as a beef Wellington—but because I wasn't sure how to go about it. My arms were too short for the hands to reach my mouth.

The raven tilted down, his tail extended for balance, and tore at the flesh with his jaws. I did the same, and with an odd memory of bobbing for apples, quite enjoyed gulping down bushels of wormy flesh, crunching through bones to get to the putrid softness inside.

After about a minute of heavenly feasting, there was a piercing screech and Raven butted me hard to distract me from the banquet. Two creatures twice *his* size were stalking toward us, teeth bared, unmistakably challenging us to defend our lunch. Raven bounded away, and I followed him. We scrambled back down the path he'd torn a few minutes before, and when we came to the end of it, crashed determinedly through the solid jungle. I looked back, and the giants weren't pursuing.

He wasn't just running away, though; he had a definite direction. The jungle thinned and we splashed across a wide shallow river, out onto an endless savannah.

On the horizon was a single black mountain. He tilted his head at it and grunted one syllable: "There."

We loped easily through the grass. I was aware that we had no real enemies here; I probably could have killed a lesser creature, like a human, with my breath alone. But we saw no other living things, which was no surprise. Our progress was as subtle as a locomotive's.

The grass thinned as we approached the mountain's slope. When it became a rocky incline, Raven stopped abruptly and turned back into a bird. I felt an odd churning inside, and became a woman again. My limbs ached pleasantly from the exercise, but I urgently needed both toothbrush and toilet.

"Here." Raven hopped over to some tufts of grass. "Chew this." I did, and it had a pleasant mild garlic flavor. Then I retreated behind a rocky outcrop, feeling a little silly for my modesty, and took my ease, then used smooth pebbles to clean up, Arab style.

I rearranged the strange clothing and returned to Raven. "Thank you. That was a fascinating experience."

"A diversion," he said, "and a quick lunch. This mountain is what we came for. You just shat upon a living creature."

"What?"

"Don't worry; we birds do it all the time. And it didn't notice." He turned to look up the slope. "It doesn't know I exist, though I've shared its mind twice. Its essence."

"What is it called?"

"It doesn't have language, with no one to talk to. I call it the Dark Man."

"Could I share its . . . essence, too?"

"That's why I brought you here. But I warn you it's disturbing."

"More so than being threatened by hungry dinosaurs?"

"Oh, quite. Being a dinosaur yourself, you knew they'd leave you be once you surrendered the food."

He was right; I hadn't been scared, just annoyed. "What is there to fear here?"

"It's not fear. Just knowledge of a special kind. Do you remember the time you first truly knew you were going to die?"

I thought. "Actually, no. I'm not sure."

"It was when you saw the Brady photographs of the ruins of Atlanta. You were ten."

The memory opened an emptiness. "All right. So this will be like that?"

"Perhaps worse. But I think you have to see it."

"Right here?"

"No. We have to fly to the top." He turned me into the eagle again. "Don't think about what you're doing. Just look at where you want to go."

It was more complicated than that, but then suddenly simple, once I let instinct take over. I flapped awkwardly a number of times, but when I was a couple of yards off the ground, realized I should tilt into the warm wind that rose up the side of the mountain of the Dark Man. Then I could spiral up almost without effort.

A shadow passed over me and I looked up to see a flying lizard about my own size. Instead of a beak, it had a mouth like a barracuda's, fangs overlapping up and down. It opened the mouth and screeched, and after a moment of terror I realized it wasn't after me; it was threatening, warning me off the smaller prey. The flying lizard dropped, talons out.

"Raven!" I cried.

Just before it reached him, Raven turned into a monstrous machine of articulated shiny metal, twice the lizard's size. The thing struck him with a clang; he slapped it off with a razor wing and it sped away in bleeding confusion.

Raven kept his metallic form until we reached the top. We both sculled onto a flat space and he turned back into a raven, and I into a woman.

"This way," he said, hopping toward a dark cave. I was annoyed that he didn't thank me for warning him about the danger. For a girl from Philadelphia, I made a pretty competent eagle. At the entrance to the cave, he stopped, and turned into old Gordon. He said a few words in Tlingit.

"Ask its permission to enter."

"I thought you said the Dark Man wasn't aware of us."

"He isn't, himself, but his body has defenses. It took me a while to figure this out: it won't admit any creature that doesn't have a language."

"Any language?"

"Just ask it permission."

The lines in bad Latin and French came to mind. "May I please come in, Dark Man?"

I guess I expected a magic door to creak open or something. But nothing changed, except for a slight cool breeze from the darkness. He changed back into a raven and hopped into the mouth of the cave, and I followed.

We picked our way through a jumbled pile of bones.

"You said it doesn't have a language. Yet it only admits people and things who do?"

"Strange, isn't it?" As if on cue, the huge toothy flying reptile skidded to a halt a few feet away, outside the cave mouth. Raven shrieked a warning at it, a painfully loud scream that reverberated in the small space. But the lizard had seen us change back into something resembling food, and of course didn't stop to consider the oddness of that. It hopped into the cave, baring its teeth, and approached the pile of bones, leathery wings dragging behind, leaving a smear of blood.

It couldn't see us. "Maybe you better change back," I whispered.

Hearing me, it tilted its head to peer into the darkness. It picked up a long bone with a taloned foot and delicately gnawed on one end. Then it dropped it and raised its wings in a kind of protective tent over its head and made a sound between a growl and a crow's caw, and stalked toward us over the bones, all teeth and terrible purpose. It got about halfway—I looked to Raven, who was watching with calm curiosity—and it suddenly stopped, cried out, and pitched forward, obviously dead.

"What happened?"

"I don't know. Want to do an autopsy?"

"But . . . how did *you* know? This is his planet, and he just walked in and died."

"It's his planet, but there's only one Dark Man on it. Creatures who find their way into the cave just die; they don't have any way to warn the next creature. Unless they have language, in which case there's no danger."

"But how did you find that out?"

"I'm always asking around. Someone on another planet told me about the Dark Man and I came here. It's an interesting experience."

"Disturbing, you said."

"That, too. Can you see me well enough to follow?"

He was black against gray. "Go ahead."

It was less scary than a cave on Earth. Cool and damp, but nothing like spiders or bats—unless they could talk, I supposed. As we moved farther in, slightly uphill, it was obvious that the walls were dimly phosphorescent. We went around a curve and there was no more light from the entrance behind us, but I could still see Raven, and rocks along the path.

We went around another bend and there was a faint flickering light. Then a steep incline, perhaps fifty yards, and we entered the large chamber from which the light was coming. It was a window to the sky. But it wasn't obviously sky—it was a bluish gray vista, on which concentric circular lines of light were superimposed, flickering.

"The circles are stars," Raven said. "Months are going by every second. This window faces what would be north, in Alaska, so we see the circumpolar stars rotating around the pole. But they're going so fast they look like streaks." He hopped up a pile of rocks that formed a natural staircase, and I followed with ease.

Below us spread the broad savannah and the thick jungle, separated by the river. The jungle seemed to vibrate, as trees died and were replaced. The river itself undulated, coiling like a slow serpent.

"It must take centuries for a river to change its course like that," I said. Raven nodded like a human, staring. Over the space of a few seconds, the savannah was transformed into pastureland. Huts of wood and stone—pieces of the Dark Man?—appeared and disappeared.

Parts of the jungle were cleared and a bridge snapped into place over the river. A town appeared and became a city, with regular streets and tall buildings on both sides of the river. Two more bridges appeared. The city spread out to the horizon, and it seemed almost to be dancing, as new buildings replaced old ones in ripples of progress.

A throbbing curve of fire on the horizon. "That's a spaceport," Raven said, "where they leave for other stars. They won't get to Earth; it's too far away. And they don't have much time."

As he said that, there was a lurch, and the city was suddenly leveled, a static jumble of ruins. The river started to move again, and widened into a lake.

In less than a minute, the jungle reclaimed the ruins on the other side of the water.

"Look at the stars," the raven said.

"I don't see anything different."

"Keep looking. Use that hill on the horizon as a reference."

I looked at the hill for a minute and saw that the circles of stars were slowly crawling to my right.

"What's happening?"

"The Dark Man is turning around to face the sun. The land nearby is moving with him."

"Is that what happened to the city—was it an earthquake when the Dark Man started to move?"

"No. They did that to themselves. Happens."

"People appeared and disappeared just like that?"

"It was actually quite a long time, to them. And they weren't people as such—as I said, mammals are just food here. They were lizards similar to the ones in the jungle—much like you were, but with longer arms and useful hands."

I remembered how it felt. "Just as vicious, though."

"Something they had in common with humans."

I looked out over the expanse, now apparently an inland sea. There was no sign of their civilization.

"The Dark Man has seen this happen before, and it may happen again. He's turning around to watch the sun because it changes on a time scale that's meaningful to him. He'll watch it die, over billions of years."

"Does this always happen?"

"Stars dying? Of course."

"No—I mean the lizards. Does civilization always bring ruin?"

"Not always. Often."

He hopped down the steps to lead me back down the corridor. "It's all timing. Once a species learns how to exchange ideas, a process is set in motion that might ultimately result in permanent peace and harmony. But it's not inevitable."

"As in our case. Humans."

"Timing, as I say. In one way of looking at it, humans discovered fire a little too early, fire and metals. From there on, it's only a matter of time before a species learns to use the forces that make stars burn. If they haven't grown past the need to wage war by then, their prospects aren't good."

I stepped carefully down the wet rocks, thinking of how I had saved my son from a senseless war, only to have him killed by a senseless man. "So you say that humanity is going to go the way of these lizards."

"You're asking me to predict the future, which is meaningless. There are many futures." He started down the corridor. "Come on. More places to see."

On the last step, I twisted my ankle and fell. He hopped back when he heard me cry out, changing into old Gordon, who gave me a hand.

We hobbled along. "It's only a couple of hundred yards to my ship. The room."

"It seems to go anywhere you want," I said through clenched teeth. "Why not just whistle for it?"

"It can't come in here. Time is funny in here, as you may have noticed."

We came out of the cave into a pelting rain. He carried me the few steps to the yellow light. Once inside, my ankle immediately stopped hurting. The place, or thing, smelled like cinnamon again.

"You should open up a clinic," I said. He'd changed back into a raven. "You'd be the richest bird on Earth."

"I already am, when I'm on Earth."

"You travel like this, most of the time?"

"Time, space." He flexed his wings in an unmistakable shrug. "I do keep moving, observing. But in a way, I'm always in Sitka. Gordon doesn't disappear for months at a time."

"I don't understand."

"You will. Soon." We both dissolved into the now-familiar transition state.

A moment later, we were back in the yellow room. "Did something go wrong?"

"No," he said. "We're never far from this place."

The door opened and I stepped toward it. "Don't go outside. Just look. I think if we went outside we couldn't get back in."

"Where are we?" It looked like a quiet woodland.

"There isn't any 'where' or 'when' here. Everybody sees something different. Tell me what you think it is."

I stepped cautiously to the door. There was a disturbing noise.

It was a quiet woodland otherwise. Birds twittering. The smell of green growing things. Buds flowering. A pear tree with a single large fruit. A snake the size of a python draped among its limbs.

"The Garden of Eden?" I said. "This can't be real."

"Whatever it is or is not, it's real. Do you see the pain yet?"

The room moved over a thick stand of bushes, toward the noise. "Stay inside," Raven repeated.

In a small clearing, a pregnant woman lay on her back. She was covered with streaks of blood, hair matted with it. She was grunting and whimpering hoarsely with exhaustion and pain. God, had I ever been there. I took an instinctive step forward.

Gordon suddenly appeared, blocking the door. "Stay. I mean it. There's nothing you can do."

"All right," I said. He turned around and looked out the door.

The woman—I couldn't think of her as "Eve"—was very close to giving birth. Her womb was dilating and I could see the top of the head, hair black as her own. Blood oozed around the crowning head. Her body writhed and she screamed, keening. "Steady," Gordon said, a hand on my shoulder.

"I've seen this before," I said. "I've done it."

"Not like this, I think."

Her womb opened impossibly wide and for a moment the screaming stopped—then in a spray of blood the head came out. It was an adult's head.

Her own head? Now *it* started screaming, even louder. With a start, I saw that the mother's head and neck had disappeared. Her womb split horribly sideways, and a bloody shoulder worked its way out. She was giving birth to herself, turning inside-out.

The screams stopped only long enough for her to take deep ragged breaths. The other shoulder worked through, distorting the mother's torso into something made of human parts but not recognizably human.

Both breasts slid out at once—and it became terrifyingly clear that the self she was giving birth to was also pregnant. I didn't know the word then, but she was everting herself. The body split and after the abdomen worked its way through, the rest was swift: the new womb and then her limbs and feet. All streaked with bright fresh blood.

The newborn mother began to whimper and clutched at the bloodied grass.

"Oh my God. She's starting over."

"You see a woman." He was Raven again.

"You don't?"

"I almost did, as Gordon. Now what I see is the Orion Nebula: the dying and birthing of stars. It goes on all the time, of course."

"But this *pain.*"

"You think the universe feels nothing, giving birth and dying? Any pain you've ever felt was only an echo of that."

I watched with horrified fascination as the process started over.

"That's only metaphor," I said. "The universe doesn't have flesh and ganglia and a brain to interpret their distress signals."

"Why do you think you have them? One of your own said, 'Pain is nature's way of telling us we're alive.' That's close to literal truth."

I was obstinate. "Pain draws our attention to something that's wrong with the body."

"What did I just say? Your body was perfectly happy when it was a scattered bunch of oxygen and hydrogen and carbon atoms. Life *is* what's wrong with it."

"Now that's a wonderful argument against suicide. When I die, the universe will be a smidgeon happier."

"This is not an argument. I'm just showing you around. What you do when we return to Sitka . . . will be what you do."

"Including . . . take my life?"

"Life was yours to give and it's yours to take. But I don't think you will kill yourself now. Let's go to one more place; then we'll start back." I shut my eyes hard and endured the whirling dislocation. It went longer than ever before, and I clenched my jaws so hard against being sick that I could hear my teeth grinding. Finally it was over.

"This is not a world," he said as I opened my eyes, "in the sense of being a planet. It's not even really a place, as your Garden of Eden was not an actual woodland." The door opened. "But I think we'll both see the same thing this time."

I stepped to the opening and took hold of the edge of the door. We were evidently floating over a landscape, drifting a few hundred yards off the ground. Dramatic mountains and cliffs, but not menacing like the first planet. Everything was subtle shades of warm gray, soft and monochromatic.

There was no horizon. The landscape stretched out forever, becoming vague with distance.

"Let's go on down," Raven said.

As we floated closer to the ground, what had appeared to be a kind of granular texture became thousands of individuals, perhaps millions.

Some few were human beings, but the overwhelming majority were otherworldly creatures. Gargoyles and sprites. Demons and floating jellyfish, an articulated metal spider and a close formation of thousands of blue bees arranged in a perfect cube. Two dinosaurs like we had been and a cluster of six of the translucent angel creatures we saw on the first planet.

"Only six?" I said.

The raven bobbed his head. "The six who elected to die."

"Wait . . . everyone here is dead? This is the afterlife?"

"They're not completely dead. But they're not really alive, in the sense of eating and breathing—if they were eating, a lot of them would eat each other; if they were breathing, they'd be breathing different atmospheres, usually poisonous to the others."

"Daniel! Is Daniel here?"

"He might be someplace. I wouldn't know where to find him, though. And you couldn't talk to him or touch him. I really don't understand this place, the where and how of it. The 'why' seems to be that it's a holding area of some kind."

"Of souls," I said. "After they die."

"They look like bodies to me."

"Waiting for something?"

"I don't know. If it's something like your Catholics' Purgatory, then I wonder where Heaven is. I've never come across it."

"Maybe your room, your ship, can't get there. Maybe you do have to die and spend some time here, first."

"Your guess is as good as mine. Almost as good, anyhow."

There didn't seem to be much order in the crowd. I tried to pick out the humans, and the nearly human, and there did seem to be a lot of the very old and the very young, as you would expect of the dead. Nobody really *looked* dead, though. No wounds or signs of disease.

But nobody was moving. It was like a photograph in three dimensions. While I was looking, two new ones appeared, one like a human woman but with spadelike appendages instead of hands, the other a kind of long-haired monkey with an extra pair of legs.

"Does everybody come here, good or bad?"

"Impossible to say. There appears to be room for about everybody." We started to rise at an accelerating rate. The individuals merged back into the granular texture and then into a smooth gray; mountains shrank to pebbles and disappeared. The horizon didn't change, though.

"What happens if you fly in one direction for a long time?"

"It doesn't seem to change. You never come to an edge. But 'a long time' doesn't mean much here. The illusion of time belongs to worlds like yours. Here, there's only will and chance."

"What do you mean by that? Time an illusion?"

"When you studied mathematics, you used the idea of infinity."

"Of course. You couldn't do calculus without it."

"And you believe the universe is infinite." I nodded. "So stars and planets and nebulae go on forever."

"Of course."

"Well, I have news for you: they don't. Within your lifetime, scientists will suspect that there's an edge to it. Within another lifetime, they'll prove there is."

"That's curious. So what's beyond it?"

"Another universe. And another and another. Every instant, from the universe's birth to its death, exists side by side, in a way. Think of it as an Edison cinematograph, writ very large: one frozen moment, then the next, and so on.

"Furthermore, every possible universe exists as well. Many where the Civil War didn't happen or was won by the South. Many where you did kill yourself Thursday evening. Many where you had biscuits for breakfast, instead of toast. With everything else in the universe unchanged. There's room for them all.

"What you perceive as time is your translation from one possible moment to the next, because of something you did or something the universe did to you."

"Free will and predestination?" I said.

"Decision and chance," the raven said, "inextricably intertwined."

We had risen so high that a featureless gray plane faded off into mist. Above the mist, blackness, no stars.

"But this place, this is beyond that?"

"Yes. This is where people go when they stop moving from moment to moment."

"So maybe this *is* Heaven?"

He just looked at me. "Close your eyes. We're going back to the angels."

I didn't close my eyes, at first—after all, while we were traveling, I didn't seem to exist as an assemblage of body parts, so what did "closed eyes" mean? In a few seconds it became pretty obvious, if not describable. Like seasickness, but somehow larger, longer, with the threat that it could last forever. I did something like closing eyes and the room disappeared, and I only felt miserable. The smell of musk changed to lemon.

Then it was cinnamon and we were there, on the Dantean planet. Through the open door, the seven angels braided together in the oven heat. "Let me speak to them first," Raven said. He hopped over to the dark soft patch he called their brain. They were momentarily still, rigid, and then resumed a rhythmic twining. "Now you," he said. "Shoes off."

The ground was like hot flour between my toes. But I remembered not to dig in when I stepped onto their coolness. At first I didn't hear or feel anything. Then there was something like a quiet song, a wordless hymn in my mind. I concentrated, but couldn't make any sense of it. Then it was gone.

"Won't you use words?" I said. But they just curled and uncurled in silence.

The raven was back in the yellow room. "I think they're done. Come on."

I crossed the hot sand, looking back at them. "Did they tell you anything?"

"Nothing I didn't already know. They like you."

I couldn't take my eyes off them, as I backed into the cube.

"Then why didn't they say anything?" It smelled of mint tea.

"They don't so much say things as do things." The yellow wall appeared. "Close your eyes."

This time I obeyed. "Are we going back?"

"Yes and no." I squeezed my eyes shut. The dislocation seemed about as long as the first one.

"You can look now." The door was open on a scene of incredible desolation, stone buildings battered to rubble, a few steel skeletons standing. Everything blackened by fire.

"Where is this?"

"Times Square, New York City." He had turned into Gordon, who blinked away tears. I had never seen him cry. "Your world, about a hundred years after you were born."

"Like . . . like the lizards' world?"

"Exactly. No human left alive." He turned to me with a kind of smile. "I feel like the Ghost of Christmas Yet to Come. This is what usually happens. Not always in the middle of the twentieth century. Sometimes it takes another hundred or even a thousand years."

"But it always happens."

"Not always." He changed back into Raven. "You don't want to go outside here. You would die. Close your eyes."

"Where are we going?"

He didn't reply, but I felt weight on my body, the compression of stays around my waist, and took one quick look. Instead of the strange skintight suit, I was wearing my warm-weather teaching clothes, the light gray Gibson Girl suit I'd mail-ordered from San Francisco.

I screwed my eyes shut again, against the rush of nausea.

"We're going back to Sitka?"

"Yes."

"I'll freeze to death in this!"

"You'll manage."

The machine stopped. I felt a breath of cool forest air and heard crickets.

We were in the woods where we'd started. But there was no snow. The light of a full moon filtered through the forest canopy. An owl called and flapped away. I stepped out onto soft humus and the yellow room disappeared behind me.

"Months have passed," I said. "It must be June or July." I slapped a mosquito.

Raven beat the air with his wings and rose to an eye-level branch. "Something has passed."

I had a chill that had nothing to do with temperature. "You said you were a guardian, but not my guardian. Are you going off to save someone else now?"

"I think I'm done here. I don't save lives. I save life. By making the smallest change I can."

"Life?"

"Think about what I've said." He hopped around in a full circle, the moonlight glinting soft rainbows off his feathers. Then he cawed, like an actual raven, and flew off into the night.

"Wait!" I said, but he was above the trees and soaring.

For a moment I was totally lost, and started to panic, but got ahold of myself. Sitka *was* an island, after all; if I walked in any direction I'd eventually come to the water, and there take my bearings.

Bears. I whistled, the way Gordon had taught me. Raven. They won't attack you if you don't surprise them. Unlike some other mammals.

I could have gone in any direction, but made the assumption that Raven's room, or ship, had come down in the same place from which it had left, in the same orientation. I picked my way through the undergrowth in a straight line for a few minutes, and was rewarded with a game trail. I turned left and walked down the hill.

I thought I knew where I was, but the place where my cabin should have been was just a small clearing. In a few more steps, though, I was on the path that turned into Lincoln Street.

The moon was high, but somewhat west. It was probably about two in the morning. The town was quiet except for faint noise drifting up from the harbor. I came to a slight rise and looked down in that direction. There were work lights arranged around one of the boats, which looked vaguely familiar.

A chill gripped me. It was the *White Nights,* and the noise was from a work crew below decks, banging rivets into the boiler. I broke into a run, as fast as my skirts would allow! I ran downhill to Baranoff Street, paused to get my breath, and walked swiftly to the Baranoff Hotel.

There was a light on in the lobby. I rushed up the steps, but the door was locked. When I tapped on the glass, the little old lady came 'round, thumb holding her place in a dime novel. She unlocked the door and a hundred wrinkles pinched into a frown. "What on earth are you doing about at this hour?"

"I couldn't sleep," I improvised, "and went down to check on the ship."

She looked at the key in her hand, evidently trying to remember having let me out. "Down to the docks after midnight," she clucked. "You're daft. But ye must have a guardian angel."

"Yes!"

I rushed by her and up the stairs to the room that Daniel and I had shared. The door was locked. I tapped, and then knocked loudly.

He opened the door and stood there bleary eyed, completely alive. I grabbed him and hugged him so hard his joints popped.

"My son . . . do I have a story to tell you."

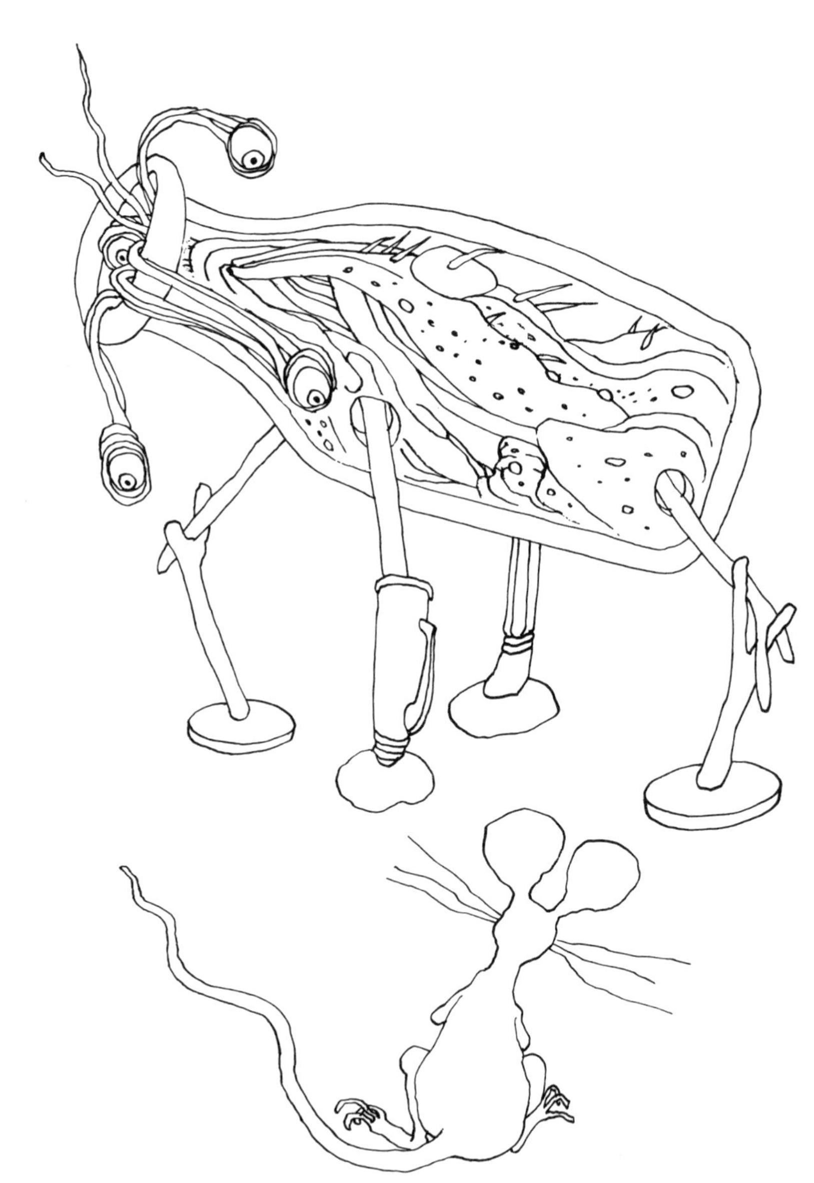

Familiar

China Miéville

A WITCH NEEDED TO impress his client. His middleman, who had arranged the appointment, told him that the woman was very old—"hundred at least"—and intimidating in a way he could not specify. The witch intuited something unusual, money or power. He made careful and arduous preparations. He insisted that he meet her a month later than the agent had planned.

His workshop was a hut, a garden shed in the shared allotments of north London. The woman edged past plots of runner beans, tomatoes, failing root vegetables and trellises, past the witch's neighbors, men decades younger than she but still old, who tended bonfires and courteously did not watch her.

The witch was ready. Behind blacked-out windows his little wooden room was washed. Boxes stowed in a tidy pile. The herbs and organic accoutrements of his work were out of the way but left visible—claws, skins like macabre facecloths, bottles stopped up and careful piles of dust and objects. The old woman looked them over. She stared at a clubfooted pigeon chained by its good leg to a perch.

"My familiar."

The woman said nothing. The pigeon sounded and shat.

"Don't meet his eye, he'll steal your soul out of you." The witch hung a black rag in front of the bird. He would not look his client clear on. "He's basilisk, but you're safe now. He's hidden."

From the ceiling was a chandelier of unshaped coat hangers and pieces of china, on which three candles scabbed with dripping were lit. Little pyramids of wax lay on the wooden table beneath them. In their guttering the witch began his consultation, manipulating scobs of gris-gris—on the photographs his client provided he sprinkled leaf flakes, dirt, and grated remnants of plastic, with an herb shaker from a pizzeria.

The effects came quickly so that even the cold old woman showed interest. Air dried up and expanded until the shed was stuffy as an airplane. There were noises from the shelves: mummied detritus moved anxious. It was much more than happened at most consultations, but the witch was still waiting.

In the heat the candles were moist. Strings of molten wax descended. They coated each other and drip-dripped in instantly frozen splashes. The stalactites extended, bearding the bottom of the candelabrum. The candles burned too fast, pouring off wax, until the wire was trimmed with finger-thick extrusions.

They built up matter unevenly, curling out away from the table, and then they sputtered and seemed not to be dripping grease but drooling it from mouths that stretched open stringy within the wax. Fluttering tongues emerged and colorless eyes from behind nictitating membranes. For moments the things were random sculptures and then they were suddenly and definitively organic. At its ends, the melted candles' runoff was a fringe of little milk-white snakes. They were a few inches of flesh. Their bodies merged, anchored, with wax. They swayed with dim predatory intent and whispered.

The old woman screamed and so did the witch. He turned his cry, though, into a declamation and wavered slightly in his chair, so that the nest of dangling wax snakes turned their attention to him. The pigeon behind its dark screen called in distress. The snakes stretched vainly from the candles and tried to strike the witch. Their toxin dribbled onto the powder of his hex, mixed it into wet grime under which the woman's photographs began to change.

It was an intercession, a series of manipulations even the witch found tawdry and immoral: but the pay was very good, and he knew that for his standing he must impress. The ceremony lasted less than an hour, the grease snakes leaking noise and fluid, the pigeon ceaselessly frightened. At the end the witch rose weakly, his profuse sweat making him gleam like the wet wax. Moving with strange speed, too fast to be struck, he cut the snakes off where their bodies became candle, and they dropped onto the table and squirmed in death, bleeding thick pale blood.

His client stood and smiled, taking the corpses of the half-snakes and her photographs, carefully leaving them soiled. She was clear-eyed and happy and she did not wince at light as the witch did when he opened the door to her and gave her instructions for when to return. He watched her go through the kitchen gardens and only closed his shed door again when she was out of sight.

The witch drew back the screen from before the terrified pigeon and was about to kill it, but he stared at the stubs of wax where the snakes had been and instead he opened a window and let the bird out. He sat at the table and breathed heavily, watching the boxes at the back of the hut. The air settled. The witch could hear scratching. It came from inside a plastic toolbox, where he had stashed his real familiar.

He had called a familiar. He had been considering it for a long time. He had had a rough understanding that it would give him a conduit to a fecundity, and that had bolstered him through the pain and distaste of what the conjuration had needed. Listening to the curious scritch-scritch he fingered the scabs on his thighs and chest. They would scar.

The information he had found on the technique was vague—passed-on vagrants' hedge-magic, notepad palimpsests, marginalia in phone books. The mechanics of the operation had never been clear. The witch consoled himself that the misunderstanding was not his fault. He had hoped that the familiar, when it came, would fit his urban practice. He had hoped for a rat, big and dirty-furred, or a fox, or pigeon such as the one he had displayed. He had thought that the flesh he provided was a sacrifice. He had not known it was substance.

With the lid off, the toolbox was a playpen, and the familiar investigated it. The witch looked at it, queasy. It had coated its body in the dust, so it no longer left wetness. Like a sea slug, ungainly, flanged with outgrowths of its own matter. Heavy as an apple, it was an amalgam of the witch's scraps of fat and flesh, coagulated with his sputum, cum, and hoodoo. It coiled, rolled itself busy into corners of its prison. It clutched toward the light, convulsing its pulp.

Even in its container, out of sight, the witch had felt it. He had felt it groping in the darkness behind him and as he did with a welling up like blood he had made the snakes come, which he could not have done before. The familiar disgusted him. It made his stomach spasm, it left him ill and confounded, and he was not sure why. He had flensed animals for his calling, alive sometimes, and was inured to that, he had eaten shit and roadkill when liturgy demanded, but that little rag of his own flesh gave him a kind of passionate nausea.

When the thing had first moved he had screamed, realizing what his familiar would be, and spewed till he was empty. And still it was almost beyond him to watch it, but he made himself, to try to know what it was that revolted him.

The witch could feel the familiar's enthusiasm. A feral fascination for things held it together, and every time it tensed and moved by peristalsis around its plastic cell the contractions of its dumb and hungry interest passed through the witch and bent him double. It was stupid: wordless and searingly curious. The witch could feel it make sense of the dust, now that it had rolled in it, randomly then deliberately, using it for something.

He wanted the strength to do again what he had done for the woman, though making the snakes had exhausted him. His familiar manipulated things, was a channel for manipulation, it lived to change, use, and know. The witch very much wanted that power it had given him, and he closed his eyes and made himself sure he could, he could steel himself. But looking at the nosing dusted red thing he was suddenly weak and uncertain. He could feel its mindless mind. To have his own effluvia maggot through him with every experience, he could not bear it, even with what it gave him. It made him a sewer. Every few seconds in his familiar's presence he was swallowing his own bile. He felt its constant eager interest like foulness, God knew why. It was not worth it. The witch decided.

It could not be killed, or if it could he did not know how. The witch took a knife to it but it investigated the blade avidly, only parting and reforming under his efforts. It tried to grip the metal.

When he bludgeoned it with a flat iron it recoiled and regrouped its matter, moved over and around the weapon, soiling it with itself and making the iron into a skate on which it tried to move. Fire only discomfited it, and it sat tranquil in acid. It studied every danger as it had dust, trying to use it, and the echo of that study turned the witch's gut.

He tipped the noisome thing into a sack. He could feel it shove itself at the fabric's pores and he moved quickly. The witch drove, hessian fumbling in the toolbox beside him (he could not put it behind him, where he could not see it, so that it might get out and conduct its investigations near his skin).

It was almost night when he stopped by the Grand Union Canal. In the municipal gardens of west London, between beat-up graffitied bridges, in earshot of the last punk children in the skate park, the witch tried to drown his familiar. He was not so stupid as to think it would work, but to drop the thing, weighted with rocks and tied up, into the cool and dirty water was a relief so great he moaned. To see it drunk up by the canal. It was gone from him. He ran.

*

Cosseted by mud, the familiar tried to learn. It sent out temporary limbs to make sense of things. It strained without fear against the sack.

It compared everything it found to everything it knew. Its power was change. It was tool-using, it had no way of knowing except to put to use. The world was infinite tools. By now the familiar understood dust well, and had a little knowledge of knives and irons. It felt the water and the fibrous weave of the bag, and did things with them to learn that they were not what it had used before.

Out of the sack, in muddy dark, it swam ugly and inefficient, learning scraps of rubbish and little life. There were hardy fish even in so grubby a channel, and it was not long before it found them. It took a few carefully apart, and learned to use them.

The familiar plucked their eyes. It rubbed them together, dangled them from their fibers. It sent out microscopic filaments that tickled into the blood-gelled nerve stalks. The familiar's life was contagious. It sucked the eyes into itself and suddenly, as visual signals reached it for the first time, though there was no light (it was burrowing in the mud), it *knew* that it was in darkness. It rolled into shallows, and with its new vitreous machines it saw streetlamp light cut the black water.

It found the corpses of the fish again (using sight, now, to help it). It unthreaded them. It greased itself with the slime on their skins. One by one it broke off the ribs like components of a model kit. It embedded them in its skin (its minute and random blood vessels and muscle fibers insinuating into the bone). It used them to walk, with the sedate pick-picking motion of an urchin.

The familiar was tireless. Over hours it learned the canal bed. Each thing it found it used, some in several ways. Some it used in conjunction with other pieces. Some it discarded after a while. With each use, each manipulation (and only with that manipulation, that change) it read meanings. The familiar accumulated brute erudition, forgetting nothing, and with each insight the next came easier, as its context grew. Dust had been the first and hardest thing to know.

When the familiar emerged from the water with the dawn, it was poured into a milk-bottle carapace. Its clutch of eyes poked from the bottleneck. It nibbled with a nail clipper. With precise little bullets of stone it had punctured holes in its glass sides, from which legs of waterlogged twig-wood and broken pens emerged. To stop it sinking into wet earth its feet were coins and flat stones. They looked insecurely attached. The familiar dragged the brown sack that had contained it. Though it had not found a use for it, and though it had no words for the emotion, it felt something like sentiment for the hessian.

All its limbs were permanently reconfigured. Even those it tired of and kicked off were wormed with organic ruts for its juices. Minuscule muscles and tendons the thickness of spider silk but vastly stronger rooted through the components of its bric-a-brac body, anchoring them together. The flesh at its center had grown.

The familiar investigated grass, and watched the birds with its inadequate eyes. It trooped industrious as a beetle on variegated legs.

Through that day and night the familiar learned. It crossed paths with small mammals. It found a nest of mice and examined their parts. Their tails it took for prehensile tentacles, their whiskers bristled it, it upgraded its eyes and learned to use ears. It compared what it found to dust, blades, water, twigs, fish ribs, and sodden rubbish: it learned mouse.

It learned its new ears, with focused fascination. Young Londoners played in the gardens and the familiar stayed hidden and listened to their slang. It heard patterns in their sequenced barks.

There were predators in the gardens. The familiar was the size of a cat, and foxes and dogs sometimes went for it. It was now too big for the bottle armor, had burst it, but had learned instead to fight. It raked with shards of china, nails, and screws—not with anger, but with its unchanging beatific interest. It was impossibly sure-footed on its numerous rubbish legs. If an attacker did not run fast enough, the familiar would learn it. It would be used. The familiar had brittle fingertips, made of dogs' teeth.

The familiar moved away from the gardens. It followed the canal bank to a graveyard, to an industrial siding, to a dump. It gave itself a shape with wheels, plunging its veins and tissue into the remnants of a trolley. When later it discarded them, pulling them out, the wheels bled.

Sometimes it used its tools like their original owners, as when it took its legs from birds (scampering over burned-out cars like a rock rabbit on four or six avian feet). It could change them. In sun, the familiar shaded its eyes with flanges of skin that had been cats' ears.

It had learned to eat. Its hunger, its feeding was a tool like dust had been: the familiar did not need to take in nourishment but doing so gave it satisfaction, and that was enough. It made itself a tongue from strips of wet towel, and a mouth full of interlocking cogs. These teeth rotated in its jaw, chewing, driving food scraps back toward the throat.

In the small hours of morning, in a waste lot stained by chemical spill, the familiar finally made a tool of the sack that had delivered it. It found two broken umbrellas, one skeletal, the other ragged, and it busied itself with them, holding them tight with hair-grip hands, manipulating them with rat tails. It secured the sack cloth to them with its organic roots. After hours of calculated tinkering, during which it spoke English words in the mind it had built itself, the shaped umbrellas spasmed open and shut on analogues of shoulders, and with a great gust the familiar flew.

Its umbrellas beat like scooping bat wings, and the greased hessian held it. It flew random as a butterfly, staring at the moon with cats' and dogs' eyes, its numerous limbs splayed. It hunted with urban bramble, thorned stalks that whipped and pinioned prey from the air and the ground. It scoured the scrubland of cats. It spasmed between tower blocks, each wing contraction jerking it through the air. It shouted the words it had learned, without sound.

There were only two nights that it could fly, before it was too large, and it loved them. It was aware of its pleasure. It used it as it grew. The summer became unusually hot. The familiar hid in the sudden masses of buddleia. It found passages through the city. It lived in wrecking yards and sewers, growing, changing, and using.

Though it replaced them regularly, the familiar kept its old eyes, moving them down itself so that its sight deteriorated along its back. It had learned caution. It was educated; two streets might be empty, but not identically so, it knew. It parsed the grammar of brick and neglected industry. It listened at doors, cupping the cones of card, the plastic funnels with which it extended its ears. Its vocabulary increased. It was a Londoner.

Every house it passed it marked like a dog: the familiar pissed out its territory with glands made from plastic bottles. Sniffing with a nose taken from a badger, it sprayed a liquid of rubbish-tip juices and the witch's blood in a rough circle across the flattened zones of the north city, where the tube trains emerged from underground. The familiar claimed the terraced landscape.

It seemed a ritual. But it had watched the little mammals of the landfills and understood that territory was a tool, and it used it and learned it, or thought it did until the night it was tracing its limits into suburban spaces, and it smelled another's trail.

The familiar raged. It was maddened. It thrashed in a yard that reeked of alien spoor, chewing tires and spitting out their rags. Eventually, it hunkered down to the intruder's track. It licked it. It bristled throughout its body of witch-flesh and patchwork trash. The new scent was sharper than its own, admixed with different blood. The familiar hunted.

The trail ran across back gardens, separated by fences that the familiar vaulted easily, trickled across toys and drying grass, over flowerbeds and rockeries. The prey was old and tough: it told in the piss. The familiar used the smell to track, and learned it, and understood that it was the newcomer here.

In the sprawl of the outer city the stench became narcotic. The familiar stalked silently on rocks like hooves. The night was warm and overcast. Behind empty civic halls, tags and the detritus of vandalism. It ended there. The smell was so strong, it was a fight drug. It blistered the familiar's innards. Cavities opened in it, rudimentary lungs like bellows: it made itself breathe, so that it could pant to murder.

Corrugated iron and barbed wire surrounds. The witch's familiar was the intruder. There were no stars, no lamplight. The familiar stood without motion. It breathed out a challenge. The breath drifted across the little arena. Something enormous stood. Debris moved. Debris rose and turned and opened its mouth and caught the exhalation. It sucked it in out of all the air, filled its belly. It learned it.

Dark expanded. The familiar blinked its eyelids of rain-wet leather offcuts. It watched its enemy unfold.

This was an old thing, an old familiar, the bull, the alpha. It had escaped or been banished or lost its witch long ago. It was broken bodies, wood and plastic, stone and ribbed metal, a constellation of clutter exploding from a mass of skinless muscle the size of a horse. Beside its wet bloody eyes were embedded cameras, extending their lenses, powered by organic current. The mammoth shape clapped some of its hand-things.

The young familiar had not known until then that it had thought itself alone. Without words, it wondered what else was in the city—

how many other outcasts, familiars too foul to use. But it could not think for long as the monstrous old potentate came at it.

The thing ran on table legs and gripped with pincers that were human jaws. They clenched on the little challenger and tore at its accrued limbs.

Early in its life the familiar had learned pain, and this attack gave it agony. It felt itself lessen, as the attacker ingested gulps of its flesh. The familiar understood in shock that it might cease.

Its cousin taught it that with its new mass it could bruise. The familiar could not retreat. Even bleeding and with arms, legs gone, with eyes crushed and leaking and something three times its size opening mouths and shears and raising flukes that were shovels, the intoxicant reek of a competitor's musk forced it to fight.

More pain and the loss of more self. The little insurgent was diminishing. It was awash in rival stink. A notion came to it. It pissed up in its adversary's eyes, spraying all the bloody muck left in it and rolling away from the liquid's arc. The hulking thing clamored silently. Briefly blinded, it put its mouth to the ground and followed its tongue.

Behind it, the familiar was motionless. It made tools of shadows and silence, keeping dark and quiet stitched to it as the giant tracked its false trail. The little familiar sent fibers into the ground, to pipework inches below. It connected to the plastic with tentacles quickly as thick as viscera, made the pipe a limb and organ, shoving and snapping it a foot below its crouching opponent. It drove the ragged end up out of the earth, its plastic jags spurs. It ground it into the controlling mass of the old familiar, into the dead center of meat, and as the wounded thing tried to pull itself free, the guileful young familiar sucked through the broken tube.

It ballooned cavities in itself, gaping vacuums at the ends of its new pipe intestine. The suction pinioned its enemy, and tore chunks of bloody matter from it. The familiar drew them through the buried duct, up into its own body. Like a glutton it swigged them.

The trapped old one tried to raise itself but its wood and metal limbs had no purchase. It could not pull itself free, and the pipe was too braced in earth to tear away. It tried to thread its own veins into the tubing and vie for it, to make its own esophagus and drink down its attacker, but the vessels of the young familiar riddled the plastic, and the dying thing could not push them aside, and with all the tissue it had lost to the usurper, they were now equal in mass, and now the newcomer was bigger, and now bigger still.

Tissue passed in fat pellets into the swelling young familiar sitting anchored by impromptu guts. Venting grave little breaths, the ancient one shriveled and broke apart, sucked into a plughole. The cobweb of its veins dried up from all its borrowed limbs and members, and they disaggregated, nothing but hubcaps again, and butcher's remnants, a dead television, tools, mechanical debris, all brittled and sucked clean of life. The limbs were arranged around clean ground, from which jagged a shard of piping.

All the next day, the familiar lay still. When it moved, after dark, it limped though it replaced its broken limbs: it was damaged internally, it ached with every step it took, or if it oozed or crawled. All but a few of its eyes were gone, and for nights it was too weak to catch and use any animals to fix that. It took none of its opponent's tools, except one of the human jaws that had been pincers. It was not a trophy, but something to consider.

It metabolized much of the flesh-matter it had ingested, burned it away (and the older familiar's memories, of self-constitution on Victorian slag heaps, troubled it like indigestion). But it was still severely bloated. It pierced its distended body with broken glass to let out pressure, but all that oozed out of it was its new self.

The familiar still grew. It had been enlarging ever since it emerged from the canal. With its painful victory came a sudden increase in its size, but it knew it would have reached that mass anyway.

Its enemy's trails were drying up. The familiar felt interest at that, rather than triumph. It lay for days in a car-wrecking yard, using new tools, building itself a new shape, listening to the men and the clatter of machines, feeling its energy and attention grow, but slowly. That was where it was when the witch found it.

An old lady came before it. In the noon heat the familiar sat loose as a doll. Over the warehouse and office roofs, it could hear church bells. The old lady stepped into its view and it looked up at her.

She was glowing, with more, it seemed, than the light behind her. Her skin was burning. She looked incomplete. She was at the edge of something. The familiar did not recognize her but it remembered her. She caught its eye and nodded forcefully, moved out of sight. The familiar was tired.

"There you are."

Wearily, the familiar raised its head again. The witch stood before it.

"Wondered where you got to. Buggering off like that."

In the long silence the familiar looked the man up and down. It remembered him too.

"Need you to get back to things. Job to finish."

The familiar's interest wandered. It picked at a stone, looked down at it, sent out veins and made it a nail. It forgot the man was there, until his voice surprised it.

"Could feel you all the time, you know." The witch laughed without pleasure. "How we found you, isn't it?" Glanced back at the woman out of the familiar's sight. "Like following me nose. Me gut."

Sun baked them all.

"Looking well."

The familiar watched him. It was inquisitive. It felt things. The witch moved back. There was a purr of summer insects. The woman was at the edge of the clearing of cars.

"Looking well," the witch said again.

The familiar had made itself the shape of a man. Its flesh center was several stone of spread-out muscle. Its feet were boulders again, its hands bones on bricks. It would stand eight feet tall. There was too much stuff in it and on it to itemize. On its head were books, grafted in spine first, their pages constantly riffling as if in wind. Blood vessels saturated their pages, and engorged to let out heat. The books sweated. The familiar's dog eyes focused on the witch, then the gently cooking wrecks.

"Oh Jesus."

The witch was staring at the bottom of the familiar's face, half-pointing.

"Oh Jesus, what you *do?*"

The familiar opened and closed the man-jaw it had taken from its opponent and made its own mouth. It grinned with thirdhand teeth.

"What you fucking *do?* Jesus *Christ.* Oh shit, man. Oh no." The familiar cooled itself with its page-hair.

"You got to come back. We need you again." Pointing vaguely at the woman, who was motionless and still shining. "Ain't done. She ain't finished. You got to come back.

"I can't *do it* on my own. Ain't got it. She ain't paying me no more. She's fucking *ruining me.*" That last he screamed in anger directed backward but the woman did not flinch. She reached out her hand to the familiar, waved a clutch of moldering dead snakes. "Come back," said the witch.

The familiar noticed the man again and remembered him. It smiled.

The man waited. "Come back," he said. "Got to come *back,* fucking *back.*" He was crying. The familiar was fascinated. "Come *back.*" The witch tore off his shirt. "You been *growing.* You been fucking *growing,* you won't stop, and I can't do nothing without you now and you're *killing* me."

The woman with the snakes glowed. The familiar could see her through the witch's chest. The man's body was faded away in random holes. There was no blood. Two handspans of sternum, inches of belly, slivers of arm-meat all faded to nothing, as if the flesh had given up existing. Entropic wounds. The familiar looked in interest at the gaps. He saw into the witch's stomach, where hoops of gut ended where they met the hole, where the spine became hard to notice and did not exist for a space of several vertebrae. The man took off his trousers. His thighs were punctuated by the voids, his scrotum gone.

"You got to come back," he whispered. "I can't do nothing without you, and you're killing me. Bring me back."

The familiar touched itself. It pointed at the man with a chicken-bone finger, and smiled again.

"Come *back,*" the witch said. "She wants you, I need you. You fucking *have* to come back. Have to *help* me." He stood cruciform. The sun shone through the cavities in him, breaking up his shadow with light.

The familiar looked down at black ants laboring by a cigarette end, up at the man's creased face, at the impassive old woman holding her dead snakes like a bouquet. It smiled without cruelty.

"Then *finish,*" the witch screamed at it. "If you ain't going to come back then fucking *finish.*" He stamped and spat at the familiar, too afraid to touch but raging. "You *fucker.* I can't stand this. Finish it for me, you *fucker.*" The witch beat his fists against his naked holed sides. He reached into a space below his heart. He wailed with pain and his face spasmed, but he fingered the inside of his body. His wound did not bleed, but when he drew out his shaking hand it was wet and red where it had touched his innards. He cried out again and shook blood into the familiar's face. "That what you *want?* That do you? You fucker. Come *back* or make it *stop.* Do *something* to *finish.*"

From the familiar's neck darted a web of threads, which fanned out and into the corona of insects that surrounded it. Each fiber snaked into a tiny body and retracted. Flies and wasps and fat bees, a crawling handful of chitin was reeled in to the base of the familiar's throat, below its human jaw. The hair-thin tendrils scored through the tumor of living insects and took them over, used them, made them a tool. They hummed their wings loudly in time, clamped to the familiar's skin.

The vibrations resonated through its buccal cavity. It moved its mouth as it had seen others do. The insectile voice box echoed through it and made sound, which it shaped with lips.

"Sun," it said. Its droning speech intrigued it. It pointed into the sky, over the nude and fading witch's shoulder, up way beyond the old woman. It closed its eyes. It moved its mouth again and listened closely to its own quiet words. Rays bounced from car to battered car, and the familiar used them as tools to warm its skin.

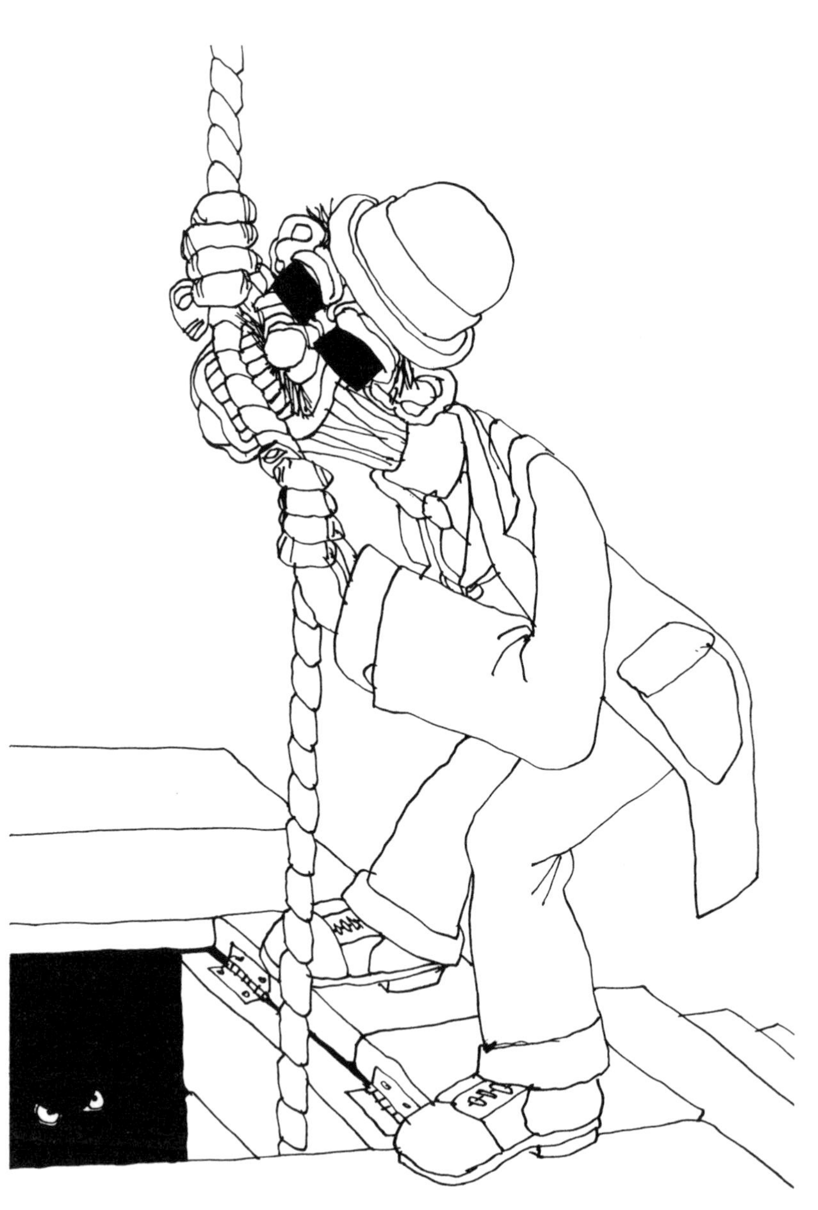

The Big Rock Candy Mountain

Andy Duncan

A RAILROAD BULL WAS IN CHARGE, of course, cane-tapping around the planks till he tripped the trap, feeling two-handed up the post to find the rope notch, hissing to himself like a slow leak.

Under the planks, six coppers were planted in a circle like fence posts. One had a bumble drilling into his shin, kicking the sawdust out behind, and another sprouted dandelions from his knobby knees. Everything grows in the Rock Candy country, even a copper's dried-out joints. I once had a toothpick bloom halfway to my mouth, and that is true, as true as the average.

Penned inside the cop ring, a little leather-faced woman in too-big overalls and a too-small porkpie hat sat in the grass, sharp chin on her knees and skinny arms wrapped around. She cussed a blue streak in a tired, raspy boy-voice, like she had wearied of it. "You withered-up hollowed-out skanktified old shits, old sons."

Me, I'd been down to the lake for a bowl of stew and was feeling belly-warm and prideful. Some miracles get stale with use and others go bad quicker than a Baptist flounder, but friends, a bowl of Big Rock stew—whether scooped from a lake or poured from a falls or welling up out of a crack in the rocks—will stay a miracle till the world looks level. So I was full of stew and full of myself when I stumbled upon the scaffold in the making. I sat beneath a cigarette tree and picked a good one and fired it up by looking at it, and, puffing, I called from the side of my mouth: "What's happening here, Muckle?"

The bull quit sniffing along the fat rope long enough to yell, "What's it look like?"—not that he knew himself, all the railroad police being blind since birth, if birth they could claim. They were all just alike, but only one came around at any given time, and he always answered to Muckle, so whether Muckle was the full-time name of an individual or a sort of migrating title like a Cherokee talking stick I'd given up wondering long before.

The setting sun flashed off Muckle's dark glasses as he sniffed his way to just the right spot. "Ahhh," he said, gnawed the rope to mark the place, and started threading it through the notch.

"What has the lady done?" I asked.

"It ain't what Dula's done, Railroad Pete," Muckle replied. "It's what Dula wants to do."

"And that would be?"

"Dula wants to." He shuddered. "Dula's trying to." He spat. "Dula's hankering to, angling to, ootching and boosting to . . . work."

"Work!" snorted the prisoner.

"Work!" groaned the coppers.

"Work!" rumbled the far-off Big Rock Candy, its glittery crystal slopes to the north for a change. The ground shimmied. The air cooled. Mr. Muckle's dickey flew up out of his Sunday vest with a ping. A dark black cloud ate the sun and rained down on us a flock of roasted ducks, burnt on one side and raw on the other.

"I ain't neither," Dula said.

"You see?" Muckle screeched. "You see what the world is coming to? Not a one of them ducks edible!" He shoved his dickey back down and straightened his celluloid collar. The bulls always dressed as if for a railroad owner's ball—I suppose to show up the rest of us stiffs. "Shrimp bushes blooming with razors, chocolate streams hardening up, ice cream turning sour before it's even out of the cow—and it's all the fault of this one, a-using around here, a-using around there, all over Hell's Half Acre, trying to talk perfectly good people into what? Into hitching the Eastbound!"

At that my cigarette lost its taste, and I put it out with a look. Heard screaming in the distance late at night, the Eastbound left your bones rattling like rails; even hearing its name at sunset was enough to give a grown man the greeny ganders. The old-timers said we'd all ridden the Eastbound to get here, and were blessed to have forgotten the details. I looked at Dula again, the set of her jaw. There was something in her face I couldn't name, something I hadn't seen in a long time.

Muckle tied the noose, his face paying no attention to his hands. They were like two crabs fighting. "There ain't no way to ride no Eastbound nohow," Muckle went on, addressing the topmost cigarette on the tree, "if you don't scheme and run and sweat and jump and climb and hide and fight and kill and that's work and to hell with it."

"Hell," groaned the coppers.

"Hell," moaned the Big Rock Candy, and blew a little airish fart. A pelter of peanuts came down, skittered off Muckle's hat brim.

"Pah! Poodle dogs," Dula muttered. "Keep on yapping, you pissant poodle dogs."

Muckle laughed like a cat getting cut the long way. No one had been hanged in the Big Rock country since the days of the one-page almanac, and he seemed to be having a high time reintroducing the custom. I'd heard many a tramp say, "Hang me if I ever work again," but I never took it, you know, for law.

I had decided to roll my own, so I snatched a paper from a passing breeze, pinched some loose tobacco off the ground, and set to work. I needed to watch that no more than Muckle needed to look at his rope ties, so I regarded the prisoner with the edge of my eye. I had identified that long-gone thing in her face. It was need. Everything a human could want lying around for the taking in the Big Rock country, and there was a face full of need. Seeing it was like climbing into a boxcar halfway between Goddamn and Nowhere and being greeted in the cattle-smelling dark by a long-gone friend, or enemy.

"Got it figured full and complete, do you, Muckle?" I asked.

"I do."

"Working is a capital offense, is it?"

"That it is, Railroad Pete."

"*Trying* to work, even?"

"So it is said. So it must be."

"Well, then, Muckle," I said, watching the little fenced-in woman watching me, "who'll be doing the honors next?"

Muckle's hands stopped, but his head swiveled on its wattled neck and trained those eyeless panes at me. I fancied I saw my cigarette reflected in those black squares, but maybe that flame wasn't on my side of the glass at all. "Whazzat?" Muckle snapped. "Honors? What honors?"

"Well, if you yourself hang this gal, then one of the coppers has to hang you next. Because all this time I've been sitting here in the shade taking my ease and smoking freeweed, you've been out there working your ass off and fixing to work even harder, hauling an easily five-stone gal, if she's a day, completely off the ground and holding her there till she's strangled dead. I call that work, and I say more stew for me."

Muckle's jaw worked away, but no sound came out. The coppers gaped, frozen in place like a prairie-dog town. I do not believe the wood in a copper stops at the hips. The Big Rock Candy heaved again, and we all got a nice dusting of powdered sugar. I knocked it off with my hat.

"But what truly gets up between my back teeth," I went on, "is this. However much work it takes you, Muckle, to hang this woman, why, it's going to take two or three times that much to hang you. So whichever copper does that job will just have to take his turn in the noose, and the copper after that, and the copper after that, and before you know it, Muckle, we'll be completely out of coppers in these parts, save one. So I'll have to do the honors on him, and then I'll have to find a passer-by to do me, and so on and so forth, and directly, why this whole country will be put plumb out of business. No, Muckle, I've studied it and studied it, and I frankly see no way out, once you've set that hellish, inexorable vortex in motion."

Coppers never talk much, but after a long, quiet time one of them rasped: "You could hang yourself, Muckle, after you do the gal, and break the cycle."

"Shut up!" Muckle said.

"We'd have to work to bury him," another copper said.

"Shut up!"

"Not if the cyclone got him," the first copper said. "The cyclone comes through here every day about five."

"We'd have to throw him in it, though, and we might miss."

"I'll do some throwing, if you don't *shut up!*"

"Maybe the gal would hang her own self."

"Hey, gal," the first copper called out. "You ain't feeling a mite sad, by any chance?"

Dula looked at me, and I looked back at her. "No, sir," she said, "feeling right as rain," and a little grape spo-de-o-dee spattered down from the sky. Some say the weather is the only thing you *can* do something about in the Big Rock country, just by thinking.

Well, the day got on, as days will, and those coppers jawed and hashed and gnawed the problem so long they took root where they were standing, and Dula just crawled out of the little thicket they had made. Bluebirds landed on their heads and sang a tune. Muckle had a hissy fit, threw down his rope, and stomped down the scaffold stairs, shaking his cane and cussing us both to a fare-thee-well.

"Well, ma'am," I told her. "I'm afraid it's the jailhouse for both of us."

We had a nice get-acquainted visit, she and I, as we led Muckle to the jailhouse, him being blind and all. We got the history out of the way early, since we couldn't remember peaturkey about our lives *before* we landed in the Big Rock country, and of course by definition nothing had happened *since*—just eating and sleeping and screwing around, and what is that to talk about? So we helped Muckle over the alky streams and the chocolate rocks and yessired him when he told us we should meditate on our sins, but we otherwise just goofed around. We laughed and laughed when we flushed a little covey of quail with bacon and fennel and buttermilk mashed potatoes, and later I blew her a smoke ring that turned into a spinning pineapple slice. She caught it on her index finger, and when she bit, the juice went everywhere.

It was a nice tin jailhouse, shining in the sun. Muckle shoved us in and slammed the door and felt around for the latch and locked it and threw away the key, which I caught and handed back to him as we came out the *other* door. "Much obliged," he muttered. "And you can just hush that laughing, Railroad Pete!" he called after us, as we strolled off nudging hips and elbows and meditating on sins yet to come. "Think you're so damn smart. Well, this troublemaker here is *your* lookout now!" Like I didn't know that already.

Sex in the Big Rock country, like all the other good things in life, is just plumb great, and we'll leave it at that. And when it's done and you roll over, right there at your elbow is a frosty mug of beer or a Cuban cigar or a straight-from-the-oven doughnut with the hot glaze sliding down. The system ain't noways Christian, but it's pretty damn workable all the same, and for a few weeks there Dula and I worked it for all it was worth.

But Dula wouldn't stop talking about the Eastbound and how to catch it, and about that fabulous land we couldn't even remember, but where—if you believed the tales—everything worth having had to be *earned,* was so hard to get, in fact, that no two people had everything the same.

"But, Dula, if that's how those poor suckers have it, why, *we're* living the life *they* dream of, right here."

"How do you know *what* they dream of? Do you remember what you dreamed of, when you were there? I don't know about you, Pete, but I damn sure wasn't dreaming about a talking mountain that strolls around firing off cherry jawbreakers."

"Woof!" huffed the Big Rock Candy.

When I woke up at night, Dula might be sitting beside me, framed by stars, stroking my face, or she might be halfway up a licorice tree, hoping to glimpse the Eastbound as it screamed by in the distance.

We fought some.

One night I woke up and sat up at the same time, all a-sweat and chilled. I'd had my first nightmare, maybe the first nightmare ever in the Big Rock country. I turned to tell Dula about it, but she was gone, and so was the memory of the dream. Only it wasn't a dream, I knew; it was my past. It was me.

"Who am I?" I said aloud.

"Who!" said the Big Rock Candy. "Whooo! Whoooooooooo!"

I got to my feet, mouth dry, and stared off toward the ridge where Dula must have gone. That wasn't the mountain's voice. That was the Eastbound, talking to *me.*

"I need to pack a bindle," I thought, and here came the memory of what a bindle was, and how I should pack it. I snatched up my blanket and shook it out and started throwing in whatever food was lying about at the time, all Bs: beluga, brie, bologna. Damn that Dula anyway. What other memories would I need before the night was through?

People that want to get around in the Big Rock country, over to Cockaigne or Lubberland or Hi-Brazil, can just walk up to one of the mail trains and sit down and lift their feet up; that's how slow those rattletraps are. Canoeing's faster, and the river runs both ways.

But the Eastbound wasn't one of those trains, and its tracks were off on the far side of the valley, nowhere near the lemonade springs, the crystal fountain, any of the sights. It was just a mile of gleaming rail running from tunnel to tunnel between two hills, with nothing to eat for a good hundred yards on either side.

You heard the whistle when the train was still miles underground, and for a half hour that sound got louder and shriller and the tunnel mouth got brighter and the gravel started dancing and the rails strummed like guitar strings and yet it was a shock when *Boom,* out of that shotgun barrel in the hill blew a big black gleaming two-header locomotive in a thunderhead of smoke and ash and sparks that burnt your eyebrows, and *Whoosh* the thing seemed to *leap* to the next tunnel where it plunged howling back into the earth for all the world like a sea monster leaving the water long enough to spout and then rolling back into the cold and the dark.

I staggered more than ran through the no-chow zone because the ground was shaking so. The two-header had already gone down, and the cars were zooming by—blinds with one side door, open gondolas, insulated reefers locked up tight. No snatching hold of this train as it passed; only your arm would swing aboard. The only way was from above. And there was Dula just where I feared—a little white smudge in the night perched on the lip of the second tunnel, looking down on the train rushing by. I ran for her and screamed her name just as she let go and dropped into one of the gondolas and not thinking I kept running up the slope into the hanging black cloud that the two-header had vomited and I choked and plunged through to the crumbling brick edge of the mouth and here came three empty gondolas in a row, maybe the last ones I'd get. I took the last big step and couldn't hear myself scream as I hit the moving floor, tumbled, slammed into the oncoming wall. Man hit twice by train, lives. I was crumpled and hurting but I was—what was the phrase—I was *holding her down.* The train hadn't shaken me yet. I rode her, I held her down, as she rolled beneath the surface of the world.

I woke up on hot greasy metal beneath the stars, pine trees whipping past. My arms and legs and fingers and head all felt awful when I moved them, but they moved. I sat up, found my bindle, sipped water, gnawed bologna. Dula had to be twenty, thirty cars up, toward the engine. But how could I know for sure? A drop into the gondola of a speeding train is pure luck. You could drop between the cars or hit the deck of a boxcar instead. And how did I know *that?*

I tied my bindle around my waist, climbed the gondola's forward wall, looked down. Good. Steel bumpers, no need to ride the coupler this time. I eased myself onto the bumper, gauged the rocking of the blind next door, then made the jump easy. Every car has its niches and platforms and handholds, for the sake of the yardmen, but between yards they have their uses, too.

I worked my way forward along the train, up and over when I could, or around the sides. My parts complained, but they did what I asked, started reaching and stepping *before* I asked. I had done this before, many times, and I could do it again and again.

No wonder the Eastbound was so fast. Car after car as I clambered along held no cargo at all. But the train wasn't empty. Not by a long shot. And I recognized just about everybody I came upon—not individual faces, but I knew their types well.

One car was full of fakers, working by lantern light on their little doodads they sucker people with. One punched holes in a sheet of tin with a nail; one pounded two bricks together and scraped the dust into paper packets; the bearded one whittled. I said no to lamp brighteners and love powders and splinters from William Jennings Bryan's church pew, but before I moved on I tossed them a couple of sinkers—as good as money when playing seven-up in a blind at night.

In the corner of another car sat two cripples, one with a pinned-up jacket sleeve, one with a strapped-on peg leg. Like all cripples who meet on the rails, they were swapping tales about the day they didn't move fast enough. They talked at once, stories sliding past each other on parallel tracks.

"I heard it go into the bucket, I did. Made a little clang like a chicken foot."

"There was three swallows of whiskey left in the bottle, and when I woke up, the doc said I could have the rest, and he didn't charge me any more than what I had in my pockets."

"I lifted it, and foot and bucket and all wasn't nearly as heavy as the foot was many a long day."

"I still reach for things with it, and sometimes the candle or bottle falls over, so a ghost hand can do that much, anyway."

"I buried it behind the Kansas City roundhouse where it's soft, 'cause I was told otherwise it wouldn't rest easy and would itch me forever. It don't itch, but that big toe still aches something fierce when the weather comes up a . . ."

In midsentence the two cripples stopped talking and started unwrapping their clothes to compare stumps, and I headed on. Some things, even in a boxcar, are just too private to watch.

Whenever I reached a gondola, I tossed in my bindle and swung over the wall, hoping to raise Dula, but time and again I had no show. All were empty until I tossed my bindle practically on top of a half dozen tramps sitting in a circle around a mushed candle. As I climbed in, they stared at me and didn't move. One held a jug ready to pour into the glass bottle held by a dough-faced old gal.

"No more!" she squawked, and the whole alky gang tensed to spring.

"I'm not thirsty," I said, quick. "Don't study about me. Just looking for a girl who dropped from a tunnel, that's all."

"No girl here! Not here!"

They stared at me some more. The old gal, satisfied, broke off looking and grunted to the stiff with the jug. He sloshed a little something into her wide-neck bottle, and she swirled it about. Another little slosh and swirl, and he stoppered the jug. They all leaned forward slack-mouthed, watching the old gal take one tee-ninchy sip from the bottle and sigh and pass it on. The water jug would cut it farther and farther around the circle till they were drinking the very memory of gin, and it would be time to go into town and raise another bottle or cup or dreg-drop of the stuff.

As the bottle went round they said a verse, taking turns at that, too.

"Sweet, sweet gin."

"Let us in."

"Sweet, sweet white."

"Light the night."

"Sweet, sweet booze."

"Tell the news."

"Throw my feet to the barroom seat."

"Gin is sweet."

Between that car and the next I crouched on the coupler and took a couple of swigs from my flask, holding the water in my cheeks and letting it seep down my throat slow. I punched the stopper three times with the side of my fist to jam it in good. Many a stiff has gone alky for lack of water.

After that I got more careful about just stepping in without an invite.

Sometimes I couldn't go over, and I couldn't go around. So I went under. It's a decent enough crawl space down there, only it's deafening loud and the sides are moving and there's nothing to crawl on but trusses and rods. I wasn't proud; I rode the trusses. But then I hit a car with no trusses, so I made like a veteran, and rode the rods.

Beneath the car and running its length was a suspended iron rod, with maybe a foot and a half of space between it and the floor above. Once again, I knew this, and knew the technique. I eased myself onto the rod until I lay full length, hands gripping the rod ahead, legs locked around the rod behind. I inchwormed forward and felt I was flying, like a witch on a broom.

Lying facedown, I knew the tracks whipped past a foot away. I couldn't see them in the pitchy black, as dense and solid as a wall. Staring at that wall like a banished child made me want to reach out, to test it with my hand, so to resist the temptation I lifted my head and looked forward, into wind like a hot greasy hand covering my face.

By turning my head to the left and sticking my neck out a little I could snatch enough outside breaths to keep from smothering, but I couldn't keep that up because it hurt my balance and because my eyes naturally focused on the most distant parts of the moonlit landscape, the parts that were moving hardly at all, as if I could just lift my topmost foot and step into them and walk away. That meant time to look down again.

I was facedown when the roaring changed tone and the stars came out below me. I gasped and was nearly gone, but my hands and feet remembered. The train was crossing a river, and as the ties of the trestle whipped past I saw through them to the water below. Then all was black and close again.

Halfway down the rod. So far, so good. We plowed through an awful smell, gone before I could gag. Something dead on the tracks. Why in the world, people reading the paper always asked, would even a drunk lie down on the tracks?

My legs and arms ached. The vibration of the rod had roiled my stomach. My teeth hurt from chattering. Not much farther.

Then I heard a new sound up ahead, against the roar of the underside. Nothing regular, just a higgledy-piggledy pinging and clanking, like a youngun tossing pennies into a train.

I had no idea what it was, but it scared me to death. I couldn't move forward, toward that noise. I lay frozen, twined around the rod, staring into the blackness ahead.

The sound getting louder, closer. Pang, ping, thonk. No rhythm at all. It was the sound of someone going mad.

Up ahead, little flickers, like fireflies. No, sparks. Flashing up first here, then there—

Then I remembered.

Back! Back!

I shinnied backward along the rod as fast as I could go. It wasn't very fast.

Someone perched at the front of the car was playing out beneath it a length of rope with a five-pound coupling pin at the end. The sounds, the sparks—those were the pin ricocheting off the wheels, the ties, the bottom of the car. A one-bullet crossfire. An old brakeman's trick to clear the undercarriage of tramps, if you can call murder a trick.

The pin lunged forward a foot at a time. Backward I inched, and inched, along a rod that was endless, beneath a car that lengthened above me like a telescope.

I inched, gasping. I tasted dust and metal filings. Kicked-up gravel cut my face.

Which would it be?

Wait for the coupling pin in the teeth?

Or just let go, and let the railbed carry me away?

My foot hit the plate at the end of the rod.

I grabbed the corner strut, one hand at a time. I brought the legs over, one at a time. I squirmed around, got head and shoulders out, grabbed the bottommost outside handhold, hauled myself out and up and onto the bumper. It wasn't easy. I sat on the bumper, worn out, shaking, happy for now to be rocked between the cars. I wasn't alone. Someone sat on the opposite bumper, facing me, rocking left when I rocked right, like a reflection. That car was a gondola, and I now saw there was a light inside it, a glow that got brighter above the wall until it crested, blinding, like the sunrise. Someone holding a lantern. I saw now the figure opposite was Dula, bound and gagged and trussed to the braces. She squirmed and kicked her feet. The man holding the lantern shouted:

"Well, butter my ass and call me a biscuit! It's the one that got away. Swam right off the hook again, eh, Railroad Pete? Proud of you, son. You've proven yourself, you've passed the test. You're home."

They clambered in till the boxcar was packed slam full of stiffs—alkys, fakers, tramps of every shape and description, jostling one another as they rocked with the walls and floor. Even the cripples, who don't do a lot of traveling between cars, were swung down from the deck in a sort of bucket. They lurched straight to the corner and picked up their conversation. Only a few of the stiffs sat near enough the lantern to be seen, but I sure hoped they were the worst of the lot. Each was big and mean and looked like he'd taken a few coupling pins in the face. They stared at the boss man like dogs waiting for scraps to fall. I figured that scrap was me.

The boss man was the highest class of stiff. He was a profesh. He wore a shiny black suit and a black shirt and a black tie and sharp black shoes and a snap-brim black hat with a black band and black horn-rimmed eyeglasses held together with black tape. Instead of sitting directly on the filthy floor, he sat on crumpled newspaper, and the edges floated up and down like slow wings in the gusts from beneath the boxcar door.

"Why, Pete," he said. "Don't tell me you don't know your old pal, your helper in time of trouble. You taught me all the rules of the road, how to ride at the top of the heap."

I sat across the lantern from him. Next to me was Dula, still bound and gagged and watching me like I was supposed to do something. I still had my bindle at my waist, so I could have a snack, I reckon, but I didn't see how that would help.

"I don't know you, mister," I said, just stalling for time. And it was true, though he did look kind of familiar, in the same vague way the others had.

"Why, I'm a profesh now, Pete, just like you. Aren't you proud?"

"I'm no profesh."

"Not on this train, no," he said. "Only one profesh per train, and that's me."

He made a move with his hand like shooing a fly, and everyone in the boxcar, from the up-front uglies to the shadows in the corners, moved closer, knives and chains and brass knucks clicking and clacking like money, or better than money. A profesh never travels alone; that's how you know he's profesh.

"Meet the guys," he said. "Meet the gals. They climb aboard, they find their way to me, and the survivors, they join up. You know how it is, Pete. Why, it's the best job available on a moving train at night, for a man who knows the score, who knows who he is. The best opportunity and, indeed, the last."

"What sort of job?" I asked. "What do they do?"

The profesh tilted his head, slowly. His voice was velvet. "They mow the lawn," he said. "They park the cars when the Astors come to tea. They do things." He made a two-handed chopping motion in the air.

"Must be hard to get good help," I said.

"Oh, there's no shortage, Pete. Didn't this train strike you as sort of, well, crowded?" He stood and paced in the lantern light. "That's how it is on a train, Pete, when people keep getting on, month after month, every stop on every line, and no one—*practically* no one, Pete—ever escapes. Think of it, Pete. Every bindle stiff, boomchaser, team-skinner, shovel bum and tong bucker, every last ring-tail tooter the whole long rusty length of the Southern P., the Central P., the U.P., the U.T.L., the C.F.T., the C.F.X., everybody and his dog from every blown-away greasewood sagebrush town thinks El Dorado and Hollywood and Daylong Screw, Nevada, are just a toot-toot train ride away." He stopped, too close, looking down at me. "And the Big Rock Candy Mountain is further, even, than those. But not quite out of reach. Is it, Pete?" When I didn't answer, he kept walking. "Last time I saw you, Pete, it was somewhere past midnight, on a fast freight from Ogden to Carson City, and we shared a boxcar, just the two of us. You'd been pretty sick, and when you finally got to sleep, I sat against the door, for fear you'd wake up wild in the night, and step out. I did not sleep, Pete. Instead, I sharpened your brass knucks, hoping to please you when you awoke. I did not sleep, the door did not open, and no one and nothing passed me. Yet when I looked up from my razor and file, I was alone in that boxcar. And I never saw you or heard tell of you again—until tonight."

I didn't remember any of that, but so what? It was no crazier than the truth of where I'd been. I didn't like the way Dula was looking at me. I said nothing.

"All these years since, Pete, I have been riding the rails, holding her down in your absence, without your help, sucking smoke and eating skeeter stew, and I have watched. And waited. And studied the scraps of newspaper that blew in during a full moon, and the chalk marks on fences and walls that no one recognizes, and squeezed old-timers for stories of ghost trains and forgotten railways and phantoms on the tracks and crowded boxcars that were empty on arrival. I've done all that, Pete, all that and worse, and never got one station, one division, one rod closer to the Big Rock Candy—until tonight." He crouched, just in the edge of the lantern light. "Now, tell me something, Pete. Tell me one thing—no, two things—and we'll let you both off at the next stop, no hard feelings, no more questions asked. Where have you been? And how did you get there?"

"Suppose I don't know?" I asked.

"Then you get out and get under. And she joins us all for the rest of the night, and repeatedly, until we're done. Sort of an employee benefit." He pulled a barber's razor from his jacket, toyed with it in his fingers. "So," he asked brightly, "how's the Big Rock stew? Good as they say? Cure what ails you?"

I don't know why I did it. Maybe I was just stalling some more. But in the same way it felt right, somehow, to go up and over that first gondola car, it felt right to pull out my bindle, toss it onto the floor, and kick it toward him.

"Taste for yourself," I said.

He sat motionless for so long that I got worried and thought Pete, your time has come. Then he shot out a hand and snatched up the bindle, slit it with one pass of the razor, and dumped everything onto the floor. His face fell.

"There's no stew here," he said, as if to himself. "Bananas . . . beets . . ." He pushed things around with the razor. He pinched and sniffed and opened jars. "Whew! That's some high-smelling cheese. And what the hell is this? *Fish* eggs? Damn." He started to giggle, a high-pitched sound I didn't care for at all. "I'll cut you for this, Pete, I swear I will, and the girl, too. I'll pass my razor to the cripples, they got plenty of experience." He speared the half-stick of bologna, held it up. "Bologna? *This* I couldn't get in any mom-and-pop in Tucum-fucking-cari?"

"Taste it," I repeated, because it still felt right, somehow.

The profesh stared at me, brought the bologna to his nose, sniffed. Sniffed again. He got interested, sawed off a hunk, nibbled it. Everyone strained forward. How long, I wondered, since they'd all eaten? The profesh chewed slowly, then more quickly, began to smile. He stuffed the whole wedge into his mouth, worked it while he cut another. "This isn't bologna," he muttered. "It tastes like . . . like . . ." He dropped the razor, lifted the stick to his face, and began to tear into it with his teeth. "The taste! Oh, my God!" He chomped and slurped and slobbered, cheeks and chin smeary with bologna grease.

His followers, excited, stood and yelled and demanded their share. What no one seemed to notice but me was that the train wasn't rocking nearly so much, the racket outside wasn't nearly so loud. This train was rolling to a stop.

While the profesh danced the bologna jig, the braver ones snatched up the other things, began their own slurping and gnawing. Then they danced, too, whooping and carrying on and shouting hallelujah.

"It's true!" the profesh yelled. "It's true!"

Now, stopping a train is a funny thing. An engine starts slowing down miles before the station, and it's going no faster than a walk when it pulls in, but at some point, that engine has got to finally stop dead. And when it does, all those hundreds of tons of steel, in all that rolling stock strung out for miles behind, collide. A fifty-car train stopping is like fifty little train wrecks in the space of a second. And if you're standing on board that train, not expecting the jolt, and you're not braced . . .

I braced—one hand on the door handle, the other arm around Dula.

Bang!

The profesh and two-thirds of the stiffs in that boxcar went flying, and I lunged forward, grabbed the razor, and cut Dula's ropes before most of them landed. I wrenched the door open and we both rolled out. I landed on hard-packed dirt, and she landed on me, mostly. We scrambled up, and ran.

The place looked like a thousand other deserted rail yards—handcars and crates, sidings and turntables, a wooden-staved water tank with only the *H* still legible, and all of it gray upon gray upon gray in the hour before dawn. We would never outrun them, once they sorted themselves out, but where could we go? Someone had to be around, however early. But all we passed were closed doors and dark windows. I stumbled once, twice. I started coughing.

Behind us the profesh screamed: "We're finally here!"

The farther I ran, the worse my coughing got. I lagged behind. I stumbled, staggered, leaned against a wall. At eye level, some hobo had chalked weird, unfamiliar signs onto the stone.

"What's wrong?"

I couldn't answer. My throat burned. My mouth tasted of copper. I bent double coughing. My drool was red in the dirt.

The profesh was right. I had been sick, powerful sick, when I landed in the Big Rock country. And now that I had left it . . .

"Go on," I said. "I'm killed already."

I found myself staring at the hobo signs—stick men, houses, arrows, circles.

"No," she said, and tried to pull me along.

The profesh ran around the corner, whooping and hollering and tearing off his clothes, eyeglasses and all. "I'll beat everybody to the lemonade springs!" he yelled. At the end of a long trail of clothes, he leaped headlong into the dirt and wallowed, barking like a seal.

I could read those signs. Of course I could. I had chalked them there in the first place.

I remembered everything.

"Dula. Those eyeglasses. And his jacket. Get them. Please."

She did. I put them on. They fit fine. For the first time, I could see the wrinkles at the corners of Dula's eyes, and the tears welling up. I plucked the razor out of the dirt where I had dropped it. It had been mine, years ago. It still felt good in my hand.

"There they are!"

The whole pack of stiffs, the uglies in the lead, came charging around the building on both sides. They all pulled up short when they saw my new clothes, my eyes, the look in my face. Swallowing another coughing jag, chest about to split, I stepped away from the wall, braced my feet, tossed the razor from hand to hand, and tried to stare them all down.

"How dare you," I whispered. Louder: "How dare you." With all the air my rattling bloody lungs could muster, I roared: "How dare you abandon me—for that!" I thrust my finger at the poor crazy profesh, then at the writing on the wall. "This is the place where I was crowned! I am Railroad Pete, and I am the King of the Tramps!"

Dead silence.

The old alky hag was the first to drop to her knees.

A second. A third.

Then, one by one, the rest. Wails and moans went up. Many lay facedown in the dirt.

"Mercy, Pete!"

"We didn't know you!"

"Help us!"

I felt a wave of dizziness, of weakness. My rattling breath was getting louder. It was like I was drowning inside.

Only the biggest, meanest-looking ugly was left standing. A badly stitched scar split his bald head like a one-track railroad. He stepped forward.

"You weren't so biggedy," he rumbled, "when I went fishing with this." He pulled from his moldy overcoat a rusty coupling pin.

I couldn't hold back the coughs anymore. I hacked and spat and bent double, lost my balance, dropped to my knees myself.

The ugly showed all the gaps in his teeth and stepped forward, swinging the thick end of the pin like a club.

"Well, this will be easy," he said. "Long live the king."

"No!" Dula screamed.

I gurgled.

Then someone screeched, in a voice like a rusty handcar:

"Alms! Alms, gentlemen! Alms for the poor and blind!"

Coupling-Pin whirled.

Tap-tap-tapping through the crowd was Muckle, cane in one hand, tip cup in the other.

Coupling-Pin raised a hand, as if Muckle could see it through those black lenses. "Back off, you old bastard. Hit the grit, or you'll get what he's getting."

"Oh, a troublemaker, eh?" Muckle said. Ignoring Coupling-Pin, he tapped over to where I lay crumpled and gasping. People in the crowd were getting up. An upside-down giant, Muckle loomed over me. He prodded me with the cane. He ratcheted himself down on one knee, joints popping, and scuttled his fingers over my face. "Oh, my goodness, yes, I know this one. He's from my side of the tracks." He struggled back up, leaning on his cane. No one offered to help. "Yes, he's a bad one and a hard case, all right," said Muckle, rubbing his hip. "One of our hardest."

"I'll fix him for you, Pops," said Coupling-Pin, stepping forward.

There was a sound like a mosquito, and then Muckle's cane was just *there,* in midair. The ugly stopped just shy of his neck hitting it, eyes big and breath held, like he'd nearly run up on barbed wire at night.

"One of *ours,* I repeat," Muckle said. The cane in his outstretched hand didn't waver a hair. "And he'll be dealt with by *us,* by me and my kin—and not by a turd like you."

The ugly whipped the coupling-pin around and harder than you'd hit a steer in a slaughterhouse slammed the blind man in the back of the head.

Muckle's glasses flew off. He hunched forward, naked face all squinched up, so many wrinkles between hairline and nose it was hard to find the two closed eyes.

No sign of blood.

No sign of damage.

He hadn't even let go of the cane.

The ugly looked at Muckle, at the pin in his hand, at Muckle again. The ugly's mouth was open.

Everyone's mouth was open.

Muckle slowly stood upright, eyes still closed but face relaxed, no longer looking hurt but just annoyed.

Everyone stepped back with a wordless sound of interest, a sort of *Hmm,* the sound a tramp makes when he sees the chalk for "Get out quick."

Muckle turned to face the crowd, wrinkly eyes still closed.

I told Dula, "Don't look."

Muckle reached up with his free hand, dug his fingers into his face, and, hauling on the skin by main force, opened his eyes.

Everyone screamed.

The screams faded away quick, like the whistle of a fast mail.

After a while I figured it was safe to open my eyes, too. The yard was empty except for Muckle and Dula and me, but there was a whole lot of dust in the air, like after a stampede.

Between the chalked wall and a rain barrel, his back to us, knelt Muckle, sliding his hands through the rubbish and weeds. His hands stopped. He grunted. He had found his glasses. He wiped them against his lapel and carefully put them on, hooked each shank over its proper ear. He stood and turned toward us, his face horribly twisted, and Dula and I held each other. His jaw clenched and dropped and clenched again and his eyebrows rode up and down and he squinched his nose.

"Goddamn things never sit right, once they get bent," Muckle said, and made another adjustment with the side of his mouth.

Next I remember, I hung off a deck, coughing red onto the gravel far below. Something was wrong with the gravel. I could see every little piece of it. It wasn't moving.

Muckle was holding me over the edge while I got it all out. We were on top of a train in the deserted yard. What little air I could squeeze into my curdled liver and lights was being cut off by my collar, knotted like a noose in long bony fingers.

"He'll be all right, won't he?" Dula called up from the yard below.

"Don't you start worrying about him *now,*" Muckle said, "after all the trouble you caused him and the Big Rock country too. Ever since he hopped the Eastbound. Streams running vinegar. Potatoes you got to dig up. Hens laying eggs what ain't even cooked. Biggest mess I ever heard tell of, on our side of the tracks. Last straw, the Big Rock Candy itself shut down. Wouldn't do nothing but peep like a chicken. Turns out it was saying, 'Pete! Pete!' Why you think we've all been out beating the bushes? Humph! But don't you fret none, he'll be fit as a fiddlehead soon as he gets back to where there ain't no *Mycobacterium tuberculosis* running around. Spit it out, son! There you go. But as for *you,* little missy—you are banished from the Big Rock country for good!"

"Well, la-de-da," Dula hollered. "That's hard news, considering I just about killed myself getting shut of the place."

I reached down a hand. "I'll miss you, Dula," I croaked out. "I'd stay here with you, really I would, if it wasn't fatal."

She stood on tiptoe and laced her fingers into mine. "Take it easy, Railroad Pete, King of the No-Count Bums. You found out who you are. Now it's my turn." She tugged away her hand. "No, Pete, I ain't gonna watch you go. It's bad luck. Go to hell, Muckle."

"You, too, honey," Muckle said with a wave of his cane.

I plucked at the edge of the roof for purchase, but the slipping was all in my mind. My view of Dula walking away was going black from the outside in, like the last picture in a Chaplin movie, right before "The End."

Muckle hocked and spat a big looey past my head. Where it splatted sprang up a purple orchid. Then Muckle snatched me from the brink and flung me to the middle of the deck like I was made of shucks.

The train jerked forward with a rusty screech. As the couplers pulled taut, a series of slams vibrated along the cars and through my sprawled body on the way to the caboose.

"You're off and rolling now, Pete," Muckle said, as we crawled beneath the water tank. He reached up, grabbed the long spout, and lifted his feet. As the groaning spout slowly swung him away, he called out: "I'll see you later, when you ain't such a mess. Right now, you're a damn sight too much like work."

Nothing special, this train, just a rattletrap old local, cars all mismatched, big letters on the sides that might spell something if hooked up right. I never saw a train you could actually read. The cars screeched and banged, and I held her down, sprawled on top, watching as the yard disappeared. It had been deserted, but as the train picked up speed, tramps sprouted from everywhere, in ones and twos and threes, scrambled from rain barrels and woodpiles and dropped from the water tank and slid down the side of the cut and ran silently alongside, tossing their bindles aboard and then making the leap and clambering on wherever they could. As we went into the cut and around the bend, three dozen shirttail-flapping tramps hung onto the boxes, every one of them my people. Up ahead, against the rising sun, was a pyramid better than fifty feet high, a sight known to every tramp in the West. It was the Ames Monument, the highest point on the U.P., all downhill from here.

*

Three months, two weeks, and four days after my return—for it was high time *someone* counted the days in the Big Rock country—I was sitting halfway up the slope of the mountain taking the air and making plans, when a cinnamon-smelling westerly wind sprang up and the photograph sailed into me, *flap!*

I peeled it off my chest. Beneath a neon sign that said AUTOMAT, Dula stood on the corner, hands on hips, dressed like a four-alarmer, from the red silk fascinator with silver webbing that wrapped her head to the single-seam stockings that must have cost $2.50—look out!—$2.75 a leg. On the back of the picture were a dried, wipe-sideways stain that smelled like spaghetti and a few lines of chicken scratch with a penny pencil.

> *Hi Pete The wind seems right today so Im throwing this off the Brooklyn Bridge hoping you get it I hope so Hows the weather Just kidding This aint no Paradise but it's still amazing what you can find just walking around Do you know the trains here got windows and seats too What will they think of next Take it easy Railroad Pete but take it—Dula—New York street New York town New York state New York everything N.Y., N.Y., N.Y., N.Y.*

Maybe I'd send a reply one day. Lace it into a shoe and drop it into the Eastbound at the tunnel, then wait for a howdy-do back to bubble up out of the stew.

I yanked a leg off a turkey bush and said aloud, by way of grace: "The day I do that will be a no-fooling strange day."

If it was easy to send word back from the Rock Candy country, why, everyone would do it, wouldn't they? And if I *could* send word, who says it wouldn't get all messed up on the way to N.Y., N.Y., N.Y., N.Y.? Just hobo signs on a wall. She wouldn't know what she was reading, what she had.

Mmm. Juicy. With a little cornbread dressing in the middle.

No, there's plenty to keep me busy right here. Got to get this place organized. Many an opportunity in the Rock Candy country, I see now, for a profesh who knows who he is.

Looky there on the ground—cranberry sauce. In a little shivery puddle with a spoon in it, Betty Boop on the handle of the spoon. All I have to do is reach out my hand.

"Boop!" said the Big Rock Candy, and peppermints peckled from the barber-striped sky.

From Knight
Gene Wolfe

The Ruined Town

The sun woke me. I still remember how warm it felt, and how good it was to be warm like that, and away from the sound of other people's voices and all the work and worry of other people's lives, the things the string kept telling me about; I must have lain in the sun for an hour before I got up.

I was hungry and thirsty when I did. Rainwater caught by a broken fountain tasted wonderful. I drank and drank; and when I straightened up, there was a knight watching me, a tall, big-shouldered man in chain mail. His helm kept me from seeing his face, but there was a black dragon on top of his helm that glared at me, and black dragons on his shield and surcoat. He began to fade as soon as I saw him, and in a couple of seconds the wind blew away what was left. It was a long time before I found out who he was, so I am not going to say anything about that here; but I do want to say something else and it will go here as well as anywhere.

That world is called Mythgarthr. I did not learn it till later, but there is no reason you should not know it now. Parka's cave was not completely there, but between Mythgarthr and Aelfrice. Bluestone Island is entirely in Mythgarthr, but before I drank the water I was not. Or to write down the exact truth, I was not securely there. That is why the knight came when he did; he wanted to watch me drinking that water. "Good lord!" I said, but there was no one to hear me.

He had scared me. Not because I thought I might be seeing things, but because I had thought I was alone. I kept looking behind me. It is no bad habit, Ben, but there was nobody there.

On the east side of the island the cliffs were not so steep. I found a few mussels and ate them raw. The sun was overhead when two fishermen came close enough to yell at. I did, and they rowed over. They wanted to know if I would help with the nets if they took me on board; I promised I would, and climbed over the gunwale. "How'd you get out there alone?" the old one wanted to know.

I wanted to know that myself, and how come they talked funny, but I said, "How would anybody get out there?" and they seemed willing to leave it at that. They split their bread and cheese with me, and a fish we cooked over a fire in a box of sand. I did not know, but that was when I started loving the sea.

At sunset, they offered me my choice of the fish we had caught for my help. I told the young one (not a lot older than me) that I would take it and share with his family if his wife would cook it, because I had no place to stay. That was okay, and when our catch had been sold, we carried the best fish and some others that had not sold into a crowded little house maybe twenty steps from the water.

After dinner we told stories, and when it was my turn I said, "I've never seen a ghost, unless what I saw today was one. So I'll tell you about that, even if it won't scare anybody like the ghost in Scaur's story. Because it's all I've got."

Everyone seemed agreeable; I think they had heard each other's stories more than once.

"Yesterday I found myself on a certain rocky island not far from here where there used to be a tower—"

"It was Duke Indign's," said Scaur, and his wife, Sha. "Bluestone Castle."

"I spent the night in the garden," I continued, "because I had something to do there, a seed I had to plant. You see, somebody important had told me to plant a seed, and I hadn't known what she meant until I found seeds in here." I showed them the pouch.

"You chopped down a spiny orange," Sha's grandfather wheezed; he pointed to my bow. "You cut a spiny orange, and you got to plant three seeds, young man. If you don't the Mossmen'll get you."

I said I had not known that.

He spat in the fire. "Folks don't, not now, and that's why there's not hardly no spiny oranges left. Best wood there is. You rub flax oil on it, hear? That'll protect it from the weather."

He held out his hand for my bow, and I passed it to him. He gave it to Scaur. "You break her, son. Break her 'cross your knee."

Scaur tried. He was strong and bent my bow nearly double but it did not break.

"See? You can't. Can't be broke." Sha's grandfather cackled as Scaur returned my bow to me. "There's not but one fruit on a spiny orange most times, and not but three seeds in it. You chop down the tree and you got to plant them in three places, else the Mossmen'll come for you."

"Go on, Able," Sha said, "tell us about the ghost."

"This morning I decided to plant the first seed in the garden of Bluestone Castle," I told them. "There was a stone bowl there that held water, and I decided I would plant the seed first and scoop up water for it. When it seemed to me I had watered it enough, I would drink what was left."

They nodded.

"I dug a little hole with my knife, dropped a seed into it, replaced the earth—which was pretty damp already—and carried water for the seed in my hands. When there was standing water in the hole, I drank and drank from the bowl, and when I looked up I saw a knight standing there watching me. I couldn't see his face, but he had a big green shield with a dragon on it."

"That wasn't Duke Indign," Scaur remarked, "his badge was the blue boar."

"Did you speak to him?" Sha wanted to know. "What did he say?"

"I didn't. It happened so fast and I was too surprised. "He—he turned into a sort of cloud, then he disappeared altogether."

"Clouds are the breath of the lady," Sha's grandfather remarked.

I asked who that was, but he only shook his head and looked into the fire.

She said, "Don't you know her name can't be spoken?"

In the morning I asked the way to Griffinsford, but Scaur said there was no town of that name thereabout.

"Then what's the name of this one?" I asked.

"Irringsmouth," said Scaur.

"I think there's an Irringsmouth near where I live," I told him. Really I was not sure, but I thought it was something like that. "It's a big city, though. The only really big city I've been to."

"Well, this is the only Irringsmouth around here," Scaur said. A passerby who heard us said, "Griffinsford is on the Griffin," and walked away before I could ask him anything.

"That's a stream that flows into our river," Scaur told me. "Go south till you come to the river, and take the River Road and you'll find it."

So I set out with a few bites of salt fish wrapped in a clean cloth, south along the little street behind the wattle house where Scaur and Sha lived, south some more on the big street it led to, and east on the high road by the river. It went through a gap without a gate in the wrecked city wall, and out into the countryside, through woods of young trees where patches of snow were hanging on in the shadows and square pools of rainwater waited for somebody to come back.

After that, the road wound among hills, where two boys older than I was said they were going to rob me. One had a staff and the other one an arrow ready—"at the nock" is how we say it here. The nock is the cut for the string. I said they could have anything I had except my bow. As I ought to have expected, they tried to take it. I held on, and got hit with the staff. After that I fought, taking my bow away from them and beating them with it. Maybe I should have been afraid, but I was not. I was angry with them for thinking they could hit me without being hit back. The one with the staff dropped it and ran; and I beat the other until he fell down, then sat on his chest and told him I was going to cut his throat.

He begged for mercy, and when I let him up he ran too, leaving his bow and quiver behind. The bow looked nice, but when I bent it over my knee it snapped. I saved the string, and slung the quiver on my back. That night I scraped away at my own bow until it needed nothing but a bath in flax oil, and put his string on it.

After that I walked with an arrow at the nock myself. I saw rabbits and squirrels, and even deer, more than once; I shot, but all I did was lose a couple of arrows until the last day. That morning, so hungry I was weak, I shot a grouse and went looking for a fire. I had a long search and almost gave up on finding any that day and ate it raw; but as evening came, I saw wisps of smoke above the treetops, white as specters against the sky. When the first stars were out, I found a hut half buried in wild violets. It was of sticks covered with hides; and its door was the skin of a deer. Since I could not knock on that, I coughed; and when coughing brought nobody, I knocked on the sticks of the frame.

"*Who's there!*" rang out in a way that sounded like the man who said it was ready to fight.

"A fat grouse," I said. A fight was the last thing I wanted.

The hide was drawn back, and a stooped and shaking man with a long beard looked out. His hand trembled; so did his head, but there was no tremor in his voice when he boomed, "Who are you?"

"Just a traveler who'll share his bird for your fire," I said.

"Nothing here to steal," the bearded man said, and held up a cudgel.

"I haven't come to rob you, only to roast my grouse. I shot and plucked it this morning, but I had no fire to cook it and I'm starved."

"Come in then." He stepped out of the doorway. "You can cook it if you'll save a piece for me."

"I'll give you more than that," I told him, and I was as good as my word: I gave him both wings and both thighs. He asked no more questions but looked at me so closely, staring and turning away, that I told him my name and age, explained that I was a stranger in his state, and asked him how to get to Griffinsford.

"Ah, the curse of it! That was my village, stripling, and sometimes I go there still to see it. But nobody lives in Griffinsford these days."

I felt that could not be true. "My brother and I do."

The bearded man shook his trembling head. "Nobody at all. Nobody's left."

I knew then that the name of our town had not been Griffinsford. Perhaps it was Griffin—or Griffinsburg or something like that. But I could not remember.

"They looked up to me," the bearded man muttered. "Some wanted to run, but I said no. Stay and fight, I said. If there's too many giants, we'll run, but we've got to try their mettle first."

I had noticed the word *giants,* and wondered what might come next.

"Schildstarr was their leader. I had my father's tall house in those days. Not like this. A big house with a half loft under the high roof and little rooms behind the big one. A big stone fireplace, too, and a table big enough to feed my friends."

"I nodded, thinking of houses I had seen in Irringsmouth.

"Schildstarr wasn't my friend, but he could've got into my house. Inside, he'd have had to stand like I do now."

"You fought them?"

"Aye. For my house? My fields and Gerda? Aye! I fought, though half run when we saw them comin' down the road. Killed one with my spear and two with my axe. They fall like trees, stripling." For a moment his eyes blazed.

"A stone . . ." He fingered the side of his head, and looked much older. "Don't know who struck me, or what it was. A stone? Don't know. Put your hand there, stripling. Feel under my hair."

His hair was thick, dark gray hair that was just about black. I felt and jerked my hand away.

"Tormented after. Water and fire. Know it? It's what they like best. Took us to a pond and built fires all round it. Drove us into the water like cattle. Threw brands at us till we drowned. All but me. What's your name, stripling?"

I told him again.

"Able? Able. That was my brother's name. Years and years ago, that was."

I knew it was not my real name, but Parka had said to use it. I asked his name.

"Found a water rat's hole," he said. "Duck and dig, come up to breathe, and the brands, burnin' and hissin'. Lost count of the duckins and the burns, but didn't drown. Got my head up into the water rat's house and breathed in there. Waited till the Angrborn thought we was all dead and went away."

I nodded, feeling like I had seen it.

"Tried to climb out, but my shadow slipped. Fell back into the pond. Still there." The bearded man shook his head. "Dreams? Not dreams. In that pond still, and the brands whizzing at me. Tryin' to climb out. Slippery, and . . . and fire in my face."

"If I slept here tonight," I suggested, "I could wake you if you had a bad dream."

"Schildstarr," the bearded man muttered. "Tall as a tree, Schildstarr is. Skin like snow. Eyes like a owl. Seen him pick up Baldig and rip his arms off. Could show you where. You really going to Griffinsford, Able?"

"Yes," I said. "I'll go tomorrow, if you'll tell me the way."

"Go too," the bearded man promised. "Haven't been this year. Used to go all the time. Used to live there."

"That'll be great," I said. "I'll have somebody to talk to, somebody who knows the way. My brother will have been mad at me, I'm pretty sure, but he'll be over that by now."

"No, no," the bearded man mumbled. "No, no. Bold Berthold's never worried about you, brother. You're no bandit."

That was how I started living with Bold Berthold. He was sort of crazy and sometimes he fell down. But he was as brave as any man I have ever known, and there was not one mean bone in his body. I tried to take care of him and help him, and he tried to take care of me and teach me. I owed him a lot for years, Ben, but in the end I was able to pay him back and that might have been the best thing I ever did.

Sometimes I wonder if that was not why Parka told me I was Able. All this was on the northern reaches of Celidon. I ought to say that somewhere.

Spiny Orange

Bold Berthold was ill the next day and begged me not to leave him, so I went hunting instead. I was not much of a hunter then, but more by luck than skill I put two arrows into a stag. Both shafts broke when the stag fell, but I salvaged the iron heads. That night while we had a feast of roast venison, I brought up the Aelf, asking Bold Berthold whether he had heard of Aelfrice, and whether he knew anything about the people who lived there.

He nodded. "Aye."

"I mean the real Aelfrice."

He said nothing.

"In Irringsmouth, a woman told a story about a girl who was supposed to get married to an Aelfking and she cheated him out of her bed. But it was just a story. Nobody thought it was real."

"Come here, betimes," Bold Berthold muttered.

"Do they? Real Aelf?"

"Aye. 'Bout as high as the fire there. Like charcoal most are, like soot, and dirty as soot, too. All sooty 'cept teeth and tongue. Eyes yellow fire."

"They're real?"

He nodded. "Seven worlds there be, Able. Didn't I never teach you?"

I waited.

"Mythgarthr, this is. Some just say land, but that's wrong. The land you walk on and the rivers you swim in. The Sea . . . Only the sea's in between, seems like. The air you breathe. All Mythgarthr, in the middle. So three above and three under. Skai's next up, or you can say sky. Both the same. Skai's where the high-flying birds go sometimes. Not little sparrows and robins, or any of that sort. Hawks and eagles and the wild geese. I even seen big herons up there."

I recalled the flying castle, and I said, "Where the clouds are."

Bold Berthold nodded. "You've got it. Still want to go to Griffinsford? Feeling better with this good meat in me. Might be better yet in the morning, and I haven't gone over to look at the old place this year."

"Yes, I do. But what about Aelfrice?"

"I'll show you the pond where they threw fire at me, and the old graves."

"I have questions about Skai, too," I told him. "I have more questions than I can count."

"More than I got answers, most likely."

Outside, a wolf howled.

"I want to know about the Angrborn and the Osterlings. Some people I stayed with told me the Osterlings tore down Bluestone Castle."

Bold Berthold nodded. "Likely enough."

"Where do the Angrborn come from?"

"Ice lands." He pointed north. "Come with the frost, and go with the snow."

"Do they come just to steal?"

Staring into the fire, he nodded again. "Slaves, too. They didn't take us 'cause we'd fought. Going to kill us instead. Run instead of fight, and they take you. Take the women and children. Took Gerda."

"About Skai—"

"Sleep now," Bold Berthold told me. "Goin' to travel, stripling. Got to get up with the sun."

"Just one more question? Please? After that I'll go to sleep, I promise."

He nodded.

"You must look up into the sky a lot. You said you'd seen eagles up there, and even herons."

"Sometimes."

"Have you ever seen a castle there, Bold Berthold?"

Slowly, he shook his head.

"Because I did. I was lying in the grass and looking up at the clouds—"

He caught me by the shoulders, just the way you do sometimes, and looked into my eyes. "You saw it?"

"Yes. Honest, I did. It didn't seem like it could be real, but I got up and ran after it, trying to keep it in sight, and it was real, a six-sided castle of white stone up above the clouds."

"You saw it." His hands were trembling worse than ever.

I nodded. "Up among the clouds and moving with them, driven by the same wind. It was white like they were, but the edges were hard and there were colored flags on the towers." The memory took me by the throat. "It was the most beautiful thing I ever saw."

Next morning Bold Berthold was up before me, and we had left his hide-covered hut far behind before the sun rose over the treetops. He could walk only slowly, leaning on his staff, but he lacked nothing in endurance, and seemed more inclined to talk while walking than he had been the night before. "Wanted to know about the Aelf last night," he said, and I nodded.

"Got to talking about Skai instead. You must've thought I was cracked. I had reasons, though."

"It was all right," I told him, "because I want to know about that, too."

The almost invisible path we had been following had led us to a clearing; Bold Berthold halted, and pointed Skaiward with his staff. "Birds go up there. You seen them."

I nodded. "I see one now."

"They can't stay."

"If—one could perch on the castle wall, couldn't it?"

"Don't talk 'bout that." I could not tell whether he was angry or frightened. "Not now and maybe not never."

"All right. I won't, I promise."

"Don't want to lose you no more." He drew breath. "Birds can't stay. You and me can't go at all. See it, though. Understand?"

I nodded.

He began to walk again, hurrying forward, his staff thumping the ground before him. "Think a bird could, too? Eagle can see better than you. Ever see a eagle nest?"

"Yes, there was one about five miles from our cabin."

"Top of a big tree?"

"That's right. A tall pine."

"Eagle's sitting there, sitting eggs, likely. Think it ever looks up 'stead of down?"

"I suppose it must." I was trotting behind him.

"Then it can go, if it's of a mind to. The Aelf's the same." One thick blue-veined finger pointed to the earth. "They're down there where we can't see, only they can see us. You and me. Hear us, too, if we talk loud. They can come up if they want to, like birds, only they can't stay."

After that we walked on in silence for half an hour or so, I pursuing almost-vanished memories. At last I said, "What would happen if an Aelf tried to stay here?"

"Die," Bold Berthold told me. "That's what they say."

"They told you that? That they couldn't live up here?"

"Aye."

Later, when we stopped to drink from a brook, I said, "I won't ask how they've been wronged, but do you know?"

He shrugged. "Know what they say."

That night we camped beside the Griffin, cheered and refreshed by its purling waters. Bold Berthold had brought flint and steel, and I collected dry sticks for him and broke them into splinters so fine that the first shower of yellow sparks set them alight. "If there wasn't no winter I could live so all my life," he said, and might have been speaking for me.

Flat on my back after our meal, I heard the distant hooting of an owl, and the soughing of the wind in the treetops, where the first green leaves had burst forth. You must understand that at that time I believed I would be home soon. I had been kidnapped, I thought, by the Aelf. They had freed me in some western state, or perhaps in a foreign country. In time, the memories of my captivity would return. Had I been wiser, I would have stayed in Irringsmouth, where I had made friends, and where there might well be a library with maps, or an American consul. As it was, there might be some clue in Griffinsford (I was not yet convinced that was not the name of our town); and if there were none, there was nothing to keep me from returning to Irringsmouth. Half destroyed, Irringsmouth remained a seaport of sorts. Maybe I could board a ship to America there. What was there to keep me from doing it? Nothing and nobody, and a ship sounded good.

"Who-o-o?" said the owl. Its voice, soft and dark as the spring night, conveyed apprehension as well as curiosity.

I too sensed the footsteps by which someone or something made its way through the forest, although one single drop of dew falling from a high limb would have made more noise than any of them.

"Who-o-o comes?"

You would get married, and I would be in the way all the time until I was old enough to live on my own. The best plan might be for me to stay out at the cabin, for the first year anyway. It might be better still for me not to come home too quickly. Home to the bungalow that had been Mom and Dad's. Home to the cabin where we had gone to hunt and fish before snow ended all that.

Yet it was spring. Surely this was spring. The stag I had killed had dropped his antlers, the grass in the forlorn little garden of Bluestone Castle had been downy and short. What had become of winter?

A lovely, pointed face lit by great lustrous eyes like harvest moons peered down into mine, then vanished.

I sat up. There was no one there except Bold Berthold, and he was fast asleep. The owl had fallen silent, but the night wind murmured secrets to the trees. Lying down again, I did my best to recall the face I had glimpsed. A green face? Surely, I thought, surely it had *looked* green.

The old trees had given way to young ones, bushes, and spindly alders when Bold Berthold said, "Here we are."

There was no town. No town at all.

"Right here." He waved his staff. "Right there's where the street run. Houses on this side, back to the water. On that other, back to the fields. This right here was Uld's house, and across from it Baldig's." He took me by the hand. "Recollect Baldig?"

I do not remember what I said, and he was not listening anyway. "Uld had six fingers, and so'd his daughter Skjena." Bold Berthold released my shoulder. "Pick up my stick for me, will you, stripling? I'll show where we met 'em."

It was some distance away, through bushes and saplings. At last he stopped to point. "That was our house, yours and mine. Only it used to be Pa's. Recollect him? Know you don't recollect her. Ma got took 'fore you was ever weaned. Mag, her name was. We'll sleep there tonight, sleep where the house stood, for the old times' sake."

I had not the heart to tell him I was not really his brother.

"There!" He led me north another hundred yards or so. "Here's the spot where I first seen Schildstarr. I'd boys like you to shoot arrows and throw stones, but they run, all of 'em. Some shot or threw first, most just run soon as the Angrborn showed their faces."

He had stayed, and fought, and fallen. Conscious of that, I said, "I wouldn't have run."

He thrust his big, bearded face into mine. "You'd have run too!"

"No."

"You'd have run," he repeated, and flourished his staff as if to strike me.

I said, "I won't fight you. But if you try to hit me with that, I'm going to take it away from you and break it."

"You wouldn't have?" He was trying not to smile.

Having convinced myself, I shook my head. "Not if they had been as tall as that tree."

He lowered his staff and leaned on it. "Wasn't. Up to that first big limb, maybe. How you know you wouldn't run?"

"You didn't," I said. "Aren't we the same?"

*

Long before sundown we had cleared a space to sleep in where the old house had stood, and built a new fire on the old hearth. Bold Berthold talked for hours about the family and about Griffinsford. I listened, mostly out of politeness at first; as the shadows lengthened, I became interested in spite of myself. There had been no school, no doctor, and no police. At long intervals, travelers had crossed the Griffin here, wading through cold mountain water that scarcely reached their knees. When the villagers were lucky, they had sold them food and lodging; when they had been unlucky, they had to fight them to protect their homes and herds.

If the Angrborn had been giants, the Osterlings who sometimes came in summer had been devils, gorging on human flesh to restore the humanity they had lost. The Aelf had come like fog in all seasons, and had vanished like smoke, "Mossmen and Salamanders, mostly," Bold Berthold confided. "Or else little Bodachan. They'd help sometimes. Find lost stock and beg blood for it." He bared his arm. "I'd stick a thorn in and give a drop or two. They ain't but mud, that kind."

I nodded to show I understood, although I did not.

"You was here with me then, only you didn't talk so high. Pa raised me, and I raised you. You got to feeling like you was in the way, I'd say, 'cause of me runnin' after Gerda. Prettiest girl I ever seen, and we had it all planned out."

I did not have to ask what happened.

"You went off, and I thought you'd be back in a year or two when we got settled. Only you never come till now. How'd you like it where you was?"

I tried to recall, but all that I could think of was that the best times in my life had come when I had been able to get out under the sky, out on a boat or among trees.

"Nothing to say?"

"Yes." I showed him the arrowheads I had saved. "Since we'll have a few more hours of daylight, I'd like to fit new shafts to them."

"Old ones broke?"

I nodded. "When the stag fell. I was thinking that if I could find more wood of the same kind as my bow, my new shafts wouldn't break."

"You'd cut one, for a couple arrows?"

I shook my head. "I'd cut a limb or two, that's all. And if I could find one of last year's fruits, I'd plant the seeds."

Laboriously he climbed to his feet. "Show you one, and it ain't gone."

He led me into the brush, and, kneeling, felt through the grass until he discovered a small stump. "Spiny orange," he said. "You planted it 'fore you went away. It was on my land, and I wouldn't let nobody cut it. Only somebody done, when I wasn't looking."

I said nothing.

"Thought it might have put up shoots." He rose again with the help of his staff. "They do, sometimes."

I knelt, took one of the two remaining seeds from my pouch, and planted it near where the earlier stump had grown. When I rose again, his face was streaked with tears. Once more he led me away, then stopped to wave his staff at the wilderness of saplings and bushes that stretched before us. "Here was my barley field. See the big tree way in back? Come on."

Halfway there he pointed out a speck of shining green. "There it is. Spiny orange don't drop its leaves like most do. Green all winter, like a pine."

Together we went to it, and it was a fine young tree about twenty-five feet high. I hugged him.

It seems to me that I should say more about the spiny orange here, but the truth is that I know little. Many of the trees we have in America are found in Mythgarthr too—oaks and pines and maples and so on. But the spiny orange is the only tree I know that grows in Aelfrice too. The sky of Aelfrice is not really strange until you look closely at it and see the people in it, and (sometimes) hear their voices on the wind. Time moves very slowly here, but we are not conscious of it. Only the trees and the people are strange at first sight. I think the spiny orange belongs here, not in Mythgarthr and not in America.

Sir Ravd

"Lad!" the knight called from the back of his tall gray. And again, "Come here, lad. We would speak to you."

His squire added, "We'll do you no hurt."

I approached warily; if I had learned one thing in my time in those woods with Bold Berthold, it was to be chary of strangers. Besides, I recalled the knight of the dragon, who had vanished before my eyes.

"You know the forest hereabout, lad?"

I nodded, giving more attention to his horse and arms than to what he said.

"We need a guide—a guide for the rest of this day and perhaps for tomorrow as well." The knight was smiling. "For your help we're prepared to pay a scield each day." When I said nothing, he added, "Show him the coin, Svon."

From a burse at his belt the squire extracted a broad silver piece. Behind him, the great bayard charger he led stirred and stamped with impatience, snorting and blowing through its lips.

"We'll feed you, too," the knight promised. "Or if you feed us with that big bow, we'll pay you for the food."

"I'll share without payment," I told him, "if you'll share with me."

"Nobly spoken."

"But how can I know you won't send me off empty-handed at the end of the day, with a cuff on the ear?"

Svon shut his fist around the scield. "How do we know you won't lead us into an ambush, ouph?"

"As for the cuff at sunset," the knight said, "I can give you my word, though you've no reason to trust it. On the matter of payment, however, I can set your mind at rest right now." A big forefinger tapped Svon's fist; when Svon surrendered the coin, the knight tossed it to me. "There's your pay for this day until sunset, nor will we take it from you. Will you guide us?"

I was looking at the coin, which bore the head of a stern young king on one side and a shield on the other. The shield displayed the image of a monster compounded of woman, horse, and fish. I asked the knight where he wanted me to take him.

"To the nearest village. What is it?"

"Glennidam," I said; I had been there with Bold Berthold.

The knight glanced at Svon, who shook his head. Turning back to me, the knight asked, "How many people?"

There had been nine houses—unmarried people living with their parents, and old people living with their married children. At a guess, three adults for each house. I asked whether I should include children.

"If you wish. But no dogs." (This, I think, may have been overheard by some Bodachan.)

"Then I'll say fifty-three. That's counting Seaxneat's wife's new baby. But I don't know its name, or hers either."

"Good people?"

I had not thought so; I shook my head.

"Ah." The knight's smile held a grim joy. "Take us to Glennidam then, without delay. We can introduce ourselves on the road."

"I am Able of the High Heart."

Svon laughed.

The knight touched the rim of his steel coif. "I am Ravd of Redhall, Able of the High Heart. My squire is Svon. Now let us go."

"If we get there today at all," I warned Ravd, "it will be very late."

"The more reason to hurry."

We camped that night beside a creek called Wulfkil, Svon and I putting up a red-and-gold tent of striped sailcloth for Ravd to sleep in. I built a fire, for I carried flint and steel now to start one, and we ate hard bread, salt meat, and onions.

"Your family may worry about you," Ravd said. "Have you a wife?"

I shook my head, and added that Bold Berthold had said I was not old enough yet.

Ravd nodded, his face serious. "And what do you say?"

I thought of school—how I might want to go to college, if I ever got back home. "A few more years."

Svon sneered. "Two rats to starve in the same hole."

"I hope not."

"Oh, really? How would *you* support a family?"

I grinned at him. "She'll tell me how. That's how I'll know when I've found her."

"She will? Well, what if she can't?" He looked to Ravd for support, but got none.

I said, "Then would she be worth marrying?"

Ravd chuckled.

Svon leveled a forefinger at me. "Someday I'll teach—"

"You must learn yourself before the day for teaching comes," Ravd told him. "Meanwhile, Able here might teach us both, I think. Who is Berthold, Able?"

"My brother." That was what we told people, Ben, and I knew Bold Berthold believed it.

"Older than yourself, since he advises you."

"I nodded. "Yes, sir."

"Where are your father and mother?"

"Our father died years ago," I told Ravd, "and my mother left soon after I was born." It was true where you are, and here as well.

"I'm sorry to hear it. Sisters?"

"No, none," I said. "Our father raised my brother, and my brother raised me."

Svon laughed again.

I was confused already, memories of home mingling with stories Bold Berthold had told me of the family here that had been his and was supposed to be mine. It was all in the past, and although America is very far from here in the present, the past is only memories, and records nobody reads, and records nobody can read. This place and that place are mixed together like the books in the school library, so many things on the wrong shelf that nobody knows what is right for it anymore.

Ravd said, "You and your brother don't live in Glennidam, from what you said. You'd know the name of Seaxneat's wife, and the name of her new child, too, since there are only about fifty people in the village. What village do you live in?"

"We don't live in any of them," I explained. "We live by ourselves, and keep to ourselves, mostly."

"*Outlaws,*" Svon whispered.

"They may be." Ravd's shoulders rose and fell by the thickness of a blade of grass. "Would you guide me to your house if I asked you, Able?"

"It's Bold Berthold's, not mine, sir." I was glaring at Svon.

"To your brother's then. Would you take us there?"

"Gladly. But it's no grand place, just a hut. It's not much bigger than your tent." I thought Svon was going to say something; he did not, so I said, "I ought to become a bandit, like Svon says. Then we'd have a nice house with thick walls and doors, and enough to eat."

"There are outlaws in this forest, Able," Ravd told me. "They call themselves the Free Companies. Do they have those things?"

"I suppose they do, sir."

"Have you seen them for yourself?"

I shook my head.

"When we met, Svon feared you would lead us into an ambush. Do you think the Free Companies might ambush us in sober fact? With three to fight?"

"Two to fight," I told him. "Svon would run."

"I would not!"

"You'll run from me before the owl hoots." I spat into the fire. "From two lame cats and a girl you'd run like a rabbit."

His hand went to his hilt. I knew I had to stop him before he drew. I jumped the fire and knocked him down. He let go of the hilt when he fell, and I drew his sword and threw it into the bushes. We fought on the ground the way you and I did sometimes, he trying to get at his dagger while I tried to stop him. We got too close to the fire and he broke loose. I thought he was going to draw it and stab me, but he jumped up and ran instead.

I tried to clean myself off a little and told Ravd, "You can have your scield back if you want it."

"*May.*" He had never stirred. "*May* governs permissions, gifts, and things of that sort. You speak too well, Able, to make such an elementary mistake."

I nodded. I had not figured him out, and I was not sure I ever would.

"Sit down, and keep my scield. When Svon returns, I'll have him give you another for tomorrow."

"I thought you'd be mad at me."

Ravd shook his head. "Svon must become a knight soon. His family expects it and so does he. So do His Grace and I, for that matter. Thus, he will. Before he receives the accolade, he has a great deal to learn. I have been teaching him, to the best of my ability."

"And me," I told him. "About *can* and *may* and other things, too."

"Thank you."

For a while after that, we sat with our thoughts. Before long I said, "Could I become a knight?"

That was the only time I saw Ravd look surprised, and it was no more than his eyes opening a little wider. "We can't take you with us, if that's what you mean."

I shook my head. "I have to stay and take care of Bold Berthold. But sometime? If I stay here?"

"You're very nearly a knight now, I believe. What makes a knight, Able? I'd like your ideas on the matter."

He reminded me of Ms. Sparreo, and I grinned. "And set them right."

Ravd smiled back. "If they need to be set right, yes. So tell me, how is a knight different from any other man?"

"Mail like yours."

Ravd shook his head.

"A big horse like Blackmane, then."

"No."

"Money?"

"No, indeed. I mentioned the accolade when we were talking about my squire. Did you understand me?"

I shook my head.

"The accolade is the ceremony by which one authorized to perform it confers knighthood. Let me ask again. What makes a man a knight, Able? What makes him different enough that we have to give him a name differing from that of an ordinary fighting man?"

"The accolade, sir."

"The accolade makes him a knight before the law, but it is a mere legality, formal recognition of something that has already occurred. The accolade says that we find this man to be a knight."

I thought about that, and about Ravd, who was a knight himself. "Strength and wisdom. Not either one by itself, but the two together."

"You're closer now. Perhaps you are close enough. It is honor, Able. A knight is a man who lives honorably and dies honorably, because he cares more for his honor than for his life. If his honor requires him to fight, he fights. He doesn't count his foes or measure their strength, because those things don't matter. They don't affect his decision."

The trees and the wind were so still then that I felt like the whole world was listening to him.

"In the same way, he acts honorably toward others, even when they do not act honorably toward him. His word is good, no matter to whom he gives it."

I was still trying to get my mind around it. "I know a man who stood his ground and fought the Angrborn, with just a spear and an axe. He didn't have a shield, or armor, a horse, or anything like that. The men with him wanted to run, and some did. He didn't. Was he a knight? This wasn't me."

"What was he fighting for, Able?" It was almost a whisper.

"For Gerda and his house. For the crops he had in his fields, and his cattle."

"Then he is not a knight, though he is someone I would like very much to count among my followers."

I asked if he had many, because he had come into that forest alone, except for Svon.

"More than I wish, but not many who are as brave as this man you know. I'd thank every Overcyn in Skai for a hundred more, if they were like that."

"He's a good man." I was picturing Bold Berthold to myself, and thinking about all that we would be able to buy with two scields.

"I believe you. Lie down now, and get some rest. We'll need you well rested tomorrow."

"I want to ask a favor first." I felt like a little kid again, and that made it hard to talk. "I don't mean anything bad by it."

Ravd smiled. "I'm sure you don't."

"I mean I'm not going to try to steal it, or hurt you with it either, or anybody. But could I look at your sword? Please? Just for a minute?"

He drew it. "I'm surprised you didn't ask when we had sunlight, when you could have seen it better. Are you sure you wouldn't prefer to wait?"

"Now. Please. I'd like to see it now. I promise I'll never ask again."

He handed it to me hilt first; and it seemed like a warm, living thing. Its long straight blade was chased with gold and double-edged; its hilt of bronze and black horsehide was topped with a gold lion's head. I studied it and gripped the sword to flourish it, and found with a sort of shock that I had stood up without meaning to.

After a minute or two of waving it around, I positioned the blade so that the firelight fell on the flat, just ahead of the guard. "There's writing here. What does it say?"

"Lut. You can't read, can you?"

I knew I could. I said, "Well, I can't read this."

"Lut is the man who made it." Ravd held out his hand, and I returned his sword. He wiped the blade with a cloth. "My sword is Battlemaid. Lut is a famous bladesmith of Forcetti, the town of my liege, Duke Marder. Your own duke, Duke Indign, is dead. Did you know?"

"I thought he must be."

"We're attempting to assimilate his lands, and finding them a bit too much to chew, I'm afraid." Ravd's smile was touched with irony.

"Was that Duke Marder on the scield you gave me?"

Ravd shook his head. "That's our king, King Arnthor."

"What was that on his shield?"

"A nykr. Lie down and go to sleep, Able. You can save the rest of your questions for tomorrow."

"Is it real?"

"Sleep!" When Ravd sounded like that, you did not argue. I lay down, turned my back to the fire, and fell asleep as soon as I shut my eyes.

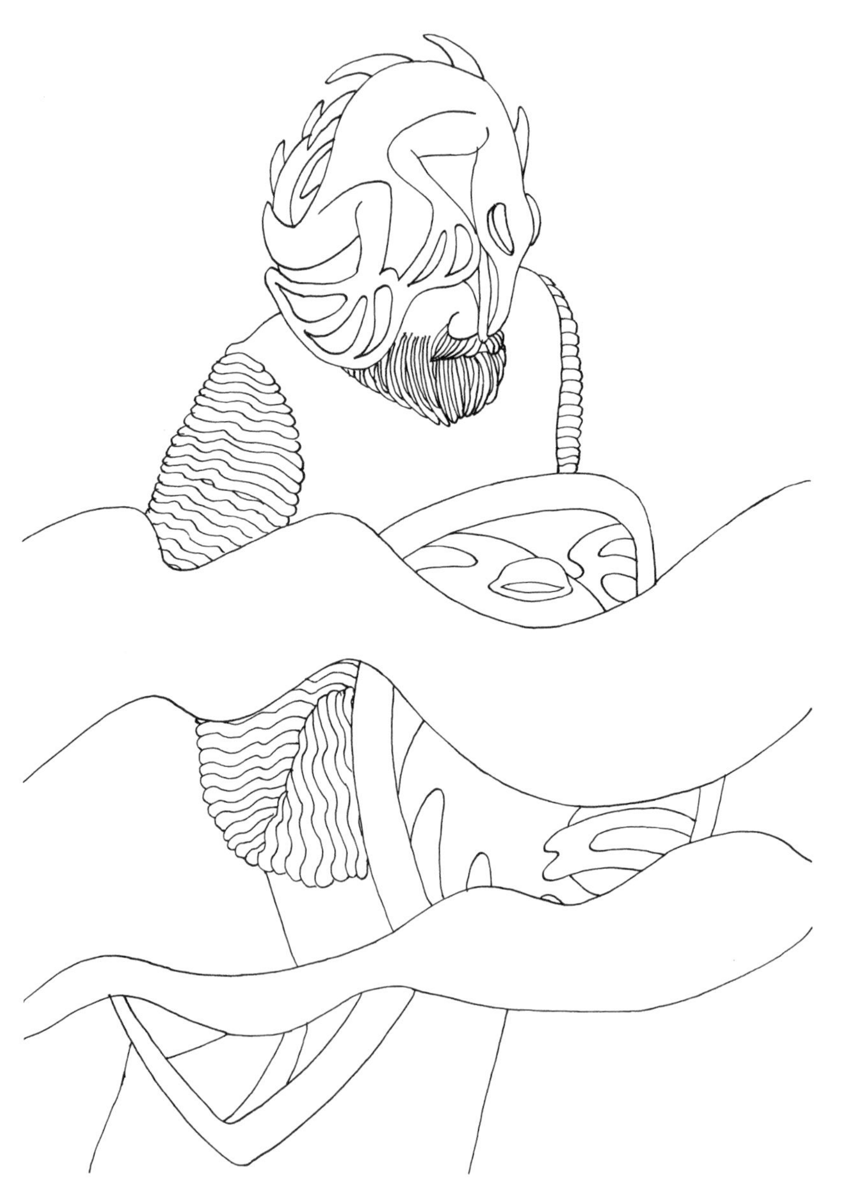

Terrible Eyes

Something that sounded like a scuffle woke me up. I heard Svon's voice and Ravd's and I decided that if I did not want to start another fight, the best thing might be for me to lie there and listen.

"I stumbled." That was Svon.

Ravd said, "No one pushed you?"

"I said I stumbled!"

"I know you did. I wish to discover whether you will verify it. It appeared to me that you had been pushed from behind. Was I wrong?"

"Yes!"

"I see. You have your sword again."

"I found it in the bushes. Do you think I'd come back here without it?"

"I don't see why not." Ravd sounded as though the question interested him. "If you mean you might need it to deal with our guide, it wasn't of great use to you an hour ago."

"We might be attacked."

"By the outlaws? Yes, I suppose we might."

"Are you going to sleep in your armor?"

"Certainly. It's one of the things a knight must learn to do." Ravd sighed. "Many years before either of us was born, a wise man said that there were only three things a knight had to learn. I believe I told you a week ago, though it may have been more. Can you tell me what they are now?"

"To ride." Svon sounded as if it were being dragged out of him. "To use the sword."

"Very good. And?"

"To speak the truth."

"Indeed," Ravd murmured. "Indeed. Shall we begin again? Or would you prefer to omit that part?"

If Svon said anything, I could not hear it.

"I've been sitting here awake since you ran away, you see. Talking to our guide at first, and talking to myself after he went to sleep. Thinking, in other words. One of the things I thought about was the way he threw your sword. I saw it. Perhaps you did as well."

"I don't want to talk about it."

"Then you need not. But I will have to talk about it more, because you won't. When a man throws a heavy object such as a sword or spear for distance, he uses his whole body—his legs and torso, as well as his arm. Able did not do that. He simply flung your sword away as a man might discard an apple core. I think—"

"Who cares what you think!"

"Why, I do." Ravd's voice was as smooth as polished steel, and sounded a good deal more dangerous. "And you must, Svon. Sir Sabel beat me twice, once with his hands and once with the flat of his sword. I was Sir Sabel's squire for ten years and two. No doubt I've told you."

Maybe Svon nodded. I could not see.

"With the flat of his sword because I attacked him. He would have been entirely justified in killing me, but he was a good and a merciful knight—a better knight than I will ever be. With his hands for something I had said to him, or something I had failed to say. I never did find out exactly what it was. He was drunk at the time—but then we all get drunk now and then, don't we?"

"You don't."

"Because he was, I found it less humiliating than I would have otherwise. Perhaps I said that I cared nothing for his thoughts. That seems likely enough.

"Able flung your sword as a man flings dung, or any such object. I believe I said that. He merely cast it from him, in other words, making no effort toward great distance or force. If you were to cast a hurlbatte so, I would chastise you. With my tongue, I mean."

Svon spoke then, but I could not hear what he said.

"It may be so. My point is that your sword cannot have been thrown far. Three or four strides, I would think. Five at most. Yet I didn't hear you searching for it in the dark, and I expected to. I was listening for it."

"I stepped on it," Svon said. "I didn't have to look for it at all."

"One resolves not to lie, but one always resolves to begin one's new truthfulness at a later time. Not now." Ravd sounded tired.

"I'm not lying!"

"Of course you are. You stepped upon your sword, four strides southeast of where I sit. You uttered no grunt of astonishment, no exclamation. You bent in silence and picked it up. You would have had to grope for the hilt, I believe, since you would not wish to lay hands on a sharp blade in the dark. You then returned it to its scabbard, a scabbard of wood covered with leather, without a sound. After that, you returned to our camp from the west, tripping over something with such violence that you almost fell into the fire."

Svon moaned like one in pain, but spoke no word.

"You must have been running to trip as hard as that and come near to falling. Were you? Running through a strange forest in the dark?"

"Something caught me."

"Ah. Now we're come to it. At least, I hope so. What was it?"

"I don't know." Svon drew breath. "I ran away. Was your churl chasing me?"

"No," Ravd said.

"Well, I thought he was, and I ran right into somebody. Only I don't think it was really a person. A—ghost or something."

"Interesting."

"There were several." Svon seemed to have taken heart. "I can't say how many. Four or five."

"Go on." I could not tell whether Ravd believed him.

"They gave me back my sword and brought me here, and they pushed me at our fire, hard, just like you said."

"Saying nothing to you?"

"No."

"Did you thank them for returning your sword?"

"No."

"Perhaps they gave you a charm or a letter? Something of that kind?"

"No."

"Did they take our horses?"

"I don't think so."

"Go now and see to them, please, Svon. See that they're well tied, and haven't been ridden."

"I don't—Sir Ravd . . ."

"Go!"

Svon cried, and right then I wanted to sit up and say something—anything—that might make him feel better. I was going to say that I would go, but that would just have made him feel worse.

When he stopped crying, Ravd said, "They frightened you very badly, whoever they were. You're more afraid of them than you are of me or our guide. Are they listening to us?"

"I don't know. I think so."

"And you're afraid that if you confide in me they'll punish you for it?"

"Yes!"

"I doubt it. If they are indeed listening, they must have heard that you *didn't* confide in me. Able, you are awake. Sit up, please, and look at me."

I did.

"How much have you heard?"

"Everything, or nearly. How did you know I was awake?"

"When you were truly asleep, you stirred in your sleep half a dozen times, and twice seemed almost to speak. Once you snored a little. When you feigned sleep, you moved not a muscle and uttered not a sound, though we were talking in ordinary tones within two strides of you. So you were awake or dead."

"I didn't want Svon to feel worse than he did already."

"Admirable."

I said, "I'm sorry I threw your sword, Svon."

"Who caught Svon and returned him to us? Do you know?"

I had no idea. I shook my head.

Svon wiped his nose. "They gave me a message for you, Able. You are to be sure that your playmate is looking out for you."

I supposed I gawked.

Ravd said, "Who are these friends of yours, Able?"

"I think . . ."

"The outlaws?"

I shook my head. "I don't think so. Couldn't it be the Aelf?"

Ravd looked thoughtful. "Svon, did you intend Able's death?"

"Yes, I did." There were no tears now; he drew his dagger and handed it to me. "I was going to kill you with this. You may keep it if you want to."

I turned it over in my hands. The tip was angled down to meet a long straight edge.

"It's a saxe." Svon sounded as if we were sharing food and passing the time. "It's like the knives the Frost Giants carry. Of course theirs are much bigger."

I said, "You were going to kill me with this?" and he nodded.

Ravd asked, "Why are you telling us this now, Svon?"

"Because I was told to give their message to him as soon as he woke up, and I think they're listening."

"So you said."

"I was hoping you'd go to sleep. Then I could have awakened him, and whispered it. That was what I wanted."

"You'd never have had to tell me what happened."

Svon nodded.

"I don't want it," I said. I gave him his dagger back. "I have a knife of my own, and I like mine better."

"You may as well tell us everything," Ravd said, and Svon did.

"I didn't run into them like I said. I ran into a tree, and hit it hard enough that I fell down. When I could I got up again and circled around your fire, keeping it only just in sight. When I was on the side where Able was, I got as close as I dared, and that was pretty close. You said you would have heard me if I had found my sword. I don't think so, because you didn't hear that. I was waiting for you to go to sleep. When I was sure you were sleeping, I was going to kill him as quietly as I could and carry his body away and hide it. I wouldn't come back until tomorrow afternoon, and you'd think he had simply run away.

"They grabbed me from behind, making less noise than I had. They had swords and bows. They took me to a clearing where I could see them a little in the moonlight, and they told me that if I hurt Able I'd belong to them. I'd have to slave for them for the rest of my life."

Ravd stroked his chin.

"They gave me that message and made me say it seven times, and swear on my sword that I'd do everything exactly the way they said."

"They had your sword?"

"Right." The kind of sarcasm I was going to get to know a lot better crept into Svon's voice. "I don't know how they got it without your hearing, but they had it."

Recalling things Bold Berthold had told me, I asked whether they were black.

"No. I don't know what color they were, but it wasn't black. They looked pale in the moonlight."

Ravd said, "Able thinks they might be Aelf. So do I. I take it they didn't identify themselves?"

"No, but—it could be right. I know they weren't people like us."

"I've never seen them. Have you, Able?"

I said, "Not that I remember, but Bold Berthold has. He said the ones who bothered him were like ashes or charcoal."

Ravd turned back to Svon. "You must tell me everything you remember about them, just as truthfully as you can. Or did they caution you not to?"

Svon shook his head. "They said to give Able their message when he woke, and never to hurt him. That was all."

"Why is Able precious to them?"

"They wouldn't tell."

"Able? Do you know?"

"No." I wished then that Ravd had not seen I was awake. "They want me to do something, but I don't know what it is."

Svon said, "Then how do you know they do?"

I did not answer.

"Our king was born in Aelfrice," Ravd told me, "as was his sister, Princess Morcaine. Since you didn't recognize his face on a scield, I doubt that you knew it."

"I didn't," I said.

"I don't believe my squire credits it—or at least, I believe he did not until now, though he may have changed his opinion."

Svon told me, "People talk as if Aelfrice were a foreign country, like Osterland. Sir Ravd says it's really another world. If it is, I don't see how people can come here from there. Or go there either."

Ravd shrugged. "And I, who have never done it, cannot tell you. I can tell you, however, that it's not wise to deny everything you can't understand. How were your captors dressed? Could you see?"

"They weren't, as far as I could see. They were as naked as poor children. They were tall, though—taller than I am, and thin." His breath caught in his throat. "They had terrible eyes."

"Terrible in what way?"

"I can't explain it. They held the moonlight and made it burn. It hurt to look at them."

Ravd sat in silence for a minute or two after that, his hand stroking his chin. "One more question, Svon, then we must sleep. All of us. It's late already, and we should be up early. You said that there were four or five of them. Was that the truth?"

"About that many. I couldn't be sure."

"Able, put a little more wood on the fire, since you're up. How many could you be sure of, Svon?"

"Four. Three were men. Males, or whatever you call them. But I think there may have been more."

"The fourth was female, I take it. Did she speak?"

"No."

"How many males did?"

"Three."

Ravd yawned, which may have been playacting. "Lie down, Svon. Sleep if you can."

Svon spread a blanket for himself and lay down on it.

Ravd said, "I believe you will be safe, Able. From Svon, at least."

I suppose I nodded, but I was thinking how another world might seem like it was just another country, and about yellow eyes that burned with moonlight like a cat's.

Gene Wolfe

Seeing Something

We reached Glennidam about midmorning, and Ravd called the people together, all the men and all the women, and some children, too. He began by driving Battlemaid into a log Svon and I fetched for him. "You are invited to swear fealty to our liege, Duke Marder," he told them. "I won't make you swear—you're free to refuse if you wish to refuse. But you should know that I will report those who do not swear to him."

After that they swore, all of them, putting their hands on the lion's head and repeating the oath after Ravd.

"Now I would like to speak with some of you, one at a time," he said, and chose six men and six women, and had Svon and me watch the rest while he talked to the first one in the front room of the biggest house in the village. An hour went by while he was talking to that first one, and the ones who were waiting got restless; but Svon put his hand to his sword and shouted until they quieted down.

The first man came out at last, sweating and unable to meet the eyes of the waiting eleven, and Ravd called for the first woman. She went inside, trembling, and the minutes ticked by. A shiny blue fly, big with carrion, buzzed around me until I chased it, then around Svon, and at last around a little black-bearded man the rest called Toug, who seemed much too despondent to chase anything.

The woman appeared in the doorway, her face streaked with tears. "Able? Which one is Able? He wants you."

I went in, and the woman sat down on a little milking stool in front of Ravd.

He, seated on a short bench with a back, said, "Able, this is Brega. Because she is a woman, I permit her to sit. The men stand. Brega tells me there is a man called Seaxneat who is well acquainted with the outlaws and entertains them at times. Do you understand why I asked you to come in?"

I said, "Yes, sir. Only I don't think I can help much."

"If we learn nothing from you, you may learn something from us." Ravd spoke to the woman. "Now, Brega, I want to explain how things are for you. In fact, I must explain that, because I doubt that you understand it."

Brega, thin and no longer young, snuffled and wiped her eyes with a corner of her apron.

"You are afraid that Able here will tell others what you've told me about Seaxneat. Isn't that so?"

She nodded.

"He won't, but your danger is much greater than that. Do you two know each other, by the way?"

She shook her head; I said, "No, sir."

"You have told me about Seaxneat, and of course I will try to find him and talk to him. Those people outside will know you've talked to me, and the longer we're together the more they will think you've told me. Do you understand what I'm saying?"

"Y-yes."

"Have you yourself, or your husband, ever been robbed?"

"They knocked me down." The tears burst forth, and flowed for some minutes.

"Do you know the name of the outlaw who knocked you down?"

She shook her head.

"But if you knew it, you would tell me, wouldn't you? It would make no sense for you to keep it from me when you have told me as much as you have. You see that, don't you?"

"It was Egil."

"Thank you. Brega, you've taken an oath, the most solemn oath a woman can take. You've acknowledged Duke Marder as your liege, and sworn to obey him in all things. If you break that oath, Hel will condemn your spirit to Muspel, the Circle of Fire. The sacrifices you've offered the Aelf can't save you. I take it you know all that."

She nodded.

"I am here because Duke Marder appointed me. If it were not for that, I would be sitting at my own table in Redhall, or seeing to my horses there. I speak for Duke Marder, just as if he were here in person. I am his knight."

She sniffled. "I know."

"Furthermore, the outlaws will avenge themselves upon you and your whole village, if they are left free to do so. Egil, who knocked you down, will do worse. This is your chance to avenge yourself, with words worth more than swords to Duke Marder and me. Do you know of anyone else here who is on good terms with the outlaws? Anyone at all?"

She shook her head.

"Only Seaxneat. What is his wife's name?"

"Disira."

"Really?" Ravd pursed his lips. "That's perilously near a queen's name some men conjure with. Do you know that name?"

"No. I don't say it."

"Does she? I will not use her name. The woman we are speaking of. Seaxneat's wife. Has she alluded to that queen in your hearing?"

"No," Brega repeated.

Ravd sighed. "Able, would you know Seaxneat if you saw him? Think before you speak."

I said, "I'm sure I would, sir."

"Describe him, please, Brega."

The woman only stared.

"Is he tall?"

"Taller than I am." She held her hands a foot apart to indicate the amount.

"A dark beard?"

"Red."

"One eye? Crooked nose? Clubfoot?"

She shook her head to all of them.

"What else can you tell us about him?"

"He's fat," she said thoughtfully, "and he walks like this." She stood up and demonstrated, her toes turned in.

"I see. Able, does this square with your recollection? Fat. The red beard? The walk?"

It did.

"When we spoke earlier, you did not name Seaxneat's wife. Was that because you didn't know her name, or because you were too prudent to voice it?"

"Because I didn't know it, sir. I'm not afraid to say Disira."

"Then it would be wise for you not to say it too often. Do you know what she looks like?"

I nodded. "She's small, with black hair, and her skin's very white. I didn't think her a specially pretty woman when Seaxneat was cheating Bold Berthold and me, but I've seen worse."

"Brega? Does he know her?"

"I think he does." The woman, who had been wiping her eyes, wiped them again.

"Very well. Pay attention, Able. If you will not listen to me about that woman's name, listen to this at least. I want you to search the village for these people. When you find either, or both, bring them to me if you can. If you can't, come back and tell me where they are. Brega will be gone by then, but I'll be talking to others, as likely as not. Don't hesitate to interrupt."

"Yes, sir."

"I want Seaxneat, of course. But I want his wife almost as much.

She probably knows less, but she may tell us more. Since she has a new child, it's quite possible she's still here. Now go."

At the outskirts of Glennidam, I halted to search its sprouting fields with my eyes. I had looked into every room of every one of the village's houses, and into every barn and shed as well, all without seeing either Seaxneat or his wife. Ravd had said I was to interrupt him if I found them, but I did not think he would like being interrupted to hear that I had not.

And Ravd had been right, I told myself. A woman with a newborn would not willingly travel far. There was every chance that when she heard a knight had come to Glennidam she had fled no farther than the nearest trees, where she could sit in the shade to nurse her baby. If I left the village to look there . . . Trying to settle the matter in my own mind, I called softly, "Disira? Disira?"

At once it seemed to me that I glimpsed her face among the crowding leaves where the forest began. On one level I felt sure it had been some green joke of sunlight and shadow; on another I knew that I had seen her.

Or at least that I had seen something.

I took a few steps, stopped a minute, still unsure, and hurried forward.

Disiri

"Help . . ." It was not so much a cry as a moan like that of the wind, and like a moaning wind it seemed to fill the forest. I pushed through the brush that crowded the forest's edge, trotted among close-set saplings, then sprinted among mature trees that grew larger and larger and more and more widely spaced as I advanced.

"Please help me. Please . . ."

I paused to catch my breath, cupped my hands around my mouth, and called, "I'm coming!" as loudly as I could. Even as I did it, I wondered how she had known there was anyone to hear her while I was still walking down the rows of sprouting grain. Possibly she had not. Possibly she had been calling like that, at intervals, for hours.

I trotted again, then ran. Up a steep ridge crowned with dreary hemlocks, and along the ridgeline until it dipped and swerved in oaks. Always it seemed to me that the woman who called could not be more than a hundred strides away.

The woman I felt perfectly certain had to be Seaxneat's wife, Disira.

Soon I reached a little river that must surely have been the Griffin. I forded it by the simple expedient of wading in where I was. I had to hold my bow, my quiver, and the little bag I tied to my belt over my head before I was done; but I got through and scrambled up the long, sloping bank of rounded stones on the other side.

There, mighty beeches robed with moss lifted proud heads into that fifth world called Skai, and there the woman who called to me sounded nearer still, no more (I thought) than a few strides off. In a dark dell full of mushrooms and last year's leaves, I felt certain I would find her. She was only on the other side of the beaver meadow, beyond all question; and after that, up on the rocky outcrop I glimpsed beyond it.

Except that when I got there I could hear her calling still, calling in the distance. I shouted then, gasping for breath between the repetitions of her name: "Disira? . . . Disira? . . . Disira?"

"Here! Here at the blasted tree!"

The seconds passed like sighs, then I saw it down the shallow valley on the farther side of the outcrop—the shattered trunk, the broken limbs, and the raddled leaves that clung to them not quite concealing something green as spring.

"It fell," she told me when I reached her. "I wanted to see if I could move it just a little, and it fell on my foot. I cannot get my foot out."

I put my bow under the fallen trunk and pried; I never felt it move, but she was able to work her foot free. By the time she got it out, I had noticed something so strange that I was certain I could not really be seeing it, and so hard to describe that I may never make it clear. The afternoon sun shone brightly just then, and the leaves of the fallen tree (which I think must have been hit by lightning), and those of the trees all around it, cast a dappled shade. Mostly we were in the shade, but there were a few splashes of brilliant sunshine here and there. I should have seen her most clearly when one fell on her.

But it was the other way: I could see her very clearly in the shade, but when the sun shone on her face, her legs, her shoulders, or her arms, it almost seemed that she was not there at all. At school Mr. Potash showed us a hologram. He pulled the blinds and explained that the darker it was in the room the more real the hologram would look. So when we had all looked at it, I moved one of the blinds to let in light, and he was right. It got dim, but it was stronger again as soon as I let the blind fall back.

"I do not think I should walk on this." She was rubbing her foot. "It does not feel right. There is a cave a few steps that way. Do you think you could carry me there?"

I did not, but I was not going to say so until I tried. I picked her up. I have held little kids who weighed more than she did, but she felt warm and real in my arms, and she kissed me.

"In there we will be out of the rain," she told me. She kept her eyes down as if she were shy, but I knew she was not really shy.

I started off, hoping I was going toward the cave she knew about, and I said that it was not going to rain.

"Yes, it is. Haven't you noticed how cool the air has gotten? Listen to the birds. To your left a trifle, and look behind the big stump."

It was a nice little cave, just high enough for me to stand up in, and there was a sort of bed made of deer skins and furs, with a green velvet blanket on top.

"Put me on that," she said, "please."

When I did, she kissed me again, and when she let me go, I sat down on the smooth, sandy floor of the cave to get my breath. She laughed at me, but she did not say anything.

For quite a while, I did not say anything either. I was thinking a lot, but I had no control of the things I thought, and I was so excited about her that I thought something was going to happen any minute that I would be ashamed of for the rest of my life. She was the most beautiful woman I had ever seen in my life (she still is) and I had to shut my eyes, which made her laugh again.

Her laugh was like nothing on earth. It was as if there were golden bells hanging among the flowers through a forest of the loveliest trees that could ever be, and a wind sighing there was ringing all the bells. When I could open my eyes again, I whispered, "Who are you? Really?"

"She you called." She smiled, not trying to hide her eyes anymore. Maybe a leopard would have eyes like those, but I kind of doubt it.

"I called Seaxneat's wife, Disira. You aren't her."

"I am Disiri the Mossmaiden, and I have kissed you."

I could still feel her kiss, and her hair smelled of new-turned earth and sweet smoke.

"Men I have kissed cannot leave until I send them away."

I wanted to stand up then, but I knew I could never leave her.

I said, "I'm not a man, Disiri, just a kid."

"You are! You are! Let me have one drop of blood, and I will show you."

By morning the rain had stopped. She and I swam side by side in the river, and lay together like two snakes on a big shady rock, only an inch above the water. I knew I was all different, but I did not know how different. I think it was the way a caterpillar feels after it has turned into a butterfly and is still drying its wings. "Tell me," I said, "if another man came, would he see you like I see you now?"

"No other man will come. Did not your brother teach you about me?"

I did not know whether she meant you or Bold Berthold, Ben, but I shook my head.

"He knows me."

"Have you kissed him?"

She laughed and shook her head.

"Bold Berthold told me the Aelf looked like ashes."

"We are the Moss Aelf, Able, and we are of the wood and not the ash." She was still smiling. "You call us Dryads, Skogsfru, Tree-brides, and other names. You may make a name for us yourself. What would like to call us?"

"Angels," I whispered, but she pressed a finger to my lips. I blinked and looked away when she did that, and it seemed to me, when I glimpsed her from the corner of my eye, that she looked different from the girl I had been swimming with and all the girls I had just made love with.

"Shall I show you?"

I nodded—and felt muscles in my neck slithering like pythons. "Good lord!" I said, and heard a new voice, wild and deep. It was terribly strange; I knew I had changed, but I did not know how much, and for a long time after I thought I was going to change back. You need to remember that.

"You won't hate me, Able?"

"I could never hate you," I told her. It was the truth.

"We are loathsome in the eyes of those who do not worship us."

I chuckled at that; the deep reverberations in my chest surprised me too. "My eyes are mine," I said, "and they do what I tell them. I'll close them before I kiss you, if we need more privacy."

She sat up, dangling her legs in the clear, cold water. "Not in this light." Her kick dashed water through a sunbeam and showered us with silver drops.

"You love the sunlight," I said. I sensed it.

She nodded. "Because it is yours, your realm. The sun gave me you, and I love you. My kind love the night, and so I love them both."

I shook my head. "I don't understand. How can you?"

"Loving me, couldn't you love some human woman?"

"No," I said. "I never could." I meant it.

She laughed, and this time it was a laugh that made fun of me. "Show me," she said.

She kicked again. The slender little foot that rose from the shimmering water was as green as new leaves. Her face was sharper, green too, three-cornered, bold and sly. Berry lips pressed mine, and when we parted I found myself looking straight into eyes of yellow fire. Her hair floated above her head.

I embraced her, lifting and holding her, and kissed her again.

PARDON

The Bearing of Light

Patrick O'Leary

I WAS THE STILL VOICE you almost heard in the middle of the night. The bearer of bad news. The sound a child makes when his momma doesn't wake. I was the promise given young girls. The hum of the crowd at a stoning. The brand on a new slave. You remember me. I was the one under your bed as you slept. I didn't have to do anything. But you knew I was there.

I say *was.* I'm retired now.

There's an old joke: a man is driving his car through the dark at the speed of light. What happens when he turns on his brights?

Light. Inescapable light. The one thing I couldn't outpace. It sought me, hounded me, followed me everywhere. So I hid in the shadowlands, between the pockets of ordinary and dark matter, on the banks of dark energy that flow like bloody rivers through this universe—places where there was only me and the big night.

Where I could be alone.

Like that dark city.

That dark alley under a blistering sun.

Where on my last day on the job in the hot shade of a concrete block building I saw a young mulatto boy pissing against a wall. The kid looked up and said, "Hey. How you been doing?"

I admired that moxie, that suave cover-up of shame. Like I was an old friend he hadn't kept in touch with lately. Well, actually, I had been acquainted with his daddy.

"You don't know how lucky you are, child."

"What chew mean?" The boy scowled beautifully as the tiny arch of yellow made a wet bloom on the gray concrete.

"I've never done what you're doing."

"Never peed? Ain't you got a dick?"

I wouldn't do that old trick. Wouldn't take out the black serpent with the red tongue. I was tired. "Where's your momma?"

The boy zipped up and scowled again. "Inside with the witch. Getting blacker."

That's when I looked up and read the new sign on the establishment.

"ELITE TANNING. FINE ORIGINAL JEWELRY. CELLULAR PAGING. METABOLITE SALE. DISCOUNT PARDONS." I reread the last two words.

"How is it that you're not with her?"

The boy gave me a hard look and said, "I don't tarry with no devils."

None that you know of, at least.

The door went ajangle as I entered the dingy, dim store and was plunged into a cloud of incense. A sickening unidentifiable tang. The pressed-tin ceiling had a row of stubby nipples—plugs where once fans turned. Perhaps, in its time, it had been a barbershop. One wall was mirrored. But I couldn't bring myself to look at my reflection. I had indulged in enough of that.

There was a glass display case stuffed with faux black velvet like folded dry lava, which held a grotesque assortment of hippie jewelry—tasteless dragons, nymphs, and griffins writhing on pins. Trinkets for fat children who never had to beg for their supper or run for their lives.

The tanning booth was behind a yellow curtain; a blue glow bled under its billowing hem. The row of pagers hung on the wall opposite the jewelry. Black boxes pasted on corkboard, price stickers above them. Below them on the counter, sample bottles of Metabolite diet pills—ugly stubby wafers—their sizes denoting one month, six months, and, apparently, a lifetime supply as big as a half gallon of milk. Take them all, I thought, and you disappear.

But they weren't why I'd come in.

The proprietor danced behind the counter, a black woman in a yellow jumpsuit swinging about to a loud Bob Marley tune. Something about Jah or Ganja. Her body shimmied and bobbled. A heavily beaded arrangement of cornrows hung to her ample waist. If she stood before the doorway to the tanning booth, I thought, they wouldn't have needed the curtain.

I suppose I envied her broad marketing strategy and her enterprise. See, I never created anything. I was a spoiler by nature. I say *was.* For honestly, how much satisfaction is there in a life of stomping sand castles, knocking over towers of blocks, pinching pets, and giving away the endings to movies?

Oh, it was a dull job.

And even the lies were no fun anymore. You are good. You are justified. You've been treated unfairly. You are beautiful. When everyone is so easily conned, where's the victory? The price I had paid for stoking the delusions of others was that I had none myself.

The Light. It was everywhere.

When did I learn to hate it?

Maybe it was my name. That was something I didn't choose.

"Come for the pardons?" the woman asked in a thick Jamaican accent.

"Yes," I said, examining the stack in the wooden out box. They appeared to be documents from another century. Brown and weathered and full of fine script interrupted by a few underlined blanks—standard contract stuff. Even a gold seal embossed in the corner. Souvenirs straining at authenticity.

"They're discounted. Fifty dollar each."

I couldn't take my eyes off them. The possibility of release—however unlikely—held me in a kind of awe. For I was tired. Tired unto death. These temporary people didn't know how lucky they were to have endings. Hadn't a clue about the gift they'd been granted. Granted. Yes, my boss had been big on freebies. It was what I hated about him most.

"Exactly what do they cover?"

She reached under the counter and brought forth a laminated list of sins. A comprehensive list. Definitive, in fact. Impressive.

"All the top ten and their variations. Just fill in the blanks, pay the cash, and yer a snow mon." Was she actually joking about my black wardrobe? She would regret that.

"Armed robbery?"

"That's a commandment," she said, nodding.

"Murder?"

"Forgot your commandments?"

"Rape?" I asked, traveling freely up her body with my eyes. I was surprised to see her smile. That wasn't the effect I was going for.

"Even that. It's a bargain."

I frowned at myself in the mirror. My long coiling hair seemed to hold less blue than usual. Ordinarily by now they felt a twinge of discomfort, as if a bee were orbiting their skulls. This one seemed not to mind my company. Smelled none of the smells. Seemed, in fact, comfortable. That could only mean she did not see me as I was.

A tanned woman came through the yellow curtain and headed for the door. Her white outfit made her skin glow. "Sister, I feel like a new woman!"

"Good on ya. Say hi to Sam."

The very brown white woman nodded.

"Tell him about the dragons," the proprietor said. "Maybe he'll come in next time."

The woman gave a stricken apologetic smile.

"It's my hair," the Jamaican said, rolling her head slightly, setting the beads atinkle. "I remind him of his daddy."

She left quickly and I examined the list, breathing through my mouth, hoping to escape the fumes that permeated the shop.

"That was a good trick."

I looked at her.

"The way you blended. I don't think she even noticed you."

Was I losing my touch? Or was it her? There was something odd about the sound of her tapping foot. Something about the way it caught the beat. And how she always seemed to be dancing, even standing still.

"I know what you're going to say. Why I have to write it down? Isn't it the thought that counts?"

I looked sharply at her. Her hand rested on the pardons, a rainbow of bracelets on her wrist. It's true: I preferred verbal agreements. Louis Mayer once said they're not worth the paper they're written on, but he was wrong. For, in my experience, to say the thing is to make it real. And I am a great listener.

I can see you're an educated mon."

"By whose authority can you issue pardons?"

"God's."

I smirked. "God gave you these contracts?"

"No, Spirit Novelties of Nebraska gave me a franchise. Most of it's carny gags. Prayer candles. Spell books. Lottery pamphlets." She tapped the stack with her meaty hand and her bracelets chinked. "But these are the Genuine Article."

"What's God got to do with it?"

"Sees all, knows all. Sins are well-cataloged phenomena. It's in all the literature, Mon."

I looked at her.

"Sacred literature," she added. "The good books."

"Books?"

"There's more than one, you know. Even the Bible's a collection."

"Some would say an anthology." I wondered if she'd read the apocrypha. "So there are no unforgivable sins?" It was a little test.

She passed. "Well, defaming the Holy Ghost."

"Yes, it is a leftover clause from the days of necromancy. Trafficking with dark forces. Perverting the spiritual nature of man."

"Yah, we were Mon then." She laughed. "When was you defrocked?"

I sighed, conceding her insight. Well, who else would her customers be but the dispensers of mercy? Those who knew the length and breadth of sin. "Ages ago."

"High rank, were ya?"

"Very high."

She shook her head. "I've had me a bishop or two. Never yet a cardinal. And the odd priest. I had a Methodist once. He had qualms."

"Qualms?"

"About buying absolution. He thought it was free. He was a good man. A good man who'd done very bad things."

Tings, she called them. Strangely, this thought did not seem to bother her. "Most people do very bad things," she said.

"True. And they know it." She smiled. "That makes 'em good."

I took the occasion to listen to her heart. I enjoy hearts. I found I could not hear it. Perhaps the Marley was too loud. My long fingers flicked the corner of the stack of documents. "One cannot purchase forgiveness. Either it's priceless or it's worthless."

"The confession," she said, crossing her arms over her heavy breasts. "That's what's priceless. That's what can't be bought."

"Then I will confess."

I set two twenties and a ten on the counter, took a deep breath, which made me feel taller. My dark hair, black T-shirt, and black jeans grew blue glistening shadows. I'll admit: I'm a bit of a ham.

I raised my right hand.

"You can fill in all the blanks, Sister. I've done them all." I let her think about that. "All." She was silent. "You want details? Two blocks from here there's an old woman who used to trust people. I killed her poodle then raped her." I savored the next phrase. "Later, I introduced Sam's father to the taste of crack. That was a slow morning."

This didn't seem news to her. That pissed me off.

"And why?" I couldn't keep the bitterness in any longer. "Because I could. Because it was allowed. Because I was his chosen and he would deny me nothing. But he would not let me share his rule. I would not be a servant in his kingdom so he let me have my own. Can you fathom that? He *let* me. He gave me dominion and I spoiled and pillaged, racked and fouled this paradise until he could smell nothing but stink. What THE FUCK IS THAT INCENSE?!" I spun about but could not see the oppressive noxious source: no rising trail of smoke, nothing burning. Placing my palms on the counter I leaned until our noses were almost touching. "I did it with his full consent. What kind of god would do that?"

Her breath was cool. "A god who loves you."

I laughed. I knew full well the power of my laugh. Usually it loosened sphincters and sprung tears. It was a sound that meant there was no way out. This was the living end. "Do you think you can instruct *me* in theology? Sister? You fat island cunt."

She didn't flinch. "Yes."

I did what I usually did instead of a smile. And my body simmered down a bit. Frankly, I was tired of shouting. Tired of everything. "Well, you can try."

She handed me a blank script and a Pentel. "Sign. I can't do it for you."

So I filled in the blanks, added *etc.* to everything, stealing a glance or two at her face, hoping to find some crack in that now solemn black edifice. I found none. And as I signed with a black *X* I knew this was no ordinary human; she had the unmistakable light. In my time I had burned real saints, watched strangers rescue lost obnoxious children, observed underpaid heroes enduring vile bosses, seen the price of goodness, and wondered why anyone took the time and trouble. But they did. And when they did an awful light came off their skin that only I could see, a sickening white light that cost them, always cost them.

Understand that until that day I had feared no one.

I began to fear her.

She sprinkled the wet ink with a saltshaker and blew the black crystals away. Opening a tiny safe behind the counter, she placed the document there. I noticed it was the only paper inside. Then she slammed the black door and twirled the combo and led me through the curtain to the tanning booth, told me to strip and lie. I stretched out under the blue neon tubing, wearing eye goggles, blind and toasting for fifteen minutes. Seven and a half each side. When I was done, I was sweating.

I had never sweated before.

When she opened the lid to let me out, she said, "Your tan is the sign of the fire that all humans must pass through. Now it is your turn."

She led me shaking to her glass case and plucked out a silver dragon.

"The beast you once were is an ornament," she said, pinning it to my T-shirt at the heart. "He is a memory of those you have burned. Here all things are made new."

She took me to the bottles of diet pills and gave me the largest. "Take one a day. In no time you will join the hunger."

Who was this creature? Gabriel? Anthrax? Sebastion?

She whirled then and my eyes caught a dizzy glimpse of gold as her pinkie toe ring flashed and she drew me to the corkboard full of pagers. She picked one, punched in a code, and clipped it to my belt. My knees went rubbery from the weight.

"You are no longer unreachable. When you are needed you will be called."

And I stood there in that little shop, my nostrils swamped with sweet incense, my eyelids twittering like an enraptured enthusiast, my mind reeling, relishing the first consecutive surprises I could remember feeling. I inspected the silver brooch, my newly golden hide, the milk carton of wafers I carried like a pigskin, and the three green digits on the face of the heavy pager. It, of all the numbers I might have tried, was the most obvious.

"That's all?" I asked.

"Nahh," she said. "That's the easy part. Now it gets bumpy."

I knew her then and was humbled that I hadn't seen it before. The white glow came out of her eyes and burned me in my deepest, hidden places, searing as it flared against my many acts, my many choices, my oblivious self. I wanted to shrink from that light, cower like a dog before an angry master. But she was not angry and there was nowhere to hide.

After an endless moment I said, "It's over?"

"Yah."

"I'm forgiven?"

"Completely."

"I did not repent."

"To say the thing is to make it real."

She touched my arm. Understand: I had never been touched like that. I hope no one ever touches you like that. "Why'd ya come back?"

Sees all, knows all. Why is she asking me?

"You wanted to be hidden. So I let you hide. You left an obvious trail, though."

"My handiwork," I said, nodding, stifling a gag that to this day I have not wholly swallowed.

"I wouldn't call it work," she said.

"No, it was more of a hobby."

"People enjoy hobbies."

I dared her eyes and got a fresh burn for my trouble. "My revenge, then," I admitted.

I could feel her waiting on my answer. An almost palpable gap, like an awful lull in conversation. I suspect it's what a conscience feels like.

"I was tired," I said finally. "Tired of being right. It's exhausting."

She smiled. "Especially when you're wrong."

Then she told me a story about a bitter man who tried to flood a home with darkness by opening all the doors of the one unlit room in the center. But as many doors as he opened, the darkness never spilled, never spread; it only paled. He found he couldn't let the dark out; he could only let the light in.

I nodded, unconsciously picking up the rhythm of her dancing body, as I contemplated the way her toes tapped, a ripple that began and ended on the little one, which bore the golden ring. With a dexterity I had only seen before in the fingers of a pianist, each toe played out a different portion of the constant reggae beat.

She opened the door and it jangled as I walked into the new day. I stopped and turned to her. "I would like to ask a favor."

"Yes?"

"I would like to take a piss."

"I understand," she said. Her nose twitched as she gave a brief sniff. "Do where the boy did."

"Thank you."

"This is love, in case you were wondering. You learn it slowly and it hurts like hell."

"Love?" It was a question I had never asked before.

"Seeing what it is and accepting it."

I will think about that for the rest of my mortal days.

"Lightbearer?"

I felt the touch of her eyes again. That hard light that I had dodged since human time began. She must have known I couldn't bear it any longer, so she spared me and looked away.

When I stopped shuddering, she said, "Don't be a stranger."

The boy's spot was still wet on the gray wall. The stink rose up as I set down the large bottle, unzipped, and released the serpent that was no longer a serpent. And I pissed. The longest, most glorious piss. A Niagara of relief. It emptied me. It plashed and pooled and snaked away. And as I pissed in the merciless shade of that dirty alley in that broken city I smiled for the first time in aeons. A real smile with none of the pretended pleasure of a smirk. And I began to laugh.

I am a fool, I thought. I gave up *this* for what? Why had it taken me so long to admit it? I had asked to be left alone. But had always hoped that somewhere he—she—was watching. That had been important. Just then I couldn't recall why.

Alone. That was all I ever wanted. If I couldn't have all of her I wanted none of her. A furious philosophy I could have learned from any two-year-old.

A dandelion stood up in a crack at my feet. A beautiful weed, I had to admit. A nuisance and a charm.

Should I pick it? Or leave it be?

I thought about it for a long time. Then I decided.

CITY
TOURS

Simon's House of Lipstick

Jonathan Carroll

HADEN WAS IN TROUBLE again. Big surprise, huh? So what else was new, right? That man wouldn't have known he had a *pulse* unless the IRA was closing in, his ex-wife was circling his field with a squadron of divorce lawyers, or a rabid dog had just bitten him on the dick.

When he opened his eyes that morning this is what immediately filled his mind: he had no money to pay the bills on his desk. His car was dying of three different kinds of automotive cancer. He had to lead a city tour today and if he didn't do it well this time, he would be fired. Earlier in his life, it was okay when Haden lost a job because there was always another around somewhere. But now, like the last pair of socks in the drawer, there were no more left. He had to wear this one with the big hole in the toe or else go barefoot, and barefoot meant even more trouble.

Sighing, he threw off the thin purple blanket he'd bought at a Chinese discount store after his wife left him and took everything, including the blankets. But she was right to leave because he was a dog in every way except loyalty. No, that's not correct. To call Haden a dog was to insult canines. Call him a rat, a weasel; call him a disease with a head. . . . Simon Haden was not a nice man, despite the fact he was a very handsome one.

His face had been the downfall of not only innumerable trusting women, but one-time friends, used car dealers who gave him a better deal than they should have, and former bosses who were proud for a while to have such a handsome guy working for them.

Why do we always, always fall for good looks? Why are we never immune to them? Is it optimism or stupidity? Maybe it's just hope—you see someone pretty and the sight convinces you if *they* can exist, then things are right in the world.

Uh huh.

Haden used to say women don't want to fuck me, they want to fuck my face and he was right. But that was history. Now few women wanted to fuck any part of him. Oh sure, sometimes one down at the end of a bar who'd had too much to drink and begun to see double saw two Hadens and thought they looked like a movie star whose name she couldn't remember at the moment. But that was rare. Now he usually drank alone and went home alone. He was a shallow, self-absorbed middle-aged man, with a fading face and an empty bank account, who gave guided tours of a city that was no longer his friend.

Why a tour guide? Because it was mindless work once you got the hang of it. And the tourists he led were so interested in what he said. Haden never got over how grateful these people were. They made him feel like he was *giving* them his city rather than just pointing out its sights.

Once in a while a good-looking woman would be part of a tour group. She'd be like an extra tip dropped in Haden's hand. What a wonderful guide he was on those days! Witty and informative, he knew everything they wanted to know. And what he didn't know, he made up. That was simple because he had been doing that sort of thing his whole life. His audience never knew the difference. Besides, his lies were so imaginative and interesting. Years later while looking at snapshots of their trip, people would say "See that dog in the portrait? It lived to be twenty-eight years old and was so loved by the Duke that its gravestone is as big as his."

A lie of course, but an interesting one.

Maybe there would be a pretty woman today. Gripping the sink with both hands, Haden stared into the bathroom mirror and said a little prayer: let there be a beautiful female face in that crowd of blue-hairs, hearing aids, and TV-sized eyeglasses. In his mind he saw them all—saw their cream-colored crepe-soled shoes the size of small hydrofoils, the perma-pressed leisure suits a thousand years out of fashion. He heard their loud voices full of whines and stupid questions—where's the castle, the toilet, the restaurant, the bus? Was one beautiful face asking so much? A daughter along for the ride, a nubile granddaughter, someone's nurse, anything to spare him a day surrounded by The House of Lipstick. He said those words slowly into the mirror, as if he were an actor learning his lines. Today he was guiding a group of people from The House of Lipstick. What was that—a store that sold only lipstick? Or a business that manufactured it? He would know more when he opened the envelope given him at work, detailing the job.

He smiled, imagining twenty old people with lipstick-smeared lips, all very attentive to what he was saying. Glistening red lips, the color of a clown's nose or a dog's rubber ball. Sighing, he picked up his toothbrush and began to prepare for the day.

Because he was a very vain man, his small closet was bursting with the best clothes—Avon Celli cashmere sweaters, one-two-three-four Richard James suits, one hundred and fifty dollar belts. He had never been to Europe but he dressed like a wealthy European. He certainly had taste and style, but neither had helped him much over the years. Yes, they had enabled him to fool some of the people some of the time. But sooner or later everyone, even the dumbbells, figured Haden out and then invariably he *was* out: out of a job, out of a marriage, out of chances.

What's most interesting about these people, even more than their pretty faces, is that they almost never understand why the world eventually ends up hating them. Haden had done terrible things to people. But for the life of him, he could not understand why he had ended up where he was now—living alone in a lousy cramped apartment, working a no-exit job, and spending way too much free time at the TV watching whatever was in front of his eyeballs. He knew which wrestlers were feuding with whom in professional wrestling. He had given serious thought to buying those Japanese steak knives on the Shopping Channel. He carefully taped his favorite daytime soap operas if he had to miss an episode.

How did I end up like *this?*

If someone had told Simon Haden that he was a colossal prick and why, he would not have understood. He would not have denied it, he would not have *understood.* Because pretty people think the world should forgive whatever their sins are simply because they exist.

He finished in the bathroom and went to the bedroom. The envelope containing the day's instructions lay on the dresser. In his underpants and sheer black socks, he picked it up and tore it open.

A little man the size of a cell phone stepped out of the envelope into his hand.

"Haden, how you doin'?"

"Broximon! Long time no see. How are you?"

Broximon, a man in a beautiful blue double-breasted suit, brushed off both arms as if being inside that envelope had dirtied them. "Can't complain, can't complain. How're you?"

Haden carefully put him down on the table and then pulled up a chair.

"Hey man, put some clothes on before we talk. I don't wanna be talkin' to a dude in his underpants."

Haden smiled and went off to choose an outfit for the day. While waiting for him, Broximon took out a tiny portable CD player and turned on some Luther Vandross.

With the music cooking in his ears, Broximon walked to the edge of the table and sat down with his legs dangling over the edge. Haden sure lived *low.* The man's apartment showed no signs of life. No texture, no soul, nothing was in it that made you go whoa, that's cool. Broximon was a firm believer in "to each his own," but when you're in a man's home, you can't help look around, right? And if you see that apartment ain't got nothing inside it but the heat, well then that's just the truth of the situation. You're not making any sort of value judgment; you're just reporting what you see. Which in this case wasn't much, that's for sure.

"So who am I showing around today? The House of Lipstick, right?" Haden came in wearing a formal white shirt and a sharp pair of black slacks that looked like they had cost serious money.

"That's right." Broximon reached into his pocket and pulled out a folded slip of paper. "A group of twelve. And the part you'll like is that they're almost all women, average age thirty."

Haden's face lit up. His prayer had been answered! He couldn't believe his luck. "What's the story with them?"

"Did you ever hear of 'Mallvelous' in Secaucus, New Jersey?"

"No." Haden looked to see if Broximon was joking with that name.

"Biggest shopping mall in the Tri-State area. Then someone started a fire in it and it became the biggest shopping-mall fire ever in the Tri-State area."

Haden checked his pockets to make sure he had everything—keys, wallet. Then he asked without much interest, "How many died in the fire?"

"Twenty-one, over half of them in The House of Lipstick. The fire started right next to their shop and they didn't have much chance of escaping."

"What was it, some kind of cosmetics store?"

"Yup. The guy who owned it—you'll meet him today—had himself a good little business because that's all he sold. Just about every brand of lipstick on earth. You know everybody's crazy for specialty shops these days. He had brands from the weirdest places, like Paraguay. You never think of women wearing lipstick in *Paraguay,* you know?"

Haden stopped walking around the room and stared at Broximon. "Why not?"

The little man was instantly embarrassed. "I don't know. Because it's—I don't know. Because it's fucking *Paraguay.*"

"So what?"

For want of anything better to do, Broximon stood and brushed off both sleeves again. "Are you ready to go or not?"

Haden stared at him a moment longer, his expression saying the other man was an idiot. The message was conveyed loud and clear. Finally he nodded.

"Good! So let's go, huh?"

Haden picked up Broximon, placed him on his right shoulder, and left the apartment.

He always met the tour bus outside the café where he ate his breakfast. The bus driver was one of those saps taken in by Haden's looks and sometimes-charm and was more than happy to detour a few blocks to pick up the tour guide.

The bus doors hissed open. Simon Haden charged up the stairs, lit from within by two cups of strong cappuccino and the optimism that comes with knowing you are going to spend the day with a bunch of young women.

The bus driver, Fleam Sule, waved one of its many tentacles in greeting at Simon. Then with another tentacle, it pressed a button to close the door. Haden had always loved octopuses. Or was it octopi? He would have to ask Fleam Sule that someday, but not right now because Women Ahoy!

Winking at the octopus bus driver, Haden put on his best, most winning smile and turned to face the passengers.

Outside on the street, Broximon stood and watched as the bus pulled away from the curb. A maple leaf blown by the wind collided with him, disappearing the tiny man completely from view for a second. He brusquely pushed it away and the leaf fled down the street. Shaking his head, he reached into his pocket and took out a cell phone the size of a pencil eraser. Speed-dialing a number, he waited for it to connect.

"Hi there, it's Brox. Yes, I was just with him." Broximon listened while the other voice said something long and involved.

Down at the corner, the traffic light turned green. The tour bus took a left and disappeared into the city.

Broximon started going up and down on his toes and looking at the sky as the other person talked on. Eventually he was able to get in,

"Look, Haden doesn't *get* it yet. It's as simple as that. He doesn't have the slightest clue. You understand what I'm saying? He's not even on the *map* yet." Broximon saw a bright red candy wrapper skittering down the street toward him. He started moving out of its way long before it arrived. Seeing it pass reminded him he hadn't had breakfast yet. That made him doubly impatient to get off the telephone and find a place to eat. "Look, I don't know how better to tell you—*he doesn't get it.* There is not one indication that Simple Simon sees the big picture."

Listening some more to the voice on the other end, Broximon was no longer paying much attention. To amuse himself, he stuck out his tongue and crossed his eyes. After holding that pose for a while, he couldn't take the other's verbal diarrhea anymore. So he said "What? Huh? What? I'm losing you. We're losing our connection here—" Then he pressed the disconnect button and turned off the phone altogether. "Enough. Breakfast time."

It took several seconds for Haden's eyes to adjust to the blue dark inside the bus. He was so eager to see that he squinted hard to distinguish who sat facing him. The first thing he saw was a cassowary in a green dress. Do you know what a cassowary is? Neither did Haden, nor did he remember the one time he had seen one at a zoo in Cincinnati. He had stopped to look at it, thinking once again how weird nature could be.

Seeing that giant bird looking at him now, his eyes narrowed. Oh no, they weren't going to do *this* to him again, were they? He remembered one tour he'd led where—

"Excuse me?"

Trying to locate the face, he worked very hard to overcome his dismay. "Yes?" He hoped his voice sounded happy and helpful.

"Is there a lavatory on this bus?"

Lavatory. When was the last time he'd heard that ridiculous word used, fourth grade? Smirking a little, he looked toward the questioner. Seeing her, the smirk died and Haden almost yawped because she was absolutely hair-raisingly beautiful. And blind.

That's right—even in that shadowy space he could plainly see the woman's eyes were so deep set in her head that they could not possibly have been functional.

"Uh yes, there's a, uh, lavatory at the back of the bus. On the left side." Absurdly and without thinking he beamed his best, most winning smile at her. Not that she could see it.

Like a crazy young dog pulling on its leash, all he wanted to do then was race down the aisle to her side and ask everything. What was her name, why she was there, where had she come from. . . . He held himself back though and tried to calm his mad-to-get-there spirit. He silently chanted to himself slowly, slowly—do this right.

For the first time since being hired to do this miserable job, Simon Haden was glad to be a tour guide; glad that today's sightseeing would last hours. It was the top-dollar, see-everything, fifteen-stops, watch-your-step-getting-off-the-bus tour. Normally he loathed it. Today with this blind angel along for the ride, it would be bliss.

Not that it mattered, but he looked over the rest of the passengers on the bus. There were a few people, a few animals, two cartoon characters, and an almost six-foot-tall bag of caramels. Nothing special, nothing new. If they had been his only customers that day, it would have taken a real effort to rise to their occasion. But with the angel sitting on the aisle in row seven, he was going to enchant them all.

He picked up the bus microphone and turned it on. Blowing into it once, he heard his short puff resound throughout the bus speakers, proof that the thing was working. Sometimes it didn't and he ended the day hoarse.

"Good morning and welcome on board."

As one, the humans, animals, and cartoon characters smiled at him. But the giant transparent bag of beige candy shuffled impatiently in its seat. Let's go, it appeared to be saying, let's get this show on the road.

Haden disliked caramels. He ate a lot of candy because he had a sweet tooth, but caramels were too much work and too much trouble. Invariably they stuck in his teeth like gluey pests and had even pulled out an expensive filling when he ate one at his parents' house. But they were very much a part of his childhood memories because his fat father loved caramels and was always eating them. His mother stationed little plates of the golden squares all around the house for her man.

"Today we're going to try and give you a pretty good overview of the city. We'll be starting in the center naturally and then working our way out—"

"Excuse me?"

He recognized her voice immediately and with a dazzling smile that could have lit the inside of the bus like a thousand-watt light bulb, he turned to the blind woman, ready to heed her every wish.

"Yes?"

"Is there a lavatory on this bus?"

The only way to make beauty ugly is to show it's crazy. Like twisting the top off a jar of something wonderful to eat, the moment we're hit by the terrible smell of it gone bad, even the hungriest person will drop the jar in the trash without a second thought.

Haden took a short quick breath as if he'd been punched in the stomach. She had already asked that question one minute ago. Was she crazy? Was all that beauty wasted because she had scrambled eggs for brains? Or maybe she just hadn't heard his response. Was that possible? Maybe she'd been distracted or thinking about something else when he had specifically said—

He stared at her, not really knowing what to say now. And as he stared, something dawned on him. He knew this woman. We rarely forget great beauty but sometimes it does happen. He ignored her question because something in him kept saying I know her face. But where do I know it from?

The bus suddenly jolted to an abrupt stop, knocking Haden way off balance. He turned to see what had made the driver slam on the brakes like that. Through the front windshield he saw a school class of young kids being shepherded across the street by a middle-aged black woman wearing a vibrantly colored dashiki and an Afro haircut that made her head look like a round, carefully trimmed hedge. When all of the kids had crossed the street and were safely on the other side, the woman raised a hand and wriggled her fingers in thanks to the bus driver for stopping.

At first Haden didn't recognize the woman, her Afro hairdo or dashiki; it was her wriggle. He *knew* that wriggle. He had lived with it for a long time at one time in his life. In a second he was absolutely sure of her. He knew the wriggle, knew the gesture, and now he knew the woman who made it.

Whipping his head around, he looked at the beautiful blind woman. He knew her too. What the hell was going on here? Why was the world too familiar to him all of a sudden?

Back a few rows, Donald Duck looked across the aisle at the cassowary and slowly raised an eyebrow. The cassowary saw it and shrugged.

"Mrs. Dugdale!" Her name fell on top of Haden's head like a brick dropped from the roof. "She was my teacher!"

The octopus bus driver looked at him. "Who was?"

Haden pointed excitedly through the windshield in the direction of where the children had just gone. "Her—the black woman who just passed with all the kids. That was my teacher in third grade!"

The driver looked in the rearview mirror a moment at the passengers. At least half of them had slid forward in their seats expectantly, as if waiting for something important to happen.

The driver feigned indifference. "Yeah, so what? Too late for me to run over her now."

"Let me out. I've got to talk to her."

"You can't leave now, Simon. We just started a tour."

"Open the door. I gotta get out. Open the door!"

"They'll fire you, man. If you walk out like this on a tour, you're history. Don't do it."

"Fleam, we're not having a discussion here, okay? Just open the damned door." Haden was a big man with impressive muscles. Fleam Sule was only an octopus and wasn't about to argue. It couldn't resist flinging a last warning at the other's back as he walked down the steps to the street. "You're in trouble now, Simon. As soon as I tell them about this at the office, they're going to fire you."

Haden wasn't listening. He didn't even hear the door hiss shut behind him and then the bus pull away from the crosswalk. He certainly did not see all of the passengers flock to one side of the bus to see what he was going to do next. Even the blind woman was there, her cheek pressed to the cold glass, listening as someone described to her what Simon Haden was doing at that very moment.

He hurried after the children and Mrs. Dugdale. It was amazing that he had abandoned the tour and even more, his chances with the beautiful blind woman. But the moment he realized who had been leading those kids across the street, Haden knew he had to talk to her.

Because his third-grade class had been so important to him?

No.

If he'd been forced on pain of death to remember one nice thing about that year in her class, all that he would have been able to come up with was she kept a goldfish in a large round bowl on her desk that was soothing to look at.

Was it because Mrs. Dugdale herself was one of those memorable teachers who change our lives forever by example?

No.

She yelled at students or threw chalk at them whenever she felt their attention was wandering, which was most of the time. Her idea of teaching was assigning individual oral reports on what was grown in Suriname. If you were bad (and most everything was bad to Mrs. Dugdale), she made you stand interminably in a corner against what she called "The Wall of Shame." In other words she was like too many teachers you had in elementary school. Haden had endured her moods and mediocrity and morsels of knowledge for a year and then moved up to fourth grade.

But there was one thing about her that he had never forgotten and it was why he was running after her now. In fact this one thing had played a large role in forming him. It was one of those rare childhood moments where we can look back and say without hesitation right there—that X marks the spot where something in me was changed forever.

When he was growing up, Haden had one great friend who happened to have the unfortunate name Clifford Snatzke. But Cliff was so utterly typical that he blended into life with only that odd name to distinguish him from X zillion other boys. For a while, until girls eventually became both visible and scrumptious, the two kids were inseparable. In Mrs. Dugdale's class they sat next to each other, which made the time with her slightly more pleasant.

Right before the school year ended and report cards were sent home, Cliff became frantic that he wasn't going to pass because he had failed too many spelling tests. He worried so much and so vocally about it that an exasperated Haden finally urged him to go see their teacher after class and just ask. After much hemming and hawing, Snatzke decided to do it—*if* his friend would wait for him outside the school building. Although Haden wanted to do ten other things, he agreed.

Not much in life bothered Clifford Snatzke and his face showed it. Usually he wore a slight smile or else a pleasant blankness that said he wasn't thinking about anything special and everything was okay.

But when he emerged from the school half an hour later, his cheeks were the red that accompanies great humiliation or a bad cry. Seeing him like that, Haden eagerly asked what had *happened* inside. At first Cliff wouldn't even make eye contact with his friend, much less tell the story. But eventually he did.

When he entered her classroom, Mrs. Dugdale was sitting at her desk looking out the window. Always one to mind his manners, Cliff waited until he was noticed. When she asked what he wanted, he told her in as few words as possible because all her students knew that Mrs. Dugdale liked a person to get right to the point.

But instead of looking in her grade book or giving him a lecture on how to improve his spelling, his teacher asked him what kind of name Snatzke was. He didn't know what she was talking about but said only that he didn't know. She asked him if he thought Snatzke was a very American name. He said he didn't know what she meant. She looked out the window again and didn't say anything for a long time. After a while he gently repeated his question.

Who knows why, who knows where such a thing came from in the woman, but Mrs. Dugdale then turned to this little boy and said "Get down on your knees and ask me, Clifford. Get on your knees and ask for your grade in spelling."

Kids are dumb. They're trusting and they have faith in what adults tell them because adults are the only authorities they have ever known. But the moment he heard this order, even dumb Clifford knew that what Mrs. Dugdale was telling him to do was both wrong and extraordinary. However he did it anyway. He got down on his knees as quickly as he could and just as quickly asked what his grade in spelling was going to be. His teacher looked at him for a few seconds and then told him to get out of her room.

That was the story. If Haden hadn't known his friend well, he would have thought Cliff made the whole thing up. But he hadn't. Before there was a chance to say or do anything, the front door of the school opened and Mrs. Dugdale emerged carrying her familiar brown leather briefcase. She saw the two boys, gave them a fake smile, and moved off.

Both boys looked at the ground for a long time. They couldn't look at each other until she was gone because of their shared knowledge of what she had just done.

Simon knew he had to act. Mrs. Dugdale had done a very bad thing to his friend. But Cliff would let it slide because he didn't have the guts to face her.

Haden *did* and for one of the only times in his life, he decided on the spot to do a genuinely selfless thing and right a wrong. Throwing Cliff a reassuring look, he trotted off in the direction of the faculty parking lot.

When he got there, Mrs. Dugdale was already in her Volkswagen and the engine was running. When she saw him coming toward her car she rolled the window down halfway. He would always remember that—the window went down only halfway; as if whatever he had to say was not important enough for her to make the effort to lower it further.

Going toward the VW, he felt as confident as a god about to fling a flaming lightning bolt at a sinful mortal. He was going to let her have it because, boy, did she deserve it.

"Yes, Simon? What would you like?"

He looked at her and panicked. Whatever godlike courage he'd brought to that moment fled. He could almost see it running crazily away in a zigzag across the parking lot, its ass on fire like Wile E. Coyote in a Road Runner cartoon. Haden loved cartoons.

"Why—," he managed to squeeze out of his terrified lungs before starting to hyperventilate. He thought he was going to have a heart attack.

"Yes, Simon? Why what?" Her first two words were friendly; the second two were a steel trap snapping shut.

"Why—" He couldn't breathe. His tongue had turned to stone.

"*Yes, Simon?*" He saw her right hand release the emergency brake. Her mouth tightened and her eyes flared when she saw he wasn't going to say anything more and that he had delayed her unnecessarily. Desperate and terrified, he did the only thing his body could do at that moment—he shrugged. Mrs. Dugdale would have said something nasty if she hadn't seen Clifford Snatzke walking toward them.

She didn't even bother to roll up the window. Putting the little car in gear, she shook her head and, gunning the engine, pulled away from Haden.

On and off for the rest of his life he thought about that moment and what he should have said and done. It haunted him, as childhood memories so often do. He even dreamed about it at night sometimes. But always, even in those dreams, when his big Cinerama, Dolby sound-surround moment came to be valiant, he chickened out.

Well not this time, by God. He had been having a rough go of it recently. Maybe seeing Mrs. Dugdale on the street now for the first time in thirty years was a test. If he passed it, things would take a turn for the better. Who knows? Life could be sneaky sometimes. The lessons it taught weren't always straightforward. Anyway, he'd like nothing more than to tell that monster what he thought of her all these years later.

As he hurried after her now, a thought blazed up in his mind like a flame flaring in total darkness: maybe many of his failures in life had been due to her and that stinking moment so long ago. If she hadn't scared him into silence, the courage he'd had on the tip of his soul that afternoon would have emerged. For the rest of his life he would have known it was there in him and real and could be used any time he needed it.

Rather than a botched, half-assed, bill-laden, dead-end life full of microwave meals and lousy smells, Haden might have been a contender—if it hadn't been for Mrs. Dugdale. He speeded up his pace.

A few moments after he caught sight of her, a car driving down the street lifted lazily off the pavement and took flight. It buzzed around overhead in a few circles before veering off out of sight behind an office building. Two large chimpanzees dressed like 1930s gangsters in double-breasted suits and black Borsalino hats came out of a nearby store smoking cigars, speaking Italian, and walking on their hands. Haden saw these things but paid no attention. Because Dugdale was near.

As he closed in, he touched the tops of her students' heads as he went. Despite his preoccupation with wanting to reach his old teacher, he couldn't help noticing how warm the children's heads were under his hand. Like little coffee pots all of them, percolating.

"Excuse me, Mrs. Dugdale?"

Her back to him, the woman turned slowly. When she saw the adult Simon Haden standing two feet away, her eyes did not ask who are you? They said I *know* who you are—so what?

"Yes, Simon, what would you like?"

Aaaugh, the exact same words she had said to him thirty years ago in the parking lot! The same unsympathetic expression on her face. Nothing had changed. Not one thing. He was almost forty but she was still looking at him as if he were a bad piece of fruit at the market.

Fuck that. His moment had come. Now was the time to act decisively. Now was the time to say something brilliant and important to show her who was boss.

Because he was in such a state of shock at her familiar words, Haden did not see that all of Mrs. Dugdale's students were frozen in place, staring at him with keen anticipation. Nor did he notice that essentially the whole world around him had come to a standstill because it too was waiting to see what he would do next. Oh sure, cars moved along the street and flies buzzed their mad circles in the air. But all of them—the flies, the drivers in the cars, the molecules in their lungs—everything and everyone had turned to Simon Haden to witness what he would do next.

He made to speak. We must give the man that. Stirring words came to him, perfectly right for the moment. The right words, the ideal tone of voice. He was all ready to go. He made to speak but then discovered he no longer had a mouth.

He worked his mouth up and down, or rather the skin on his face where his mouth had previously been. It stretched, it moved, but that was only because it was skin and he was working the muscles beneath it. Muscles that should have controlled a mouth but he did not have one anymore. He had only skin there—smooth flat skin like the long expanse on a cheek.

He put both hands up to touch it but that only confirmed what he already feared—no mouth. Unwilling to believe what they felt, his fingers kept groping around there as if they were searching for a light switch in the dark.

He glanced at Mrs. Dugdale. Her expression made that terrible moment worse. Scorn. The only thing on her face was scorn. Scorn for Haden, scorn for his cowardice, and scorn for whomever he was now in her eyes. He was reliving his thirty-year-old moment of truth with her in the school parking lot. And this time he *would* have prevailed if he'd only had a mouth.

But he didn't. Frantically he slapped the space on his face where a mouth *should* have been. While doing that he glared at this woman, this villain in an Afro who was winning again. The only weapon he had to use now was his eyes. But eyes are not meant for this kind of warfare. A dirty look doesn't have the firepower, the megatonnage a ripping good sentence does.

Somewhere in a far corner of his mind, Haden knew that he had been here before, right smack in the middle of this moment and exact situation, mouthless. But his fury and exasperation combined brushed aside this déjà vu. So what if he had been here before—he still had to handle it now. Still had to find a way to defeat Dugdale and show her that he was not the idiot her mocking eyes said he was.

Desperation growing, he looked around for something, anything that he could use. His eyes fell on a little girl. Her name was Nelly Weston and she was one of Mrs. Dugdale's students. The girl was tormented too often by the teacher for being too slow, too sloppy, too dreamy for Dugdale's liking.

Haden picked up Nelly and slid his hand under the back of her sweatshirt. It happened so fast that she didn't have a chance to protest. But when he touched her bare back she understood instantly what he was doing and smiled like she had never smiled before in her teacher's presence.

Nelly looked at Mrs. Dugdale and opened her mouth wide like the ventriloquist's dummy she had just become. It was all right though because she knew what was about to happen. Out of her little girl's mouth came a man's deep voice—calm but a little threatening too—Simon Haden's voice.

"You mean old bitch! You haven't changed at all in thirty years. I'm sure you're still torturing your students when no one is watching. When your door is closed and you think you're safe. Remember Clifford Snatzke, huh? Remember what you did to him? Well, surprise! You're not safe and some of us do know *exactly* what you do, Bully. Shithead."

Nelly mouthed his words perfectly. She could feel Haden's hand on her back manipulating her, but she didn't need to because the two of them were wholly in synch with the words. What he wanted to say she wanted to say, and she did.

When he was finished and staring triumphantly at Dugdale's stunned and then frightened face, Haden barely heard a voice nearby say, "Well, it's about time. Bravo."

He shifted his eyes over and down and there was dapper little Broximon, hands on hips, a big smile on his face. Where had *he* suddenly come from?

A million or a billion synapses and connections and whatever else suddenly jumped across Haden's brain. Something big was taking form in there, something was coming clear. He suddenly looked at life around him. At the street, the cars, the people, the sky, the world. An instant later, Simon Haden understood.

He gasped through a mouth that reappeared the moment he made his discovery. He lowered Nelly Weston to the ground.

This city, this planet, this life around him was his own invention. He had created all of it. He knew that now. Where had he created it? In the dreams he had every night while he slept.

He looked at Mrs. Dugdale and was almost as surprised to see she was smiling at him and nodding. So was Broximon. So was every person nearby. A small dog on a leash was staring and smiling at him too. He knew the dog's name—Birmy. He knew it because he had made it up one night. He had made up this entire world.

Simon Haden finally realized that he was surrounded by a land, a life, a world that he had created every night of his life in his dreams.

Everything here was either fashioned by him, or taken from his conscious world and carried over into his dream world so that he could play with it, fight with it, or try to resolve it in a place of his own.

At forty, Simon Haden had had more than fourteen thousand dreams. A lot of material there to build a world on.

"I'm dead." He stated this—he did not ask it as a question. He looked at Broximon. The little man kept smiling but now he nodded too.

"That's what death is—everyone makes their own when they're alive. Then we die and all of our dreams come together and form a place, a land. And that's where we go when we die." This time Haden looked at his old third-grade teacher for corroboration and she nodded too.

"And you live in that dreamland you created until you recognize what it really is, Simon." She said it cheerfully in the same tone of voice one would use to proclaim it was a beautiful day.

Thoughts, images, and particularly memories shot back and forth across Haden's mind like tracer bullets in a night firefight. Octopus bus drivers, cars that flew, beautiful blind women—

"That blind woman—I remember her now. I remember the dream she was in. She was always saying the same thing again and again. It drove me nuts. I had the dream right after I got married. I dreamed—"

Broximon waved the rest away. "It doesn't matter, Simon. So long as you realize what this is all about, you can fit the individual pieces together later."

"But I definitely *am* dead?" For some reason, Haden looked at little Nelly Weston this time for the answer. She gave a child's big up and down nod to make sure that he understood.

He gestured with both hands at the world around them. "And this is death?"

"*Your* death, yes." Broximon chuckled. "And you created almost all of us at one time or another. That is, except for Mrs. Dugdale and things like that giant bag of caramels on the bus. Remember how much your father loved caramels?"

Haden was very afraid to ask the next question but he knew that he must. In a low voice, almost a whisper, he asked, "How long have I been here?"

Broximon looked at Dugdale who looked at Nelly who looked at Broximon. He sighed, puffed out his cheeks, and said, "Let's just say you've had this meeting with Mrs. Dugdale a lot but before this, she's always won."

"Answer me, Broximon. How long have I been here?"

"A long time, pal. A very, *very* long time."

Haden shuddered. "And I'm just realizing now what it's all about?"

"Who cares how long it's taken, Simon. You know now."

The woman and the girl nodded vigorously in agreement. Haden noticed that the rest of those around them were nodding too in much the same way—everyone clearly agreed on this point.

"Well what am I supposed to *do* with it? What am I supposed to do now?"

Mrs. Dugdale crossed her arms over her chest and wore a very familiar expression on her face. Haden remembered it well. "You finally passed first grade, Simon. Now you move on to second."

An icy chill tiptoed up Simon Haden's spine. "Death is like *school?*"

Again, every one and every thing grew the same smile and looked very pleased at his progress.

The Invisible Empire

John Kessel

—Inspired by Karen Joy Fowler's story "Game Night at the Fox and Goose"

When Henrietta and Hiram Patterson arrived at church that Sunday, Henrietta's arm was bound to a splint, tied up in a sling made from a blue kerchief. In the quiet chat of the congregation before we entered, Henrietta allowed as how she had been kicked by the mule, but I was not the only observer to notice Hiram's sidelong watchfulness, and the fact that their two boys kept their mother between themselves and their father at all times.

The congregation was more subdued than usual in the wake of the news of that week. Robert and I sat in the third pew; Sarah sat with her husband and three children a row ahead of us. Lydia Field, her black hair piled high beneath a modest straw hat, kept watch from the choir loft. Beautiful Iris sat in front with her beau, Henry Fletcher. Louellen was not a churchgoer, and Sophonsiba attended the colored church.

As the Pattersons took seats in our pew, I nodded toward them. Hiram, shaved clean and his hair parted neatly in the middle, nodded gravely back. Henrietta avoided my gaze. Their older boy took up a hymnal and paged through it.

The service began with the singing of "When Adam Was Created."

When Adam was created,
He dwelt in Eden's shade;
As Moses has related,
Before a bride was made.

I looked up at Lydia in the choir. Her eyes closed, she sang as sweetly as an angel; one would think her the picture of feminine submission. Another angel was Sarah, mother and homemaker. Certainly Henry Fletcher considered Iris an angel sent from heaven to entice him.

I felt for Robert's hand, and held it as I sang.

. . . This woman was not taken
From Adam's head, we know;
And she must not rule o'er him,
It's evidently so.

The husband is commanded
To love his loving bride;
And live as does a Christian,
And for his house provide.
The woman is commanded
Her husband to obey,
In every thing that's lawful,
Until her dying day.

As the song ended, the Reverend Hines climbed to the pulpit. He stared down for some time without speaking, the light from the clerestory gleaming off his bald pate. Finally he began.

"I take my text, on this day of retribution, from the letter of St. Paul to the Ephesians, chapter 5, verses 22 through 24. 'Wives, submit to your husbands, as to the Lord. For the husband is the head of the wife, as also Christ is head of the church; and he is the Savior of the body. Therefore, just as the church is subject to Christ, so let the wives be to their own husbands in everything.'"

The minister rested his hand on the Bible. "My brothers and sisters, the sword of a righteous God is raised over the heads of those rebellious women who walk among us today. They think that by hiding in the dark, we will not see them. But to the Lord God Almighty, there is no darkness but the darkness of eternal perdition to which those women condemn themselves. God saw Eve when she ate of the forbidden fruit; he sees you now."

Did God see when a father in Bristol, Connecticut, knocked the teeth of his eighteen-year-old daughter down her throat because she entertained the attentions of a boy he did not approve? Did he see when Charles S. Smith, a married man, got with child the simple-minded eleven-year-old Edith Wilson in Otsego County, New York?

"But my message today is not only to the wives," Hines went on. "Brothers, I ask you: why was Adam cast from the garden? It was not because he ate of the apple! I put it to you that he was cast out because he sacrificed his judgment to that of his wife. The minute Adam saw Eve with the apple of which she had eaten, he knew she was damned. Adam's sin was that he loved Eve too much. He loved her so much that, despite his knowledge that in violating the injunction of the Lord God she had committed the gravest crime, he could not bear to see her damned by herself. So he ate of the apple too, and damned himself, and all of his posterity, with her.

"From that one act of submission to a wrongheaded woman have come five thousand years of suffering.

"My word today to you wives is obvious: obey your husband. He is born to a wisdom you cannot grasp; his hand is the hand of the Lord. When you turn against a man, you turn against the utmost power of the universe. If you have transgressed, the Lord demands you confess. Remember, Jesus forgave even the woman taken in adultery; he awaits your repentance with arms open in sweet forgiveness. But for those whose hearts are hardened, only the angel of death awaits. Speak now, and be saved, or hold your tongues and be damned for all eternity.

"My word today to you husbands, in particular and most direly to those who know of the sins of your wives yet keep silent out of love, is simply this: you must act! You bear the burden of the Lord's command, to be the head of your wife. Your own salvation, her salvation, and the salvation of the community depend on it. Do not think that, by protecting her, you show mercy, any more than by joining Eve, Adam did. By protecting evil, you condemn yourself, and your children, and the children of every other man to evil.

"All across our land, in these days of rebellion, this challenge is put to all, male and female. 'Be not deceived; God is not mocked: for whatsoever a man soweth, that shall he also reap.'

"Let us pray."

As Reverend Hines led the Lord's Prayer, I bowed my head and recited the words with the others, but my ears were burning. Beside me, Robert's eyes were closed. I glanced up and saw Lydia's head held rigidly forward.

After the prayer, the reverend called on the congregation to testify. "Now is the time! Do not be afraid of your neighbors' reaction. Do not wait, thinking perhaps that tomorrow, or next week, will be soon enough. Tomorrow or next week you may be dead and burning in hell; no man knows the hour of his judgment!"

He waited. The church lay silent. I saw Iris's golden head tremble; Iris is a foolish girl. I remembered how she had fretted at the talk she had aroused when she'd worn red bloomers to the cotillion. Her commitment went little farther than reading smuggled copies of *Woodhull and Claflin's Weekly.* But she did not rise.

In the end, no one did. Reverend Hines's scowl told all that was needed of his displeasure.

After the service, as we stood beneath the huge oak outside the church, I made a special point to take the reverend's hand. I thanked him for calling us to our conscience and deplored the lack of a response from the congregation.

"God have mercy on their souls," he said. "For I will have none."

"I hope their silence only signifies the personal repentance that must precede the public one," I said, and stepped aside.

As Robert shook hands with Hines, Lydia Field touched my arm, and mentioned to me that the quilting circle needed to get together soon.

Robert is a carpenter: he built our house with his own hands, on an acre of ground a mile outside of town. It is a finer house than our income warrants, with extra bedrooms that we have not had cause to use. In truth, the house, like our lives, is a work in progress, perhaps never to be finished. In the evenings, after quitting his shop, Robert works mounting crown molding, laying oak flooring, trimming windows.

I fell in love with Robert when I saw him work. He is never a talkative man, but in his workshop he becomes a silent one, except for the aimless and off-key tunes that he hums, unaware.

He leans over the bench, feeds a long strip of maple through the saw, pumping the treadle steadily with his foot. He inspects the result, measures it, marks it, and slides it into the miter box. His eyes are quiet. His lips are closed in an expression that is the faintest prelude to a smile, but not a smile itself. His hands are precise. He takes up a box saw. He does not hurry, he does not dawdle. A shock of hair falls into his eyes, he brushes it away, and it falls back. In the mornings I shake sawdust from his pillow.

After we had returned from the church and had eaten our dinner, Robert changed out of his Sunday suit and went to work on the stair rail in the front hall.

"It's Sunday," I said, wiping my hands. "The day of rest."

"But we aren't the sort who regulate our lives by the Bible, are we?"

He did not return my stare. "Would you have me be the kind of woman Jordan Hines prefers?"

He shrugged the canvas strap from his shoulder and set down his long toolbox. "I don't look to Jordan Hines for my conscience. But some things are wrong. Killing a man in cold blood is wrong."

"But killing a woman in hot passion is all right. And breaking her arm is not worth notice."

"Don't put words in my mouth."

"Henrietta Patterson is a mouse; she wouldn't take a step outside her kitchen without her husband's leave—more's the pity. Name a man in this town who has been killed."

"Susannah, can you blame me if I am troubled? This cannot go on much longer before you are found out."

"For every woman found out a hundred more will rise. Laura D. Fair was murdered by a mob in Seneca Falls ten years ago. Did that stop anything?"

He knelt beside the box and took up one of the balusters he had turned on the lathe that week. "I did not marry Laura D. Fair. At least, I didn't think I was marrying her. I married for love and a family, not revenge and violence."

I turned from him and went to the kitchen. He laid down the baluster and followed me. As I stood at the counter, my back to him, he touched my shoulder.

"I didn't mean it that way," he said. "If we never have a child, I'll still have you. That's why I'm worried. I could not bear to lose you."

I had not seen my woman's bleeding in more than a month, but I wouldn't get our hopes up only to suffer another loss. "I won't sit by and watch a woman like Henrietta Patterson pretend to be kicked by a mule when everyone in town knows it was her drunken husband." I turned from him and went to our room.

"Susannah!"

I closed the door and lay on the bed, dry eyed, heavy with sudden fatigue. He did not follow. After a while I heard the sound of his boots in the hall, and the snick of the folding rule as he measured the stairway. Dinah, our cat, jumped onto the bed and curled up beside me. As the afternoon declined I fell asleep.

When I woke it was evening. I took off my dress and donned a pair of men's trousers and a man's shirt. Worn, sturdy shoes, leather work gloves. I found Robert in the kitchen, the sleeves of his work shirt rolled to his elbows, eating bread and cheese. On the table lay the newspaper from the day before.

John Kessel

'SISTERS OF FURY' EXECUTED

◆

Presidential Assassins Hanged in Philadelphia

◆

The 'Drop' Falls at Three Minutes Past Six O'Clock

◆

President Hendricks Declares 'Justice Done'

◆

Female Protests Quelled

Philadelphia, July 22

The last chapter of the conspiracy to assassinate the President is finished.

Saturday, at six in the morning, the twelve women convicted of treason and murder in the assassination of President Cleveland were put to death. In execution of the sentence of the Military Commission, duly approved by the President, the prisoners were hanged by the neck until dead in the courtyard of the federal penitentiary in Philadelphia, Pennsylvania.

The painful scene was unattended by either extraordinary accident or incident, and was conducted in the most solemn and quiet manner.

Witnesses report that the last words of Helen Araminta Macready, leader of the hooded women who assaulted the President last May during the monthly tea held on the White House lawn, were "Death to all seducers."

Robert looked up at me. His eyes slowly passed over my clothing. He didn't speak.

"I am going out tonight," I told him. "Don't wait up for me."

The six of us gathered at the barn at the Compson place at midnight. In the hardscrabble fields remained only twisted, dry stalks of last year's corn; the burnt shell of the house stood stark in the moonlight, the brick chimney rising like a sentinel over the ruin.

Sophonsiba crawled into the hearth and pulled our robes out of the chimney. She hurried back to the barn, her dark face gleaming, and handed around the robes and hoods.

Lydia had brought the horses, and we mounted and rode east. I am not the best rider—Lydia has been a horsewoman since her youth—but my skill exceeded that of the awkward Sarah and Louellen. Still, we had all made progress in the last year. It was a hot night; the air hung heavy with not a breath of breeze. I felt the sweat gather at the back of my neck. The sound of cicadas in the oaks was deafening.

The Patterson farm stood near the junction of Swift Creek and the Manahoc, forty poorly tended acres of cleared forest planted to corn and beans. We tied the horses in the woods near the road and moved silently up to the ramshackle house.

The back door was open. We crept through the kitchen, past the room where the boys slept, to their parents' room. Henrietta lay on her back cradling the broken forearm against her breast, waiting for us, her eyes glinting in the dark.

Sarah motioned her to be quiet. Patterson stank of whiskey, and snored loudly, lost to the world. We fell upon him: one woman to each arm, and a pillow over his face.

"No!" Henrietta cried. "Don't hurt him!" But it was mostly show.

"Megaera!" Lydia told Louellen. "Hold her back." Louellen pulled Henrietta away from the bed. Patterson struggled, but in a moment we had him bound and gagged. Lydia lit a lamp; when he saw the hooded figures standing around the bed, his eyes went wide.

We dragged him to his feet and pushed him out into the yard. "No, please," Henrietta whimpered.

The oldest boy, no more than eight or nine, woke and ran after us. His mother had to hold him back, wrapping her good arm about him. He stood barefoot in the dirt watching us with big eyes. His little brother came out and clutched his mother's nightgown. "Mama?" he asked.

"Hush," his mother said, weeping.

Sarah and Iris fetched the horses. Sophonsiba knocked Patterson's feet out from under him and the drunken man fell hard. He cursed through the gag, rolling in the dust as Lydia tied him by a long rope to the pommel of her saddle.

We dragged him out to the bridge over the creek. There we stripped him naked and tied him to the bridge.

"His figure falls far short of the Greek ideal," Iris said slyly.

"Be quiet, Tisiphone," Lydia commanded in a guttural voice. I do think that Lydia could find work as a medium, and it would not be a show—for I had seen enough of her to know that, when she spoke like this, she was indeed being moved by some spirit that was not quite herself.

"Hiram Patterson. We are the ghosts of women dead at the hands of men. We are told you come of a good family. If that is so, it is time for you to get down on your knees in church next Sunday, confess your sins, and beg the forgiveness of your dear wife. You are marked. We will be watching. If you fail, rest assured that there is no place in Greene County that is beyond our reach."

Lydia extended her arm, pointing a black-gloved finger at him. "You will not receive another warning. We *will* have good husbands, or we will have none."

Then she turned to me. "Alecto," she said. "Do your work."

Sophonsiba advanced with the torch. I took out the straight razor and unfolded the blade. When Patterson saw the torchlight gleam along it, he let out a muffled howl and lost control of his bladder. The urine splashed down the front of my robe. I slapped his face.

Disgusted, I crouched before him. He writhed. "Keep still, or this will not go well for you!" I said. He legs trembled like those of a man palsied. When I touched the razor to his groin, he fainted. His body slumped, and he fell against the blade. Blood welled and ran down his leg.

"I'm afraid I have nicked him," I said.

"Finish quickly."

He bled a deal, but the wound was far from mortal. I shaved his pubic hair, and delicately cut a circle and dependent cross on his chest.

I was withdrawing the bloody razor from my work when Louellen hissed, "Someone's coming!"

A half dozen horses came galloping down the road.

Sophonsiba hurled the torch into the creek while the rest of us ran to our mounts. My horse shied from the flash of our robes, tossing his head and flipping the reins from my fingers. I stumbled forward and grasped them, then awkwardly pulled myself into the saddle.

"Halt!" one of the men shouted. A gunshot rang out; Sarah's head snapped back and she dropped like a stone from her horse, her foot caught in her stirrup. The horse began to run, dragging her.

Sophonsiba pulled a pistol from beneath her robe and fired at the men; at the sound of the shot her horse reared, almost throwing her. The men drew up and fired back. Louellen and Iris were already gone, and Sophonsiba kicked her horse's flanks and surged away. I hesitated, thinking of Sarah, but Lydia grabbed my robe and tugged. "Ride!" she shouted, and we were off.

We set off down the road toward Parson's Knob, away from the creek. A couple more shots whizzed past us. When we crested the ridge, I spied Sophonsiba, Louellen, and Iris ahead of us. Instead of following, Lydia veered right, into the trees.

"This way," she called. I jerked the reins, almost losing my saddle, and swerved with her between the trees.

Clouds had blown in, and a wind had picked up. In the dark it was hard to see the branches that whipped across us; I ducked and dodged trying to keep up. We descended through a series of gullies toward the river. After ten frantic minutes Lydia halted, and held up a hand for me to be quiet. We heard further shots in the distance.

"The men must have been covering the road," Lydia said. "They wanted us to flee that way. Louellen rode them right into an ambush."

"Will they tell?" We had all vowed death before betrayal.

Lydia's masked face turned toward me. "Louellen will not. Sophonsiba most definitely will not. Iris would—if she hasn't already."

"What?"

"Do you think they fell upon us by accident? They were forewarned. We have a traitor among us."

"It can't be. If they knew, why weren't they waiting when we came for Patterson?"

"I don't know."

We rode north along the river, picking our way quietly through the trees. The foliage was so thick here we had to dismount and lead the horses, and eventually we moved away from the river so as not to come out onto the road near the ferry landing.

Leaves rustled in the stiffening breeze, broken by the occasional hoot of an owl. The temperature was falling and it felt like rain.

I pondered what had happened to the other women. Sarah was surely dead. If caught, Sophonsiba would be summarily shot—and the others? Last winter the Martyred Marys had been hanged in Trenton. The governor had vowed "to expunge the viper of female vigilance organizations" from the state. Victoria Woodhull's press had been destroyed; even Bloomer's timid *The Lily* was forced to print in secret. In the aftermath of the president's assassination, every man in the country would be on the alert.

My horse nickered nervously, tossed his head, and I shortened my grip on the reins. Lydia held up a hand. "Willet's Road," she whispered and, handing me her horse's reins, crept forward to peer into the clearing in the trees, looking, in her black robe, for all the world like some monstrous crow.

She came back. "It's clear. Let's try to make it to the barn. I'll take the horses from there and we can creep back into town before first light."

We remounted and rode west, away from the river. The road was deserted, and the sinking moon, dipping beneath the cloud cover, shone eerily, the oak trees with their sprays of leaves black against the sky. Twenty minutes later, as the Compson place arose out of the darkness, we heard the sound of horses.

"Quickly!" Lydia hissed, and kicked her horse into a canter, heading for the barn just as the clouds opened and the rain began. I raced after her, and we jumped off the horses, pulling them inside. We peered out toward the road a hundred yards away through the increasing downpour as three horsemen trotted by from the direction we had come. One of them was towing a horse that looked as if it might have a body thrown over the saddle.

The rain drummed on the roof, drizzling through gaps in the boards. Neither of us spoke for some time. Lydia took off her robe and tucked it under her saddle pad. Mine reeked of Patterson's urine. I buried it in some rotting straw in the corner of a stall and tucked the hood into the waistband of my trousers. "I'll take the horses back to Martha's stable," Lydia said. "You can get back to town on foot."

"Who do you think those men were?" I asked. "I don't see them coming from our town."

"I expect they were from Statesberg. Maybe joined by a few from town, but not many. We'll find out tomorrow."

"I don't believe Iris betrayed us. The men fired as soon as they saw us. Would they shoot at their own informer?"

"I would not hazard a guess as to what a man might do," Lydia said.

I sat back in the straw of the barn's floor, and watched the glint of a spider's web in the corner of the doorway. "I begin to wonder if we can ever change them."

Lydia turned to me; her voice was fierce. "If men were capable of change, then reason would have done it years ago. For most, the only answer is death."

"How can you say that?"

"You and your precious Robert! What do you think we have been doing? We aren't changing their minds—we're forcing them to stop abusing us because they know if they don't stop they will be punished."

"That's a counsel of despair. If you're right, men and women will never live together in peace."

"Do you think Hiram Patterson is capable of having his mind changed?"

"Maybe Hiram Patterson isn't—but other men."

"Any men persuaded are regarded by others with contempt. Men like Patterson and Hines run the world."

I wanted to protest, to point out that no one had come forward in answer to Hines's call at church. Instead I brooded. "If it comes down to open war between men and women, women will lose."

She tugged at the hood at my waist. "Why do you think you wear this?"

Just then my horse neighed and backed up into the darkness. I turned and saw men in the road. They pulled up, sitting motionless in their saddles, and stared at the barn. I prayed they would pass. Instead they moved off the road toward us through the steady rain.

Lydia grabbed her horse's reins, fitted her boot into the stirrup, and pulled herself astride. "Sneak out the back. Stick to the woods. I'll ride out front and outrun them."

Without waiting for my protest she kicked her horse's flanks, crouched behind his head, and raced out of the barn. The men were startled; Lydia veered past them and out to the road. One drew a pistol and fired; I saw the muzzle flash in the dark.

I did not wait to see what happened next. I crawled out the back of the barn and ran slipping through the mud for the tree line thirty yards away through Compson's abandoned corn field. I did not look back until I was under the trees; the men were gone, chasing after Lydia down the Statesville Road.

I ran for a long time. I had played in these woods as a girl, running with the boys, climbing trees, building forts, fighting General Lee and Napoleon and wicked King John in a thousand childish games. But though I knew the woods well, in the darkness and rain it was hard for me to keep my direction, and I became lost. I was still stunned by Sarah's death. Perhaps it was a delayed reaction, or fear, or some late understanding of how mad our project had been, but I found myself sitting beneath the trees, soaked to the skin, sobbing.

It must have been approaching dawn when the rain stopped and the clouds blew away. I could make out my surroundings and realized I was not far from home. I tried to stand, but a wave of nausea swept over me and I leaned one hand against the bole of a tree, bent over, vomiting.

I had emptied my stomach and was wiping my hand against my mouth when I was seized from behind and thrown to the ground.

"Susannah Mueller! Does your husband know you are out here at night?"

I twisted my head and saw, standing above me, Everett Smith, who hung around the dry goods store and had occasionally done odd jobs for Robert. He had a bottle in his left hand and a pistol in his right.

"Anyone might take you for a wicked girl," Smith said. He waved the pistol at my outfit. "In such a mannish mode of dress."

"All right, Everett," I said. "You've captured me. You'd best take me to the sheriff."

"What's the sheriff ever done for me?" he said.

He took a swig from the bottle, emptied it, and flung it aside, where it hit the tree and shattered. His pistol still on me, he fell to his knees, grabbed the front of my shirt, and yanked it up. When I tried to struggle, he slapped me across the face.

We wrestled in the wet leaves, but he was too strong for me. He tore at my clothes, his hot breath stinking of whiskey, his forearm across my neck. Unable to move him, I felt with my hands in the ground around us, hoping for a rock or tree limb. My hand fell upon the neck of the broken bottle.

Without a thought, I jabbed the bottle neck into his throat. He yelped and surged up, clutching at his neck, and I could feel the hot blood spurting over my cheek and shoulder. Smith fell back, making sounds like a hurt dog.

"What—what've you done?" he gasped. His hand fumbled for the pistol.

I kicked it away from him. He coughed, shuddered, and leaned back against the trunk of the tree. After a moment I crawled to him and tried to stanch the bleeding with my hood, with mud and leaves, with my hands. Nothing worked. I could barely make out his eyes as they glazed over. I sat watching as he bled to death.

I stuffed my bloody hood into a hollow log and made my way in the lessening darkness back home. My legs were heavy with weariness, yet my mind whirled. When I closed my eyes, I again saw Sarah's head snap back from the force of the shot. I prayed that Lydia was wrong about Iris. I wondered if the others had escaped, and realized that, if they had not, it would be better for me if they had been killed. Yet how could I face the day hoping for such a disaster, and knowing that Everett Smith's body lay half a mile from our house?

When I reached home, I crept quietly into the kitchen, undressed, and washed the blood from my face and hands with water from the kitchen pump. Dinah came in and sat on her haunches, watching me with feline imperturbability. I crammed my shirt and trousers into the woodstove, where the coals quickly set them afire.

As I climbed back into bed, Robert lifted his head. "Thank God you're back. I've been lying awake all night. Will this ever stop, Susannah?"

"It's stopped," I said, resting my head in the crook of his arm.

"Are you all right?" he asked.

"I'm fine."

He kissed me on the cheek, and fell asleep. I lay there waiting for the dawn, my hand resting on my belly, thinking about whether I wanted it to be a boy, or a girl, or nothing at all.

The Further Adventures of the Invisible Man

Karen Joy Fowler

— For Ryan

MY MOTHER LIKES TO REFER to 1989 as the year I played baseball, as if she had nothing to do with it, as if nothing *she* did that year was worth noting. She has her unamended way with too many of the facts of our lives, especially those occurring before I was born, about which there is little I can do. But this one is truly unfair. My baseball career was short, unpleasant, and largely her fault.

For purposes of calibration where my mother's stories are concerned, you should know that she used to say my father had been abducted by aliens. My mother and he made a pact after *Close Encounters of the Third Kind* that if one of them got the chance they should just go and the other would understand, so she figured right away that this is what had happened. He hadn't known I was coming yet or all bets would have been off, my mother said.

This was before *X-Files* gave alien abduction a bad name; even so my mother said we didn't need to go telling everyone. There'd be plenty of time for that when he returned, which he would be doing, of course. If he could. It might be tricky. If the aliens had faster-than-light spaceships, then he wouldn't be aging at the same rate as we; he might even be growing younger; no one knew for sure how these things worked. He might come back as a boy like me. Or it was entirely possible that he would have to transmutate his physical body into a beam of pure light in order to get back to us, which, honestly, wasn't going to do us a whole lot of good and he probably should just stay put. In any case, he wouldn't want us pining away, waiting for him—he would want us to get on with our lives. So that's what we were doing and none of this is about my father.

My mother worked as a secretary over at the college in the department of anthropology. Sometimes she referred to this job as her fieldwork. I could write a book, she would tell Tamara and me over dinner, I could write a book about that department that would call the whole theory of evolution into question. Tamara lived with us to help pay the rent. She looked like Theda Bara, though of course I didn't know that back then. She wore peasant blouses and ankle bracelets and rings in her ears. She slept in the big bedroom and worked behind the counter at Cafe Roma and sometimes sang on open mike night. She never did her dishes, but that was okay, my mom said. Tamara got enough of that at work and we couldn't afford not to be understanding. The dishes could be *my* job.

My other job was to go to school, which wasn't so easy in the sixth grade when this particular installment takes place. A lot of what made it hard was named Jeremy Campbell. You have to picture me, sitting in my first row desk, all hopeful attention. I just recently gave up my Inspector Gadget lunchbox for a nonpartisan brown bag. I'm trying to fit in. But that kid with the blond hair who could already be shaving, that's Jeremy Campbell. He's at the front of the room, so close I could touch him, giving his book report.

"But it's too late," Jeremy says, looking at me to be sure I know he's looking at me. "Every single person in that house is dead." He turns to Mrs. Gruber. "That's the end."

"I guess it would have to be," Mrs. Gruber says. "Are you sure this is a book you read? This isn't just some story you heard at summer camp?"

"*The Meathook Murders.*"

"Written by?"

Jeremy hesitates a moment. "King."

"Stephen King?

"Stanley King."

"It's not on the recommended list."

Jeremy shakes his head sadly. "I can't explain that. It's the best book I ever read."

"All right," says Mrs. Gruber. "Take your seat, Jeremy."

On his way past my desk Jeremy deliberately knocks my books onto the floor. "Are you trying to trip me, Nathan?" he asks.

"Take your seat, Jeremy," Mrs. Gruber says.

"I'll talk to you later," Jeremy assures me.

After school, having no friends to speak of, I sometimes biked to my mom's office. The bike path between my school and hers took me past the Little League fields, the Mormon temple, some locally famous hybrid trees—a very messy half walnut–half elm created by Luther Burbank himself just to see if he could—and the university day care, where I once spent all day every day finger painting and was a much happier camper.

I came to a stop sign at the same time as a woman in a minivan. (Maybe this was the same day as Jeremy's book report, maybe not. I include it so you'll know the sort of town we live in.) Even though I came to a complete stop, even though I didn't know her from Adam, she rolled down her window to talk to me. "You should be wearing a helmet," she said. *That* kind of town. Someone had graffitied the words BASEBALL SPAWNS HATE onto the Little League snack bar. This is a story about baseball, remember?

My mom's desk was in the same room as the faculty mailboxes. A busy place, but she liked that, she always liked to talk to people. On my way into the office I passed one of the other secretaries and two profs. By the time I got to my mom I'd been asked three times how school was and three times I'd said it was fine. There was a picture of me on her desk, taken when I was three and wearing a Batman shirt with the batwings stretched over my fat little three-year-old stomach, and also my most recent school picture, no matter how bad.

"Hey, cookie." My mom was always happy to see me; it's still one of the things I like best about her. "How was school?" I think she was pretty, but most kids think that about their moms; maybe she wasn't. Her hair was blonde back then and cut extremely short, her eyes a light, light blue. She had a little snow globe on her desk only instead of a snow scene there was a miniature copy of the sphinx inside, and instead of snow there was gold glitter. I picked it up and shook it.

"Have you ever heard of a book called *The Meathook Murders?*" I asked. I was just making conversation. Mom's not much of a reader.

Sure enough, she hadn't. But it reminded her of a movie she'd seen and she started to tell me the plot, which took some time, being complicated and featuring nuns with hooks for hands. My mom went to Catholic school.

She kept forgetting bits of it and the whole time she was talking to me she was also typing a letter, up until the climax, which required both hands. My mom showed me how the sleeve of the habit fell so that you saw the hook, but only for a second, and then the nun said, "Are you here to confess?" just to get into the confessional where no one could see. And then it turned out not to be the nun with the hook, after all. It turned out to be the policeman, dressed in the wimple with a fake hook. He ended up stabbed with his own fake hook, which was, my mom assured me, a very satisfying conclusion.

Somewhere in the middle of her recitation Professor Knight came in to pick up his mail. Back in the fifth grade, during the Christmas concert, when we all had reindeer horns on our heads and jingle bells in our hands and our parents were there to see us, Bjorn Benson told me that Professor Knight was my father. "Everyone knows," Bjorn said. But Professor Knight had a daughter named Kate who was just a year older than me, and I'm betting she didn't know, nor his wife neither. Kate and I were at the same school then, where I could keep an eye on her. But by now she was at the junior high and I only saw her downtown sometimes. She was a skinny girl with cow eyes who sucked on her hair. "Stop staring at me" is about the only thing she ever said to me. She didn't *look* like my sister.

I kept meaning to ask my mom, but I kept chickening out. I wasn't ever really supposed to believe in the alien abduction story; it was just there to be something funny to say, but mainly to stop me asking anything outright. Which I certainly couldn't do then, not when she was working so hard to keep me distracted and entertained. Besides, Professor Knight didn't even glance our way; if he was my father I think he would've wanted to know how school was. But then I was suspicious all over again, because the moment he left, my mom started talking about my dad. The wonders he was seeing! The friends he was making! "On the planet Zandoor," she told me, "they only wish they had hooks for hands. Instead, they have herrings. Your dad could get stuck there a long time just dialing their phones for them."

She ran out of steam, all at once, her mouth sagging so she looked sad and tired. My response to this was complicated. I felt sorry for her, but it made me angry, too. I was just a kid, it didn't seem fair to make me see this. So I gave her the note Mrs. Gruber had said to take right home to her a couple of weeks ago. I was just being mean. I'd already read it. It said Mrs. Gruber wondered if I didn't need a male role model.

And then I was relieved that Mom didn't seem to mind. She crumpled the note and hooked it over her head into the wastebasket. "I've got a job to do, cupcake," she said, so I went home and played *The Legend of Zelda* until dinnertime.

But she was more upset than she let on. Later that night Victor Wong dropped by, and I heard them talking. Victor worked in the computer department at Pacific Gas and Electric and was my mom's best friend. He was a thin-faced, delicate guy. I liked him a lot, maybe partly because he was the one man I knew for sure wasn't my dad—wrong race—and wasn't ever going to be my dad. He'd been coming around for a long time without it getting romantic. I always thought he liked Tamara though he never said so, even to my mom. If you believe her.

"Hey, don't look at me," Victor said when she brought up Mrs. Gruber's note. "I'm a heterosexual man and everyone who meets me assumes I'm gay. I'm a hopeless failure at both lifestyles."

"There's not a damn thing wrong with Nathan," my mom said, which was nice of her, especially since she didn't know I was listening. "He's a great kid. He's never given me a speck of trouble. Where does she get off?"

"Maybe the note wasn't aimed at Nathan. Maybe the note was aimed at you."

"I don't know what you're talking about."

"I think you do," Victor said. But I certainly didn't, although I spent a fair amount of time puzzling over it. I could make a better guess now. Apparently my mother used to flirt outrageously during PTA meetings in a way some people felt distracted from the business at hand. Or so Bjorn Benson says. He's still a font of information, but he's a CPA now, I doubt he'd lie.

"How you doing, Nathan?" Victor asked me later on his way to the bathroom. I was still playing *The Legend of Zelda.*

"I just need a magic sword," I told him.

"Who doesn't?" he said.

This brings us up to Saturday afternoon. The car wouldn't start; it put my mom in a very bad mood. She was always sure our mechanic was ripping her off. She had a date that evening, a fix-up from a friend, some guy named Michael she'd never even seen. So I left her getting ready and biked over to Bertilucci's Lumber and Drugs. My plan was to price a new game called *The Adventures of Link.* Even though I was such a great kid, and had never given her a speck of trouble, my mother had steadily refused to buy this game for me. I already spent too much time playing *The Legend of Zelda,* she said, as if getting me *The Adventures of Link* wouldn't solve that problem in a hot second. Anyway we couldn't afford it, especially not now that the car had to be repaired again.

Somewhere in the distance, a farmer was burning his fields. The sky to the south was painted with smoke and the whole town smelled sweetly of it. On my way to the store I passed the Yamaguchis'. Ms. Yamaguchi took self-defense with my mother and was very careful about gender-engendering toys. Her four-year-old son, Davey, was on the porch with his doll. As I biked by, he held the doll up, sighted along it. "Ack-ack-ack-ack," he said, picking me off cleanly.

I spent maybe fifteen minutes mooning over the video games. I wanted *The Adventures of Link* so bad I didn't even notice that Jeremy Campbell had come into the store, although if I'd looked into the shoplifting mirrors I could've seen him before he snuck up behind me. He put a hand on my shoulder and spun me around. He was with Diego Ruiz, a kid who'd never been anything but nice to me till this. "Come with me," Jeremy said.

We went to the front of the store where Mr. Bertilucci had temporarily abandoned the counter and Jeremy went around it and pulled the new copy of *Playboy* out from underneath. "Have you ever seen this before?" he asked me. He'd already flipped open the centerfold and he put it right on my face; I was actually breathing into her breasts, which was maybe all that kept me from hyperventilating.

"My mom says I have to get right home," I told him.

"Do pictures of naked women always make you think of your mom?" he asked. "Does your mom have tits like these?"

"I've seen his mom," Diego said. "No tits at all."

"Sad." Jeremy put an arm around me. "I'll tell you what," he said. "Take this magazine out of the store for me"—he tucked it inside my jacket while he talked—"and I'll owe you one."

I would have offered to buy it, but I didn't have money and Mr. Bertilucci wouldn't have sold it to me if I did. I really didn't see how I had a choice in the matter so I zipped my jacket up, but then it occurred to me that if I was going to shoplift anyway I should get something I wanted, so I went back for *The Adventures of Link.*

Soon I was at the police department, talking with a cop named Officer Harper. I got my one phone call and caught my mom just as she and Michael were about to leave the house. Since my mom had no car she was forced to ask Michael to drive her to the police station. Since they were planning on a classy restaurant she arrived in her blue dress with dangly earrings in the shape of golden leaves, shoes with tiny straps, and heels that clicked when she walked, tea rose perfume on her neck. Michael had long hair and a Star Trek tie.

We all sat and watched a videotape of me sticking the game under my jacket. Apparently most theft occurred at the video games; it was the only part of the store televised. There was no footage at all of Jeremy, at least none that we saw. I was more scared of Jeremy than Officer Harper, so I kept my mouth shut. Officer Harper told my mom and Michael to call him Dusty.

"He's never done anything like this before, Dusty," my mom said. "He's a great kid."

Dusty had a stern look for me, a concerned one for my mother. "You and your husband," he began.

"I'm not her husband," Michael said.

"Where's his father?"

Apparently we weren't telling the police about the alien abduction. "He's not part of the picture," was all my mother would say about that.

"Is there any other man taking an interest in him?" Dusty asked. He was looking at Michael.

"Christ." Michael blocked the look with his hands, waved them about. "This is our first date. This is me, meeting the kid for the first time. How do you do, Nathan."

"Don't kids with fathers ever shoplift?" my mother asked. She was looking so nice, but her voice had a tight-wound sound to it.

"I'm only asking because of the *Playboy.*" Dusty had confiscated the magazine and inventoried it with the other officers. Now he put it, folded up discreetly, on the metal desk between us.

This was the first my mother had heard about the *Playboy.* I could see her taking it in and, unhappy as she already was, I could see it made an impact. "I do have a suggestion," Dusty said.

It was a terrible suggestion. Dusty coached a Little League team called the Tigers. He thought Mr. Bertilucci might not press charges if Dusty could tell him he'd be keeping a personal eye on me. "I don't like baseball," I said. I was very clear about this. I would rather have gone to jail.

"A whole team of ready-made friends," Dusty said encouragingly. You could see he was an athlete himself. He had big shoulders and a sunburned nose that he rubbed a lot. There were bowling trophies on the windowsill and a memo pad with golf jokes on the desk.

"And I suck at it."

"Maybe we can change that."

"Really suck."

My mother was looking at me, her eyes narrow, and her earrings swinging. "I think it's a wonderful idea." The words came out without her hardly opening her mouth. "We're so grateful to you, Dusty, for suggesting it."

So I was paroled to the Tigers. I was released into my mother's custody, and she wouldn't let me bike home by myself, and she was feeling bad about Michael's spoiled evening. So she hissed me into Michael's car, apologizing the whole time to him. She suggested that we could maybe all go to the miniature golf course together. Michael agreed, but it wasn't his idea, and he and my mom were still dressed for a first impression.

I couldn't have been more miserable. I was hoping hard that Michael would turn out to be a jerk so that I would only have ruined the date, and not the rest of my mother's life. I hated him the minute I saw him, but you can't go by that. I could pretty much be counted on to hate every guy my mom went out with. This was easy since they were all jerks.

My mom was so mad at me that she couldn't miss. By the time we got to the fourth hole she was already three strokes under par. The fourth hole was the castle.

"I still don't get what not having a father has to do with shoplifting." There was a perfect little thwock sound when she hit the ball. She was clicking along on her two-inch heels and she *owned* this golf course.

Michael had been holding his tongue, but this was about the eighth time she'd said this. "It's not my business," he offered.

"But . . ."

Michael banked the ball off the side of the castle door and it rolled all the way back to his feet. "I just don't think his father would be letting him off so easy."

"What does that mean?"

"It means, here he is. Two hours ago the police picked him up for shoplifting. Is he being punished? No. You take him out for a game of miniature golf."

"Oh, he's not having a good time," my mom said. She turned to me. "Are you?"

"No, ma'am," I assured her.

"He stole something. If that'd been me, my father would have made real sure it never happened again," Michael said. "With his belt he would have made sure." Another ball missed the opening by inches.

"I have raised this kid all by myself for eleven years," my mother said. She was below us now, on the second half of the hole, sinking her putt. "I've done a great job. This is a great kid."

I saw the glimmer of a chance. "Don't make me play baseball, Mom." I put my heart into my voice.

"You. Don't. Even. Speak to me," she answered.

By the time we got to the sixteenth hole, the anthill, we were really not getting along. "*Playboy!*" My mother was so far ahead there was no way for her to lose now. She'd forgotten about the dressed-up mousse in her hair, hair snot, she calls this. Sometime around hole seven she'd run her hand through it. Now it was sticking up in odd tufts. Of course, neither Michael nor I could tell her this even if we'd wanted to. She sank another ball. "I picketed the campus bookstore for carrying *Playboy.* Did you remember that, Nathan?"

I was hitting my balls too softly. I couldn't get them over the lip of the hole. Michael was hitting his balls too hard. They bounced into the hole and out again. He'd put his hair behind his ears, but it wouldn't stay there.

"There, you see . . . ," Michael said.

"What?"

"Not that it's my business."

"Go ahead." My mom's voice was a wonder of nasty politeness. "Don't hold back."

"I just think a desire to look at *Playboy* magazine is pretty natural at his age. I think his father would understand that."

"I think *Playboy* promotes a degraded view of women. I think it's about power, not about sex. And I think Nathan knows how I feel."

Michael lined up his ball. He looked at the anthill, back down at his ball, looked at the anthill again. He took a little practice swing. "At a certain age, boys start to see breasts everywhere they look." He hit the ball too hard. "It's no big deal."

"I think that's six strokes," my mother said. "That would be your limit." She was snarling at him, her hair poking out of her head like pinfeathers.

His ears turned red. He snarled back. "It's not a real game."

"I think I've had six strokes, too," I said.

My mother retrieved her ball from the hole. "Don't *you* even speak to me."

*

Michael dropped us at home and we never saw him again. In my mind he lives forever, talking about breasts and taking that sad practice swing in his Star Trek tie. Because it was already midseason it took most of the next week to get me added to the Tigers' roster. Dusty let my mom know he was probably the only coach in town who could've accomplished it. His own son was the Tigers' top pitcher, a pleasant, pug-nosed kid named Ryan. Jeremy Campbell played third base.

My first game came on a Thursday night. So far I'd done nothing but strike out in practice and let ground balls go through my legs. While I was getting into my uniform my mom tossed a bag onto my bed. "What's this?" I asked. I opened it up. I was looking at something like a small white surgical mask, only rigid and with holes in it.

"Little something your coach said you might need," my mother told me.

"What is it?"

"An athletic cup."

"A *what?*"

"You wear it for protection."

I was starting to get it. What I was getting was horrifying. "I'm going to be hit in the balls? Is that what you're telling me?"

"Of course not."

"Then why am I wearing this?"

"So you don't have to worry even for a minute about it." Which of course I wasn't until this cup appeared. "I can show you how to wear it," my mom said. "On my hand."

"No!" I slammed the door. I couldn't get it comfortable, and I didn't know if this was because I wasn't wearing it right, or because it was just uncomfortable. In a million years I wouldn't ask my mother. I took it off and stowed it under the mattress.

Victor drove us to the game since we still didn't have a car. "It looks to me like your distributor got a bit wet," the mechanic had told my mom. "We could just dry it out, if that was all it was. But it looks to me like somebody just kept trying to start it and trying to start it until the starter burned out. Now your starter is shot and you're going to need a new battery too since it looks to me as if somebody tried to charge up the battery and thought they could just attach those jumper cables any which way. I wish you'd called us first thing when we could just have dried it out." He'd made my mom so mad she told him not to touch the car, but he'd let her leave it anyway, since we all knew she'd have to back down eventually.

So Victor drove us, and I tried to appeal to him. No way, I thought, could he have played baseball any better than I did. But he betrayed me, he was a scrappy little player, or so he chose to pretend. I've never yet met a grown man who'll admit he couldn't play ball. And then he added a second betrayal. "You watch too much television, Nathan." He had his arm stretched out comfortably across the seat back, driving with one hand. Nothing on his conscience at all. "This'll be good for you."

Tamara met us, since they all insisted on being in the stands for my debut. Because I was on the bench, I was practically sitting with them. I could hear them having a good time behind me, heading for the snack bar every couple of minutes, and I could have been having a good time too, except that I knew I had to go on the field eventually. Everyone plays, those were the stupid rules.

Ryan took the mound. A guy from the college was umping, a big, good-looking, long-armed cowboy of a guy named Chad. I heard my mom telling Tamara and Victor she thought he was cute and I was suddenly afraid she was going to like Little League way too much. Ryan warmed up and then the first batter stepped into the box. Ryan threw. "Strike!" Chad said.

"Good call, blue," my mother told him from the stands.

The other coach, a man with a red face, gray hair, and his ears sticking out on the outside of his baseball cap, called for a time-out. He spoke with Chad. "They're using an ineligible pitcher," he said. "We're filing a protest."

"You can talk to me," Dusty told him. "I'm right here. What the hell do you mean?"

"You pitched him Monday. All game. You can't use him again for four days."

Dusty counted on his fingers. "Monday, Tuesday, Wednesday, Thursday."

"You can't count Monday. You pitched him Monday."

"Did he pitch Monday?" Chad asked.

"Yes," Dusty said.

"Oh, you bet he did." The other coached pushed his hat back from his puffy, red face. "Thought I wouldn't notice?"

"I thought it was four days."

"Game goes to the Senators," Chad said.

"Wait. I'll pitch someone else," Dusty offered. "It was an honest mistake. Come on, he's only thrown a single pitch. The kids are all here to play. We'll start over."

"Not a chance." The other coach told the Senators to line up. "Shake their hands," he told them. "Give the Tigers a cheer. Let's show a little sportsmanship."

Back in the stands I could hear Victor saying how much better Little League would be if the kids made up the rules and didn't tell them to the parents. Whenever the parents started to figure them out, Victor suggested, the kids could change them.

But I thought this had worked out perfectly. Chad was already picking up the bases. My mom called to him that he umped one hell of a game. "Don't give me such a hard time, lady," he said, but he was all smiling when he said it; he came over to talk to her. Dusty took the team out for ice cream. There was a white owl in the air and a cloud of moths around the streetlights. A breeze came in from the almond orchards. I was one happy ballplayer.

Of course they wouldn't all be like that. Sooner or later I could see I was going to be out in right field with the ball headed for my uncupped crotch, the game on the line, and Jeremy Campbell watching me from third.

On Friday my mother called and told the garage to go ahead and fix the car. This was a defeat and she took it as such. I didn't have another game until Monday, but I did have practice on Friday so I was not as happy as I could have been either. The practice field was on the way home from the garage so Mom drove by later after she'd picked up the car. The weather was hot and the team was just assembling. She stopped for a moment to watch and then the car wouldn't start. "Jesus Christ!" she said. She banged the horn once in frustration; it gave a startled caw.

Jeremy came biking in beside her. He started to pedal past, then swung around. "Pop the hood," he told her.

"I picked this car up from the garage about two minutes ago. I won't even tell you what I just paid that crook."

Jeremy lifted the hood. "Your ground strap came off." He did something I couldn't see; when my mom turned the key, it started right up.

"What a *wonderful* boy," she said to me. To him, "You're a wonderful boy."

"Forget it." Jeremy was all gracious modesty.

She took off then, engine churning like butter, and we'd just barely started passing the ball around when Dusty got called away on a 911. The assistant coach hadn't arrived yet, so Dusty told us all to go straight on home again. After Dusty left, Jeremy chased me into Putah Creek Park, where my bicycle skidded out from under me when I tried to make a fast, evasive turn. He threw my bike down into the creek gully. He left me lying on the ground, hating myself for being afraid to even stand up, thinking of ways I could kill him. I could run him through with a magic sword. I could hang him from a meathook. I could smother him with his own athletic cup. If I bashed his skull with a baseball bat, no one would ever suspect it was me.

The bank of the creek was steep. I slid all the way down it. Then I slipped in the mud trying to get myself and the bicycle out again. The creek was already covered with summer slime and I got slick, green, fish-smelling streaks of it on my pants. My shoes were ruined. The front wheel of the bike was bent and I had to carry it home, rolling it on the back tire.

This was a long, hard, hot walk. I loved my bicycle, but there were many, many moments when I considered just walking off and leaving it. I'd hit my knees and my hands on the pavement when I fell, and my injuries stung and throbbed while I was walking. I told my mother I'd fallen off the bike, which was certainly true, and she bought it, even though I'd never fallen off my bike before, and certainly not into the creek.

Tamara was singing at Cafe Roma that evening and my mother had mentioned it to Chad, so she was thinking he might show. It had her distracted and she didn't make the fuss over my injuries that I expected. She was busy borrowing clothes from Tamara and moussing up her hair. This was a good thing, I thought, fewer questions to deal with and it probably meant I was growing up. But the lack of attention made me even more miserable than I already was. It would have all been worthwhile if my injuries had kept me out of Monday's game, but they didn't.

When everyone had left the house I took a hammer to the athletic cup. I meant to prove the cup wasn't up to much, but I found out otherwise. The blows bounced off it without leaving a mark. To make sure the hammer wasn't defective I tested it on the floor in my room. I left a ding like a crescent in the linoleum inside my closet. I smashed up a bunch of old crayons and put a hole in the bedroom wall behind the bed. I took an apple I hadn't eaten at lunch outside and crushed it like an egg. I was more and more impressed with the cup. I just needed a whole suit of the stuff.

This was all about the same time Boston third baseman Wade Boggs went on national TV and told the world he was addicted to sex.

We had a game Monday against the Royals and, like a nightmare, suddenly, there we were, down by one run, two outs, sixth and final inning, with Bjorn Benson on first base and me at bat. So far I'd only connected with the ball once and that was a feeble foul. Jeremy came out to the box to give me a little pep talk. "This used to be a good team before you joined," he said. "But you suck. If you cost us this game you'll pay in ways you can't even imagine, faggot." He smelled of cigarettes, though no one in my town smoked; it was like a town ordinance. Jeremy spit into the dust beside my cleats. I turned to look at the stands and I saw my mother watching us.

Dusty came and took the bat out of my hand. He went to the umpire, who wasn't Chad. "Ryan batting for Nathan," he said. He sent me back to the bench. It took Ryan seven pitches to strike out, which is surely four more pitches than it would have taken me.

Our car wasn't working again and Victor had dropped us off, but he couldn't stay for the whole game, so my mom asked Dusty's wife, Linda, a pretty woman who wore lipstick even to the ballpark, for a ride home.

When we got in the car we were all quiet for awhile. Dusty finally spoke. "You played a good game, Nathan. You too, Ryan."

Linda agreed. "It was a good game. Nothing to be ashamed of."

"Usually you can hit off Alex," Dusty said to Ryan. "I wonder what happened tonight."

"He didn't get to bed until late," Linda suggested. "Were you tired, honey?"

"I don't think Alex was pitching as fast as he usually does. I thought he was tiring. I thought you'd hit off him."

"That was a lot of pressure, putting him in then," Linda observed. "But usually he would have gotten a hit. Were you tired, honey?"

"One more pitch, we would have had him, right, Tigers?"

Ryan looked out the window and didn't say much. There was a song on the radio, "Believe It or Not," and his lips were moving as if he was singing along, but I couldn't hear him.

They let us off and we went inside. Like Ryan, my mom had been quiet the whole way home. I went to clean up and then she called me into the kitchen. "Couple of things," she said. "First of all, you're scared of that boy. The one who fixed our car. Why?"

"Because he's scary?" I offered. "Because he's a huge, mean, cretinous freak who hates me?" I was relieved, but mortified that she knew. I was also surprised. It was too much to feel all at once. I made things worse by starting to cry, loudly, and with my shoulders shaking.

My mom put her arms around me and held me until I stopped. "I love you," she said. She kissed the top of my head.

"I love you, too."

"I loved you first." Her arms tightened on me. "So there's a rumor on the street that you don't want to play baseball anymore."

I pushed away to look at her face. She stuck out her tongue and crossed her eyes.

"You mean it?" I asked. "I can quit?"

"I'll call Dusty tonight and tell him he's short one little Tiger."

It turned out to be a little more complicated. My mom called Dusty, but Dusty said he needed to see me, said he needed to hear it from me. He'd made representations to Mr. Bertilucci, he reminded us. He didn't want those to have been false representations. He thought we owed it to him to listen to what he had to say. He asked us to come to the house.

My mom agreed. By now we had the car back again. My mother drove and on the way over she warned me about the good cop/bad cop routine she thought Dusty and Linda might be planning to pull. She promised she wouldn't leave me alone with Dusty and she was as good as her word even when Linda tried to entice her outside to show her where the new deck was going to go. Ryan had obviously made himself scarce.

We sat in the living room, which was done country style, white ruffles and blue-and-white checks. Someone, I'm guessing Linda, collected ceramic ducks. She stood at the kitchen door smiling nervously at us. The TV was on in the background, the local news with the affable local anchor. Dusty muted her to talk to me. "You haven't really given the team or yourself a chance," Dusty said. His face had a ruddy, healthy glow.

"I just don't like baseball."

"You don't like it because you think you're no good at it. Give yourself time to get better." He turned to my mother. "You shouldn't let him give up on himself."

"He's not giving up on himself. He's being himself."

"He was improving every game," Linda said.

"He never wanted to play. I made him."

Dusty leaned forward. "And I remember why you made him. You want that to happen again?"

"That's a separate issue."

"I don't think so," Dusty turned to me again. "Don't let yourself become one of the quitters, Nathan. Don't walk out on your team. The values you learn on the playing field, those are the values that make you a success in everything you do later in life."

"I never played on a team," my mom observed. "How ever do I manage to get through the day?"

It was a snotty comment. Really, she was the one who started it. Dusty was the one to go for the throat. "I'm sure his father wouldn't want him taught to be a quitter."

There was a long, slow, loud silence in the room. Then my mom was talking without moving her mouth again. "His father is none of your damn business."

"Would anyone like a cup of coffee?" Linda asked. Her sandals tapped anxiously as she started into the kitchen, then came back out again. "I made brownies! I hope everyone likes them with nuts!"

Neither my mom nor Dusty showed any sign of hearing her. Neither would take their eyes off the other. "He didn't quit on you, Dusty," my mom said. "You quit on him."

"What does that mean?"

"It was his turn to bat."

"That was okay with me," I pointed out. "I was really happy with that."

"That was a team decision," Dusty said. "That's just what I'm talking about. If you'd ever played on a team you wouldn't be questioning that decision."

My mother stood, taking me by the hand. "You run your team. Let me raise my kid," she said. And we left the house and one of us left it hopping mad. "On the planet Zandoor," she told me, "Little League is just for adults. Dusty wouldn't qualify. Of course it's not like Little League here. You try to design a glove that fits on a Zandoorian."

The other one of us was so happy he was floating. When we got home Victor, Tamara, and Chad were sitting together on our porch. "I'm not a baseball player anymore," I told them. I couldn't stop grinning about it.

"Way to go, champ," Tamara said. She put her arms around me. Her body was much softer than my mom's and her black hair fell over my face so I smelled her coconut shampoo. It was a perfect moment. I remember everything about it.

"What do you think of that?" my mom asked Chad.

Through the curtain of Tamara's hair I watched him shrug. "If he doesn't like to play, why should he play?"

They were staring at each other. I thought he was a little young for her, besides being a fat jerk, but no one was asking me. "Saturday night," she told him, "there's a Take Back the Night march downtown. Victor, Tamara and I are going. Do you want to come?"

Chad looked at Victor. "This is a test, isn't it?" he asked.

"You already passed the test," my mother said.

The next day she spotted Jeremy while she was dropping me at school. She waved him over and he actually came. "I'm so glad to see you," she told him. "I didn't thank you properly for helping with the car the other day. You were great. Where did you learn to do that?"

"My dad," Jeremy said.

"I'm going to call him up and thank him, too. Tell him what a great kid he has. And you should come to dinner. I owe you that much. Honestly, you'd be doing me a favor. I'm thinking of buying a new car, but I need someone knowledgeable advising me." She was laying it on so thick the air was hard to breathe.

Jeremy suggested a Mustang convertible, or maybe a Trans Am. He was walking away before she'd turn and see the look I was giving her. "That's wonderful," I said. "Jeremy Campbell is coming to dinner. That's a dream come true." I gathered up my homework, slammed the car door, stormed off. Then I came back. "And it won't work," I told her. "You don't know him like I do."

"Maybe not," my mom said. "But it's hard to dislike someone you've been good to, someone who's depending on you. It's an old women's trick. I think it's worth a try."

Let me just take a moment here to note that it did not work. Jeremy Campbell didn't even show up for the dinner my mom cooked specially for him. He did ease off for a bit until whatever it was about me that provoked him provoked him again. Not a thing worked with Jeremy until Mr. Campbell was laid off and the whole Campbell family finally had to move three states east. The last time I saw him was June of 1991. He was sitting on top of me, pinning my shoulders down with his knees, stuffing dried leaves into my mouth. He had an unhappy look on his face as if he didn't like it any more than I did, and that pissed me off more than anything.

Then he turned his head slightly and a beam of pure light came streaming through his ears, lighting them up, turning them into two bright red fungi at the sides of his head. It helped a little that he looked ridiculous, even though I was the only one in the right position to see. It's the picture I keep in my heart.

So that's the way it really was and don't let my mother tell you differently. Saturday turned out to be the night I won at *The Legend of Zelda*. I was alone in the house at the time. Mom and Tamara were off at their rally, marching down Second Street, carrying signs. The Playboy Bunny logo in a red circle with a red slash across its face. On my computer the theme played and the princess kissed the hero, again and again. These words appeared on the screen: *You have destroyed Ganon. Peace has returned to the country of Heryl.*

And then the words vanished and were replaced with another message. *Do you wish to play again?*

What I wished was that I had *The Adventures of Link*. But before I could get bitter, the phone rang. "This is really embarrassing," my mom said. "There was a little trouble at the demonstration. We've been arrested."

"Arrested for what?" I asked.

"Assault. Mayhem. Crimes of a violent nature. None of the charges will stick. We were attacked by a group of nazi frat boys and I did nothing but defend myself. You know me. Only thing is, Dusty is in no mood to cut me any slack. I don't think I'm getting out tonight. What a vindictive bastard he's turned out to be!"

"Are you all right?"

"Oh, yeah. Hardly a scratch." There was a lot of noise in the background. I could just make out Tamara, she was singing that Merle Haggard song "Mama Tried." "There's a whole bunch of us here," my mother said. "It's the crime of the century. I might get my picture in the paper. Anyway, Victor wasn't arrested. You know Victor. So he's on his way to stay with you tonight. I just wanted you to hear from me yourself."

I didn't like to think of her spending the night in jail, even if it did sound like a slumber party over there. I could already hear Victor's car pulling up out front. I was glad he was staying; I wouldn't have liked to be alone all night. Sometime in the dark I'd have started thinking about nuns with hooks for hands. Now I could see him through the window and he was carrying a pizza. Good on Victor! "Just as long as you're all right," I told her.

"I must say you're being awfully nice about this," my mother said.

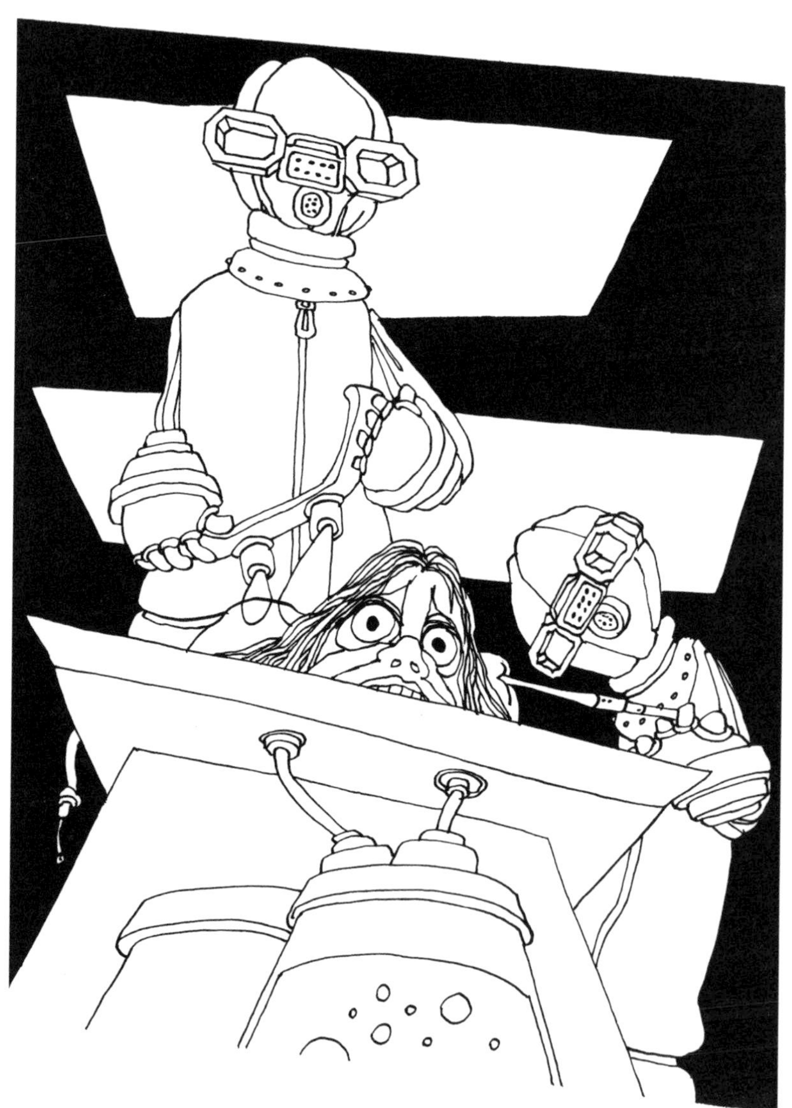

Abduction

Paul Park

THESE CREATURES—I HESITATE to call them people—since my capture they have taken away my rights. I sit and sit. The screens can be manipulated and changed, so in the library I go as far back as I can, looking for something I can hold in my hand. Last week I read a book almost two hundred years old. When they talked about the mowers in the corn, how all the animals and bugs were pressed into a shrinking space—that's a description of where I used to live. Is it any wonder we bolted when we should have stayed, surrendered when we should have fought? Two hundred years ago the farmers carried scythes and flails in their own hands. Later it was all machines—no hunger and no blood lust either. Robots and automata step by my door.

This was in what used to be known as British Columbia. I won't tell you the place—there was a lot of open country. But even when I first arrived, the woods were full of people who'd been chased there from all over. Women, like me, who'd been abused as children. Lesbians and straight—almost my first night, I went up to the youth hostel and got into a conversation with a man at the campfire. There'd been some northern lights. Just as easily as telling me his name, he started into a story about how a space ship had landed in his back yard, big as his house. The pilot was someone he already knew, someone who was working to save us. Gandhi, Martin Luther King, and Abraham Lincoln were all members of this same race, living undercover. They kept installations at the magnetic poles to prevent the world from tilting on its axis.

He was a large man with a pleasant face, sitting on a rock. Later I got to know him before he moved away, and he would tell me versions of the same story any time I liked. Maybe he felt he had to keep working on it because he could never get it to sound like the truth. Or maybe he was making conversation—to believe, not to believe, it's not really required when you listen to most things.

But just because it's easy to make fun of stupidity doesn't mean there isn't something there. The first knowledge I got, the first sniff of something real, came from my job.

For a long time I'd been on relief because of my disability. I'd pick my checks up once a month at the post office. When the laws changed, I had to go to work at the new settlement. We all had to go to work. My best friend, Rose, used to shoot some of her own food. But they took her shotgun away and put her to work planting trees. Cold, dead hands, she'd said, but there she was, bending over in the evening mist, her bag full of seedlings.

I saw her from the window of the bus. Because of my disability, I'd chosen domestic work. They picked us up in front of the store and took us to the place down a new logging road. We were in a battered yellow school bus. Like most people, I'd gotten the ligation when I went for government assistance. There weren't many children in our town. So it felt strange to be bouncing on the long mud ruts, my dinner in a brown bag, going to someplace new, and there were a lot of leaves and crumpled-up pieces of paper on the floor. It was the beginning of September, dark at seven o'clock or so. The driver turned on the dome lights as we came through the gate. Or else it's not a gate but a disturbance in the air. You can see a shimmering over the mud and feel something in your teeth, even though they turned the current off. There's a firebreak in the trees on either side.

When I got off that bus the first time, I needed some information, because it was hard for me to make sense of what I was seeing. This was in a place I'd lived for most of my life. I'd moved to Canada with my husband twenty years before. We'd had a lot of reasons—food additives, computerized commercials, manipulated images. Then Stephen moved away and used to write me from Milwaukee, but nothing he said made me want to join him there. Instead, my friend Rose helped me build my house in the woods, where there was a real community. But we were isolated, too. When the world came to us, we weren't equipped to understand it very well—I see that now. Maybe there's no one who understands more than bits and pieces, and everything is just a tiny piece of something else. Nothing ever changes, and then you look back and it's different. It's true I did have trouble sleeping, and terrible, strange dreams. I woke up feeling drugged and tired, and sometimes I'd have earaches or ringing in my ears. Sometimes I'd have bruises, and painful menstruations, and sore genitals that couldn't be explained.

I spoke to Rose the next morning. "They've clear-cut in a circle about half a mile in diameter. Above your head it looks like sky, but I don't think it is. I think we came in through an invisible wall, and there was a pressure on the inside. You could feel it in your ears.

There wasn't any breeze. Smells—there was an antiseptic, hospital kind of smell, very faint. It never really got dark. You couldn't see the stars."

"And what was inside?"

"Grass. The road changed to a surface like poured concrete, and then ended in a circle. There were some white, square, stucco buildings that looked prefabricated."

We were sitting in Rose's house. It had an octagonal cupola on top, a sleeping loft with windows on all sides. She'd lit the stove and we were having some mint tea, sitting side by side on the daybed. I was looking at her boots and shoes, lined up perfectly along the drying slat—typical Virgo, I thought, not for the first time. There was just the one room.

"And . . . ?"

"We went inside. There are four apartments in each building, two on a floor. I went upstairs to meet my family—I'm going to be helping them. Cooking, cleaning, looking after the kiddies. You know."

"It's degrading."

I shrugged. "I've done worse," I said, which wasn't exactly true. Because of the focusing disorder, my work history has been kind of spotty.

"So?" she said, and I realized I'd been letting the conversation die, settling into long pauses while I looked stupidly at her boots, the bare studs of the wall, the tar paper showing through the knotholes, and the short, patternless tips of the nails. Rose was my best friend, but to tell the truth, I've never been much good at explaining things, talking to people. So maybe it was my fault when she started to get the wrong idea. I sat rubbing my face and staring at the long oak floorboards that she'd stolen from someplace, and which I had helped her sand, stain, and polyurethane in fifteen much-diluted coats.

She took the cups to the sink and washed them, then slid them into the wooden drying rack, otherwise empty. I sat looking at her scrawny back in the orange shirt they'd given her, while in my mind I was trying to think about my new family, whom I'd met for the first time the evening before.

The father was named Mr. Kang, a tall, thin man. He never smiled. He always wore a business suit. He was bald, with a weak chin, flat nose, and black slanted eyes. He stood very close to me, and I had to look up at his hairless face, the skin so smooth and shiny it was like porcelain. It had a greenish tinge. Because I was working for him, he thought he owned me, owned my body. Even that first night he put his long hand on my back as he showed me the washing machine. He brushed against my breast, and I was terrified—no.

Here in my jail cell, I have time to think. For a few months this was part of my memory, part of my dreams, how he used to push me against the wall. But wouldn't I have told Rose the next morning, wouldn't I have complained, and wouldn't she have comforted me? Memories can be inserted like fertilized eggs. Whenever I picture Mr. Kang in my mind, he is always arrogant, distant, cold. Except for the last time, when he was hurt and bleeding—no.

"I met the father first," I said, looking at Rose's gray hair, tied at the nape of her neck. She washed the cups, laid them in the rack, then dried them, put them away in the high cupboard. I could see neat rows of jars and bottles.

"What was he like?"

I shivered. "It's like he's not real. His face is like a mask, and you never know what he's thinking. His voice is soft, like a whisper. He gave me the worst creeps."

Did I really say these things? I looked at the empty gun rack by the door. Rose dried her hands, then rolled down her sleeves and buttoned them. Her wrists were long and thin.

"Oh, but the child," I said. "She is a darling. Oh, my God, I feel sorry for her. It's like she's in a cage and doesn't know it. You should just see her, she is so sweet."

Rose took off her glasses, washed the lenses, and polished them. "What kind of a place is it?" she asked. "I mean, what are they doing here?"

I shrugged. "It's for executives. It's a paid vacation or a reward. He's got some kind of transmitter, so he can still be at the office, which is in Hong Kong. He's up all night, then he goes fishing. It's for the wife and child, he told me. The girl—Opal—she has asthma. There are some other kids, and they play together. There's a nice play structure."

One way to talk about Rose would be to say that she was paranoid about authority. Otherwise you could say she was made up of circles or concentric spheres. Outside, the yard is a mess: overgrown, full of broken cars and machines. The paint is peeling, the tar paper is rotting, and the house looks like a shack. Then inside there's not a grain of dust. But she herself doesn't bathe much, and her clothes are pretty dirty. If you touch her, she gets tense. But she'd do anything for me, as I found out.

Now she rearranged her glasses on her sharp nose. "Let's go see."

"What?"

"I want to see. It's not so far away."

"I don't think we're allowed."

But she never cared about that. She pulled on her socks and boots, closed down the stove. Then she was out through the ripped screen door, while I tied my own laces. I heard her firing up the truck, a rusted old Dodge, though the inside was swept out.

I was surprised she wanted to waste the energy. She knew all the old roads through the woods. We came into the place through the back side, and walked half a mile through the spruce trees. I showed her where the play structure was, on the other side of the wavy, shimmery line. The kids were all out, and I don't think they could see us, though we stood a hundred feet away.

"There she is," I said. Opal was sitting by herself on a swing, a little girl in a red sweater.

"She doesn't look Chinese," Rose said.

Was it then that she first told me "You've got the same coloring"? No, that's not it exactly. "She must take after her mother."

I shook my head. Then we stood staring for a little while longer next to the wavy line. Rose had a greedy look. As I say, we hadn't seen many children in that area.

The truth is, women have been kidnapped and violated, the eggs stripped out of their bodies. They have been subjected to cruel tests by expressionless monsters. Over and over again they tell the same story, which had come out of therapy sessions with a psychiatrist at Harvard University. Rose showed me a copy of the book. The cover was gone, because it was sixty years old and had been passed from hand to hand so many times.

Rose laughed at the inconsistencies, but I couldn't tell what she was thinking. She was trying to be supportive. When I told her some of my stories, suddenly it turned out she had more than one book on this subject. I was surprised because I'd never seen anything to read in her little house, even though like me she'd been to college a long time before. Now she showed me an illustrated book of some woman's experiences: the reimplantation process, the generations of hybrids in their crèche, each one closer to humanity.

I had been telling her about my nightmares. Babies and children stolen away—"Do you believe this stuff?" she asked.

"No."

"Me neither. It's just a fantasy to get people through menopause. Women who haven't had any children and are thinking about it now." She showed me a picture of a naked woman on her back in a doctor's office, tubes up her nose, while the alien put his hands inside of her. "It's just a metaphor."

I thought this was a cruel thing to say. If she wanted to reassure me, she didn't succeed. Didn't it all turn out to be true, almost, in cold fact? I remembered how on aurora borealis nights, sometimes I'd made fun of the fat man with his space ships. Now I was too horrified to read the story printed on the page. Nothing is more credible than printed words, and nothing is more personal than a woman's story of her own distress. I too had crippling headaches, and a burning sensation beneath my right eye. I too am susceptible, easily hypnotized.

"It's a way of blaming other people for our own choices," Rose said. "Everyone is a victim." Later: "I swear she looks just like you. She could be your daughter."

"Who?"

"Opal."

"Don't say that."

But it was true. The child had my yellow hair, blue eyes. Over the days I had gotten to be friends with her mother, a dark-skinned woman of the type that used to be known as African-American. She was a hesitant, shy woman about twenty-eight years old, and her name was Emily Blaine. She wasn't used to having someone work for her, and sometimes I would find her vacuuming as I arrived. Other times she would make me coffee, ask me to sit, while Opal watched the screens. "I'm lonely here," she said.

I was surprised they'd stayed so long. When the job was first explained to me, I was made to think I'd have a different family every week.

"I hate this weather," she said. "It's so cold in these mountains."

What weather was she talking about? The air seemed warmer inside the settlement. A strange, white glow came from the window. "Mr. Kang is very frustrated," she said. "He thinks he's being punished."

Normally I didn't say much during these conversations. I thought if I said nothing, after a while, Emily would break down and tell me the truth, that Mr. Kang was physically violent to her. Once I had seen a bruise on Emily's arm.

I looked in through the doorway to where Opal was sitting on the carpet, surrounded by the flowing screens. Even there were images above her head. The sound was a low whisper. A pretty blonde girl with bleached skin, she sat inside a glowing box.

"I swear it's like a jail here," Emily continued. "You don't know how lucky you are. No one tells my husband anything—it makes him crazy. Then he blames her and me."

"Why?"

She shrugged. "It's not rational. Maybe she's not perfect. You only get the one chance."

We were sitting in the kitchen drinking coffee. We sat on plastic stools. I hadn't tasted coffee in fifteen years, but I was liking it now. I had washed the floor that morning, which hadn't taken long. I'd scarcely had to rinse out the sponge.

"Is she your child?"

Emily gave me an angry look. "What do you mean?"

I didn't answer. Her talk went someplace else, then it came back. "I know up here you live like animals. It's not like that for us—we couldn't get a permit for a son. We didn't want anyone who looked like me. So we settled for an actress in an old movie."

The screens went dark, and Opal came running out. I'd left the vacuum cleaner on the floor, and I don't think she could see it till her eyes adjusted. She tripped over the hose and barked her skin, tore her white stockings—there were tears. Emily ran to her and gathered her up, kissed her, comforted her, while I sat with my hand on the polished surface of the table. She was always tender with that girl, I thought.

Rose told me to write down my dreams. "They're trying to teach you something," she said. "If you write them down, they'll get more real."

That was so stupid, it makes me angry even now. What was happening to me at night, I called it dreaming just to make it less frightening. But I was standing in my own flesh. Here's something I wrote down dutifully near the end of September: *I came home late at night from work, and my headache was so bad I had to smoke a joint to get to sleep. I wasn't even aware of lying down. But there was a white light outside my window and when I opened the door, I could see the shadows of the trees thrown back. There was a frost, and the leaves were dry under my feet. I walked out into the light and I could see the men, see their shadows coming toward me. Then as usual they forced me down on my stomach, put something in my mouth, fastened my hands. I must have lost consciousness, and when I woke up I was on a metal table with my cheek flat against it. Doctors stood around me, and I could see them in the mirrored wall. They had scalpels made of colored lasers, and they were making incisions all along my back, so that they could look inside and probe me with their fingers. They wore masks and rubber gloves. I couldn't feel anything, even though I knew they were touching the deep cuts, shining their lights inside. I could hear a hissing sound like gas escaping, and the beating of my heart.*

After something like that, I was too tired to do anything, and so Rose came over and took care of me. She made me dried bean soup. I tried to reward her by hugging her, but she was awkward, stiff. So I lay back down, curled up in my sleeping bag. "Describe them," she said.

I didn't want to talk about it, but she persisted. "There are a couple of different kinds," I said at last. "They've got a leader who's taller than the others. He has a body like an insect or a praying mantis. He can make you think what he wants, feel what he wants. The others do what he says. There are smaller ones, much darker, and a woman who seems to pity me. Once she offered me a pair of precious stones. The children are very small, and hungry for some kind of human contact. They grow the fetuses in a laboratory."

"Wow."

Was she stupid? She must have been able to see the connection with my job. But she didn't say anything about that. I lay on my futon, and she sat cross-legged on the floor beside me. She was stirring the soup and blowing on it. How would she have reacted if I had told her about another dream I had? Two of the doctors went into a consultation room. I slid off my bed and followed them in there, pulled the masks away. Rose was one of them, and Mr. Kang. He carried a stainless steel speculum—is it any wonder I was nervous around him? The next evening, just as my shift began, he took me away from the kitchen where I was making sautéed beans. He pretended to have a question about the delicate cycle, and he led me down the back corridor to the laundry room. "I don't want to embarrass you," he said. In the narrow space he told me he had left some paper currency on his bedside table. Terrified, I stared up at his hairless chin receding into his long neck. Was he offering me money? He had enormous slanted eyes. His tie was a narrow strip of plastic, and he had taken his jacket off. Then suddenly he grabbed hold of my shoulders and turned me to the wall so I'd be quiet. He was groping me, his hands under my shirt. I was too frightened to say anything, even when Emily came running down the hall to rescue me, I thought. Mr. Kang was accusing me of terrible things, and now he pushed me away and ducked into the laundry room where I had left my bag. He pulled out my apple, my sandwich wrapped in paper, my prescription bottle—there was nothing for him there to use against me. But then he rummaged through my coat, hanging where I'd left it, and he found nineteen dollars. Worse still, he found a pair of malachite and silver earrings from Hong Kong. It was cheap stuff, not valuable, but I started to cry. I saw Emily clutch at her own earlobes as I slumped down against the wall. The little girl was there. She was looking at me curiously until her mother pulled her away.

Here in this place, humiliating memories return to me. I sit with my book, waiting for my supper, listening to the murmur of the television in the lounge. My cell is rectangular, a toilet in the corner, the window too thick to break. My room is warm in winter, cool in summer—not true of my cabin in the woods. The fire had gone out, and I was lying in my sleeping bag when Rose brought me the termination notice from the bureau of assistance.

"Not good," she said.

Dreams can be a clue, a fantasy of guilt. Of all the screens that divide us from ourselves, they are the easiest to penetrate. The last one I wrote down, they made me read it to the judge.

"There's a complaint," Rose said. "He says you threatened him. But he won't press charges."

I winced at the memory. "It's a lie. He had to make something up."

I meant I would have paid the money back. But it was hard to explain that to Rose. So I came up with a metaphor. "He had to get rid of me," I said. "I was going to tell someone."

I had to make her draw it out of me and so I waited. "What?" she said. "That he was always trying to feel you up?"

I almost laughed at the quaint phrase. "Worse than that. I don't care about myself."

She had to pull it out of me, what I suspected. She couldn't stand to hear about a child suffering. She was a tenderhearted person deep inside.

"What about the mother?"

I shook my head. "She closes her eyes to it. Without him she's got nothing."

I remember all these words were like sharp pieces of metal in my mouth. I couldn't wait to spit them out. But even now I chew and chew. We all have our humiliations, and Rose had hers—she was too smart to be taken in. I tell myself that now, sitting at the window when I can't sleep, trying to get a look at the night sky. But there are floodlights in the parking lot. If Abraham Lincoln wanted to bring his ship in there, he'd have ample room.

I swear I missed that little girl so much. Blonde hair. Blue eyes. She was sort of clumsy, the way she walked. After Mr. Kang threw me out, I was too sick to get out of bed, and at first I didn't realize why that was. I moped around the house, and in the mornings I'd write down my dreams. Once a week or so the men would come for me, and I'd be on the table, and dark-skinned nurses would steal away my baby. Awake, it sickened me to think of her being raised by a monster and a woman who couldn't protect her. My own family was like that, and I know all about it.

"I'm afraid they are just going to send for him, and they'll take her away, back to Hong Kong or someplace else, and I'll never see her again. It breaks my heart. I think if she could just be with us, and we could take your truck and drive away somewhere."

"Where would we go?" asked Rose. She meant because of the new laws. Already by that time, outside the settlement was smaller than the inside, and it was shrinking all the time. To go anywhere we'd have to cross the line, which was something Rose talked about. She'd acquired another gun.

But I felt so sad when I pictured that little girl, alone in her box of screens, I couldn't think rationally. The closest I came was when I thought I could ransom her, hold her for ransom. Those executives have a lot of money, I thought, and Mr. Kang had robbed me of my benefits.

Sometimes I thought up plans that involved violence. Even so, it didn't reassure me when Rose used to take out the new gun, a nickel-plated .22 caliber pistol she had bought on the black market. She used to carry it in the pocket of her old canvas coat when sometimes we would walk up to the settlement. Except for the first and last time, Opal wasn't at the playground. But in October when the frost had come, Rose and I walked up to the shimmering line and she was there, swinging on the swings. Mr. Kang and Emily were there too, and they were having an argument. Mr. Kang grabbed hold of Emily's wrist. He was furious, a tall man, much taller than she, with thin arms and legs. Though Rose had never met him, she recognized him at once, and shouted at him to leave his wife alone. He must have heard something, because he turned toward us. Rose had taken out her gun and was behaving very stupidly, I felt, gesturing and swaggering. Once she even twirled it on her finger. And Mr. Kang must have seen something, because he came up to the wall on the other side and stood close to us, just a few yards away. And Rose stepped out to meet him with the gun held in front of her. She also was tall and thin.

There was a mirrored wall between them, a wavy, shimmering disturbance in the air that kept us safe. But then maybe a bus or car pulled through the gate, or else the current was interrupted, and in a single moment the wall flickered and disappeared. Rose stood with the gun held out.

Now I sit by the window of my little cell inside the wall, looking out into the lighted parking lot. If there are northern lights above me, I can't see them. The belly of the mother ship could drift above my head, and I'd be unaware. I'm making a joke, of course—I can tell what is reality and what is fantasy. The reality is what I wrote down later: *I thought I could recognize the two doctors above me. I knew I wasn't pregnant, but I didn't say a word. I was listening to them argue, a professional disagreement, I could tell by the tone. But then I couldn't pay attention, because I was looking at the child they had brought. The nurse had earrings that looked beautiful against her skin, and she was leading the child away from me. Above me the doctors were still arguing, and one of them reached over and cut the other on his shoulder so the blood poured out. He screamed, and at that moment the restraints fell away from me, and I jumped through the door. The men were trying to close the door, but I jumped through. The doctors were still screaming when I grabbed hold of the child.*

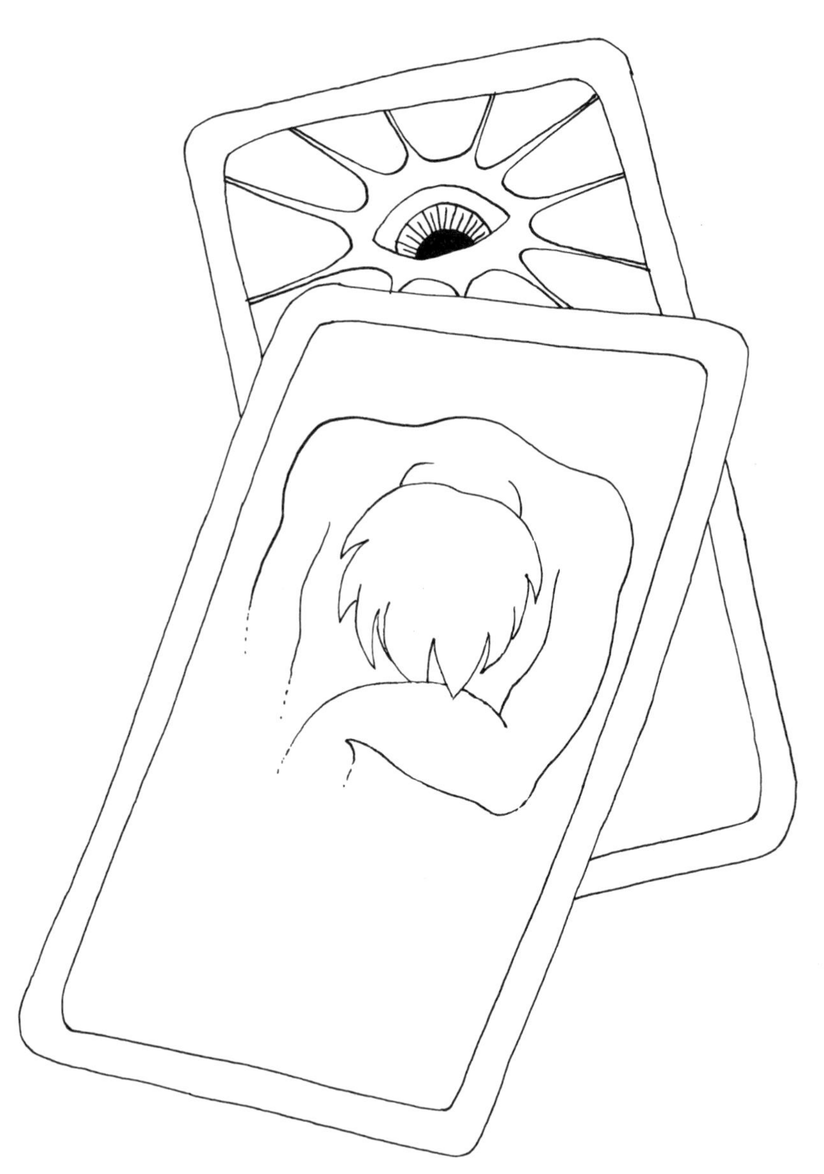

The Least Trumps
Elizabeth Hand

IN THE LONELY HOUSE there is a faded framed *LIFE* magazine article from almost half a century ago, featuring a color photograph of a beautiful woman with close-cropped blonde hair and rather sly gray eyes, wide crimson-lipsticked mouth, a red-and-white striped bateau-neck shirt. The woman is holding a large magnifying lens and examining a very large insect, a plastic scientific model of a common black ant, *Formica componatus,* posed atop a stack of children's picture books. Each book displays the familiar blocky letters and illustrated image that has been encoded into the dreamtime DNA of generations of children: that of a puzzled-looking, goggle-eyed ant, its antenna slightly askew as though trying, vainly, to tune in to the signal from some oh-so-distant station.

Wise Aunt or Wise Ant? reads the caption beneath the photo. *Blake E. Tun Examines a Friend.*

The woman is the beloved children's book author and illustrator, Blake Eleanor Tun, known to her friends as Blakie. The books are the six classic Wise Ant books, in American and English editions and numerous translations. *Wise Ant, Brave Ant, Curious Ant; Formi Sage, Weise Ameise, Una Ormiga Visionaria.* In the room behind Blakie, you can just make out the figure of a toddler, out of focus as she runs past. You can see the child's short blonde hair cut in a page-boy, and a tiny hand that the camera records as a mothlike blur. The little girl with the Prince Valiant haircut, identified in the article as Miss Tun's adopted niece, is actually Blakie's illegitimate daughter, Ivy Tun. That's me.

Here in her remote island hidey-hole, the article begins, *Blake Eleanor Tun brings to life an imaginary world inhabited by millions.*

People used to ask Blakie why she lived on Aranbega. Actually, just living on an island wasn't enough for my mother. The Lonely House stood on an islet in Green Pond, so we lived on an island on an island.

"Why do I live here? Because enchantresses always live on

islands," she'd say, and laugh. If she fancied the questioner she might add, "Oh, *you* know. Circe, Calypso, the Lady in the Lake. . . ."

Then she'd give her, or very occasionally him, one of her mocking sideways smiles, lowering her head so that its fringe of yellow hair would fall across her face, hiding her eyes so that only the smile remained.

"The smile on the face of the tiger," Katherine told me once when I was a teenager. "Whenever you saw that smile of hers, you'd know it was only a matter of time."

"Time till what?" I asked.

But by then her attention had already turned back to my mother: the sun to Katherine's gnomon, the impossibly beautiful bright thing that we all circled, endlessly.

Anyway, I knew what Blakie's smile meant. Her affairs were notorious even on the island. For decades, however, they were carefully concealed from her readers, most of whom assumed (as they were meant to) that Blake E. Tun was a man—that *LIFE* magazine article caused quite a stir among those not already in the know. My mother was Blakie to me as to everyone else. When I was nine she announced that she was not my aunt but my mother, and produced a birth certificate from a Boston hospital to prove it.

"No point in lying. It would however be more *convenient* if you continued to call me Blakie." She stubbed out her cigarette on the sole of her tennis shoe and tossed it over the railing into Green Pond. "But it's no one's business who you are. Or who I am in relation to you, for that matter."

And that was that. My father was not a secret kept from me; he just didn't matter that much, not in Blakie's scheme of things. The only thing she ever told me about him was that he was very young.

"Just a boy. Not much older than you are now, Ivy," which at the time was nineteen. "Just a kid."

"Never knew what hit him," agreed my mother's partner, Katherine, as Blakie glared at her from across the room.

It never crossed my mind to doubt my mother, just as it never crossed my mind to hold her accountable for any sort of duplicity she might have practiced, then or later. The simple mad fact was that I adored Blakie. Everyone did. She was lovely and smart and willful and rich, a woman who believed in seduction, not argument; when seduction failed, which was rarely, she was not above abduction, of the genteel sort involving copious amounts of liquor and the assistance of one or two attractive friends.

The Wise Ant books she had written and illustrated when she was in her twenties. By her thirtieth birthday they had made her fortune. Blakie had a wise agent named Letitia Thorne and a very wise financial adviser named William Dunlap, both of whom took care that my mother would never have to work again unless she wanted to.

Blakie did not want to work. She wanted to seduce Dunlap's daughter-in-law, a twenty-two-year-old Dallas socialite named Katherine Mae Moss. The two women eloped to Aranbega, a rocky spine of land some miles off the coast of Maine. There they built a fairy-tale cottage in the middle of a lake, on a tamarack- and fern-covered bump of rock not much bigger than the Bambi Airstream trailer they'd driven up from Texas. The cottage had two small bedrooms, a living room and dining nook and wraparound porch overlooking the still silvery surface of Green Pond. There was a beetle-black cast-iron Crawford woodstove for heat and cooking, kerosene lanterns and a small red hand pump in the slate kitchen sink. No electricity; no telephone. Drinking water was pumped up from the lake. Septic and gray water disposal was achieved through an ancient holding tank that was emptied once a year.

They named the cottage the Lonely House, after the tiny house where Wise Ant lived with her friends Grasshopper and Bee. Here they were visited by Blakie's friends, artistic sorts from New York and Boston, several other writers from Maine, and by Katherine's relatives, a noisy congeries of cattle heiresses, disaffected oilmen and Ivy league dropouts, first-wave hippies and draft dodgers, all of whom took turns babysitting me when Blakie took off for Crete or London or Taos in pursuit of some new *amour.* Eventually, of course, Katherine would find her and bring her home: as a child I imagined my mother engaged in some world-spanning game of hide-and-seek, where Katherine was always It. When the two of them returned to the Lonely House, there would always be a prize for me as well. A rainbow map of California, tie-dyed on a white bedsheet; lizard-skin drums from Angola; a meerschaum pipe carved in the likeness of Richard Nixon.

"You'll never have to leave here to see the world, Ivy," my mother said once, after presenting me with a Maori drawing on bark of a stylized honeybee. "It will all come to you, like it all came to me."

My mother was thirty-seven when I was born, old to be having a baby, and paired in what was then known as a Boston marriage. She and Katherine are still together, two old ladies now living in a posh assisted-living community near Rockland, no longer scandalizing anyone. They've had their relationship highlighted on an episode of *This American Life,* and my mother is active in local liberal causes, doing benefit readings of *The Vagina Monologues* and signings of *Wise Ant* for the Rockland Domestic Abuse Shelter. Katherine reconciled with her family and inherited a ranch near Goliad, where they still go sometimes in the winter. The Wise Ant books are now discussed within the context of midcentury American lesbian literature, a fact which annoys my mother no end.

"I wrote those books for *children,*" she cries whenever the topic arises. "They are *children's books,*" as though someone had confused the color of her mailbox, red rather than black. "For God's sake."

Of course Wise Ant will never be anything more than her antly self—wise, brave, curious, kind, noisy, helpful—just as Blakie at eighty-two remains beautiful, maddening, forgetful, curious, brave; though seldom, if ever, quiet. We had words when I converted the Lonely House to solar power—

"You're spoiling it. It was never *intended* to have electricity—"

Blakie and Katherine were by then well established in their elegant cottage at Penobscot Fields. I looked at the room around me—Blakie's study, small but beautifully appointed, with a Gustav Stickley lamp that she'd had rewired by a curator at the Farnsworth, her laptop screen glowing atop a quartersawn oak desk; Bose speakers and miniature CD console.

"You're right," I said. "I'll just move in here with you."

"That's not the—"

"Blakie. I need electricity to work. The generator's too noisy, my customers don't like it. And expensive. I have to work for a living—"

"You don't have to—"

"I *want* to work for a living." I paused, trying to calm myself. "Look, it'll be fun—doing the wiring and stuff. I got all these photovoltaic cells, when it's all set up, you'll see. It'll be great."

And it was. The cottage is south facing: two rows of cells on the roof, a few extra batteries boxed in under the porch, a few days spent wiring, and I was set. I left the bookshelves in the living room, mostly my books now, and a few valuable first editions that I'd talked Blakie into leaving. Eliot's *Four Quartets* and some Theodore Roethke; *Gormenghast;* a Leonard Baskin volume signed *For Blakie.* One bedroom I kept as my own, with a wide handcrafted oak cupboard bed, cleverly designed to hold clothes beneath and more books all around. At the head of the bed were those I loved best, a set of all six Wise Ant books and the five volumes of Walter Burden Fox's unfinished *Five Windows One Door* sequence.

The other bedroom became my studio. I set up a drafting table and autoclave and lightbox, a shelf with my ultrasonic cleaner and driclave. On the floor was an additional power unit just for my machine and equipment; a tool bench holding soldering guns, needle bars, and jigs; a tall stainless steel medicine cabinet with enough disinfectant and bandages and gloves and hemostats to outfit a small clinic; an overhead cabinet with my inks and pencils and acetates. Empty plastic caps await the colored inks that fill the machine's reservoir. A small sink drains into a special tank that I bring to the Rockland dump once a month, when everyone else brings in their empty paint cans. A bookshelf holds albums filled with pictures of my own work and some art books—Tibetan stuff, pictures from Chauvet Cavern, Japanese woodblock prints.

But no flash sheets; no framed flash art; no fake books. If customers want flash, they can go to Rockland or Bangor. I do only my own designs. I'll work with a customer, if she has a particular image in mind, or come up with something original if she doesn't. But if somebody has her heart set on a prancing unicorn, or Harley flames, or Mister Natural, or a Grateful Dead logo, I send her elsewhere.

This doesn't happen much. I don't advertise. All my business is word of mouth, through friends or established customers, a few people here on Aranbega. But mostly, if someone wants me to do her body work, she *really* has to want me, enough to fork out sixty-five bucks for the round-trip ferry and at least a couple hundred for the tattoo, and three hundred more for the Aranbega Inn if she misses the last ferry, or if her work takes more than a single day. Not to mention the cost of a thick steak dinner afterward, and getting someone else to drive her home. I don't let people stay at the Lonely House, unless it's someone I've known for a long time, which usually means someone I was involved with at some point, which usually means she wouldn't want to stay with me in any case. Sue is an exception, but Sue is seeing someone else now, one of the other occupational therapists from Penobscot Fields, so she doesn't come over as much as she used to.

That suits me fine. My customers are all women. Most of them are getting a tattoo to celebrate some milestone, usually something like finally breaking with an abusive boyfriend, leaving a bad marriage, coming to grips with the aftermath of a rape. Breast cancer survivors—I do a lot of breast work—or tattoos to celebrate coming out, or giving birth. Sometimes anniversaries. I get a lot of emotional baggage dumped in my studio, for hours or days at a time; it always leaves when the customers do, but it pretty much fulfills my need for any kind of emotional connection, which is pretty minimal anyway.

And, truth to tell, it fulfills most of my sexual needs too; at least any baseline desire I have for physical contact. My life is spent with skin: cupping a breast in my hand, pulling the skin taut between my fingers while the needle etches threadlike lines around the aureole, tracing yellow above violet veins, turning zippered scars into coiled serpents, an explosion of butterfly wings, flames or phoenixes rising from a puckered blue-white mound of flesh; or drawing secret maps, a hidden cartography of grottoes and ravines, rivulets and waves lapping at beaches no bigger than the ball of my thumb; the ball of my thumb pressed there, index finger there, tissue film of latex between my flesh and hers, the hushed drone of the machine as it chokes down when the needle first touches skin and the involuntary flinch that comes, no matter how well she's prepared herself for this, no matter how many times she's lain just like this, paper towels blotting the film of blood that wells, nearly invisible, beneath the moving needle bar's tip, music never loud enough to drown out the hum of the machine. Hospital smells of disinfectant, blood, antibacterial ointment, latex.

And sweat. A stink like scorched metal: fear. It wells up the way blood does, her eyes dilate and I can smell it, even if she doesn't move, even if she's done this enough times to be as controlled as I am when I draw the needle across my own flesh: she's afraid, and I know it, needle-flick, soft white skin pulled taut, again, again, between my fingers.

I don't want a lot of company, after a day's work.

I knew something was going to happen the night before I found the Trumps. Sue teases me, but it's true, I can tell when something is going to happen. A feeling starts to swell inside me, as though I'm being blown up like a balloon, my head feels light and somehow cold, there are glittering things at the edges of my eyes. And sure enough, within a day or two someone turns up out of the blue, or I get a letter or e-mail from someone I haven't thought of in ten years, or I see something—a mink, a yearling moose, migrating elvers—and I just know.

I shouldn't even tell Sue when it happens. She says it's just a manifestation of my disorder, like a migraine aura.

"Take your fucking medicine, Ivy. It's an early warning system: take your Xanax!"

Rationally I can understand that, rationally I know she's right. That's all it is, a chain of neurons going off inside my head, like a string of firecrackers with a too-short fuse. But I can never explain to her the way the world looks when it happens, that green glow in the sky not just at twilight but all day long, the way I can see the stars sometimes at noon, sparks in the sky.

I was outside the Lonely House, cutting some flowers to take to Blakie. Pink and white cosmos; early asters, powder blue and mauve; white sweet-smelling phlox, their stems slightly sticky, green aphids like minute beads of dew beneath the flower heads. From the other shore a chipmunk gave its warning *cheeet.* I looked up, and there on the bank a dozen yards away sat a red fox. It was grinning at me; I could see the thin black rind of its gums, its yellow eyes shining as though lit from within by candles. It sat bolt upright and watched me, its white-tipped brush twitching like a cat's.

I stared back, my arms full of asters. After a moment I said, "Hello there. Hello. What are you looking for?"

I thought it would lope off then, the way foxes do, but it just sat and continued to watch me. I went back to gathering flowers, putting them into a wooden trug and straightening to gaze back at the shore. The fox was still there, yellow eyes glinting in the late-summer light. Abruptly it jumped to its feet. It looked right at me, cocking its head like a dog waiting to be walked.

It barked—a shrill, bone-freezing sound, like a child screaming. I felt my back prickle; it was still watching me, but there was something distracted about its gaze, and I saw its ears flatten against its narrow skull. A minute passed. Then, from away across Cameron Mountain there came an answer, another sharp yelp, higher-pitched and ending in a sort of yodeling wail. The fox turned so quickly it seemed to somersault through the low grass, and arrowed up the hillside toward the birch grove. In a moment it was gone. There was only the frantic chatter of red squirrels in the woods and, when I drew the dory up on the far shore a quarter-hour later, a musky sharp smell like crushed grapes.

I got the last ferry over to Port Symes, me and a handful of late-season people from away, sunburned and loud, waving their cell phones over the rail as they tried to pick up a signal from one of the towers on the mainland.

"We'll *never* get a reservation," a woman said accusingly to her husband. "I *told* you to have Marisa do it before she left—"

At Port Symes I hopped off before any of them, heading for where I'd left Katherine's car parked by an overgrown bank of dog roses. The roses were all crimson hips and thorns by now, the dark green leaves already burning to yellow; there were yellow beech leaves across the car's windshield, and as I drove out onto the main road I saw acorns like thousands of green-and-bronze marbles scattered across the gravel road. Summer lingers for weeks on the islands, trapped by pockets of warmer air, soft currents and gray fog holding it fast till mid-October some years. Here on the mainland it was already autumn.

The air had a keen winey scent that reminded me of the fox. As I headed down the peninsula toward Rockland I caught the smell of burning leaves, the dank odor of smoke snaking through a chimney that had been cold since spring. The maples were starting to turn, pale gold and pinkish red. There had been a lot of rain in the last few weeks; one good frost would set the leaves ablaze. On the seat beside me Blakie's flowers sat in their mason jar, wrapped in a heavy towel; one good frost and they might be the last ones I'd pick this year.

I got all the way to the main road before the first temblors of panic hit. I deliberately hadn't taken my medication—it made me too sleepy, I couldn't drive, and Sue would have had to meet me at the ferry, I would be asleep before we got to her place. The secondary road ended; there was a large green sign with arrows pointing east and west.

THOMASTON
OWL'S HEAD
ROCKLAND

I turned right, toward Rockland. In the distance I could see the slate-covered reach of Penobscot Bay, a pine-pointed tip of land protruding into the waters, harsh white lights from Rockland Harbor; miles and miles off, a tiny smudge like a thumbprint upon the darkening sky.

Aranbega. I was off island.

The horror comes down, no matter how I try to prepare myself for it, no matter how many times I've been through it: an incendiary blast of wind, the feeling that an iron helmet was tightening around my head. I began to gasp, my heart starting to pound and my entire upper body going cold. Outside was a cool September twilight, the lights of the strip malls around Rockland starting to prick through the gold-and-violet haze, but inside the car the air had grown black, my skin icy. There was a searing fire in my gut. My T-shirt was soaked through. I forced myself to breathe, to remember to exhale: to think *You're not dying, nobody dies of this, it will go, it will go. . . .*

"Fuck." I clutched the steering wheel and crept past the Puffin Shop convenience store, past the Michelin tire place, the Dairy Queen; through one set of traffic lights, a second. *You won't die, nobody dies of this; don't look at the harbor.*

I tried to focus on the trees—two huge red oaks, there, you could hardly see where the land had been cleared behind them to make way for a car wash. *It's just a symptom, you're reacting to the symptoms, nobody dies of this, nobody.* At a stop sign I grabbed my cell phone and called Sue.

"I'm by the Rite-Aid." *Don't look at the Rite-Aid.* "I'll be there, five minutes—"

An SUV pulled up behind me. I dropped the phone, feeling like I was going to vomit; turned sharply onto the side street. My legs shook so I couldn't feel the pedals under my feet. *How can I drive if my legs are numb?*

The SUV turned in behind me. My body trembled, I hit the gas too hard and my car shot forward, bumping over the curb then down again. The SUV veered past, a great gray blur, its lights momentarily blinding me. My eyes teared and I forced my breath out in long hoots, and drove the last few hundred feet to Sue's house.

She was in the driveway, still holding the phone in one hand.

"Don't," I said. I opened the car door and leaned out, head between my knees, waiting for the nausea to pass. When she came over I held my hand up and she stopped, but I heard her sigh. From the corner of my eye I could see the resigned set to her mouth, and that her other hand held a prescription bottle.

Always before when I came over to visit my mother, I'd stay with Sue and we'd sleep together, comfortably, not so much for old time's sake as to sustain some connection at once deeper and less enduring than talk. Words I feel obliged to remember, skin I can afford to forget. A woman's body inevitably evokes my own, small wet mouths, my own breath, my own legs, breasts, arms, shoulders, back. Even after Sue started seeing someone else, we'd ease into her wide bed with its wicker headboard, cats sliding to the floor in a gray heap like discarded laundry, radio playing softly, *Tea and oranges, So much more.*

"I think you'd better stay on the couch," Sue said that night. "Lexie isn't comfortable with this arrangement, and . . ."

She sighed, glancing at my small leather bag, just big enough to hold a change of underwear, hairbrush, toothbrush, wallet, a battered paperback of *Lorca in New York.* "I guess I'm not either. Anymore."

I felt my mouth go tight, stared at the mason jar full of flowers on the coffee table.

"Yup," I said.

I refused to look at her. I wouldn't give her the satisfaction of seeing how I felt.

But of course Sue wouldn't be gleeful, or vindictive. She'd just be sad, maybe mildly annoyed. I was the one who froze and burned; I was the one who scarred people for a living.

"It's fine," I said after a minute, and, looking at her, smiled wryly. "I have to get up early anyway."

She looked at me, not smiling, dark brown eyes creased with regret. *What a waste,* I could hear her thinking. *What a lonely wasted life.*

I think the world is like this: beautiful, hard, cold, unmoving. Oh, it turns, things change—clouds, leaves, the ground beneath the beech trees grows thick with beechmast and slowly becomes black fragrant earth ripe with hellgrammites, millipedes, nematodes, deer mice. Small animals die, we die; a needle moves across honey-colored skin and the skin turns black, or red, or purple. A freckle or a mole becomes an eye; given enough time an eye becomes an earthworm.

But change, the kind of change Sue believes in—Positive Change, Emotional Change, Cultural Change—I don't believe in that. When I was young, I thought the world *was* changing: there was a time, years-long, when the varicolored parade of visitors through the Lonely House made me believe that the world Outside must have changed its wardrobe as well, from sere black suits and floral housedresses to velvet capes and scarlet morning coats, armies of children and teenagers girding themselves for skirmish in embroidered pants, feathered headdresses, bare feet, bare skin. I dressed myself as they did—actually, they dressed *me,* as Blakie smoked and sipped her whiskey sour, and Katherine made sure the bird feeders and woodbox were full. And one day I went out to see the world.

It was only RISD—the Rhode Island School of Design—and it should have been a good place, it should have been a Great Place for me. David Byrne and a few other students were playing at someone's house, other students were taking off for Boston and New York, squatting in Alphabet City in burned-out tenements with a toilet in the kitchen, getting strung out, but they were doing things, they were having adventures, hocking bass guitars for Hasselblad cameras, learning how to hold a tattoo machine in a back room on St. Mark's Place, dressing up like housewives and shooting five hours of someone lying passed out in bed while a candle flickered down to a shiny red puddle and someone else laughed in the next room. It didn't look like it at the time, but you can see it now, when you look at their movies and their photographs and their vinyl forty-fives and their installations: it didn't seem so at the time, but they were having a life.

I couldn't do that. My problem, I know. I lasted a semester, went home for Christmas break and never went back. For a long time it didn't matter—maybe it never mattered—because I still had friends, people came to see me even when Blakie and Katherine were off at the ranch, or bopping around France. Everyone's happy to have a friend on an island in Maine. So in a way it was like Blakie had told me long ago: the world *did* come to me.

Only of course I knew better.

Saturday was Sue's day off. She'd been at Penobscot Fields for eleven years now and had earned this, a normal weekend; I wasn't going to spoil it for her. I got up early, before seven, fed the cats and made myself coffee, then went out.

I walked downtown. Rockland used to be one of the worst-smelling places in the United States. There was a chicken-processing plant, fish factories, the everyday reek and spoils of a working harbor. That's all changed, of course. Now there's a well-known museum, and tourist boutiques have filled up the empty storefronts left when the factories shut down. Only the sardine-processing plant remains, down past the Coast Guard station on Tilson Avenue; when the wind is off the water you can smell it, a stale odor of fishbones and rotting bait that cuts through the scents of fresh-roasted coffee beans and car exhaust.

Downtown was nearly empty. A few people sat in front of Second Read, drinking coffee. I went inside and got coffee and a croissant, walked back onto the sidewalk and wandered down to the waterfront. For some reason seeing the water when I'm on foot usually doesn't bother me. There's something about being in a car, or a bus, something about moving, the idea that there's *more* out there, somewhere; the idea that Aranbega is floating in the blue pearly haze and I'm here, away: disembodied somehow, like an astronaut untethered from a capsule, floating slowly beyond that safe closed place, unable to breathe and everything gone to black, knowing it's just a matter of time.

But that day, standing on the dock with the creosote-soaked wooden pilings beneath my sneakers, looking at orange peels bobbing in the black water and gulls wheeling overhead—that day I didn't feel bad at all. I drank my coffee and ate my croissant, tossed the last bit of crust into the air and watched the gulls veer and squabble over it. I looked at my watch. A little before eight, still too early to head to Blakie's. She liked to sleep in, and Katherine enjoyed the peace and quiet of a morning.

I headed back toward Main Street. There was some early-morning traffic now, people heading off to do their shopping at Shaw's and Wal-Mart. On the corner I waited for the light to change, glanced at a storefront, and saw a sign taped to the window.

ST. BRUNO'S EPISCOPAL CHURCH
ANNUAL RUMMAGE SALE
SATURDAY, SEPTEMBER 7
8 A.M. – 3:00 P.M.
LUNCH SERVED FROM 11:30

Penobscot Fields had once been the lupine-strewn meadow behind St. Bruno's; proximity to the church was one of the reasons Blakie and Katherine had first signed on to the retirement community. I wasn't a churchgoer, but during the summer I was an avid hunter of yard sales in the Rockland area. You don't get many of them after Labor Day, but the rummage sale at St. Bruno's almost makes up for it. I made sure I had wallet and checkbook in my bag then hurried to get there before the doors opened.

There was already a line. I recognized a couple of dealers, a few regulars who smiled or nodded at me. St. Bruno's is a late-nineteenth-century neo-Gothic building, designed in the late Arts and Crafts style by Halbert Liston; half-timbered beams, local dove gray fieldstone, slate shingles on the roof. The rummage sale was not in the church, of course, but the adjoining parish house. It had whitewashed walls rather than stone, the same half-timbered upper story, etched with arabesques of dying clematis and sere Virginia creeper. In the door was a diamond-shaped window through which a worried elderly woman peered out every few minutes.

"Eight o'clock!" someone called good-naturedly from the front of the line. Bobby Day, the graying hippie who owned a used bookstore in Camden. "Time to go!"

From inside, the elderly woman gave one last look at the crowd, then nodded. The door opened; there was a surge forward, laughter and excited murmurs, someone crying, "Marge, look out! Here they come!" Then I was inside.

Long tables of linens and clothing were at the front of the hall, surrounded by women with hands already full of flannel sheets and crewelwork. I scanned these quickly, then glanced at the furniture. Nice stuff—a Morris chair and old oak settle, some wicker, a flax wheel. Episcopalians always have good rummage sales, better quality than Our Lady of the Harbor or those off-brand churches straggling down toward Warren.

But the Lonely House was already crammed with my own nice stuff, besides which it would be difficult to get anything back to the island. So I made my way to the rear of the hall, where Bobby Day was going through boxes of books on the floor. We exchanged hellos, Bobby smiling but not taking his eyes from the books; in deference to him I continued on to the back corner. An old man wearing a canvas apron with a faded silhouette of St. Bruno on it stood over a table covered with odds and ends.

"This is whatever didn't belong anywhere else," he said. He waved a hand at a hodgepodge of beer steins, Tupperware, mismatched silver, shoeboxes overflowing with candles, buttons, mason jar lids. "Everything's a dollar."

I doubted there was anything there worth fifty cents, but I just nodded and moved slowly down the length of the table. A chipped Poppy Trails bowl and a bunch of ugly glass ashtrays. Worn Beanie Babies with the tags clipped off. A game of Twister. As I looked, a heavyset woman barreled up behind me. She had a rigidly unsmiling face and an overflowing canvas bag—I caught glints of brass and pewter, the telltale dull green glaze of a nice Teco pottery vase. A dealer. She avoided my gaze, her hand snaking out to grab something I'd missed, a tarnished silver flash hidden behind a stack of plastic Easter baskets.

I tried not to grimace. I hated dealers and their greedy bottom-feeder mentality. By this afternoon she'd have polished the flask and stuck a seventy-five-dollar price tag on it. I moved quickly to the end of the table. I could see her watching me whenever my hand hovered above something; once I moved on she'd grab whatever I'd been examining, give it a cursory glance before elbowing up beside me once more. After a few minutes I turned away, was just starting to leave when my gaze fell upon a swirl of violet and orange tucked within a Pyrex dish.

"Not sure what that is," the old man said as I pried it from the bowl. Beside me the dealer watched avidly. "Lady's scarf, I guess."

It was a lumpy packet a bit larger than my hand, made up of a paisley scarf that had been folded over several times to form a thick square, then wrapped and tightly knotted around a rectangular object. The cloth was frayed, but it felt like fine wool. There was probably enough of it to make a nice pillow cover. Whatever was inside felt compact but also slightly flexible; it had a familiar heft as I weighed it in my palm.

An oversized pack of cards. I glanced up to see the dealer watching me with undisguised impatience.

"I'll take this," I said, and handed the old man a dollar. "Thanks."

A flicker of disappointment across the dealer's face. I smiled at her, enjoying my mean little moment of triumph, and left.

Outside the parish hall a stream of people were headed for the parking lot, carrying lamps and pillows and overflowing plastic bags. The church bell tolled eight-thirty. Blakie would just be getting up. I killed a few more minutes by wandering around the church grounds, past a well-kept herb garden and stands of yellow chrysanthemums. Behind a neatly trimmed hedge of boxwood I discovered a statue of St. Bruno himself, standing watch over a granite bench. Here I sat with my paisley-wrapped treasure, and set about trying to undo the knot.

For a while I thought I'd have to just rip the damn thing apart, or wait till I got to Blakie's to cut it open. The cloth was knotted so tightly I couldn't undo it, and the paisley had gotten wet at some point then shrunk—it was like trying to pick at dried plaster, or Sheetrock.

But gradually I managed to tease one corner of the scarf free, tugging it gently until, after a good ten minutes, I was able to undo the wrappings. A faint odor wafted up, the vanilla-tinged scent of pipe tobacco. There was a greasy feel to the frayed cloth, sweat, or maybe someone had dropped it on the damp grass. I opened it carefully, smoothing its folds till I could finally see what was tucked inside.

It was a large deck of cards, bound with a rubber band. The rubber band fell to bits when I tried to remove it, and something fluttered onto the bench. I picked it up: a scrap of paper with a few words scrawled in pencil.

The least trumps

I frowned. The Greater Trumps, those were the picture cards that made up the Major Arcana in a tarot deck—the Chariot, the Magician, the Empress, the Hierophant. Eight or nine years ago I had a girlfriend with enough New Age tarots to channel the entire Order of the Golden Dawn. Marxist tarots, lesbian tarots, African, Zen, and Mormon tarots; Tarots of the Angels, of Wise Mammals, poisonous snakes and smiling madonni; Aleister Crowley's tarot, and Shirley Maclaine's; the dread Feminist Tarot of the Cats. There were twenty-two Major Arcana cards, and the lesser trumps were analogous to the fifty-two cards in an ordinary deck, with an additional four representing knights.

But the least trumps? The phrase stabbed at my memory, but I couldn't place it. I stared at the scrap of paper with its rushed scribble, put it aside, and examined the deck.

The cards were thick, with the slightly furry feel of old pasteboard. Each was printed with an identical and intricate design of spoked wheels, like old-fashioned gears with interlocking teeth. The inks were primitive, too-bright primary colors, red and yellow and blue faded now to periwinkle and pale rose, a dusty gold like smudged pollen. I guessed they dated to the early or mid-nineteenth century. The images had the look of old children's picture books from that era, at once vivid and muted, slightly sinister, as though the illustrators were making a point of not revealing their true meaning to the casual viewer. I grinned, thinking of how I'd wrested them from the clutches of an antiques dealer, then turned them over.

The cards were all blank. I shook my head, fanning them out on the bench before me. A few of the cards had their corners neatly clipped, but others looked as though they had been bitten off in tiny crescent-shaped wedges. I squinted at one, trying to determine if someone had peeled off a printed image. The surface was rough, flecked with bits of darker gray and black, or white, but it didn't seem to have ever had anything affixed to it. There was no trace of glue or spirit gum that I could see, no jots of ink or colored paper.

A mistake then. The deck had obviously been discarded by the printer. Not even a dealer would have been able to get more than a couple of bucks for it.

Too bad. I gathered the cards into a stack, started wrapping the scarf around them when I noticed that one card was thicker than the rest. I pulled it out; not a single card after all, but two that had become stuck together. I set the rest of the deck aside, safe within the paisley shroud, then gingerly slid my thumbnail between the stuck cards. It was like prizing apart sheets of mica—I could feel where the pasteboard held fast toward the center, but if I pulled at it too hard or too quickly the cards would tear.

But very slowly, I felt the cards separate. Maybe the warmth of my touch helped, or the sudden exposure to air and moisture. For whatever reason, the cards suddenly slid apart so that I held one in each hand.

"Oh."

I cried aloud, they were that wonderful. Two tiny, brilliantly inked tableaux like medieval tapestries, or paintings by Brueghel glimpsed through a rosace window. One card was awhirl with minute figures, men and women but also animals, dogs dancing on their hind legs, long-necked cranes and crabs that lifted clacking claws to a sky filled with pennoned airships, exploding suns, a man being carried on a litter and a lash-fringed eye like a greater sun gazing down upon them all. The other card showed only the figure of a naked man, kneeling so that he faced the viewer, but with head bowed so that you saw only his broad back, a curve of neck like a quarter-moon, a sheaf of dark hair spilling to the ground before him. The man's skin was painted in gold leaf; the ground he knelt upon was the dreamy green of old bottle glass, the sky behind him crocus yellow, with a tinge upon the horizon like the first flush of sun, or the protruding tip of a finger. As I stared at them I felt my heart begin to beat, too fast too hard but not with fear this time, not this time.

The Least Trumps. The term was used, just once, in the first chapter of the unfinished, final volume of *Five Windows One Door.* I remembered it suddenly, the way you recall something from early childhood, the smell of marigolds towering above your head, a blue plush dog with one glass eye, thin sunlight filtering through a crack in a frosted glass cold frame. My mouth filled with liquid and I tasted sour cherries, salt and musk, the first time my tongue probed a girl's cunt. A warm breeze stirred my hair. I heard distant laughter, a booming bass note that resolved into the echo of a church clock tolling nine.

> Only when he was certain that Mabel had fallen fast asleep beside him would Tarquin remove the cards from their brocade pouch, her warm limbs tangled in the stained bedcovers where they emitted a smell of yeast and limewater, the surrounding room suffused with twilight so that when he held the cards before her mouth, one by one, he saw how her breath brought to life the figures painted upon each, as though she breathed upon a winter windowpane where frost-roses bloomed: *Pavell Saved From Drowning, The Bangers, One Leaf Left, Hermalchio and Lachrymatory, Villainous Saltpetre, The Ground-Nut, The Widower:* all the recusant figures of the Least Trumps quickening beneath Mabel's sleeping face.

Even now the words came to me by heart. Sometimes, when I couldn't fall asleep, I would lie in bed and silently recite the books from memory, beginning with Volume One, *The First Window: Love Plucking Rowanberries,* with its description of Mabel's deflowering that I found so tragic when I first read it. Only later in my twenties, when I read the books for the fifth or seventh time, did I realize the scene was a parody of the seduction scene in *Rigoletto.* In this way Walter Burden Fox's books eased my passage into the world, as they did in many others. Falling in love with fey little Clytie Winton then weeping over her death; making my first forays into sex when I masturbated to the memory of Tarquin's mad brother Elwell taking Mabel as she slept; realizing, as I read of Mabel's great love affair with the silent film actress Nola Flynn, that there were words to describe what I did sometimes with my own friends, even if those words had a lavender must of the attic to them: *tribadism, skylarking, sit Venus in the garden with Her Gate unlocked.*

My mother never explained any of this to me: sex, love, suffering, patience. Probably she assumed that her example alone was enough, and for another person it might well have been. But I never saw my mother unhappy, or frightened. My first attack came not long after Julia Sa'adah left me. Julia who inked my life Before and After; and while at the time I was contemptuous of anyone who suggested a link between the two events, breakup and crackup, I can see now that it was so. In Fox's novels, love affairs sometimes ended badly, but for all the lessons his books held, they never readied me for the shock of being left.

That was more than eleven years ago. I still felt the aftershocks, of course. I still dream about her: her black hair, so thick it was like oiled rope streaming through my fingers; her bronzy skin, its soft glaucous bloom like scuppernongs; the way her mouth tasted. Small mouth, smaller than my own, cigarettes and wintergreen, tea oil, coriander seed. The dream is different each time, though it always ends the same way, it ends the way it ended: Julia looking at me as she packs up her Rockland studio, arms bare so I can see my own apprentice work below her elbow, vine leaves, stylized knots. My name there, and hers, if you knew where to look. Her face sad but amused as she shakes her head. "You never happened, Ivy."

"How can you *say* that?" This part never changes either, though in my waking mind I say a thousand other things. "Six years, how can you fucking *say* that?"

She just shakes her head. Her voice begins to break up, swallowed by the harsh buzz of a tattoo machine choking down; her image fragments, hair face eyes breasts tattoos spattering into bits of light, jabs of black and red. The tube is running out of ink. "That's not what I mean. You just don't get it, Ivy. *You* never happened. *You.* Never. Happened."

Then I wake and the panic's full-blown, like waking into a room where a bomb's exploded. Only there's no bomb. What's exploded is all inside my head.

It was years before anyone figured out how it worked, this accretion of synaptic damage, neuronal misfirings, an overstimulated fight-or-flight response; the way one tiny event becomes trapped within a web of dendrites and interneurons and triggers a cascade of cortisol and epinephrine, which in turn wakes the immense black spider that rushes out and seizes me so that I see and feel only horror, only dread, the entire world poisoned by its bite. There is no antidote—the whole disorder is really just an accumulation of symptoms, accelerated pulse rate, racing heartbeat, shallow breathing. There is no cure, only chemicals that lull the spider back to sleep. It may be that my repeated tattooing of my own skin has somehow oversensitized me, like bad acupuncture, caused an involuntary neurochemical reaction that only makes it worse.

No one knows. And it's not something Walter Burden Fox ever covered in his books.

I stared at the illustrated cards in my hands. Fox had lived not far from here, in Tenants Harbor. My mother knew him years before I was born. He was much older than she was, but in those days—this was long before e-mail and cheap long-distance servers—writers and artists would travel a good distance for the company of their own kind, and certainly a lot further than from Tenants Harbor to Aranbega Island. It was the first time I can remember being really impressed by my mother, the way other people always assumed I must be. She had found me curled up in the hammock, reading *Love Plucking Rowanberries.*

"You're reading Burdie's book." She stooped to pick up my empty lemonade glass.

I corrected her primly. "It's by Walter Burden Fox."

"Oh, I know. Burdie, that's what he liked to be called. His son was Walter too. Wally, they called him. I knew him."

Now, behind me, St. Bruno's bell rang the quarter hour. Blakie would be up by now, waiting for my arrival. I carefully placed the two cards with their fellows inside the paisley scarf, put the bundle inside my bag, and headed for Penobscot Fields.

Blakie and Katherine were sitting at their dining nook when I let myself in. Yesterday's *New York Times* was spread across the table, and the remains of breakfast.

"Well," my mother asked, white brows raised above calm gray eyes as she looked at me. "Did you throw up?"

"Oh, hush, you," said Katherine.

"Not this time." I bent to kiss my mother, then turned to hug Katherine. "I went to the rummage sale at St. Bruno's, that's why I'm late."

"Oh, I meant to give them my clothes!" Katherine stood to get me coffee. "I brought over a few boxes of things, but I forgot the clothes. I have a whole bag, some nice Hermès scarves, too."

"You shouldn't give those away." Blakie patted the table, indicating where I should sit beside her. "That consignment shop in Camden gives us good credit for them. I got this sweater there." She touched her collar, dove gray knit, three pearl buttons. "It's lamb's wool. Bonwit Teller. They closed ages ago. Someone must have died."

"Oh hush," said Katherine. She handed me a coffee mug. "Like we need credit for *clothes.*"

"Look," I said. "Speaking of scarves . . ."

I pulled the paisley packet from the purse, clearing a space amidst the breakfast dishes. For a fraction of a second Blakie looked surprised, then she blinked, and along with Katherine leaned forward expectantly. As I undid the wrappings the slip of paper fell onto the table beside my mother's hand. Her gnarled fingers scrabbled at the table, finally grabbed the scrap.

"I can't read this," she said, adjusting her glasses as she stared and scowled. I set the stack of cards on the scarf, then slid them all across the table. I had withheld the two cards that retained their color; now I slipped them into my back jeans pocket, carefully, so they wouldn't get damaged. The others lay in a neat pile before my mother.

"'The Least Trumps.'" I pointed at the slip of paper. "That's what it says."

She looked at me sharply, then at the cards. "What do you mean? It's a deck of cards."

"What's written on the paper. It says, 'The Least Trumps.' I don't know if you remember, but there's a scene in one of Fox's books, the first one? The Least Trumps is what he calls a set of tarot cards that one of the characters uses." I edged over beside her, and pointed at the bit of paper she held between thumb and forefinger. "I was curious if you could read that. Since you knew him? I was wondering if you recognized it. If it was his handwriting."

"Burdie's?" My mother shook her head, drew the paper to her face until it was just a few inches from her nose. It was the same pose she'd assumed when pretending to gaze at Wise Ant through a magnifying glass for *LIFE* magazine, only now it was my mother who looked puzzled, even disoriented. "Well, I don't know. I don't remember."

I felt a flash of dread, that now of all times would be when she started to lose it, to drift away from me and Katherine. But no. She turned to Katherine and said, "Where did we put those files? When I was going through the letters from after the war. Do you remember?"

"Your room, I think. Do you want me to get them?"

"No, no. . . ." Blakie waved me off as she stood and walked, keeping her balance by touching chair, countertop, wall on the way to her study.

Katherine looked after her, then at the innocuous shred of paper, then at me. "What is it?" She touched one unraveling corner of the scarf. "Where did you get them?"

"At the rummage sale. They were wrapped up in that, I didn't know what they were till I got outside and opened it."

"Pig in a poke." Katherine winked at me. She still had her silvery hair done every Thursday, in the whipped-up spray-stiffened bouffant of her Dallas socialite days—not at the beauty parlor at the retirement center, either, but the most expensive salon in Camden. She had her nails done too, even though her hands were too twisted by arthritis to wear the bijoux rings she'd always favored, square-cut diamonds and aquamarines and the emerald my mother had given her when they first met. "I'm surprised you bought a pig in a poke, Ivy Bee."

"Yeah. I'm surprised too."

"Here we are." My mother listed back into the room, settling with a thump in her chair. "Now we can see."

She jabbed her finger at the table, where the scrap of paper fluttered like an injured moth, then handed me an envelope. "Open that, please, Ivy dear. My hands are so clumsy now."

It was a white letter-sized envelope, unsealed, tipsy typed address.

```
Miss Blakie Tun,
The Lonely House,
Aranbega Island, Maine
```

Before zip codes, even, one faded blue four-cent stamp in one corner. The other corner with the typed return address: `W. B. Fox, Sand Hill Road, T. Harbor, Maine.`

"Look at it!" commanded Blakie.

Obediently I withdrew the letter, unfolded it, and scanned the handwritten lines, front and back, until I reached the end. Blue ink, mouse-tail flourish on the final *e. Very Fondly Yours, Burdie.*

"I think it's the same writing." I scrutinized the penmanship, while trying not to actually absorb its content. Which seemed dull in any case, something about a dog, and snow, and someone's car getting stuck, and *Be glad when summer's here, at least we can visit again.*

Least. I picked up the scrap of paper to compare the two words.

"You know, they *are* the same," I said. There was something else, too. I brought the letter to my face and sniffed it. "And you know what else? I can smell it. It smells like pipe tobacco. The scarf smells like it, too."

"Borkum Riff." My mother made a face. "Awful sweet stuff, I

couldn't stand it. So."

She looked at me, gray eyes narrowed, not sly but thoughtful. "We were good friends, you know. Burdie. Very lovable man."

Katherine nodded. "Fragile."

"Fragile. He would have made a frail old man, wouldn't he?" She glanced at Katherine—two strong old ladies—then at me. "I remember how much you liked his books. I'm sorry now we didn't write to each other more, I could have given you his letters, Ivy. He always came to visit us, once or twice a year. In the summer."

"But not after the boy died," said Katherine.

My mother shook her head. "No, not after Wally died. Poor Burdie."

"Poor Wally," suggested Katherine.

It was why Fox had never completed the last book of the quintet. His son had been killed in the Korean War. I knew that; it was one of the only really interesting, if tragic, facts about Walter Burden Fox. There had been one full-length biography, written in the 1970s, when his work achieved a minor cult status boosted by the success of Tolkien and Mervyn Peake, a brief vogue in those days for series books in uniform paperback editions. *The Alexandria Quartet, Children of Violence, A Dance to the Music of Time. Five Windows One Door* had never achieved that kind of popularity, of course, despite the affection for it held by figures like Anaïs Nin, Timothy Leary, and Virgil Thomson, themselves eclipsed now by brighter, younger lights.

Fox died in 1956. I hadn't been born yet. I could never have met him.

Yet, in a funny way, he made me who I am—well, maybe not *me* exactly. But he certainly changed the way I thought about the world; made it seem at once unabashedly romantic and charged with a sense of imminence, as ripe with possibility as an autumn orchard is ripe with fruit. Julia and I were talking once about the 1960s—she was seven years older than me, and had lived through them as an adult, communes in Tennessee, drug dealing in Malibu, before she settled down in Rockland and opened her tattoo studio.

She said, "You want to know what the sixties were about, Ivy? The sixties were about *It could happen.*"

And that's what Fox's books were like. They gave me the sense that there was someone leaning over my shoulder, someone whispering *It could happen.*

So I suppose you could say that Walter Burden Fox ruined the real world for me, when I didn't find it as welcoming as the one inhabited by Mabel and Nola and the Sienno brothers. Could there ever have been a real city as marvelous as his imagined Newport? Who would ever choose to bear the weight of this world? Who would ever want to?

Still, that was my weakness, not his. The only thing I could really fault him for was his failure to finish that last volume. But, under the circumstances, who could blame him for that?

"So these are his cards? May I?" Katherine glanced at me. I nodded, and she picked up the deck tentatively, turned it over, and gave a little gasp. "Oh! They're blank—"

She looked embarrassed and I laughed. "Katherine! *Now* look what you've done!"

"But were they like this when you got them?" She began turning the cards over, one by one, setting them out on the table as though playing an elaborate game of solitaire. "Look at this! They're every single one of them blank. I've never seen such a thing."

"All used up," said Blakie. She folded the scarf and pushed it to one side. "You should wash that, Ivy. Who knows where it's been."

"Well, where *has* it been? Did he always go to church there? St. Bruno's?"

"I don't remember." Blakie's face became a mask: as she had aged, Circe became the Sphinx. She was staring at the cards lying faceup on the table. Only of course there were no faces, just a grid of gray rectangles, some missing one or two corners or even three corners. My mother's expression was watchful but wary; she glanced at me, then quickly looked away again. I thought of the two cards in my back pocket but said nothing. "His wife died young, he raised the boy alone. He wanted to be a writer too, you know. Probably they just ended up in someone's barn."

"The cards, you mean," Katherine said mildly. Blakie looked annoyed. "There. That's all of them."

"How many are there?" I asked. Katherine began to count, but Blakie said, "Seventy-three."

"Seventy-three?" I shook my head. "What kind of deck uses seventy-three cards?"

"Some are missing, then. There's only seventy." Katherine looked at Blakie. "Seventy-three? How do you know?"

"I just remember, that's all," my mother said irritably. She pointed at me. "*You* should know. You read all his books."

"Well." I shrugged and stared at the bland pattern on the dining table, then reached for a card. The top right corner was missing; but how would you know it was the top? "They were only mentioned once. As far as I recall, anyway. Just in passing. Why do you think the corners are cut off?"

"To keep track of them." Katherine began to collect them back into a pile. "That's how card cheats work. Take off a little teeny bit, just enough so they can tell when they're dealing 'em out. Which one's an ace, which one's a trey."

"But these are all the same," I said. "There's no point to it."

Then I noticed Blakie was staring at me. Suddenly I began to feel paranoid, like when I was a teenager out getting high, walking back into the Lonely House and praying she wouldn't notice how stoned I was. I felt like I'd been lying, although what had I done, besides stick two cards in my back pocket?

But then maybe I was lying, when I said there was no point; maybe I was wrong. Maybe there *was* a point. If two of the cards had a meaning, maybe they all did; even if I had no clue what their meaning was. Even if nobody had a clue: they still might mean something.

But what? It was like one of those horrible logic puzzles—you have one boat, three geese, one fox, an island: how do you get all the geese onto the island without the fox eating them? Seventy-three cards; seventy that Katherine had counted, the pair in my back pocket: where was the other one?

I fought an almost irresistible urge to reveal the two picture cards I'd hidden. Instead I looked away from my mother, and saw that now Katherine was staring at me, too. It was a moment before I realized she was waiting for the last card, the one that was still in my hand. "Oh. Thanks—"

I gave it to her, she put it on top of the stack, turned, and gave the stack to Blakie, who gave it to me. I looked down at the cards and felt that cold pressure starting to build inside my head, helium leaking into my brain, something that was going to make me float away, talk funny.

"Well." I wrapped the cards in the paisley scarf. It still smelled faintly of pipe tobacco, but now there was another scent too, my mother's Chanel No. 5. I stuck the cards in my bag, turned back to the dining table. "What should we do now?"

"I don't have a clue," said my mother, and gave me the smile of an octogenarian tiger. "Ivy? You decide."

*

Julia's father was Egyptian, a Coptic diplomat from Cairo. Her mother was an artist manqué from a wealthy Boston family that had a building at Harvard named for it. Her father, Narouz, had been married and divorced four times; Julia had a much younger half brother and several half sisters. The brother died in a terrorist attack in Egypt in the early nineties, a year or so before she left me. After her mother's death from cancer the same year, Julia refused to have anything else to do with Narouz or his extended family. A few months later, she refused to have anything to do with me as well.

Julia claimed that *Five Windows One Door* could be read as a secret text of ancient Coptic magic, that there were meanings encoded within the characters' ceaseless and often unrequited love affairs, that the titles of Nola Flynn's silent movies corresponded to oracular texts in the collections of the Hermitage and the Institut Français d'Archeologie Orientale in Cairo, that the scene in which Tarquin sodomizes his twin is in fact a description of a ritual to leave a man impotent and protect a woman from sexual advances. I asked her how such a book could possibly be conceived and written by a middle-aged communicant at St. Bruno's in Maine, in the middle of the twentieth century.

Julia just shrugged. "That's why it works. Nobody knows. Look at Lorca."

"Lorca?" I shook my head, trying not to laugh. "What, was he in Maine, too?"

"No. But he worked in the twentieth century."

That was almost the last thing Julia Sa'adah ever said to me. This is another century. Nothing works anymore.

I caught an earlier ferry back than I'd planned. Katherine was tired; I had taken her and my mother to lunch at the small café they favored, but it was more crowded than usual, with a busload of blue-haired leaf-peepers from Newburyport who all ordered the specials so that the kitchen ran out and we had to eat BLTs.

"I just hate that." Blakie glowered at the table next to us, four women the same age as she was, scrying the bill as though it were tea leaves. "Look at them, trying to figure out the tip! Fifteen percent, darling," she said loudly. "Double the tax and add one."

The women looked up. "Oh, thank you!" one said. "Isn't it pretty here?"

"I wouldn't know," said Blakie. "I'm blind."

The woman looked shocked. "Oh, hush, you," scolded Katherine. "She is not," but the women were already scurrying to leave.

I drove them back to their tidy modern retirement cottage, the made-for-TV version of the Lonely House.

"I'll see you next week," I said, after helping them inside. Katherine kissed me and made a beeline for the bathroom. My mother sat on the couch, waiting to catch her breath. She had congestive heart disease, payback for all those years of smoking Kents and eating heavily marbled steaks.

"You could stay here if you wanted," she said, and for almost the first time I heard a plaintive note in her voice. "The couch folds out."

I smiled and hugged her. "You know, I might do that. I think Sue wants a break from me. For a little while."

For a moment I thought she was going to say something. Her mouth pursed and her gray eyes once again had that watchful look. But she only nodded, patting my hand with her strong cold one, then kissed my cheek, a quick furtive gesture like she might be caught.

"Be careful, Ivy Bee," she said. "Goodbye."

On the ferry I sat on deck. The boat took no cars, and there were only a few other passengers. I had the stern to myself, a bench sheltered by the engine house from spray and chill wind. The afternoon had turned cool and gray. There was a bruised line of clouds upon the horizon, violet and slate blue; it made the islands look stark as a Rockwell Kent woodblock, the pointed firs like arrowheads.

It was a time of day, a time of year, I loved; one of the only times when things still seemed possible to me. Something about the slant of the late year's light, the sharp line between shadows and stones, as though if you slid your hand in there you'd find something unexpected.

It made me want to work.

I had no customers lined up that week. Idly I ran my right hand along the top of my left leg, worn denim and beneath it muscle, skin. I hadn't worked on myself for a while. That was one of the first things I learned when I was apprenticed to Julia: a novice tattoo artist practices on herself. If you're right-handed, you do your left arm, your left leg; just like a good artist makes her own needles, steel flux and solder, jig and needles, the smell of hot tinning fluid on the tip of the solder gun. That way people can see your work. They know they can trust you.

The last thing I'd done was a scroll of oak leaves and eyes, fanning out above my left knee. My upper thigh was still taut white skin.

I was thin and rangy like my mother had been, too fair to ever have tanned. I flexed my hand, imagining the weight of the machine, its pulse a throbbing heart. As I stared at the ferry's wake, I could see the lights of Rockland Harbor glimmer then disappear into the growing dusk. When I stuck my head out to peer toward the bow, I saw Aranbega rising from the Atlantic, black firs and granite cliffs buffed to pink by the failing sun.

I stood, keeping my balance as I gently pulled the two cards from my back pocket. I glanced at both, then put one into my wallet, behind my driver's license; sat and examined the other, turning so that the wall of the engine house kept it safe from spray. It was the card that showed only the figure of a kneeling man. A deceptively simple form, a few fluid lines indicating torso, shoulders, offertory stance—that crescent of bare neck, his hands half hidden by his long hair.

Why did I know it was a man? I'm not sure. The breadth of his shoulders, maybe; some underlying sense that any woman in such a position would be inviting disaster. This figure seemed neither resigned nor abdicating responsibility. He seemed to be waiting.

It was amazing, how the interplay of black and white and a few drops of gold leaf could conjure up an entire world. Like Pamela Colman Smith's designs for the Waite tarot—the High Priestess; the King of Wands—or a figure that Julia had shown me once. It was from a facsimile edition of a portfolio of Coptic texts on papyrus, now in the British Library. There were all kinds of spells—

> For I am having a clash with a headless dog, seize him when he comes. Grasp this pebble with both your hands, flee eastward to your right, while you journey on up.
>
> A stinging ant: In this way, while it is still fresh, burn it, grind it with vinegar, put it with incense. Put it on eyes that have discharge. They will get better.

The figure was part of a spell to obtain a good singing voice. Julia translated the text for me as she had the others:

> Yea, yea, for I adjure you in the name of the seven letters that are tattooed on the chest of the father, namely AAAAAAA, EEEEEEE, EEEEEEE, IIIIIII, OOOOOOO, UUUUUUU, OOOOOOO. Obey my mouth, before it passes and another one comes in its place! Offering: wild frankincense, wild mastic, cassia.

The Coptic figure that accompanied the text had a name: DAVI-THEA RACHOCHI ADONIEL. It looked nothing like the figure on the card in front of me; it was like something you'd see scratched on the wall of a cave.

Yet it had a name. And I would never know the name of this card.

But I would use it, I decided. *The least trumps.* Beneath me the ferry's engine shifted down, its dull steady groan deepening as we drew near Aranbega's shore. I slid the card into the Lorca book I'd brought, stuffed it into my bag, and waited to dock.

I'd left my old GMC pickup where I always did, parked behind the Island General Store. I went inside and bought a sourdough baguette and a bottle of Tokaji. I'd gotten a taste for the wine from Julia; now the store ordered it especially for me, though some of the well-heeled summer people bought it as well.

"Working tonight?" said Mary, the store's owner.

"Yup."

Outside it was full dusk. I drove across the island on the rugged gravel road that bisected it into north and south, village and wild places. To get to Green Pond you drive off the main road, following a rutted lane that soon devolves into what resembles a washed-out streambed. Soon this rudimentary road ends, at the entrance to a large grove of hundred-and-fifty-year-old pines. I parked here and walked the rest of the way, a quarter mile beneath high branches that stir restlessly, making a sound like the sea even on windless days. The pines give way to birches, ferns growing knee-high in a spinney of trees like bones. Another hundred feet and you reach the edge of Green Pond, before you the Lonely House rising on its gray islet, a dream of safety. Usually this was when the last vestiges of fear would leave me, blown away by the cool wind off the lake and the sight of my childhood home, my wooden dory pulled up onto the shore a few feet from where I stood.

But tonight the unease remained. Or no, not unease exactly; more a sense of apprehension that, very slowly, resolved into a kind of anticipation. But anticipation of what? I stared at the Lonely House with its clumps of asters and yellow coneflowers, the ragged garden I deliberately didn't weed or train. Because I wanted the illusion of wilderness, I wanted to pretend I'd left something to chance. And suddenly I wanted to see something else.

If you walk to the other side of the small lake—I hardly ever do—

you find that you're on the downward slope of a long boulder-strewn rise, a glacial moraine that eventually plummets into the Atlantic Ocean. Scattered white pines and birches grow here, and ancient white oaks, some of the very few white oaks left in the entire state, in fact, the rest having been harvested well over a century before, as masts for the great schooners. The lesser trees—red oaks, mostly, a few sugar maples—have been cut, for the Lonely House's firewood and repairs, so that if you stand in the right place you can actually look down the entire southeastern end of the island and see the ocean: scumbled gray cliffs and beyond that nothing, an unbroken darkness that might be fog, or sea, or the end of the world.

The right place to see this is from an outcropping of granite that my mother named the Ledges. On a foggy day, if you stand there and look at the Lonely House, you have an illusion of gazing from one sea island to another. If you turn, you see only darkness. The seas are too rough for recreational sailors, far from the major shipping lanes, too risky for commercial fishermen. The entire Grand Banks fishery has been depleted, so that you can stare out for hours or maybe even days and never see a single light, nothing but stars and maybe the blinking red eye of a distant plane flying the Great Circle Route to Gander or London.

It was a vista that terrified me, though I would dutifully point it out to first-time visitors, showing them where they could sit on the Ledges.

"On a clear day you can see Ireland," Katherine used to say; the joke being that on a Maine island you almost never had a clear day.

This had not been a clear day, of course, and with evening high gray clouds had come from the west. Only the easternmost horizon held a pale shimmer of blue-violet, lustrous as the inner curve of a mussel shell. Behind me the wind moved through the old pines, and I could hear the rustling of the birch leaves. Not so far off a fox barked. The sound made my neck prickle.

But I'd left a single light on inside the Lonely House, and so I focused on that, walking slowly around the perimeter of Green Pond with the little beacon always at the edge of my vision, until I reached the far side, the eastern side. Ferns crackled underfoot; I smelled the sweet odor of dying bracken, and bladder wrack from the cliffs far below. The air had the bite of rain to it, and that smell you get sometimes, when a low pressure system carries the reek of places much farther south—a soupy, thick smell, like rotting vegetation, mangroves or palmettos. I breathed it in and thought of Julia, and realized that for the first time in years, an hour had gone by and I had not thought about her at all. From the trees on the other side of Green Pond the fox barked again, even closer this time.

For one last moment I stood, gazing at the Ledges. Then I turned and walked back to where my dory waited, clambered in and rowed myself home.

The tattoo took me till dawn to finish. Once inside the Lonely House I opened the bottle of Tokaji, poured myself a glassful, and drank it. Then I went to retrieve the card, stuck inside that decrepit New Directions paperback in my bag. The book was the only thing of Julia's I had retained. She'd made a point of going through every single box of clothes and books I'd packed, through every sagging carton of dishware, and removed anything that had been hers. Anything we'd purchased together, anything that it had been her idea to buy. So that by the time she was done, it wasn't just like I'd never happened. It was like she'd never happened, either.

Except for this book. I found it a few months after the breakup. It had gotten stuck under the driver's seat of my old Volvo, wedged between a broken spring and the floor. In all the years I'd been with Julia, I'd never read it, or seen her reading it; but just a few weeks earlier I started flipping through the pages, casually, more to get the poet's smell than to actually understand him. Now I opened the book to the page where the card was stuck, and noticed several lines that had been highlighted with yellow marker.

> The *duende,* then, is a power and not a construct, is a struggle and not a concept. That is to say, it is not a question of aptitude, but of a true and viable style—of blood, in other words; of creation made act.

A struggle, not a concept. I smiled, and dropped the book on the couch; took the card and went into my studio to work.

I spent over an hour just getting a feel for the design, trying to copy it freehand onto paper before giving up. I'm a good draftsman, but one thing I've learned over the years is that the simpler a good drawing appears to be, the more difficult it is to copy. Try copying one of Picasso's late minotaur drawings and you'll see what I mean. Whoever did the design on this particular card probably wasn't Picasso, but the image still defeated me. There was a mystery to it, a sense of waiting that was charged with power, like that D. H. Lawrence poem, *those who have not exploded.* I finally traced it on my light board, the final stencil image exactly the same size as that on the card, outlined in black hectograph ink.

Then I prepped myself. My studio is as sterile as I can make it. There's no carpet on the bare wood floor, which I scrub every day. Beneath a blue plastic cover, the worktable is white formica, so blood or dirt shows, or spilled ink. I don't bother with an apron or gloves when I'm doing myself, and between the lack of protection and a couple of glasses of Tokaji, I always get a slightly illicit-feeling buzz. I feel like I'm pulling something over, even though there's never anyone around but myself. I swabbed the top of my thigh with seventy percent alcohol, used a new, disposable razor to shave it; swabbed it again, dried it with sterile gauze soaked in more alcohol. Then I coated the shaved skin with betadine, tossing the used gauze into a small metal biohazard bin.

I'd already set up my inks in their plastic presterilized caps—black, yellow and red to get the effect of gold leaf, white. I got ready to apply the stencil, rubbing a little bit of stick deodorant onto my skin, so that the ink would adhere, then pressing the square of stenciled paper and rubbing it for thirty seconds. Then I pulled the paper off. Sometimes I have to do this more than once, if the customer's skin is rough, or the ink too thick. This time, though, the design transferred perfectly.

I sat for a while, admiring it. From my angle, the figure was upside down—I'd thought about it, whether I should just say the hell with it and do it so I'd be the only one who'd ever see it properly. But I decided to go with convention, so that now I'd be drawing a reverse of what everyone else would see. I'm a bleeder, so I had a good supply of Vaseline and paper towels at hand. I went into the living room and knocked back one last glass of Tokaji, returned to the studio, switched on my machine, and went at it.

I did the outlines first. There's always this *frisson* when the needles first touch my own skin, sterilized metal skimming along the surface so that it burns, as though I'm running a flame-tipped spike along my flesh. Before Julia did my first tattoo I'd always imagined the process would be like pricking myself with a needle, a series of fine precise jabs of pain.

It's not like that at all. It's more like carving your own skin with the slanted nib of a razor-sharp calligraphy pen, or writing on flesh with a soldering iron. The pain is excruciating, but contained: I look down at the vibrating tattoo gun, its tip like a wasp's sting, and see beneath the needles a flowing line of black ink, red weeping from the black: my own blood. My left hand holds the skin taut—this also hurts like hell—while my right fingers manipulate the machine and the wad of paper towel that soaks up blood as the needle moves on, its tip moving in tiny circles, being careful not to press too hard, so it won't scab. I trace a man's shoulders, a crescent that becomes a neck, a skull's crown above a single thick line that signals a cascade of hair. Then down and up to outline his knees, his arms.

When the pain becomes too much I stop for a bit, breathing deeply. Then I smooth Vaseline over the image on my thigh, take a bit of gauze and clean the needle tip of blood and ink. After twenty minutes or so of being scarred with a vibrating needle your endorphins kick in, but they don't block the pain; they merely blur it, so that it diffuses over your entire body, not just a few square inches of stretched skin burning like a fresh brand. It's perversely like the aftermath of a great massage, or great sex; exhausting, unbearable, exhilarating. I finished the outline and took a break, turning on the radio to see if WERU had gone off the air. Two or three nights a week they sign off at midnight, but Saturdays sometimes the DJ stays on.

This was my lucky night. I turned the music up and settled back into my chair. My entire leg felt sore, but the outline looked good. I changed the needle tip and began to do the shading, the process that would give the figure depth and color. The tip of the needle tube is flush against my skin, but only for an instant; then I flick it up and away. This way the ink is dispersed beneath the epidermis, deepest black feathering up to create gray.

It takes days and days of practice before you get this technique down, but I had it. When I was done edging the figure's hair, I cleaned and changed the needle tube again, mixing gamboge yellow and crimson until I got just the hue I wanted, a brilliant tiger-lily orange. I sprayed the tattoo with disinfectant, gave it another swipe of Vaseline, then went to with the orange. I did some shading around the man's figure, until it looked even better than the original, with a numinous glow that made it stand out from the other designs around it.

It was almost two more hours before I was done. At the very last I put in a bit of white, a few lines here and there, ambient color, really, the eye didn't register it as white but it charged the image with a strange, almost eerie brilliance. White ink pigment is paler than human skin; it changes color the way skin does, darkening when exposed to the sun until it's almost indistinguishable from ordinary flesh tone.

But I don't spend a lot of time outside; inks don't fade much on my skin. When I finally put down the machine, my hand and entire right arm ached. Outside, rain spattered the pond. The wind rose, and moments later I heard droplets lashing the side of the house. A barred owl called its four querulous notes. From my radio came a low steady hum of static. I hadn't even noticed when the station went off the air. Soon it would be 5:00 A.M., and the morning DJ would be in. I cleaned my machine and work area quickly, automatically; washed my tattoo, dried it, and covered the raw skin with antibacterial ointment, and finally taped on a Telfa bandage. In a few hours, after I woke, I'd shower and let the warm water soften the bandage until it slid off. Now I went into the kitchen, stumbling with fatigue and the postorgasmic glow I get from working on myself.

I'd remembered to leave out a small porterhouse steak to defrost. I heated a cast-iron skillet, tossed the steak in and seared it, two minutes on one side, one on the other. I ate it standing over the sink, tearing off meat still cool and bloody in the center. There are some good things about living alone. I knocked back a quart of skim milk, took a couple of ibuprofen and a high-iron formula vitamin, went to bed, and passed out.

The central conceit of *Five Windows One Door* is that the same story is told and retold, with constantly shifting points of view, abrupt changes of narrator, of setting, of a character's moral or political beliefs. Even the city itself changed, so that the bistro frequented by Nola's elderly lover, Hans Liep, was sometimes at the end of Tufnell Street; other times it could be glimpsed in a cul-de-sac near the Boulevard El-Baz. There were madcap scenes in which Shakespearean plot reversals were enacted—the violent reconciliation between Mabel and her father; Nola Flynn's decision to enter a Carmelite convent after her discovery of the blind child Kelson; Roberto Metropole's return from the dead; even the reformation of the incomparably wicked Elwell, who, according to the notes discovered after Fox's death, was to have married Mabel and fathered her six children, the eldest of whom grew up to become Amantine, Popess of Tuckahoe and the first saint to be canonized in the Reformed Catholic Church.

Volume Five, *Ardor ex Cathedra,* was unfinished at the time of

Fox's death. He had completed the first two chapters, and in his study was a box full of hand-drawn genealogical charts and plot outlines, character notes, a map of the city, even names for new characters—Billy Tyler, Gordon MacKenzie-Hart, Paulette Houdek, Ruben Kirstein. Fox's editor at Griffin/Sage compiled these remnants into an unsatisfactory final volume that was published a year after Fox died. I bought a copy, but it was a sad relic, like the blackened lump of glass that is all that remains of a stained-glass window destroyed by fire. Still, I kept it with its brethren on a bookshelf in my bedroom, the five volumes in their uniform dust jackets, scarlet letters on a brilliant indigo field with the author's name beneath in gold.

I dreamed I heard the fox barking, or maybe it really was the fox barking. I turned, groaning as my leg brushed against the bedsheet. The bandage had fallen off while I slept. I groped under the covers till I found it, a clump of sticky brown gauze; tossed it on the floor, sat up, and rubbed my eyes. It was morning. My bedroom window was blistered with silvery light, the glass flecked with rain. I looked down at my thigh. The tattoo had scabbed over, but not much. The figure of the kneeling man was stark and precise, its orange nimbus glazed with clear fluid. I got up and limped into the bathroom, sat on the edge of the tub and laved my thigh tenderly, warm water washing away dead skin and dried blood. I patted it dry and applied another thin layer of antibiotic ointment, and headed for the kitchen to make coffee.

The noise came again—not barking at all but something tapping against a window. It took me a minute to figure out what it was: the basket the Lonely House used as a message system. Blakie had devised it forty years ago, a pulley and old-fashioned clothesline, strung between the Lonely House and a birch tree on the far shore. A small wicker basket hung from the line, with a plastic ziplock bag inside it, and inside the bag Magic Markers and a notepad. Someone could write a note on shore, then send the basket over; it would bump against the front window, alerting us to a visitor. A bit more elegant than standing on shore and shouting, it also gave the Lonely House's inhabitants the chance to hide, if we weren't expecting anyone.

I couldn't remember the last time someone had used it. I had a cell phone now, and customers made appointments months in advance. I'd almost forgotten the clothesline was there.

I went to the front window and peered out. Fog had settled in during the night; on the northern side of the island the foghorn moaned. No one would be leaving Aranbega today. I could barely discern the other shore, thick gray mist striated with white birch trees. I couldn't see anyone.

But sure enough, there was the basket dangling between the window and the front door. I opened the window and stuck my hand out, brushing aside a mass of cobwebs strung with dead crane flies and mosquitoes to get at the basket. Inside was the ziplock bag and the notebook, the latter pleached with dark green threads. I grimaced as I pulled it out, the pages damp and molded into a block of viridian pulp.

But stuck to the back of the notebook was a folded square of yellow legal paper. I unfolded it and read the message written in strong square letters.

Ivy—
Christopher Sa'adah here, I'm staying in Aran. Harbor, stopped by to say hi. You there? Call me @ 462-1117. Hope you're okay.

C.

I stared at the note for a full minute. Thinking, this is a mistake, this is a sick joke; someone trying to torment me about Julia. Christopher was dead. Nausea washed over me, that icy chill like a shroud, my skin clammy and the breath freezing in my lungs.

"Ivy? You there?"

I rested my hand atop the open window and inhaled deeply. "Christopher." I shook my head, gave a gasping laugh. "Jesus—"

I leaned out the open window. "Christopher?" I shouted. "Is that really you?"

"It's really me," a booming voice yelled back.

"Hold on! I'll get the dory and come right over—"

I ran into the bedroom and pulled on a pair of loose cutoffs and faded T-shirt, then hurried outside. The dory was where I'd left it, pulled up on shore just beyond the fringe of cattails and bayberries. I pushed it into the lake, a skein of dragonflies rising from the dark water to disappear in the mist. There was water in the boat, dead leaves that nudged at my bare feet; I grabbed the oars and rowed, twenty strong strokes that brought me to the other shore.

"Ivy?"

That was when I saw him, a tall figure like a shadow breaking from the fog thick beneath the birches. He was so big that I had to blink to make sure that this, too, wasn't some trick of the mist: a black-haired, bearded man, strong enough to yank one of the birch saplings up by the roots if he'd wanted to. He wore dark brown corduroys, a flannel shirt, and brown Carhartt jacket; heavy brown work boots. His hair was long and pushed back behind his ears; his hands were shoved in his jacket pockets. He was a bit stooped, his shoulders raised in a way that made him look surprised, or unsure of himself. It made him look young, younger than he really was; it made him look like Christopher, Julia's thirteen-year-old brother.

He wasn't thirteen anymore. I did the math quickly, bringing the boat round and grabbing the wet line to toss on shore. Christopher was Narouz Sa'adah's son by his third wife. He was eighteen years younger than Julia; that would make him eleven years younger than me, which would make him—

"Little Christopher!" I looked up at him from the dory, grinning. "How the hell old are you?"

He shrugged, leaned down to grab the end of the line and loop it around the granite post at the shoreline. He took out a cigarette and lit it, inhaled rapidly—nervously, I see now—and let his arm dangle so that the smoke coiled up around his wrist.

"I'm thirty-four." He had an almost comically basso voice that echoed across Green Pond like the foghorn. An instant later I heard a loon give its warning cry. Christopher dropped his cigarette and stubbed it out, cocking his head toward the dory. "Is that the same boat you used to have?"

"Sure is." I hopped into the water, wincing at the cold, then waded to shore. "Jesus. Little Christopher. I can't believe it's you. You—Christ! I—well, I thought you were dead."

"I got better." He stared down at me and for the first time smiled, his teeth still a little crooked and nicotine stained, not Julia's teeth at all; his face completely guileless, close-trimmed black beard, long hair falling across tawny eyes. "After the bombing? I was in hospital for a long time, outside Cairo. It wasn't just you—everyone thought I was dead. My father finally tracked me down and brought me back to Washington. I think you and Julia had broken up by then."

I just stared at him. I felt dizzy: even though it was a small piece of the world, of history, it meant everything was different. Everything was changed. I blinked and looked away from him, saw the birch leaves spinning in the breeze, pale gold and green, goldenrod past its prime, tall stalks of valerian with their flower heads blown to brown vein. I looked back at Christopher: everything was the same.

He said, "I can't believe it's you either, Ivy."

I threw my arms around him. He hugged me awkwardly—he was so much bigger than I was!—and started laughing in delight. "Ivy! I walked all the way over here! From the village, I'm staying at the inn. That lady at the general store?"

"Mary?"

"Right, Mary—she remembered me, she said you still lived here—"

"Why didn't you call?"

He looked startled. "You have a phone?"

"Of course I have a phone! Actually, it's a cell phone, and I only got it a year ago, after they put up a tower over on Blue Hill." I drew away from him, balancing on my heels to make myself taller. "Jeez, you're all growed up, Christopher. I'm trying to think, when was the last time I saw you—"

"Twelve years ago. I was just starting grad school in Cairo. I came to see you and Julia in Rockland before I left. Remember?"

I tried, but couldn't; not really. I'd never known him well. He'd been a big ungainly teenager, extremely quiet and sitting at the edges of the room, where he always seemed to be listening carefully to everything his older sister or her friends said. He'd grown up in D.C. and Cairo, but he spent his summers in the States. I first met him when he was twelve or thirteen, a gangly kid into Dungeons & Dragons and *Star Wars,* who'd recently read Tolkien and had just started on Terry Brooks.

"Jesus, don't read *that,*" I'd said, snatching away *The Sword of Shannara* and shoving my own copy of *Love Plucking Rowan-berries* into his big hands. For a moment he looked hurt. Then, "Thanks," he said, and gave me that sweet slow smile. He spent the rest of that summer in our apartment overlooking Rockland Harbor, hunched into a wicker chair on the decrepit back deck as he worked his way through *Sybylla and the Summer Sky, Mellors' Plasma Bistro, Love Regained in Idleness,* and finally the tattered remnants of *Ardor ex Cathedra.*

"Of course I remember," I said. I swiped at a mosquito, looked up, and grinned. "Gosh. You were still a kid then. How're you doing? *What* are you doing? Are you married?"

"Divorced." He raised his arms, yawning, and stretched. His silhouette blotted out the gray sky, the blurred shapes of trees and boulders. "No kids, though. I'm at the Center for Remote Sensing at B.U., coordinating a project near the Chephren Quarries, in the Western Desert. Upper Egypt."

He dropped his arms and looked down at me again. "So Ivy—would you—how'd you feel about company? I could use a cup of coffee. We can walk back to town if you want. Have a late lunch. Or early dinner. . . ."

"Christ, no." I glanced at my raw tattoo. "I should clean that again, before I do anything. And I haven't even had breakfast yet."

"Really? What were you doing? I mean, are you with a customer or something?"

I shook my head. "I was up all night, doing this—" I splayed my fingers above the figure on my thigh. "What time is it, anyway?"

"Almost four."

"Almost *four?*" I grabbed his hand and twisted it to see his wristwatch. "I don't believe it! How could I, I—" I shivered. "I slept through the whole day."

Christopher stared at me curiously. I was still holding his wrist, and he turned his hand, gently, his fingers brushing mine. "You okay, Ivy? Did I get you in the middle of something? I can come back."

"I don't know." I shook my head and withdrew my hand from his, but slowly, so I wouldn't hurt his feelings. "I mean no, I'm fine, just—"

I looked at my thigh. A thread of blood ran down my leg, and as I stared a damselfly landed beneath the tattoo, its thorax a metallic blue needle, wings invisible against my skin. "I was up all night, doing that—"

I pointed at the kneeling man; only from my angle he wasn't kneeling but hanging suspended above my knee, like a bat. "I—I don't think I finished until five o'clock this morning. I had no idea it was so late. . . ."

I could hear the panic in my own voice. I took a deep breath, trying to keep my tone even, but Christopher just put one hand lightly one my shoulder and said, "Hey, it's okay. I really can come back. I just wanted to say hi."

"No. Wait." I counted ten heartbeats, twelve. "I'm okay. I'll be okay. Just, can you row us back?"

"Sure." He stooped to grab a leather knapsack leaning against a tree. "Let's go."

With Christopher in it, the dory sat a good six inches lower in the water, and it took a little longer with him rowing. Halfway across the brief stretch of pond I finally asked him.

"How is Julia?"

My voice was shaky, but he didn't seem to notice. "I don't know. One of my sisters talked to her about five years ago. She was in Toronto, I think. No one's heard from her." He strained at the oars, then glanced at me measuringly. "I never really knew her, you know. She was so much older. I always thought she was kind of a bitch, to tell you the truth. The way she treated you . . . it made me uncomfortable."

I was silent. My leg ached from the tattoo, searing pain like a bad sunburn. I focused on that, and after a few minutes I could bear to talk.

"Sorry," I said. The dory ground against the shore of the islet. The panic was receding; I could breathe again. "I get these sometimes. Panic attacks. Usually it's not at home, though; only when I go off island."

"That's no fun." Christopher gave me an odd look. Then he clambered out and helped me pull the dory into the reeds. He followed me through the overgrown stands of phlox and aster, up the steps and into the Lonely House. The floor shuddered at his footsteps. I closed the door, looked up at him, and laughed.

"Boy, you sure fill this place up—watch your head, no, wait—"

Too late. As he turned he cracked into a beam. He clutched his head, grimacing. "Shit—I forgot how small this place is—"

I led him to the couch. "Here, sit—I'll get some ice."

I hurried into the kitchen and pulled a tray from the freezer. I was still feeling a little wonky. For about twenty-four hours after you get tattooed, it's like you're coming down with the flu. Your body's been pretty badly treated; your entire immune system fires up, trying to heal itself. I should have just crawled back into bed. Instead I called, "You want something to drink?"

I walked back in with a bowl of ice and a linen towel. Christopher was on the sofa, yanking something from his knapsack.

"I brought this." He held up a bottle of tequila. "And these—"

He reached into the knapsack again and pulled out three limes. They looked like oversized marbles in his huge hand. "I remember you liked tequila."

I smiled vaguely. "Did I?" It had been Julia who liked tequila, going through a quart every few days in the summer months. I sat beside him on the couch, wrapped the ice in the towel, and held it out. He lowered his head, childlike, and after a moment I very gently touched it. His hair was thick and coarse, darker than his sister's; when I extended my fingers I felt his scalp, warm as though he'd been sitting in the sun all day. "You're hot," I said softly, and felt myself flush. "I mean your head—your skin feels hot. Like heatstroke."

He kept his head lowered, saying nothing. His long hair grazed the top of my thigh. He reached to take my hand, and his was so much bigger, it was as though my own hand was swallowed in a heated glove, his palm calloused, fingertips smooth and hard; soft hairs on the back of his wrist. I said nothing. I could smell him, an acrid smell, not unpleasant but strange; he smelled of limes and sweat, and raw earth, stones washed by the sea. My mouth was dry, and as I moved to place the ice-filled towel on his brow I felt his hand slip from mine, to rest upon the couch between us.

"There." I could feel my heart racing, the frantic thought. *It's just a symptom, there's nothing to be scared of, it's just a symptom, it's just—*

"Christopher," I said thickly. "Just—sit. For a minute."

We sat. My entire body felt hot, and damp; I was sweating now myself, not cold anymore, my heartbeat slow and even. From outside came the melancholy sound of the foghorn, the ripple of rain across the lake. The room around us was full of that strange, translucent green light you get here sometimes: being on an island on an island suspended in fog, droplets of mist and sea and rain mingling to form a shimmering glaucous veil. Outside the window the world seemed to tremble and break apart into countless motes of silver, steel-gray, emerald, then cohere again into a strangely solid-looking mass. As though someone had tossed a stone into a viscous pool, or probed a limb with a needle; that sense of skin breaking, parting then closing once more around the wound, the world, untold unseen things flickering and diving, ganglia, axons, otters, loons. A bomb goes off, and it takes twelve years to hear its explosion. I lifted my head and saw Christopher watching me. His mouth was parted, his amber eyes sad, almost anguished.

"Ivy," he said. When his mouth touched mine I flinched, not fear but shock at how much bigger it was than my own, than Julia's, any woman's. I had not touched a man since I was in high school, and that was a boy, boys; I had never kissed a man. His face was rough; his mouth tasted bitter, of nicotine and salt. And blood, too—he'd bitten his lip from nervousness, my tongue found the broken seam just beneath the hollow of his upper lip, the hollow hidden beneath soft hair, not rough as I had thought it would be, and smelling of some floral shampoo.

It was like nothing I had imagined—and I *had* imagined it, of course. I'd imagined everything, before I fell in love with Julia Sa'adah. I'd fallen in love with *her*—her soul, her *duende,* she would have called it—but in a way it had almost nothing to do with her being another woman. I'd seen movies, porn films even, lots of them, watching with Julia and some of her friends, the ones who were bisexual, or beyond bisexual, whatever that might be; read magazines, novels, pornography, glanced at sites online; masturbated to dim images of what it was like, what I thought it might be like. Even watched once as a couple we knew went at it in our big untidy bed, slightly revved-up antics for our benefit, I suspect, a lot of whimpering and operatic sound effects.

This was nothing like that. This was slow, almost fumbling; even formal. He seemed afraid, or maybe it was just that he couldn't believe it, that it wasn't real to him, yet.

"I was always in love with you." He was lying beside me on the couch; not a lot of room left for me, but his broad arm kept me from rolling off. Our shirts were stuffed behind our heads for pillows, I still wore my cutoffs, and he still had his corduroy jeans on. We hadn't gotten further than this. On the floor beside us was the half-empty bottle of tequila, Christopher's pocketknife, and the limes, cloven in two so that they looked like enormous green eyes. He was tracing the designs on my body; the full sleeve on my left arm, Chinese water dragons, stylized waves, all in shades of turquoise and indigo and green. Green is the hardest ink to work with—you mix it with white, the white blends into your skin tone, you don't realize the green pigment is there and you overdo, going over and over until you scar. I'd spent a lot of time with green when I started out; yellow too, another difficult pigment.

"You are so beautiful. All this . . ." His finger touched coils of vines, ivy that thrust from the crook of my elbow and extended up to my shoulder. His own body was unblemished, as far as I could see. Skin darker than Julia's, shading more to olive than bronze; an almost hairless chest, dappled line of dark hair beneath his navel. He tapped the inside of my elbow, tender soil overgrown with leaves. "That must have hurt."

I shrugged. "I guess. You forget. All you remember afterward is how intense it was. And then you have these—"

I ran my hand down my arm, turned to sit up. "This is what I did last night." I flexed my leg, pulled up the edge of my shorts to better expose the new tattoo. "See?"

He sat up, ran a hand through his black hair, then leaned forward to examine it. His hair spilled down from his forehead; he had one hand on my upper thigh, the other on his own knee. His broad back was to me, olive skin, a paler crescent just above his shoulders where his neck was bent: a scar. There were others, jagged smooth lines, some deep enough to hide a fingertip. Shrapnel, or glass thrown off by the explosion. His long hair grazed my leg, hanging down like a dark waterfall.

I swallowed, my gaze flicking from his back to what I could glimpse of my tattoo, a small square of flesh framed between his arms, his hair, the ragged blue line of my cutoffs. A tall man, leaning forward so that his hair fell to cover his face. A waterfall. A curtain. Christopher lifted his head to stare at me.

A veil, torn away.

"Shit," I whispered. "Shit, shit . . ."

I pushed away from him and scrambled to my feet. "What? What is it?" He looked around as though expecting to see someone else in the room with us. "Ivy—"

He tried to grasp me but I pulled away, grabbing my T-shirt from the couch and pulling it on. "Ivy! What happened?" His voice rose, desperate; I shook my head, then pointed at the tattoo.

"This—" He looked at the tattoo, then at me, not comprehending. "That image? I just found it yesterday. On a card. This sort of tarot card, this deck. I got it at a rummage sale—"

I turned and ran into my studio. Christopher followed.

"Here!" I darted to my work table and yanked off the protective blue covering. The table was empty. "It was here—"

I whirled, went to my light table. Acetates and sheets of rag paper were still strewn across it, my pencils and inks were where I'd left them. A dozen pages with failed versions of the card were scattered across the desk, and on the floor. I grabbed them, holding up each sheet and shaking it as though it were an envelope, as though something might fall out. I picked up the pages from the floor, emptied the stainless steel wastebasket, and sifted through torn papers and empty ink capsules. Nothing.

The card was gone.

"Ivy?"

I ignored him and ran back into the living room. "Here!" I yanked the paisley-wrapped deck from my purse. "It was like this, it was one of these—"

I tore the scarf open. The deck was still there. I let the scarf fall and fanned the cards out, facedown, a rainbow arc of labyrinthine wheels; then twisted my hand to show the other side.

"They're blank," said Christopher.

"That's right. They're all blank. Only there was one—last night—"

I pointed at the tattoo. "That design. There was one card with that design. I copied it. It was with me in the studio, I had it on my drafting table. I ended up tracing it for the stencil."

"And now you can't find it."

"No. It's gone." I let my breath out in a long, low whoosh, I felt sick at my stomach, but it was more like seasickness than panic, a nausea I could override if I wanted to. "It's—I won't find it. It's just gone."

My eyes teared. Christopher stood beside me, his face dark with concern. After a minute he said, "May I?"

He held out his hand, and I nodded and gave him the cards. He riffled through them, frowning. "Are they all like this?"

"All except two. There's another one—" I gestured at my purse. "I put it aside. I got them at the rummage sale at St. Bruno's yesterday. They were—"

I stopped. Christopher was still examining the cards, holding them up to the light as though that might reveal some hidden pattern. I said, "You read Walter Burden Fox, right?"

He glanced up at me. "Sure. *Five Windows One Door?* You gave it to me, remember? That first summer I stayed with you down at that place you had by the water. I loved those books." His tone softened; he smiled, a sweet, sad half smile, and held the cards up as though to show a winning hand. "That really changed my life, you know. After I read them; when I met you. That's when I decided to become an archaeologist. Because they were—well, I don't know how to explain it. . . ."

He tapped the cards thoughtfully against his chin. "I loved those books so much. I couldn't believe it, when I got to the end? That he never finished them. I used to think, if I had only one wish, it would be that somehow he finished that last book. Like maybe if his son hadn't died, or something. Those books just amazed me!"

He shook his head, still marveling. "They made me think how the world might be different than what it was; what we think it is. That there might be things we still don't know, even though we think we've discovered everything. Like the work I do? We scan all these satellite images of the desert, and we can see where ancient sites were, under the sand, under the hills. Places so changed by wind erosion you would never think anything else was ever there—but there were temples and villages, entire cities! Empires! Like in the third book, when you read it and find out there's this whole other history to everything that happened in the first two. The entire world is changed."

The entire world is changed. I stared at him, then nodded. "Christopher—these cards are from his books. The last one. 'The least trumps.' When I got them, there was a little piece of paper—"

My gaze dropped to the floor. The scrap was there, by Christopher's bare foot. I picked up the scrap and handed it to him. "'The least trumps.' It's in the very first chapter of the last book, the one he never finished. Mabel's in bed with Tarquin and he takes out this deck of cards. He holds them in front of her, and when she breathes on them it somehow makes them come alive. There's an implication that everything that happened before has to maybe do with the cards. But he died before he ever got to that part."

Christopher stared at the fragment of paper. "I don't remember," he said at last. He looked at me. "You said there's one other card. Can I see it?"

I hesitated, then went to get my bag. "It's in here."

I took out my wallet. Everything around me froze; my hand was so numb I couldn't feel it when I slid my finger behind my license. I couldn't feel it, it wasn't there at all—

But it was. The wallet fell to the floor. I stood and held the card in both hands. The last one: the least trump. The room around me was gray, the air motionless. In my hands a lozenge of spectral color glimmered and seemed to move. There were airships and flaming birds, two old women dancing on a beach, an exploding star above a high-rise building. The tiny figure of a man was not being carried in a litter, I saw now, but lying in a bed borne by red-clad women. Above them all a lash-fringed eye stared down.

I blinked and rubbed my eye, then gave the card to Christopher. When I spoke my voice was thick. "I—I forgot it was so beautiful. That's it. The last one."

He walked over to the window, leaned against the wall, and angled the card to catch the light. "Wow. This is amazing. Was the other one like it? All this detail . . ."

"No. It was much simpler. But it was still beautiful. It makes you realize how hard it is, drawing something that simple."

I looked down at my leg and smiled wryly. "But you know, I think I got it right."

For some minutes he remained by the window, silent. Suddenly he looked up. "Could you do this, Ivy? On me?"

I stared at him. "You mean a tattoo? No. It's far too intricate. It would take days, something like that. Days, just to make a decent stencil. The tattoo would probably take a week, if you were going to do it right."

"This, then." He strode over to me, pointing to the sun that was an eye. "Just that part, there—could you do just that? Like maybe on my arm?"

He flexed his arm, a dark sheen where the bicep rose, like a wave. "Right there—"

I ran my hand across the skin appraisingly. There was a scar, a small one. I could work around it, make it part of the design. "You should think about it. But yeah, I could do it."

"I have thought about it. I want you to do it. Now."

"Now?" I looked at the window. It was getting late. Light was leaking from the sky, everything was fading to lavender-gray, twilight. The fog was coming in again, pennons of mist trailing above Green Pond. I could no longer see the far shore. "It's kind of late. . . ."

"Please." He stood above me; I could feel the heat radiating from him, see the card glinting in his hand like a shard of glass. "Ivy—"

His deep voice dropped, a whisper I felt more than heard. "I'm not my sister. I'm not Julia. Please."

He touched the outer corner of my eye, where it was still damp. "Your eyes are so blue," he said. "I forgot how blue they are."

We went into the studio. I set the card on the light table, with the deck beside it, used a loupe to get a better look at the image he wanted. It would not be so hard to do, really, just that one thing. I sketched it a few times on paper, finally turned to where Christopher sat waiting in the chair beside my worktable.

"I'm going to do it freehand. I usually don't, but this is pretty straightforward, and I think I can do it. You sure about this?"

He nodded. He looked a little pale, there beneath the bright lights I work under, but when I walked over to him he smiled. "I'm sure."

I prepped him, swabbing the skin, then shaving his upper arm twice, to make sure it was smooth enough. I made sure my machine was thoroughly cleaned, and set up my inks. Black, cerulean and cobalt, Spaulding and Rogers Bright Yellow.

"Ready?"

He nodded, and I set to.

It took about four hours, though I pretty much lost track of the time. I did the outline first, a circle. I wanted it to look very slightly uneven, like this drawing by Odile Redon I liked—you can see how the paper absorbed his ink, it made the lines look powerful, like black lightning. After the circle was done I did the eye inside it, a half circle of white, because in the card the eye is looking down, at the world beneath. Then I did the flattened ovoid of the pupil. Then the flickering lashes all around it. Christopher didn't talk. Sweat ran in long lines from beneath his arms; he swallowed a lot, and sometimes closed his eyes. There was so much muscle beneath his skin that it was difficult to keep it taut—no fat, and the skin wasn't loose enough—so I had to keep pulling it tight. I knew it hurt.

"That's it, take a deep breath. I can stop, if you need to take a break. I need to take a break, anyway."

But I didn't. My hand didn't cramp up; there was none of that fuzzy feeling that comes after holding a vibrating machine for hours at a stretch. Now and then Christopher would shift in his chair, never very much. Once I moved to get a better purchase on his arm, sliding my knee between his legs: I could feel his cock, rigid beneath his corduroys, and hear his breath catch.

He didn't bleed much. His olive skin made the inks seem to glow, the blue-and-gold eye within its rayed penumbra, wriggling lines like cilia. At the center of the pupil was the scar. You could hardly see it now, it looked like a shadow, the eye's dark heart.

"There." I drew back, shut the machine off, and nestled it in my lap. "It's finished. What do you think?"

He pulled his arm toward him, craning his head to look. "Wow. It's gorgeous." He looked at me and grinned ecstatically. "It's fucking gorgeous."

"All right then." I stood and put the machine over by the sink, turned to get some bandages. "I'll just clean it up, and then—"

"Not yet. Wait, just a minute. Ivy."

He towered above me, his long hair lank and skin sticky with sweat, pink fluid weeping from beneath the radiant eye. When he kissed me I could feel his cock against me, heat arcing above my groin. His leg moved, it rubbed against my tattoo, and I moaned but it didn't hurt, I couldn't feel it, anything at all, just heat everywhere now, his hands tugging my shirt off then drawing me into the bedroom.

Not like Julia. His mouth was bigger, his hand; when I put my arms around him my fingers scarcely met, his back was so broad. The scars felt smooth and glossy; I thought they would hurt if I touched them but he said no, he liked my fingernails against them, he liked to press my mouth against his chest, hard, as I took his nipple between my lips, tongued it then held it gently between my teeth, the aureole with its small hairs radiating beneath my mouth. He went down on me and that was different too, his beard against the inside of my thighs, his tongue probing deeper; my fingers tangled in his hair and I felt his breath on me, his tongue still inside me when I came. He kissed me and I tasted myself, held his head between my hands, his beard wet. He was laughing. When he came inside me he laughed again, almost shouted; then collapsed alongside me.

"Ivy. Ivy . . ."

"Shhh." I lay my palm against his face and kissed him. The sheet between us bore the image of a blurred red sun. "Christopher."

"Don't go." His warm hand covered my breast. "Don't go anywhere."

I laughed softly. "Me? I never go anywhere."

We slept. He breathed heavily, but I was so exhausted I passed out before I could shift toward my own side of the bed. If I dreamed, I don't remember; only knew when I woke that everything was different, because there was a man in bed beside me.

"Huh." I stared at him, his face pressed heavily into the pillow. Then I got up, as quietly as I could. I tiptoed into the bathroom, peed, washed my face and cleaned my teeth. I thought of making coffee, and peered into the living room. Outside all was still fog, dark gray, shredded with white to mark the wind's passing. The clock read 6:30. I turned and crept back to the bedroom.

Christopher was still asleep. I sat on the edge of the bed, languidly, and let my hand rest upon my tattoo. Already it hurt less; it was healing. I looked up at the head of the bed, where my mother's books were, and Walter Burden Fox's. The five identical dust jackets, deep blue, with their titles and Fox's name in gold letters.

Something was different. The last volume, the one completed posthumously by Fox's editor, with the spine that read **ARDOR EX CATHEDRA * WALTER BURDEN FOX.**

I yanked it from the shelf, holding it so the light fell on the spine.

ARDOR EX CATHEDRA * WALTER BURDEN FOX & W. F. FOX

My heart stopped. Around me the room was black. Christopher moved on the bed behind me, yawning. I swallowed, leaning forward until my hands rested on my knees as I opened the book.

ARDOR EX CATHEDRA

By Walter Burden Fox
Completed by Walter F. Fox

"No," I whispered. Frantically I turned to the end, the final twenty pages that had been nothing but appendices and transcriptions of notes.

Chapter Seventeen: The Least Trumps.

I flipped through the pages in disbelief, and yes, there they were, new chapter headings, every one of them—

Pavell Saved From Drowning. One Leaf Left. Hermalchio and Lachrymatory. Villainous Saltpetre. The Scars. The Radiant Eye. I gasped, so terrified my hands shook and I almost dropped it, turning back to the frontispiece.

Completed by Walter F. Fox

I went to the next page—the dedication.

To the memory of my father

I cried out. Christopher sat up, gasping. "What is it? Ivy, what happened—"

"The book! It's different!" I shook it at him, almost screaming. "He didn't die! The son—he finished it, it's all different! *It's changed.*"

He took the book from me, blinking as he tried to wake up. When he opened it I stabbed the frontispiece with my finger.

"There! See—it's all changed. *Everything has changed.*"

I slapped his arm, the raw image that I'd never cleaned and never bandaged. "Hey! Stop—Ivy, stop—"

I started crying, sat on the edge of the bed with my head in my hands. Behind me I could hear him turning pages. Finally he sighed, put a hand on my shoulder, and said, "Well, you're right. But—well, couldn't it be a different edition? Or something?"

I shook my head. Grief filled me, and horror; something deeper than panic, deeper even than fear. "No," I said at last. My voice was hoarse. "It's the book. It's everything. We changed it, somehow—the card . . ."

I stood and walked into my studio, slowly, as though I were drunk. I put the light on and looked at my worktable.

"There," I said dully. In the middle of the table, separate from the rest of the deck, was the last card. It was blank. "The last one. The last trump. Everything is different."

I turned to stare at Christopher. He looked puzzled, concerned but not frightened. "So?" He shook his head, ventured a small smile. "Is that bad? Maybe it's a good book."

"That's not what I mean." I could barely speak. "I mean, everything will be different. Somehow. Even if it's just in little ways—it won't be what it was. . . ."

Christopher walked into the living room. He looked out the window, then went to the door and opened it. A bar of pale gold light slanted into the room and across the floor, to end at my feet. "Sun's coming up." He stared at the sky. "The fog is lifting. It'll be nice, I think. Hot, though."

He turned and looked at me. I shook my head. "No. No. I'm not going out there."

Christopher laughed, then gave me that sad half-smile. "Ivy—"

He walked over and tried to put his arms around me, but I pushed him away and walked into the bedroom. I began pulling on the clothes I'd worn last night. "No. No. Christopher—I can't, I won't."

"Ivy." He watched me, then shrugged and came into the room and got dressed, too. When he was done, he took my hand.

"Ivy, listen." He pulled me to his side, with his free hand pointed at the book lying on the bed. "Even if it *is* different—even if *everything* is different—why does that have to be so terrible? Maybe it's not. Maybe it's better."

I began to shake my head, crying again. "No, no, no . . ."

"Look—"

Gently he pulled me into the living room. Full sun was streaming through the windows now; outside, on the other side of Green Pond, a deep blue sky glowed above the green treetops. There was still mist close to the ground but it was lifting. The pines moved in the wind, and the birches; I heard a fox barking, no, not a fox: a dog. "Look," Christopher said, and pointed at the open front door. "Why don't we do this—you come with me, I'll stay right by you—shit, I'll *carry* you if you want—we'll just go look, okay?"

I shook my head no, but when he eased slowly through the door I followed, his hand tight around mine but not too tight: I could slip free if I wanted. He wouldn't keep me. He wouldn't make me go.

"Okay," I whispered. I shut my eyes, then opened them. "Okay, okay."

Everything looked the same. A few more of the asters had opened, deep mauve in the misty air. One tall yellow coneflower was still in bloom. We walked through them, to the shore, to the dory. There were dragonflies and damselflies inside it, and something else. A butterfly, brilliant orange edged with cobalt blue, its wings fringed, like an eye. We stepped into the boat and the butterfly lifted into the air, hanging between us then fluttering across the water, toward the western shore. My gaze followed it, watching as it rose above the Ledges then continued down the hillside.

"I've never been over there," said Christopher. He raised one oar to indicate where the butterfly had gone. "What's there?"

"You can see." It hurt to speak, to breathe, but I did it. I didn't die. You can't die, from this. "Katherine—she always says you can see Ireland from there, on a clear day."

"Really? Let's go that way, then."

He rowed to the farther shore. Everything looked different, coming up to the bank; tall blue flowers like irises, a yellow sedge that had a faint fragrance like lemons. A turtle slid into the water, its smooth black carapace spotted with yellow and blue. As I stepped onto the shore I saw something like a tiny orange crab scuttling into the reeds.

"You all right?" Christopher cocked his head and smiled. "Brave little ant. Brave Ivy."

I nodded. He took my hand, and we walked down the hillside. Past the Ledges, past some boulders I had never even known were there; through a stand of trees like birches only taller, thinner, their leaves round and shimmering, silver-green. There was still a bit of fog here but it was lifting, I felt it on my legs as we walked, a damp, cool kiss upon my left thigh. I looked over at Christopher, saw a golden rayed eye gazing back at me, a few flecks of dried blood beneath. Overhead the trees moved and made a high rustling sound in the wind. The ground beneath us grew steeper, the clefts between rocks overgrown with thick masses of small purple flowers. I had never known anything to bloom so lushly this late in the year. Below us I could hear the sound of waves, not the crash and violent roar of the open Atlantic but a softer sound; and laughter, a distant voice that sounded like my mother's. The fog was almost gone but I still could not glimpse the sea; only through the moving scrim of leaves and mist a sense of vast space, still dark because the sun had not struck it yet in full, pale gray-blue, not empty at all, not anymore. There were lights everywhere, gold and green and red and silver, stationary lights and lights that wove slowly across the lifting veil, as through wide streets and boulevards, haloes of blue and gold hanging from ropes across a wide sandy shore.

"There," said Christopher, and stopped. "There, do you see?"

He turned and smiled at me, reached to touch the corner of my eye, blue and gold; then pointed. "Can you see it now?"

I nodded. "Yeah. Yeah, I do."

The laughter came again, louder this time; someone calling a name. The trees and grass shivered as a sudden brilliance overtook them, the sun breaking at last from the mist behind me.

"Come on!" said Christopher, and, turning, he sprinted down the hill. I took a deep breath, looked back at what was behind us. I could just see the gray bulk of the Ledges, and beyond them the thicket of green and white and gray that was the Lonely House. It looked like a picture from one of my mother's books, a crosshatch hiding a hive, a honeycomb, another world. "Ivy!"

Christopher's voice echoed from not very far below me. "Ivy, you have to see this!"

"Okay," I said, and followed him.

October in the Chair
Neil Gaiman

—For Ray Bradbury

OCTOBER WAS IN THE CHAIR, so it was chilly that evening, and the leaves were red and orange and tumbled from the trees that circled the grove. The twelve of them sat around a campfire roasting huge sausages on sticks, which spat and crackled as the fat dripped onto the burning applewood, and drinking fresh apple cider, tangy and tart in their mouths.

April took a dainty bite from her sausage, which burst open as she bit into it, spilling hot juice down her chin. "Beshrew and suck-ordure on it," she said.

Squat March, sitting next to her, laughed, low and dirty, and then pulled out a huge, filthy handkerchief. "Here you go," he said.

April wiped her chin. "Thanks," she said. "The cursed bag-of-innards burned me. I'll have a blister there tomorrow."

September yawned. "You are *such* a hypochondriac," he said, across the fire. "And such *lan*guage." He had a pencil-thin mustache, and was balding in the front, which made his forehead seem high, and wise.

"Lay off her," said May. Her dark hair was cropped short against her skull and she wore sensible boots. She smoked a small brown cigarillo, which smelled heavily of cloves. "She's sensitive."

"Oh puhlease," said September. "Spare me."

October, conscious of his position in the chair, sipped his apple cider, cleared his throat, and said, "Okay. Who wants to begin?" The chair he sat in was carved from one large block of oak wood, inlaid with ash, with cedar, and with cherrywood. The other eleven sat on tree stumps equally spaced about the small bonfire. The tree stumps had been worn smooth and comfortable by years of use.

"What about the minutes?" asked January. "We always do minutes when I'm in the chair."

"But you aren't in the chair now, are you, dear?" said September, an elegant creature of mock solicitude.

"What about the minutes?" repeated January. "You can't ignore them."

"Let the little buggers take care of themselves," said April, one hand running through her long blonde hair. "And I think September should go first."

September preened and nodded. "Delighted," he said.

"Hey," said February. "Hey-hey-hey-hey-hey-hey-hey. I didn't hear the chairman ratify that. Nobody starts till October says who starts, and then nobody else talks. Can we have maybe the tiniest semblance of order here?" He peered at them, small, pale, dressed entirely in blues and grays.

"It's fine," said October. His beard was all colors, a grove of trees in autumn, deep brown and fire orange and wine red, an untrimmed tangle across the lower half of his face. His cheeks were apple red. He looked like a friend, like someone you had known all your life. "September can go first. Let's just get it rolling."

September placed the end of his sausage into his mouth, chewed daintily, and drained his cider mug. Then he stood up and bowed to the company and began to speak.

"Laurent DeLisle was the finest chef in all of Seattle; at least, Laurent DeLisle thought so, and the Michelin stars on his door confirmed him in his opinion. He was a remarkable chef, it is true—his minced lamb brioche had won several awards, his smoked quail and white truffle ravioli had been described in the *Gastronome* as 'the tenth wonder of the world.' But it was his wine cellar . . . ah, his wine cellar . . . that was his source of pride and his passion.

"I understand that. The last of the white grapes are harvested in me, and the bulk of the reds: I appreciate fine wines, the aroma, the taste, the aftertaste as well.

"Laurent DeLisle bought his wines at auctions, from private wine lovers, from reputable dealers: he would insist on a pedigree for each wine, for wine frauds are, alas, too common, when the bottle is selling for perhaps five, ten, a hundred thousand dollars, or pounds, or euros.

"The treasure—the jewel—the rarest of the rare and the *ne plus ultra* of his temperature-controlled wine cellar was a bottle of 1902 Château Lafitte. It was on the wine list at $120,000, although it was, in true terms, priceless, for it was the last bottle of its kind."

"Excuse me," said August politely. He was the fattest of them all, his thin hair combed in golden wisps across his pink pate.

September glared down at his neighbor. "Yes?"

"Is this the one where some rich dude buys the wine to go with the dinner, and the chef decides that the dinner the rich dude ordered isn't good enough for the wine, so he sends out a different dinner, and the guy takes one mouthful, and he's got, like, some rare allergy and he just dies like that, and the wine never gets drunk after all?"

September said nothing. He looked a great deal.

"Because if it is, you told it before. Years ago. Dumb story then. Dumb story now." August smiled. His pink cheeks shone in the firelight.

September said, "Obviously pathos and culture are not to everyone's taste. Some people prefer their barbecues and beer, and some of us like—"

February said, "Well, I hate to say this, but he kind of does have a point. It has to be a new story."

September raised an eyebrow and pursed his lips. "I'm done," he said abruptly. He sat down on his stump.

They looked at each other across the fire, the months of the year.

June, hesitant and clean, raised her hand and said, "I have one about a guard on the X-ray machines at LaGuardia Airport, who could read all about people from the outlines of their luggage on the screen, and one day she saw a luggage X ray so beautiful that she fell in love with the person, and she had to figure out which person in the line it was, and she couldn't, and she pined for months and months. And when the person came through again she knew it this time, and it was the man, and he was a wizened old Indian man and she was pretty and black and, like twenty-five, and she knew it would never work out and she let him go, because she could also see from the shapes of his bags on the screen that he was going to die soon."

October said, "Fair enough, young June. Tell that one."

June stared at him, like a spooked animal. "I just did," she said.

October nodded. "So you did," he said, before any of the others could say anything. And then he said, "Shall we proceed to my story, then?"

February sniffed. "Out of order there, big fella. The man in the chair only tells his story when the rest of us are through. Can't go straight to the main event."

May was placing a dozen chestnuts on the grate above the fire, deploying them into patterns with her tongs. "Let him tell his story if he wants to," she said. "God knows it can't be worse than the one about the wine. And I have things to be getting back to. Flowers don't bloom by themselves. All in favor?"

"You're taking this to a formal vote?" February said. "I cannot believe this. I cannot believe this is happening." He mopped his brow with a handful of tissues, which he pulled from his sleeve.

Seven hands were raised. Four people kept their hands down—February, September, January, and July. ("I don't have anything personal on this," said July apologetically. "It's purely procedural. We shouldn't be setting precedents.")

"It's settled then," said October. "Is there anything anyone would like to say before I begin?"

"Um. Yes. Sometimes," said June, "sometimes I think somebody's watching us from the woods and then I look and there isn't anybody there. But I still think it."

April said, "That's because you're crazy."

"Mm," said September, to everybody. "She's sensitive but she's still the cruelest."

"Enough," said October. He stretched in his chair. He cracked a cobnut with his teeth, pulled out the kernel, and threw the fragments of shell into the fire, where they hissed and spat and popped, and he began.

There was a boy, October said, who was miserable at home, although they did not beat him. He did not fit well, not his family, not his town, nor even his life. He had two older brothers, who were twins, older than he was, and who hurt him or ignored him, and were popular. They played football: some games one twin would score more and be the hero, and some games the other would. Their little brother did not play football. They had a name for their brother. They called him the Runt.

They had called him the Runt since he was a baby, and at first their mother and father had chided them for it.

The twins said, "But he *is* the runt of the litter. Look at *him.* Look at *us.*" The boys were six when they said this. Their parents thought it was cute. A name like "the Runt" can be infectious, so pretty soon the only person who called him Donald was his grandmother, when she telephoned him on his birthday, and people who did not know him.

Now, perhaps because names have power, he was a runt: skinny and small and nervous. He had been born with a runny nose, and it had not stopped running in a decade. At mealtimes, if the twins liked the food they would steal his; if they did not, they would contrive to place their food on his plate and he would find himself in trouble for leaving good food uneaten.

Their father never missed a football game, and would buy an ice cream afterward for the twin who had scored the most, and a consolation ice cream for the other twin, who hadn't. Their mother described herself as a newspaperwoman, although she mostly sold advertising space and subscriptions: she had gone back to work full-time once the twins were capable of taking care of themselves.

The other kids in the boy's class admired the twins. They had called him Donald for several weeks in first grade, until the word trickled down that his brothers called him the Runt. His teachers rarely called him anything at all, although among themselves they could sometimes be heard to say that it was a pity the youngest Covay boy didn't have the pluck or the imagination or the life of his brothers.

The Runt could not have told you when he first decided to run away, nor when his daydreams crossed the border and became plans. By the time he admitted to himself that he was leaving he had a large Tupperware container hidden beneath a plastic sheet behind the garage, containing three Mars bars, two Milky Ways, a bag of nuts, a small bag of licorice, a flashlight, several comics, an unopened packet of beef jerky, and thirty-seven dollars, most of it in quarters. He did not like the taste of beef jerky, but he had read that explorers had survived for weeks on nothing else, and it was when he put the packet of beef jerky into the Tupperware box and pressed the lid down with a pop that he knew he was going to have to run away.

He had read books, newspapers, and magazines. He knew that if you ran away you sometimes met bad people who did bad things to you; but he had also read fairy tales, so he knew that there were kind people out there, side by side with the monsters.

The Runt was a thin ten-year-old, with a runny nose, and a blank expression. If you were to try to pick him out of a group of boys, you'd be wrong. He'd be the other one. Over at the side. The one your eye slipped over.

All through September he put off leaving. It took a really bad Friday, during the course of which both of his brothers sat on him (and the one who sat on his face broke wind, and laughed uproariously) to decide that whatever monsters were waiting out in the world would be bearable, perhaps even preferable.

Saturday, his brothers were meant to be looking after him, but soon they went into town to see a girl they liked. The Runt went around the back of the garage and took the Tupperware container out from beneath the plastic sheeting. He took it up to his bedroom. He emptied his schoolbag onto his bed, filled it with his candies and comics and quarters and the beef jerky. He filled an empty soda bottle with water.

The Runt walked into the town and got on the bus. He rode west, ten-dollars-in-quarters worth of west, to a place he didn't know, which he thought was a good start, then he got off the bus and walked. There was no sidewalk now, so when cars came past he would edge over into the ditch, to safety.

The sun was high. He was hungry, so he rummaged in his bag and pulled out a Mars bar. After he ate it he found he was thirsty, and he drank almost half of the water from his soda bottle before he realized he was going to have to ration it. He had thought that once he got out of the town he would see springs of fresh water everywhere, but there were none to be found. There was a river, though, that ran beneath a wide bridge.

The Runt stopped halfway across the bridge to stare down at the brown water. He remembered something he had been told in school: that, in the end, all rivers flowed into the sea. He had never been to the seashore. He clambered down the bank and followed the river. There was a muddy path along the side of the riverbank, and an occasional beer can or plastic snack packet to show that people had been that way before, but he saw no one as he walked.

He finished his water.

He wondered if they were looking for him yet. He imagined police cars and helicopters and dogs, all trying to find him. He would evade them. He would make it to the sea.

The river ran over some rocks, and it splashed. He saw a blue heron, its wings wide, glide past him, and he saw solitary end-of-seaon dragonflies, and sometimes small clusters of midges, enjoying the Indian summer. The blue sky became dusk gray, and a bat swung down to snatch insects from the air. The Runt wondered where he would sleep that night.

Soon the path divided, and he took the branch that led away from the river, hoping it would lead to a house, or to a farm with an empty barn. He walked for some time, as the dusk deepened, until, at the end of the path, he found a farmhouse, half tumbled down and unpleasant-looking. The Runt walked around it, becoming increasingly certain as he walked that nothing could make him go inside, and then he climbed over a broken fence to an abandoned pasture, and settled down to sleep in the long grass with his schoolbag for his pillow.

He lay on his back, fully dressed, staring up at the sky. He was not in the slightest bit sleepy.

"They'll be missing me by now," he told himself. "They'll be worried."

He imagined himself coming home in a few years' time. The delight on his family's faces as he walked up the path to home. Their welcome. Their love. . . .

He woke some hours later, with the bright moonlight in his face. He could see the whole world—as bright as day, like in the nursery rhyme, but pale and without colors. Above him, the moon was full, or almost, and he imagined a face looking down at him, not unkindly, in the shadows and shapes of the moon's surface.

A voice said, "Where do you come from?"

He sat up, not scared, not yet, and looked around him. Trees. Long grass. "Where are you? I don't see you."

Something he had taken for a shadow moved, beside a tree on the edge of the pasture, and he saw a boy of his own age.

"I'm running away from home," said the Runt.

"Whoa," said the boy. "That must have taken a whole lot of guts."

The Runt grinned with pride. He didn't know what to say.

"You want to walk a bit?" said the boy.

"Sure," said the Runt. He moved his schoolbag, so it was next to the fence post, so he could always find it again.

They walked down the slope, giving a wide berth to the old farmhouse.

"Does anyone live there?" asked the Runt.

"Not really," said the other boy. He had fair, fine hair that was almost white in the moonlight. "Some people tried a long time back, but they didn't like it, and they left. Then other folk moved in. But nobody lives there now. What's your name?"

"Donald," said the Runt. And then, "But they call me the Runt. What do they call you?"

The boy hesitated. "Dearly," he said.

"That's a cool name."

Dearly said, "I used to have another name, but I can't read it anymore."

They squeezed through a huge iron gateway, rusted part open, part closed into position, and they were in the little meadow at the bottom of the slope.

"This place is cool," said the Runt.

There were dozens of stones of all sizes in the small meadow. Tall stones, bigger than either of the boys, and small ones, just the right size for sitting on. There were some broken stones. The Runt knew what sort of a place this was, but it did not scare him. It was a loved place.

"Who's buried here?" he asked.

"Mostly okay people," said Dearly. "There used to be a town over there. Past those trees. Then the railroad came and they built a stop in the next town over, and our town sort of dried up and fell in and blew away. There's bushes and trees now, where the town was. You can hide in the trees and go into the old houses and jump out."

The Runt said, "Are they like that farmhouse up there? The houses?" He didn't want to go in them, if they were.

"No," said Dearly. "Nobody goes in them, except for me. And some animals, sometimes. I'm the only kid around here."

"I figured," said the Runt.

"Maybe we can go down and play in them," said Dearly.

"That would be pretty cool," said the Runt.

It was a perfect early October night: almost as warm as summer, and the harvest moon dominated the sky. You could see everything.

"Which one of these is yours?" asked the Runt.

Dearly straightened up proudly, and took the Runt by the hand. He pulled him over to an overgrown corner of the field. The two boys pushed aside the long grass. The stone was set flat into the ground, and it had dates carved into it from a hundred years before. Much of it was worn away, but beneath the dates it was possible to make out the words DEARLY DEPARTED WILL NEVER BE FORG.

"Forgotten, I'd wager," said Dearly.

"Yeah, that's what I'd say too," said the Runt.

They went out of the gate, down a gully, and into what remained of the old town. Trees grew through houses, and buildings had fallen in on themselves, but it wasn't scary. They played hide-and-seek. They explored. Dearly showed the Runt some pretty cool places, including a one-room cottage that he said was the oldest building in that whole part of the country. It was in pretty good shape, too, considering how old it was.

"I can see pretty good by moonlight," said the Runt. "Even inside. I didn't know that it was so easy."

"Yeah," said Dearly. "And after a while you get good at seeing even when there ain't any moonlight."

The Runt was envious.

"I got to go to the bathroom," said the Runt. "Is there somewhere around here?"

Dearly thought for a moment. "I don't know," he admitted. "I don't do that stuff anymore. There are a few outhouses still standing, but they may not be safe. Best just to do it in the woods."

"Like a bear," said the Runt.

He went out the back, into the woods which pushed up against the wall of the cottage, and went behind a tree. He'd never done that before, in the open air. He felt like a wild animal. When he was done he wiped himself with fallen leaves. Then he went back out the front. Dearly was sitting in a pool of moonlight, waiting for him.

"How did you die?" asked the Runt.

"I got sick," said Dearly. "My maw cried and carried on something fierce. Then I died."

"If I stayed here with you," said the Runt, "would I have to be dead too?"

"Maybe," said Dearly. "Well, yeah. I guess."

"What's it like? Being dead."

"I don't mind it," admitted Dearly. "Worst thing is not having anyone to play with."

"But there must be lots of people up in that meadow," said the Runt. "Don't they ever play with you?"

"Nope," said Dearly. "Mostly, they sleep. And even when they walk, they can't be bothered to just go and see stuff and do things. They can't be bothered with me. You see that tree?"

It was a beech tree, its smooth gray bark cracked with age. It sat in what must once have been the town square, ninety years before.

"Yeah," said the Runt.

"You want to climb it?"

"It looks kind of high."

"It is. Real high. But it's easy to climb. I'll show you."

It was easy to climb. There were handholds in the bark, and the boys went up the big beech tree like a couple of monkeys, like pirates, like warriors. From the top of the tree one could see the whole world. The sky was starting to lighten, just a hair, in the east.

Everything waited. The night was ending. The world was holding its breath, preparing to begin again.

"This was the best day I ever had," said the Runt.

"Me too," said Dearly. "What are you going to do now?"

"I don't know," said the Runt.

He imagined himself going on, walking across the world, all the way to the sea. He imagined himself growing up and growing older, bringing himself up by his bootstraps. Somewhere in there he would become fabulously wealthy. And then he would go back to the house with the twins in it, and he would drive up to their door in his wonderful car, or perhaps he would turn up at a football game (in his imagination the twins had neither aged nor grown) and look down at them, in a kindly way. He would buy them all—the twins, his parents—a meal at the finest restaurant in the city, and they would tell him how badly they had misunderstood him and mistreated him. They would apologize and weep, and through it all he would say nothing. He would let their apologies wash over him. And then he would give each of them a gift, and afterward he would leave their lives once more, this time for good.

It was a fine dream.

In reality, he knew, he would keep walking, and be found tomorrow, or the day after that, and go home and be yelled at and everything would be the same as it ever was, and day after day, hour after hour, until the end of time he'd still be the Runt, only they'd be mad at him for leaving.

"I have to go to bed soon," said Dearly. He started to climb down the big beech tree.

Climbing down the tree was harder, the Runt found. You couldn't see where you were putting your feet, and had to feel around for somewhere to put them. Several times he slipped and slid, but Dearly went down ahead of him, and would say things like "Just a little to the right now," and they both made it down just fine.

The sky continued to lighten, and the moon was fading, and it was harder to see. They clambered back through the gully. Sometimes the Runt wasn't sure that Dearly was there at all, but when he got to the top, he saw the boy waiting for him.

They didn't say much as they walked up to the meadow filled with stones. The Runt put his arm over Dearly's shoulder, and they walked in step up the hill.

"Well," said Dearly. "Thanks for stopping by."

"I had a good time," said the Runt.

"Yeah," said Dearly. "Me too."

Down in the woods somewhere a bird began to sing.

"If I wanted to stay—?" said the Runt, all in a burst. Then he stopped. *I might never get another chance to change it,* thought the Runt. He'd never get to the sea. They'd never let him.

Dearly didn't say anything, not for a long time. The world was gray. More birds joined the first.

"I can't do it," said Dearly eventually. "But *they* might."

"Who?"

"The ones in there." The fair boy pointed up the slope to the tumbledown farmhouse with the jagged broken windows, silhouetted against the dawn. The gray light had not changed it.

The Runt shivered. "There's people in there?" he said. "I thought you said it was empty."

"It ain't empty," said Dearly. "I said nobody lives there. Different things." He looked up at the sky. "I got to go now," he added. He squeezed the Runt's hand. And then he just wasn't there any longer.

The Runt stood in the little graveyard all on his own, listening to the birdsong on the morning air. Then he made his way up the hill. It was harder by himself.

He picked up his schoolbag from the place he had left it. He ate his last Milky Way and stared at the tumbledown building. The empty windows of the farmhouse were like eyes, watching him.

It was darker inside there. Darker than anything.

He pushed his way through the weed-choked yard. The door to the farmhouse was mostly crumbled away. He stopped at the doorway, hesitating, wondering if this was wise. He could smell damp, and rot, and something else underneath. He thought he heard something move, deep in the house, in the cellar, maybe, or the attic. A shuffle, maybe. Or a hop. It was hard to tell.

Eventually, he went inside.

Nobody said anything. October filled his wooden mug with apple cider when he was done, and drained it, and filled it again.

"It was a story," said December. "I'll say that for it." He rubbed his pale blue eyes with a fist. The fire was almost out.

"What happened next?" asked June nervously. "After he went into the house?"

May, sitting next to her, put her hand on June's arm. "Better not to think about it," she said.

"Anyone else want a turn?" asked August. There was no reply. "Then I think we're done."

"That needs to be an official motion," pointed out February.

"All in favor?" said October. There was a chorus of "Ayes." "All against?" Silence. "Then I declare this meeting adjourned."

They got up from the fireside, stretching and yawning, and walked away into the wood, in ones and twos and threes, until only October and his neighbor remained.

"Your turn in the chair next time," said October.

"I know," said November. He was pale, and thin lipped. He helped October out of the wooden chair. "I like your stories. Mine are always too dark."

"I don't think so," said October. "It's just that your nights are longer. And you aren't as warm."

"Put it like that," said November, "and I feel better. I suppose we can't help who we are."

"That's the spirit," said his brother. And they touched hands as they walked away from the fire's orange embers, taking their stories with them back into the dark.

Malebolge, Or the Ordnance of Genre

Gary K. Wolfe

NOT ALL POPULAR GENRES are meant to blow up. We pretty much expect from mysteries today something of the same thrill that readers expected a century ago; tempestuous romances only seem to get more tempestuous; and the western long ago quietly faded away into elegiac ghost towns waiting for the likes of Cormac McCarthy to turn up with fresh ammo. But the fantastic genres of horror, science fiction, and fantasy have been unstable literary isotopes virtually since their evolution into identifiable narrative modes, or at least into identifiable market categories, a process which began a century or more ago and has not entirely worked itself through even yet. Although at times they have seemed in such bondage to formula and convention that they were in danger of fossilization, these genres are in fact wired more like those ticking, blinking time bombs which, in the final moments of bad suspense movies, must be disarmed by cutting either the red wire or the green wire: make the wrong choice and the movie inadvertently gets a better ending, as its fundamental assumptions are shot to hell and what had seemed one thing is now another. (Never mind, for the moment, that bad movies never actually end this way. We are discussing fiction here, and one of the curses visited upon such fiction is that it is too often and too easily confused with the film genres of the same names.)

A good deal of cavalier wire-cutting is going on these days among writers using the resources of what were once fairly clearly delineated genres, and for the most part this is a salutary and exhilarating development, bringing with it a sense of breached ramparts and undiscovered terrain. What had seemed to be one thing is becoming another. But in order to fully understand the implications of this shift, this new superposition of fictional states, we have to understand a bit about how the bomb got in the basement in the first place, and what its components are. An important key to this understanding, I would argue, involves revisiting not only what is written under the various rubrics of science fiction, fantasy, and horror, but what is *read,* and how it is read, and how certain selective vacancies of sensibility have distorted our capacity to receive the fantastic as a viable mode of literary exploration. In particular, what I hope to do here is trace, in broad outline, an account of how over nearly two centuries we *unlearned* to read fantastic stories, of what became of such stories as a result, and of how the fantastic has begun to reemerge in varying ways in recent decades from the cauldron to which it was once consigned, bringing with it distinctive modes of apprehension and style.

This brief history might as well begin with a real-life anecdote. Toward the end of my graduate studies at the University of Chicago, a number of students who had participated in a Theory of Fiction seminar launched into a rambling coffeehouse debate that lasted most of the academic year, turning on the question of what formally constituted a novel. After a raft of theoretical models had been considered and ultimately rejected, after principles of exclusion had been refined and multiplied in what we might now recognize as a fractal pattern of growth, several members of the group—perhaps even the entire group, I don't remember—arrived at a consensus: the formal novel, they decided, the *properly* formal novel, meaning one that satisfied all the rules of exclusion, consisted of a set that included *Middlemarch* and excluded everything else. Whatever simple delights might have been offered by earlier narratives, these were invariably contaminated by the viruses of romance, Gothicism, sensation, satire, social documentarianism, allegory, and even myth. At their best, they only represented the forward slope of this peak experience, this *Überroman,* while subsequent efforts represented only refinements of style, form, and structure, if not outright abandonment of the ideal in the guise of Modernism and all that came after. At that time, I counted myself as much an admirer of *Middlemarch* as anyone in the room, but at the same time I knew that I'd derived substantial degrees of pleasure and discovery from stories that not only demonstrated no effort whatsoever to look like *Middlemarch,* but that seemed to be part of another, more distant mountain range altogether. I was also aware that Eliot herself had written such a story in "The Lifted Veil" (1859), one of the more compelling psychic fantasy tales to emerge from Victorian literature.

More than thirty years later, I received an e-mail from the daughter of a close friend, who had enrolled in another literary theory seminar, this one at Oberlin College. The text which had come up for discussion was Stephen King's *'Salem's Lot,* and the immediate cause of the e-mail was a discussion during which one of her classmates had dismissed the novel as "meaningless pleasure" and the rest had more or less agreed that the book's genre origins, along with its manifest intent to entertain, all but precluded any further discussion of it in aesthetic terms. In what amounted to a kind of discovery brief, my friend's daughter e-mailed a number of writers and critics familiar with genre fiction (including King himself) to seek refutations of this argument—or at least to expose the subtext of passionately held but unexamined assumptions which, as is often the case in undergraduate English courses, had passed for literary debate in her class. Had it been possible, through some time warp, for these Oberlin students to get together with my own University of Chicago classmates from three decades earlier, they might well have voted *'Salem's Lot* a good candidate for the Anti-*Middlemarch,* a work so steeped in sensation and story that it more closely echoed the primitive thrills of a lesser age than the psychological subtleties of high Victorian domestic realism. (It's not, to my mind, one of King's most compelling works, but that's beside our immediate point.)

To the best of my knowledge, none of the participants in my *Middlemarch* discussion, most of whom later became professors of English, ever published a version of their argument (though the Oberlin student, Emma Straub, did publish the responses to her survey in an online magazine called the *Spook*), but they didn't need to: the fundamental assumptions that powered this debate had been laid out more than a century earlier, among Victorian critics and essayists who sought evidence that literature, like technology and industry, could be measured according to the forward thrust of evolutionary progress. "A scientific, and somewhat skeptical age," wrote an essayist in the *Westminster Review* in 1853, "has no longer the power of believing in the marvels which delighted our ruder ancestors," just as it might prosecute a necromancer for "obtaining money under false pretenses" or a showman for "exhibiting a giant at a fair." "Falsehood is so easy, truth so difficult," added Eliot herself in *Adam Bede* (1859, the same year as "The Lifted Veil"). "The pencil is conscious of a delightful facility in drawing a griffin—the longer the claws, and the larger the wings, the better; but that marvelous facility which we mistook for genius is apt to forsake us when we want to draw a real unexaggerated lion." Both Emma Straub, who had grown up in a house frequented by genre writers of every stripe, and I, who had spent many years enjoying science fiction, fantasy, and horror fiction, had found ourselves deposited, Oz-like, in the realm of the unexaggerated lion. It's a familiar story to many, and as Emma's case illustrates, it's far from closed.

At first blush, comments such as Eliot's might simply seem to be fanfares for the rise of domestic realism as a dominant aesthetic for the Victorian novel, or the literary equivalent of Herbert Butterfield's Whig fallacy of history, but the groundwork being laid here also helped set the terms of discourse concerning fantastic literature in all its forms for the next century and a half. Prior to the rise of this characteristically Victorian aesthetic, the fantastic had gained sufficient prominence in Romantic-era criticism and art as to virtually constitute an alternate mode of seeing. In 1741, Johann Jakob Bodmer, a German philologist and translator, claimed of the imagination that it "not only places the real before our eyes in a vivid image and makes distant things present, but also, with a power more potent than that of magic, it draws that which does not exist out of the state of potentiality, gives it a semblance of reality and makes us see, hear, and feel these new creations." More than a century and a half later, when Joseph Conrad invoked similar terms while articulating his artistic goal in his famous preface to *The Nigger of the Narcissus*—"to make you hear, to make you feel—it is, before all, to make you *see*"—he was referring not to "new creations" but to the representation of the simple efforts of a laborer in a nearby field. What had happened? How had the skills of evocation become so circumscribed?

Between 1798 and 1800 in Germany, the brothers A. W. and Friedrich Schlegel devoted a good deal of space in their journal *Das Athenaeum* to debates over the rules of fairy tales and other forms of fantastic literature, a debate eventually joined by such then-prominent fantasists as Novalis, E. T. A. Hoffmann, and Ludwig Tieck (whose three-volume 1844 collection *Phantasus* is given a frame story in which characters also debate the aesthetics of *Märchen*); one recurring tenet of these debates was that the fantastic might well demand a separate mode of understanding from more clearly representational forms of narrative, as well as from homilies and allegories (which instantly subvert their own fantastic elements by reminding us, for example, that a talking fox is not a talking fox, but a lesson). William Blake, in "A Vision of the Last Judgment," set imagination or "visionary fancy" apart from the cruder modes of fable or allegory—a distinction that would remain crucial in discussions of fantasy for decades to come—and, most famously, Samuel Taylor Coleridge offered his argument, in the early chapters of *Biographia Literaria,* that "fancy and imagination were two distinct and widely different faculties." Fancy, for Coleridge, was "no other than a mode of Memory emancipated from the order of time and space"—much as Blake disdained fable and allegory as "daughters of Memory"—whereas imagination was "the living Power and prime Agent of all human Perception."

Within decades, such notions had come to be regarded largely as peculiar artifacts of Romanticism, even though versions of them continued to be argued by novelists and critics such as George MacDonald, G. K. Chesterton, E. M. Forster, and eventually, of course, by more nearly contemporary and contemporary writers such as J. R. R. Tolkien, C. S. Lewis, and Ursula K. Le Guin. For the most part, however—as these examples attest—the articulation of the fantastic as a mode of storytelling became the province of the storytellers themselves rather than of the critics. The critics, for the most part, were elsewhere. By the end of the century, the notion of fantastic or dreamlike narratives as remnants of a more primitive consciousness even gained something of the patina of scientific authority, as Freud's description of what he called "primary process" thinking (in *The Interpretation of Dreams,* 1900) made it clear that this was something of far more importance to small children and savages than to more rational adults, who wisely banished it to the unconscious and went about their business guided by the logic and causality of secondary process thinking. (It wasn't really until the 1960s, under the influence of Pinchas Moy and others, that analytic theory began to recognize "primary process" as an important component of the sense of selfhood.)

Ironically, this devaluation, or at least devalorization, of the fantastic began at a time when the outlines of the modern popular genres of the fantastic were first being laid down in a series of seminal works: the Gothic novel and the stories of Poe provided a rough template for what would become horror fiction; Mary Shelley's *Frankenstein* (also derived largely from the Gothic, but with the crucial distinction that her protagonist rejected supernaturalism and alchemy in favor of experimental science) established many of the preconditions of science fiction; the extended fairy-tale narratives of the German Romantics and their English imitators (which included Thackeray and Ruskin as well as MacDonald) first articulated the portaled alternate realities that became a key element of modern fantasy. Each of these works spawned substantial numbers of imitators during the next century; genre literary historians have now pretty firmly established lengthy bibliographies of scientific romances before H. G. Wells, of supernatural horror tales before Bram Stoker and

H. P. Lovecraft, of large-scale visionary fantasies before J. R. R. Tolkien. Many of these works are even worth reading today, and some are absolutely startling. Few, however, have survived outside the narrow interests of collectors and genre historians.

Despite the temptation for champions of the fantastic to seek conspiracies of suppression—suggesting that residual Puritanism led Victorian readers to view the unfettered imagination with something akin to panic, for example, or that fantastic tales implied a kind of mutability of history and reality that the dogma of realism could not subsume—the fact is that the protocols for reading the fantastic were not so much suppressed as diverted: into children's literature, into historical novels, into false medieval narratives, into the literature of sensation, sometimes even into the substrata of the tale being told (this is more or less what happens to Gothic supernaturalism in the novels of the Brontës). The once-estimable Lord Bulwer-Lytton may have written science fiction (*The Coming Race,* 1871) or weirdly cockeyed spiritualist fantasy (*A Strange Story,* 1862), but his most famous end-of-the-world tale remains *The Last Days of Pompeii* (1834), in which the apocalyptic vision is mitigated by the comforting conceit that the world being destroyed isn't ours, and that the events described with such obvious relish aren't going to happen to us, but already happened to someone else, someone not English. Victorian apocalypses offered something of the same lascivious *frisson* as those popular marble sculptures of nubile slave girls in chains—the rationale may have been historical representation, but at the level of pure voyeuristic sensation, the intent was unmistakable: I only read *Playboy* for the stonework. George MacDonald may have written two of the seminal adult fantasy novels in English, *Phantastes* (1858) and *Lilith* (1895), but the wider popularity of his children's fairy tales such as "The Golden Key" (1867) and *At the Back of the North Wind* (1871) permitted many readers to regard these fairly radical nonconformist visions as little more than aberrant offshoots of his career as a children's writer (though he did write a number of realistic provincial Scottish novels as well). Lest we suspect that this particular strategy of marginalization was peculiar to the Victorians, we might take a look at Edmund Wilson's famous 1956 *Nation* review of Tolkien's *The Lord of the Rings,* which he easily dismissed as "a children's book that has somehow got out of hand, since, instead of directing it at the 'juvenile' market, the author has indulged himself in developing the fantasy for its own sake." The notion that "fantasy for its own sake" is a kind of aberrant indulgence is a succinct expression of what had happened to the reading of the fantastic over the preceding century.

The act of reading fantastic literature became marginalized not only ideologically, by virtue of its content, but commercially, by virtue of its venues of publication. The two are not unrelated: each of the emergent genres of the fantastic (fantasy, horror, science fiction) included tropes and images which were highly sensational, and therefore highly degradable. Despite the wishful thinking of many science fiction historians, Mary Shelley's *Frankenstein,* with its Gothic trappings, didn't immediately give rise to intellectual works of science fiction about the possibilities of science or the nature of artificial life, but rather to a series of often lurid stage adaptations (two separate productions were already onstage when she returned to England in 1823) that continued throughout the nineteenth century and segued into the movies throughout the twentieth. The Gothic novel itself seemed to split into two streams: on the one hand, the brooding, atmospheric tales of the Brontës and their successors, some of which eventually earned canonical status; on the other, such penny dreadfuls or "bloods" as *Varney the Vampire* by (probably) John Malcolm Rymer, which ran endlessly and almost plotlessly for some 109 weekly installments between 1847 and 1849, and which may still represent some sort of low point in the history of horror fiction, which has more than its share of low points. (To be sure, there was a middle ground, characterized by the classic English ghost story and by such writers as Wilkie Collins and Joseph Sheridan Le Fanu, though Collins is now principally remembered as a precursor of the mystery novel and Le Fanu as a writer of popular romances.) And fantasy, as we've already seen, tended largely to remain associated with children's books, although Arthurian and other pseudomedieval fictions remained popular throughout the century, emerging as full-fledged fantasy narratives in the prose work of William Morris by late in the century.

In America, the question of commercial marginalization of the fantastic genres would eventually express itself even more dramatically, with the rise of the pulp magazines and the attendant culture of pulp. The Gothic novel had quickly found a home in the American wilderness in the work of Charles Brockden Brown, Nathaniel Hawthorne, and Edgar Allan Poe, though for the most part these writers shied away from overt supernaturalism, and certain works by Poe and Hawthorne are even frequently cited as precursors of science fiction (Poe's "Mellonta Tauta," for example, or Hawthorne's

"Rappacini's Daughter"). But science fiction as something resembling a genre in the modern sense became much more visible in the pages of the dime novels—a particularly delicious and often-imitated example was Edward Ellis's 1868 *The Steam Man of the Prairie,* featuring a human-shaped steam engine chuffing about the Wild West—and eventually in the pages of the cheaply made magazines published by Frank Munsey and others (some date the beginning of the "pulp era" to 1896, when Munsey transformed a former boys' weekly paper into an all-adventure-fiction magazine called the *Argosy*). By the 1920s, the outlines of what would become the familiar pop genres of horror and science fiction were being sketched out in two important pulps: the former in *Weird Tales,* founded in 1923, and the latter in *Amazing Stories,* founded in 1926. *Weird Tales* published a fair amount of fantasy of the "sword-and-sorcery" variety (most notably Robert E. Howard's "Conan the Barbarian" stories in the 1930s), but it wasn't until 1939 that a fairly serious—though short-lived—attempt was made to create a modern fantasy pulp tradition with the publication of *Unknown,* intended as a fantasy companion to editor John W. Campbell, Jr.'s successful science fiction magazine, *Astounding.*

From a purely literary standpoint, the pulp tradition didn't do anyone much good. All we have to do is look at the adjectives in the titles of these pulps to figure out what was going wrong: *Weird, Amazing, Astounding,* and dozens more: *Wonder Stories, Marvel Tales, Terror Tales, Horror Stories, Eerie Mysteries, Fantastic Adventures, Startling Stories, Strange Stories, Astonishing Stories, Bizarre, Stirring Science Stories, Thrilling Stories* (and later *Thrilling Wonder Stories*), *Gripping Terror, Imaginative Tales, Rocket Stories, Planet Stories,* and on and on, an endless parade of gerundives and adjectives that seemed to promise their readers passivity: these are not stories that you have to read, these are stories that will *do things to you,* that will leap off the page unmediated by any readerly acts of decoding, grab you by the suspenders, and pummel you into submission. Your task is not to understand—to see, feel, or hear—it is merely to be horrified, astounded, amazed, astonished, terrified, stirred, gripped, and thrilled. Don't ask what's behind the curtain: we're exhibiting a giant at a fair here. It shouldn't be surprising that the famously lurid cover art for these pulps (which has become a fetish in itself among collectors) shares certain principles of color, composition, and draftsmanship with the art of sideshow posters and traveling circuses.

More important than their appearance, though, was the manner in which the pulp magazines turned their stories into perishable goods, complete with sell-by dates. The history of literary ephemera dates back centuries, of course, but even in the dime novels and the Salisbury Square bloods, the stories *were* the products; one presumably picked up the next installment of *Varney the Vampire* because it *was Varney the Vampire,* because the text was roughly coequal with the text-product being sold. But readers of *Weird Tales,* even though they would quickly develop favorite writers, picked up the next copy because it was *Weird Tales,* trusting the editors to fill the magazine with stories that fulfilled some often unarticulated template of what the magazine represented. In the science fiction field, at least, this led to enormous power devolving on the editors, who essentially took over the debate as to what the field was or ought to be. Even today, the Hugo Awards presented at the annual world convention of science fiction fans are named after the field's first famous editor, Hugo Gernsback, who founded *Amazing Stories* in 1926, and readers often refer to the genre's "golden age"—the period which introduced such now-revered authors as Isaac Asimov and Robert Heinlein—as "the Campbell era," after John W. Campbell, Jr., who began editing *Astounding Stories* (which he quickly renamed *Astounding Science Fiction*) in 1937. The authors, on the other hand, were sometimes reduced to writing stories on demand to satisfy an idea of the editors, or in more demeaning cases to writing stories that would exactly fill a hole in the next month's issue or that would somehow make sense of a prepurchased cover illustration. This is a tradition that would continue for years after the pulps had been replaced by the only slightly less garish digest-sized magazines of the 1950s. And few if any writers for these magazines had any reason to believe that their stories would survive beyond the few weeks that the magazines containing them remained on the stands. What passed for literary debate about the nature of the fantastic was by now purely proletarian: in the letter columns of the magazines, a farmer from Kansas might have an equal platform with the writers and editors themselves, and might even have an edge, since he (or she) was holding next month's quarter.

For most serious readers, the fiction in the pulps was all but invisible, at best a guilty pleasure, at worst an assault on the moral order. But at the same time, amid all the lurid tales of hungry elder gods looking for a snack and galaxy-busting backyard scientists, a kind of outsider aesthetic was being forged, just as it had been forged among the Victorian children's fantasists or the inheritors of the Gothic tradition. This aesthetic didn't really begin to be articulated until some of these ephemeral tales began to be collected in books. H. P. Lovecraft, for example, died in 1937 after building a considerable following as well as a circle of imitators in the pulps, but it wasn't until two years later that two of these imitators, August Derleth and Donald Wandrei, founded a publishing firm called Arkham House with the express intent of preserving Lovecraft's work, which they had been unable to interest mainstream publishers in. Even before that, an early horror anthology titled *Creeps by Night* had been assembled by no less a luminary than Dashiell Hammett in 1931, and Lovecraft himself had been reprinted (along with other *Weird Tales* regulars such as Robert E. Howard and Clark Ashton Smith) in a British anthology series, originally titled *Not at Night,* edited by Christine Campbell Thomson between 1925 and 1937. In 1943, the first science fiction anthology to be labeled as such was Donald A. Wollheim's *The Pocket Book of Science Fiction,* presented as one of the wildly eclectic series of one-off special-interest titles which also included *The Pocket Book of Home Canning* and *The Pocket Book of Crossword Puzzles.* By the end of the 1940s, however, larger and more comprehensive anthologies began to appear. Science fiction saw Raymond J. Healy and J. Francis McComas's *Adventures in Time and Space* (1946), while horror fiction, in addition to Lovecraft, saw Herbert A. Wise and Phyllis M. Fraser's *Great Tales of Terror and the Supernatural* (1944); both eventually gained lasting influence by remaining in print for years as part of Random House's Modern Library. The indefatigable anthologist Groff Conklin mined both genres in a series of some forty-one anthologies over a twenty-two–year period, ending with his death in 1968. Genre fantasy, having never quite established a firm foothold in the pulps, didn't fare as well, although there were such occasional titles as *The Saturday Evening Post Fantasy Stories,* edited by someone named Barthold Fles in 1951, and a collection of tales from the short-lived *Unknown Worlds* in 1948.

The major significance of these anthologies was to provide a distillation of pulp and other stories which then began circulating among new generations of readers. But at the same time, there was evident in many of them a sense that these fields had become "ghettoized," isolated from the literary mainstream, and a concomitant sense that the anthologists were about the business of establishing a kind of de facto canon, as well as a de facto literary history. Some of these anthologies actively hungered for respect: Hammett's collection of horror tales, for example, included Faulkner's "A Rose for Emily," while a 1950 anthology by August Derleth (the same one who had set about resurrecting Lovecraft) tried mightily to establish a pedigree by including selections from Plato, Rabelais, Swift, and Bacon. Judith Merril, who edited the most popular "year's best" anthologies of science fiction and fantasy in the 1950s, found ways to include stories by Eugene Ionesco, Robert Nathan, John Steinbeck, and even Walt Kelly and Garson Kanin in her generous definitions of these genres. This search for a usable past and respectable relatives continued well into the 1970s when genre fantasy, now established as a viable market segment in the wake of the Tolkien craze of the sixties, began to seek its own roots: the Ballantine Adult Fantasy series, edited by Lin Carter from 1969 through 1974, reprinted works by William Morris, James Branch Cabell, and George Meredith together with classic genre and pulp writers; surely one of the irreproducible moments of the lingering 1960s was discovering a mass-market prose translation of Book I of Ariosto's *Orlando Furioso* at the local newsstand in January of 1973.

In the end, though, the renascence of the fantastic would not emerge from its search for illustrious relations, its efforts to carve makeshift canons from pulp fiction, or even the befuddled gaze of academia, which eventually produced a sizable body of postmodernist theorizing, three or four academic journals devoted to science and fantasy fiction, and college courses in which *'Salem's Lot* could be assigned, as well as works by Lovecraft, Tolkien, Heinlein, Le Guin, or the most recent favorite among science fiction academics, Philip K. Dick. Instead, the signal development of the last few decades has been the emergence of a generation of writers—though "generation" is a misnomer, since these writers currently range in age from the twenties to the seventies—whose ambitions lay in what we might call recombinant genre fiction: stories which effectively decompose and reconstitute genre materials and techniques together with materials and techniques from an eclectic variety of literary traditions, even including the traditions of domestic realism. This eclecticism became most famously visible in the science fiction field in the 1960s with the "New Wave" associated with Britain's *New Worlds* magazine, which showcased experimental work by such authors as J. G. Ballard, Brian W. Aldiss, and M. John Harrison—each of whom, in their later careers, moved comfortably between mainstream fiction, genre work, and more indefinable literary fabulation.

Science fiction has since been visited by a number of other such movements—the cyberpunks of the 1980s in the wake of William Gibson's *Neuromancer,* the "new humanists" who reacted to the cyberpunks, the "literary hard science fiction" ("hard science fiction" being an older term for stories that adhere rigorously to limitations imposed by physical science) of such authors as Greg Bear, Joe Haldeman, and Gregory Benford. Today, M. John Harrison is one of the touchstones of literary science fiction in the United Kingdom, just as Gene Wolfe is a touchstone in the United States; both authors, significantly, began their careers as genre writers in genre magazines, and Wolfe is still known mostly within the science fiction community for his complex, ornate, and infinitely subtle novels of distant futures.

Horror and fantasy, perhaps less politically organized than science fiction, have been less susceptible to manifestos and movements, but they are not without their schools, from the "Lovecraft circle" of the 1930s to the "splatterpunks" of the 1990s—whose fiction was pretty much what the label suggests—or the current Goths, who seem to regard horror as a lifestyle as much as a body of fiction; the fiction is often a mechanism for validating the attitude. Fantasy, at least of the broadly commercial variety, has been so dominated by the quest structure of Tolkien's *Lord of the Rings* that it barely leaves room for movements (though there have been a few, such as the "urban fantasy" associated with writers like Charles de Lint); some popular current fantasy series have long since left the simple quest-trilogy structure behind, and generate not so much sequels as metastases. But these fields as well have given rise to touchstone authors whose works seem to demand a reinvention of the ways in which we read genre. Peter Straub's 1979 novel *Ghost Story* may seem to offer a veritable motif index of supernatural tropes, but in fact is a serious and ambitious interrogation of the notion of the ghost story in all its forms, told in a complexly structured narrative which belies the notion that such tropes can support only linear tales of single-minded revelation. Angela Carter, in *The Bloody Chamber and Other Stories* (1979), revealed that the fairy-tale redaction—itself virtually a subgenre of modern fantasy—could unpack deep and troubling conflicts of culture and gender, while her novels freely manipulated time and space using techniques drawn from surrealism, magic realism, and science fiction. John Crowley, who began his career clearly identified as a science fiction writer, virtually exploded the possibilities of several familiar fantasy tropes in his iconically titled 1981 novel *Little, Big,* in which the title refers not only to the notion of an ever-expanding inner world within the framework of the outer, but to the structuring of the novel itself; and in the *Aegypt* sequence of novels (1997–2000), which expands the notion to reveal a complex secret history of the world. Elizabeth Hand (who like Crowley began by writing science fiction), in novels such as *Waking the Moon* (1994) and *Black Light* (1999), has found ways of bringing the familiar tropes of ancient warring supernatural forces and the resurrection of a goddess into the domestic arenas of the college novel or the arts novel, without sacrificing the characterological demands of either. None of these writers, I would argue, can be read fully without an appreciation of their use of genre materials—of the valorization of Story that remains at the center of the fantastic genres even in their most demeaned forms—but none can be fully read with *only* an appreciation of those genre materials, either.

But matters grow yet more complex, in the work of these writers and others, as the borders of genre themselves begin to dissolve, along with the borders between genre fiction and literary fiction. Jonathan Carroll's first novel, *The Land of Laughs* (1980), was read by some as a horror novel, with its strange small Missouri town haunted—and perhaps formed—by the imagination of a writer who once lived there, but subsequent novels have made such easy readings all but impossible, as Carroll combines ghosts, time travel, supernatural agents, aliens, and even such hard science concepts as cold fusion into narratives that at times seem cavalierly unconcerned with what genre they might properly belong to. Jonathan Lethem's first novel, *Gun, with Occasional Music* (1994), uses the form of the hard-boiled detective tale, but is set in a postliterate, drug-dazed twenty-first century dystopia filled with talking animals that function much like cartoon characters; his later novels have moved increasingly further from traditional genre structures, but have never quite abandoned the skillful structural use of genre iconography. China Miéville's second and third novels, *Perdido Street Station* (2000) and *The Scar* (2002), are set in a densely grotesque fantasy world—his New Crobuzon is one of the great urban environments of modern fantasy—but a world whose inhabitants and whose technology seem a chaotic mix of figures from science fiction, horror, and alchemy. Patrick O'Leary's 1997 novel, *The Gift,* seems a fairly conventional fantasy, until we note mention of spacecraft and personality matrices, while his 2001 novel, *The Impossible Bird,* is a posthumous fantasy of brotherly love in which the fantasy premise is rationalized by an appeal to alien conspiracies and information-laden hummingbirds. Even Stephen King, in what may turn out to become the most ambitious work of his career, combines classic quest fantasy motifs with apocalyptic science fiction and his more familiar trademark horror effects in his "Dark Tower" sequence, which began more than twenty years ago and shows few signs of being completely unfolded yet.

At the same time that genre materials begin flowing freely into one another, we begin to see evidence of an even more peculiar development: the nongenre genre story. By this I don't mean those attempts at using genre material by writers from "outside," such as the occasional ill-conceived science fiction novel by P. D. James, John Updike, or Paul Theroux, but rather those stories so closely informed by genre-based structures and sensibilities that they may convey the *feel* of a particular genre, and may open up to genre readings in a way different from how they open up to conventional readings, even though they lack traditional genre markers. Examples of this in—or near—the horror genre include Peter Straub's 1988 novel *Koko,* which shares with genre horror a concern for portraying extreme experience as almost mystically transformative, but lacks the direct supernatural elements that had once been regarded as a defining element of the genre. (Despite this, and perhaps as a sign of the changing times, the novel won a World Fantasy Award for best novel, and one of its competing nominees was the equally unsupernatural *The Silence of the Lambs,* by Thomas Harris.) By a similar token, novels such as Bruce Sterling's *Zeitgeist* (2000) and Neal Stephenson's *Cryptonomicon* (1999) bear all the hallmarks of good near-future science fiction—the world slightly estranged from our own by new developments in technology and exaggerated social trends, the elements of absurdist social satire, the sense of history as malleable—but in fact neither novel is even set in the future nor makes much use of the surface machinery of science fiction. The Stephenson concerns cryptography and early computer theory at Bletchley Park during World War II, combined with a contemporary tale of data espionage; the latter is about a cynically manufactured multicultural pop group designed to maximize the profit potential of the premillennium *zeitgeist,* and to be disbanded at the turn of the century. Both novels, however, are rife with the science fictional habits of treating speculative thought as though it were heroic action, and of manipulating ideas as though they were characters.

So now we have a situation in which novels containing no material fantasy at all are nominated for and receive fantasy awards, in which novels with little or no science fiction content gain huge followings among science fiction readers who recognize in them something of their own, in which growing numbers of writers view the materials forged in genre as resources rather than as constraints, in which the edges of the genres themselves bleed into one another, in which authors gleefully and knowingly cut the wrong wire. There is perhaps a certain danger in this, in drawing so freely on material that was once condemned to exile, in assembling story-machines that demand a wider repertoire of sensibilities on the part of readers, and it may not be an exaggeration to describe these writers as courageous. Genre writers still complain of the "ghetto" in which they see themselves forced to toil, but an only slightly more overbaked metaphor might be hell itself, and even a particular region of hell: in Dante's *Inferno,* it's curious to note how many of the sinners gathered together in the eighth circle, the *Malebolge,* or ditches of evil, seem to be guilty of crimes of genre: the fortune-tellers and diviners, who pretend to see the future; the alchemists, who claimed their art could transform base materials into something wonderful; the sowers of discord; the evil counselors who sinned by glibness of tongue; the panderers and seducers; and, in the central pit, the giant Nimrod, the builder of the Tower of Babel. For the myriad distinctive voices that make up the postgenre fantastic, the voices heard after the explosion, there is yet the risk of that baleful gaze from the moral poet, still suspecting the crime of fantasy for its own sake no matter how elegant the tale. Dante may never have read a word of Tolkien or Lovecraft or Heinlein, but he knew a shell game when he saw one.

Beyond the Pale

John Clute

1. MISS MIMESIS IN THE FOGGY DEW

IN ORDER TO GET a running start on our subject, which is the fantastic in 2002, the state of the fantastic in cusp country, it might be an idea to back off a century, and begin with Joseph Conrad.

In early 1899, after an intense and feverish spate of work, Conrad published "Heart of Darkness" in *Blackwood's Magazine.* It was the greatest novella he would ever write, and the last of the great English-language novellas of the 1890s; those of interest for us include Arthur Machen's "The Great God Pan" (1894), H. G. Wells's *The Time Machine* (1895), and Henry James's "The Turn of the Screw" (1898). Of these, it is almost certainly Conrad's premonitory masterpiece that has had the deepest influence over the past hundred years. "Heart of Darkness" remains a profoundly *visible* book, a map of the long portage the Western World would make through the twentieth century (which is the second of the two centuries that have most made us). And even now the tale is present to us, a shape of story timed to catch us in the act.

Conrad's great novella is also, of course, as we have been taught, a central text in the etiology of Modernism, in the analysis of late European imperialism; and it has become a taproot for the study of postcolonial literatures. These discourses extractable from the text are, we know, justly studied. But when we look at "Heart of Darkness" in situ, we find that the seemingly extractable elements of the tale twist in the mind's eye like chimerae, illusions of available content. When we gaze into the overwhelmingly dense dreamtime of story that is "Heart of Darkness," we find our attention focusing instead upon the highly foregrounded, indeed spectacular way it is actually told, upon the presentness of the storytelling even now, a hundred years further into the anxiety of the world, for the hypnopompic drama Marlow recounts, and the hypnopompic experience of reading the tale, are as one. Reading "Heart of Darkness" is like spelunking the century it adumbrates. It is Conrad's central stab at a task hardly undertaken by writers before him, and rarely by those who have followed: the task of understanding a world contemporaneous with the world he is writing in.

But here's the rub. This *yarn*, which has told a century, itself wants explication; but when we turn to the professional literary critics of the last hundred years, whose job it is to give us the likes of Conrad whole, we find too often what seems a real disinclination (not only on the part of E. M. Forster or F. R. Leavis) to address precisely the *way* of "Heart of Darkness," or for that matter the nature of Conrad's subsequent decline into the dignified English gentleman who created the Whited Sepulchre of *Chance* (1913). There is something tight-sphinctered in this critical vacancy of response, almost as though twentieth-century critics were embarrassed to admit that, in "Heart of Darkness," echt proto-pre-Modernist Joseph Conrad had achieved his greatest effects, had understood most deeply the world of his time and ours, through *subliterary means:* because "Heart of Darkness" takes its incipit from the tale of adventure, whose roots do not lie in realism, whose access to the Ocean of Story is uncensored.

Club Story, a term which describes one late form of a story type found throughout that vast repertory, might come in useful at this point; it is one of several terms which a critic of the fantastic—in contradistinction to a critic of establishment literatures—might comfortably apply to "Heart of Darkness." Under various names, precursor versions of the Club Story have existed since the first story was told about a storyteller telling stories. It dates from the *Decameron* and *The Thousand and One Nights* and before; seminal texts in the literature of the fantastic—including Ludwig Tieck's *Phantasus* (1812–1816, three volumes), which Gary Wolfe refers to above (in "Malebolge, Or the Ordnance of Genre"), and E. T. A. Hoffmann's *The Serapion Brothers* (1819–1821, four volumes)—are presented in a format very similar to that of the Club Story proper, which flourished for half a century or so after Robert Louis Stevenson published *The New Arabian Nights* (1882, two volumes), becoming more and more popular as new magazines like the *Strand* found that the form attracted a continuing readership.

The Club Story is simple enough to describe: it is a tale or tales recounted orally to a group of listeners forgathered in a venue safe from interruption. Its structure is normally twofold: there is the tale told; and encompassing that a frame which introduces the teller of the tale—who may well claim to have himself lived the story he's telling—along with its auditors and the venue. At its most primitive, the Club Story usefully frames Tall Tales in a way that eases our suspension of disbelief during the duration of the telling—the Mulliner stories by P. G. Wodehouse and the Jorkens tales by Lord Dunsany are examples of this form of subjunctive allowance—but surrender the tale to the judgment of the world once it has been told. At all levels of sophistication, the Club Story form enforces our understanding that *a tale has been told.*

It is not a term which forms, to my knowledge, any large part of the twentieth-century critical response to "Heart of Darkness," though it does seem that any critic of the literature of the 1890s in English might plausibly have asked, long before now, why the four greatest novellas published during that period—the Machen, the Wells, the James, and "Heart of Darkness" itself—were Club Stories. *The Time Machine* and "The Turn of the Screw" and "Heart of Darkness" are straightforward enough, though "The Great God Pan" might be described as a recomplicated example of the form, one whose story implicates and whose outcome is affected by those who have listened to the early stages of the tale. The 1890s was a decade of denial and boast, recessional and augur, a decade during the course of which, to the exilic perception of Joseph Conrad, Europe must visibly have begun to distend with Empire like a balloon, a snake that had swallowed the Underworld, and soon to burst asunder. It was a decade that begged alarum. So it is noteworthy that the great augur-loaded novellas of the decade are texts conspicuously shaped as vessels for the mandatory reception of story: stories which enforce witness.

In "Heart of Darkness," the auditors of Marlow's tale—the Director and the Lawyer and the Accountant and the narrator (an implied author who is probably Conrad himself)—hear him out on a sloop becalmed upon the estuarial Thames, east of babylonic London, just as the tide is about to turn from the West and the sloop to slide down darkness into Ocean. These auditors, who seem to have bestrid the world, may pretend to refuse to hear Marlow, but it's too late for that, the story has been told: Marlow's deposition about the fate of the Western World has been so presented that the rulers of that world (and the readers of "Heart of Darkness") have had to witness it. Like any Club Story, "Heart of Darkness" is both a story and a device to mandate its reception. It may be that the "impurity" of this element of reportage at the heart of the Club Story accounts for the fact that literary theorists seem to scant it. Critics of the fantastic, dealing as they do with a set of genres intensely sensitive to the world, should have no such compunction.

We come to time, the conversation between time past and time present. The Club Story frame bears within it a double relationship to time, for it bears—like a Mask enclosing its Twin—a tale which, though it must logically have taken place before being told, now bursts by virtue of its means of telling through the Whited Sepulchre of the conventional world into the present tense, demanding witness. So "Heart of Darkness," as we've noted already, happens at the time the author is writing it: right there in the present tense of the end of the nineteenth century as the Western World edges toward cusp country, that badlands for humans which we may now, after a two-century dance to the music of time, be leaving:

> Marlow ceased, and sat apart, indistinct and silent, in the pose of a meditating Buddha. Nobody moved for a time. "We have lost the first of the ebb," said the Director suddenly. I raised my head. The offing was barred by a black bank of clouds, and the tranquil waterway leading to the uttermost ends of the earth flowed sombre under an overcast sky—seemed to lead into the heart of an immense darkness.

To describe "Heart of Darkness" as a Club Story is not to say that Conrad is locked into any literal reiteration of the modes of the tale of adventure, like poor H. Rider Haggard stuck to his salt lick down She way. "Heart of Darkness" is a deeply *unlocked* manifestation of story. In the revolutionary balance it achieves between the fantastic and the mundane, it is circumscribed neither by previous models, nor by propriety, nor by any sense of moral gradient between one mode of understanding the universe and another. The perturbation of the tale in 1899 still shakes us today, still opens into a world unparsable by any one set of tools (it might be noted that the strategies of several stories assembled here in *Conjunctions* are similarly strategies of equipoise).

Equipoise, then, is also a term of use to critics of the fantastic. It takes into account, but goes beyond, Tzvetan Todorov's famous definition of the fantastic as the "duration of uncertainty" until an implied reader (safely decontextualized in time and place) decides whether a particular story is to be read as uncanny (that is, mundane but creepy) or marvelous (that is, impossible according to the rules of the world at the time the story was written down). But just as theories of the "pure" novel can end up describing only *Middlemarch,* Todorov's theory ends up describing (insecurely) little more than

"The Turn of the Screw." This may be acute, but it is a knife too sharp for sense. Critics of science fiction have the same problem with Darko Suvin, who defines science fiction as "cognitive estrangement within a novum." But Suvin's diktat can be tamed into a description of the actual time-governed world, if we define science fiction as that set of texts which makes cognitive estrangement storyable. It should also be possible to domesticate Todorov in a similar fashion: if we focus upon "hesitation" (his term) or equipoise, we can expand his version of the fantastic into a description of something storytellers do in time.

Equipoise as used here is not a term normally applicable to fantasy, which may be described as comprising stories set in worlds which are impossible but which the story believes; nor, at a hazard, does it seem to be much use in understanding the epistemology games of science fiction, which have much more to do with suspense. But it certainly applies to works—like "Heart of Darkness" or "The Turn of the Screw" or James's otherwise inexplicable *The Sacred Fount* (1901)—which are built upon sustained narrative negotiations of uncertainty, without coming to any necessary decision as to what is real.

The ultimate problem with Todorov is the problem of twentieth-century critics in general: their unspoken assumption that the fantastic cannot be told as a given, that it is a moral/aesthetic/cultural hot potato requiring decisive action, that equipoise is obscurely untruthful. The heartwood indeterminacy of "Heart of Darkness" has seemed invisible to them—see Gary Wolfe's comments on "vacancies of sensibility"—because they have been able only to conceive of Conrad's active, unresolved (and perhaps unresolvable) equipoise between the fantastic and the mundane in terms of *vacillation:* as a wobbling between the inadmissible and mimesis, between subliterary genres of adventure and mature renderings of the "seeable" world, with a not exactly hidden rider that the choice between the fantastic and the real is in the first instance necessary, and in the second constitutes a choice between recidivism and progress. But the suspendedness of "Heart of Darkness" cannot be defined as sensationalism awaiting moral restitution. There is no moral gradient in the range of Marlow's perception of the phenomena. What Marlow tells us is the case of the story. Kurtz himself—twinning Marlow and Mephistopheles—is not a metaphor, he does not stand for anything but the case and the position of himself: he hovers, he is equipoise.

As do its 1890s cohorts, "Heart of Darkness" hovers between

protocols of story, between centuries, between fin de siècle and aftermath, between Ruin and Futurity. It is a tale about enduring the vertigo of unknowing, forever; its example paces within the stories of *Conjunctions,* which have also been written at a time of change, when it is, perhaps, as important—as gallant—to know how to inhabit conflicting protocols as it is to know the truth about things.

Portal/Cloaca. Portal, a term commonly found in the criticism of the fantastic, generally designates an opening—whether rabbit hole or wardrobe or borderline or cave or tornado—from one reality to another. Portals are *penetrated* by children or heroes in their quest, beyond the fields we know, for a world consubstantial with the heart's desire. As Marlow's tale begins we learn that the liminal beings who inhabit the Whited Sepulchre of Brussels have given him the OK to cross the borderline into the unknown, and that initially he thinks of the Congo as a vast gate or portal into the great darkness he thinks he wishes to plumb. Though, in his telling of the tale, Marlow mutes and ironizes this frame of mind of his, it is pretty clear that the beginning of his long trip up the Congo toward Kurtz follows a basic fantasy story: that of the quest undertaken through a portal. Soon, however, a hovering "insecurity" of language cues us to suspect that this initial story may be under serious attack, that a darker model of story may be overwriting it.

Horror and Fantasy, as grammars of story, can be understood as mirror reversals. Such a mirror stands athwart "Heart of Darkness," and when Marlow passes through that mirror he passes into a black Wonderland, and Portal becomes a Cloaca down which the raw world pours. Marlow's Quest becomes its mirror opposite, a Hook (the hook that gaffs the fish), which compels him to continue, keelhauling him on the rind of the world (the world the Congo exhales) till he drowns. The only way Marlow can avoid fatal immersion (by now the world has literally infected him with a fever) is to leap up the Cloaca like a spawning salmon, toward the dark within which the demon twin resides. The oneiric plunges of elision which mark the storyline of "Heart of Darkness" might have been more fruitfully registered by critics if they had been able to understand without derision that the profound metamorphosis in Marlow comes about through a reversal of story type. E. M. Forster famously derided as contentless the language Conrad uses here to trace this deep transfiguration of his tale. The truth, of course, is that Conrad's language here is not a meditation but a grammar, and that certain tools of understanding will find that grammar invisible.

Terms useful for analysis, like Portal/Cloaca, are of course grossly simpler than the works they cartoon. But they are pointers. It does seem, for instance, that something like a Portal/Cloaca transformation—some systole and diastole of interchange between optimism and pessimism, between conquering and being overwhelmed, between fix and consequence, initiative and atrocity, Gesamptkunstwerk and the Absurd, Papa Joe and Koba the Dread—does singularly mark the last century, which is the second century to be so singed with time that its inhabitants could think of the world as an engine pounding. So the grammar of "Heart of Darkness" prefigures the rhythm of the century it opens; deep within that grammar, or so it still seems to readers in 2002, lies a body English of the terrible anxiety of time (at least one story assembled here in *Conjunctions*—John Crowley's "The Girlhood of Shakespeare's Heroines," see below—can be understood as a tragic description of the unwriting of Portal in a lamed world, as though Marlow's boat had simply sunk). Nor is it at all strange that the genres of the fantastic of the West refract, with allergenic sensitivity, this pulsation of the world, for they were created when it began to turn, round about 1800. The fantastic in the West is time's child. The genres of the fantastic—and stories like "Heart of Darkness," whose shape is the shape of the openness to the world of the Ocean of Story—have ever since taken the world's pulse.

Twins, or Doubles, or Shadows, are the wake of that pulse. In horror stories—and in tales like "Heart of Darkness," which evoke the modes of horror—they represent a locus for some original part of our lives that remains in situ when the world turns so fast we leave something of ourselves behind, something torn from us unfinished. Twins haunt texts, therefore, whose ostensible heroes—like Marlow before the Congo turns on him and he must learn to swim, or Dr. Jekyll, or Dorian Gray, or Miles Teagarden in *If You Could See Me Now* (1977) by Peter Straub, or Humbert Humbert, or the witch in China Miéville's "Familiar," another *Conjunctions* story—are hollow men.

This sense of a hollowness surrounding an inner self is, I think, modern. It is a modern experience to be bifurcated by the world into mask and twin, to experience *évolué* guilt for no greater sin than that of attempting to match the beat of a world which will not stop. Any litany of malaises of twentieth-century Western man—anomie, estrangement, alienation, one-dimensionality, all the hysterias (from consumerism to recovered memories), dissociations of sensibility (including the dissociative calving off of mimetic literature from its amniotic twin, the fantastic that surrounds it), the lonely crowd, vastation, the death of God—adds up in the end to a statement that, in the end, it is impossible to keep up. The approaches to "Heart of Darkness" that we have been describing all point to this anxiety of ceaselessness, this amnesia consequent upon fracture. The literatures of the fantastic—which were born in 1800 or so, when time began to split us, and which "Heart of Darkness" taps—are topiary growths in the pulse of time: they are the body English of what has happened to us.

Under rubrics of this sort, a critic of the fantastic in literature might approach a text not normally interpreted as a citizen of the Ocean of Story. For it does seem clear that Conrad—at least in 1899—was as opportunistic as any great artist in his choice of ways to tell. The artistic creed he first published as a preface to the magazine release in 1897 of *The Nigger of the "Narcissus,"* and republished in 1902, seems anomalous in this frame of understanding, or perhaps it is "Heart of Darkness" itself which is anomalous in his career. Certainly it's the case that a phrase like "before all, to make you see," by seeming to restrict evocation to the mundane (as Wolfe notes in "Malebolge"), does little to describe the author's attempts, in "Heart of Darkness," to give tongue to an equipoise which limns the abyss of Kurtz. It is a credo whose republication three years after "Heart of Darkness" reads more like retraction than advocacy.

The creed won in the end, however, and Conrad retracted into the English gentleman of *Chance*—an odyssey of diminishment that took from us a writer of greatness—and we are left with a masterwork whose gravamen, in the eyes of those whose task it has been to marshall our understanding, is either illicit or indetectable.

But it is not only "Heart of Darkness" that has been misprisioned or ignored through the critical exclusion of the fantastic from the organon of literature, an exclusion which fatally slights the centrality of story in any wider understanding of what it is we do when we tell. By creating a restrictive paling around the residue which is deemed real and therefore tellable, the literary critics of the past two centuries have created a canon so focused on the simple end of the spectrum of story that most of world literature has vanished out of ken.

The operators of this exclusionary theoretic, in terms of which texts respond to the world the way a snail responds to salt, have signally failed to understand the underlying project of the genres of the fantastic over the past two centuries, the centuries of world change and species anxiety. As a whole, to put it into a nutshell, the project of the fantastic since 1800, a project which underlies the pulp and the junk as well as "Heart of Darkness," the meretricious and the mechanically repetitive as well as (say) Stephen Spielberg's hugely misunderstood *AI* (2001), is that of making storyable our profound anxieties about a world whose claws are Time.

2. "HURRY, HURRY, THE EARTH'S TURNING"

So we were wrong at the beginning. "Heart of Darkness" is more than a running start into the cusp country we inhabit here in 2002 like blind men in the belly of an elephant: "Heart of Darkness" is a twin of now. If it were reprinted here in *Conjunctions,* it would segue seamlessly into (say) Neil Gaiman's "October in the Chair," a Club Story in which the months forgather to tell one another seasonal tales, each tale telling the nature of the month who tells it as the great year turns; or (say) Kelly Link's "Lull," a tale which might be described as Club Story wrought to its uttermost. The first half is constructed as an immensely complex frame—as the first half of a palindrome—that introduces the second half, which comprises a tale told to the forgathered Auditors by a woman who usually does telephone sex at four bucks a minute, but who also does Story if asked. Into the shattered lull of the lives depicted in the frame, this unseen voice of Story tells a tale (which contains further tales within tales) that seems to reverse the stalled lives of the characters who witness its telling, but in the end does not: for the figure of the palindrome at the heart of the working of the overall tale is a figure with no exit, and the cast of "Lull" is in hell.

John Crowley's "The Girlhood of Shakespeare's Heroines," which we've already mentioned, might also share a book with "Heart of Darkness," for both are tales dependent for their outcomes on a handling of Equipoise (as is M. John Harrison's "Entertaining Angels Unawares," which hovers between two angels of death, the fearless boss who dreams of decapitating whole populations but whose life is a giving, and the protagonist, the wannabe angel whose ungivingness fails to qualify him to share the dream). Where Conrad keeps his tale open as to the nature of Kurtz—who cannot therefore be decided upon, so that the oneiric latency of the tale, its hovering between the mimetic and the fantastic, the personal and the world-historical, remains uncensorably witnessable—Crowley closes his novella to any final possibility that there may be more than one story of the world, that there may be a story of the world in which story is true. "The Girlhood of Shakespeare's Heroines" closes into a tragedy of aftermath almost as soon as its Kurtz figure, the festival sponsor whose name cannot be remembered after he evanesces from view, poisonously suggests that Shakespeare is nothing but Mask, that the true hidden progenitor of the magic words about to play on stage is Bacon the Twin. This litany is poisonous, almost devilish, because it is literally *false:* it takes from the narrator and his young lover in 1959 a world athrum with storyline, reducing sense of potential—that Equipoise—into a world of false codes, lamings of Story. That the protagonists of the story are themselves gallant only intensifies the vastation they inhabit as their time closes. Hurry, the narrator thinks, contemplating his lover's adult attempts to recapture through photographs a world unspoliated by code death: hurry, hurry, the earth's turning. But the earth continues to turn, like a clock. This is genuinely tragic; but it is a rendering of tragedy that can best—perhaps only—be understood when it is understood *how* "The Girlhood of Shakespeare's Heroines" is not a fantasy.

For if there is an ascertainable deep structure to twentieth-century fantasy, it is something that Crowley bids farewell to in his novella. What we now recognize as fantasy (as distinguished from other modes of the fantastic like supernatural fiction or horror) was created out of the wound of aftermath of World War I by a wide range of writers—from E. R. Eddison to J. R. R. Tolkien to C. S. Lewis to Hugh Lofting to David Lindsay and beyond—who shared little but a need to close the wound. For them, fantasy begins in suture. From their works as a whole, and from the works of those influenced by them, comes a sense of the underlying movement of fantasy as a loosening of bondage—history loosening into story—a process I've found convenient to articulate as a four-part discourse, one that fantasy texts themselves, in the flesh, translate into storyable form. The first two terms of that discourse constitute a negotiation with history: which impinges upon the world of the story as a sense of Wrongness (which in seasonal terms can be understood as the end of Summer), and metastasizes into a cancerous Thinning (which is Autumn) of the created land. Thinning—which is often manifested in the tale as a kind of cultural and personal amnesia: which is the bondage of losing who we were—often takes up much of the action of typical fantasy novels (genre fantasy series, set in rigid Fantasylands, never really pass beyond Thinning), and conveys an affect of terrible, impoverishing, senseless affray, rather like trench warfare. But then—in No Man's Land, in the Waste Land—the Story speaks at last, rescue is nigh, light at the end of the tunnel, and the story opens into Recognition (Winter), where we learn who we are, and what Story is telling us. Recognition itself exfoliates finally into Return (Spring), but relatively few fantasy stories give much space to achieved pastoral, perhaps because just governance (like utopias) can hardly be told at all. Twentieth-century fantasy, in other words, is a literature of refusal. It is subversive. It is a counter-story to the world. It tells us that history has gone *wrong,* and must be left behind, or we are lost. Fantasy in this light is an escape (as J. R. R. Tolkien suggested in 1947) from prison.

"The Girlhood of Shakespeare's Heroines," like "Lull," ends in prison; no loosening is possible. A revisionist fantasy like Andy Duncan's "The Big Rock Candy Mountain" reverses the pattern of discourse: its protagonist escapes the just governance of his 1930s Paradise, and undergoes a Recognition in reverse, discovering who he was in the world of time; only at that point, before tuberculosis thins him stone dead, is he storied back to bliss. A fantasy like Elizabeth Hand's "The Least Trumps" may share a starting point with Crowley—a recognizable world populous with characters drawn with a loving attentiveness more frequently associated with "realist" texts—but translates itself almost imperceptibly into a tale that illuminates the discourse of fantasy, for its protagonist recovers her lost Story by tattooing it literally onto her own skin: an extremely neat rendering of the act of Recognition.

But Hand has not written a fantasy of Recognition because it was *expected* of her, any more than Crowley was expected to describe a world that becomes tragic, that cannot be retold; or Gaiman to conceive the reverse, to imagine Story as the key to season; or Link to create a loop out of horror, out of the raw materials of the mundane, a house of mirrors with no exit; or Duncan to create, on the other hand, a loop which becomes rescue. If any of these stories obey any expectations, they do so by choice. The whole range of works offered here in *Conjunctions* demonstrates the ruthless opportunism of the writers of 2002 when it comes to deciding how to tell, when it comes to choosing how to conjunct with the pulse of the world.

The extremes are great. Karen Joy Fowler's "The Further Adventures of the Invisible Man" invokes the fantastic only to refuse it, in order (I'd guess) to simplify the task of understanding a protagonist already overburdened with story. Peter Straub's "Little Red's Tango," on the other hand, could be understood to begin in the mundane world—and a critic of nonfantastic literature might readily understand the movement of the story as a gradual intensification of its metaphorical content, and read the tale as mundane to the end. But years ago, Samuel R. Delany argued with great cogency that the reading protocols of the fantastic demanded that we be open to the *literal:* that in the literatures of the fantastic a cigar is what the story says it is. Sometimes it is only a cigar. Sometimes it is a spaceship. Sometimes it is a stogie in God's mouth. If the cigar inhales us, it is a Portal; if it drowns us in contaminants, it is a Cloaca. If it occupies two worlds, but remains a cigar in both, it is a conjunction. What the cigar almost never is, is a metaphor. "Little Red's Tango" is, in other words, exactly what Straub tells us it is, in a form of telling (the story reads as a parody of scripture) that underlines the literalness of his intent: Little Red is literally a Christ of our days, a benign hemorrhage of giving, a being who decreases entropy. His substance, which is explicitly bread and wine, feeds us.

There is more. "Little Red's Tango," after our reading of the literal tale, gives us more: the pleasure of the text is markedly enhanced when we understand that the story evokes a central dynamic of horror—a transfer of substance from the hollow to the hungry—but is itself not horror. Our joy in understanding that Little Red is plenitude comes from our knowledge of the alternatives Straub chooses not to follow, that he has written a tale of counterhorror. Like so many stories of the present era, "Little Red's Tango" is a conversation with the Ocean of Story: in a world of convulsive instability, the world it is the task of the fantastic to make storyable, it knows its place. A more orthodox transfer of substance governs the action of China Miéville's "Familiar," though with the twist that the familiar is consubstantial with its host—the Twin consubstantial with its Mask—so that when the abandoned familiar gains ontological conglomeration by literally hollowing its maker into a pattern of holes penetrating a few "handspans of sternum, inches of belly," this transfer of substance is revealed as a deep pun, an ideogram of the nature of the hunger of the Twin since long before Hyde. Like "Little Red's Tango," like every story assembled in *Conjunctions,* "Familiar" is itself a kind of pun: an autonomous story that has not ever been told before, that is, at the same time, a conversation with siblings.

Clues to the depth of that conversation surface throughout the texts on view. Gene Wolfe's "Knight," for instance—which comprises a substantial excerpt from a long novel to be published next year—may seem at first glance to inhabit a straightforward medieval secondary world with seers and swords, just another Arthurized Version of fantasyland. What we soon discover, of course, is that the Land into which Able of the High Heart irrupts from his childhood on Earth resembles fantasyland only superficially, and for just a few pages; and that the Portal Able reaches the Land through is no run-of-the-mill Portal. The Land, we discover, is molten with metamorphosis, and on our learning that it stands fourth in a sevenfold hierarchy of superimposed realities, we begin to think we may be conversing with the Cabbala, with something (we think vaguely) hermetic. And the Portal—which Wolfe first describes in an introductory chapter not printed here—remains part of the flow of the story, invisible but immanent, a continuing grammar for the continuance of Able upon his course. At this point, keeping in mind that Portal sufficiently elongated becomes Pilgrimage, we notice other things as well. The oddly named inhabitants of the Land whom Able meets—Scaur and Ravd and the others—seem clearly to have been set in place in order for him to meet them; they are vividly real on the page, but they are also *exemplary*. So the seeming transparency of telling of "Knight" is a snare, and—like any other tale here assembled—cannot be read as innocent of the Ocean of Story in which it bathes. Like any conscious work of art in the literatures of the fantastic in 2002, it is a conversation: which may be enough to go on till the full tale unfolds. But one can make an interim guess. "Knight" is a pilgrimage through a clade of worlds toward the truth, a progress which subjects Able's knightliness to a series of tests and temptations to linger. The text that "Knight" seems most conversant with, at this moment, seems to be David Lindsay's *A Voyage to Arcturus* (1920). But the conversation will not stop there, though we do.

The stories touched upon here were convenient to the arguments suggested. If those arguments had been uttered differently—for there is more than one story of the world, more than one way to address the natures of the world—every other story in the book could have been as ruthlessly cited for grist: because they are all conversant. The final lesson of any examination of the fantastic is connection. Touch one story and we touch them all.

Touch David Lindsay, back in the maelstrom of Europe between the wars, and we touch Joseph Conrad, back before the drowning he saw coming down. For we are touching the Ocean of Story. These two speak in different voices, with different ends in view, but they join in the project of the past two hundred years in the West, that of fishing for ways to tell us what is happening, here and now, as the daily unprecedented world turns that we inherit. And so here we are, us and the world, beyond the pale. So let us make some talk together, us and the world, and our tales witnessing.

NOTES ON CONTRIBUTORS

JONATHAN CARROLL's latest novel is *White Apples* (Tor Books). Among his other novels are *Sleeping in Flame* (Vintage), *The Land of Laughs* (St. Martin's Press), and *Bones of the Moon* (Century Hutchinson Limited).

JOHN CLUTE's recent books include a novel, *Appleseed* (Tor Books), and a collection of reviews and essays, *Look at the Evidence* (John D. Barry Design).

JOHN CROWLEY is the author of *Little, Big* (Orion Publishing Group), a family chronicle; the *Aegypt* series (Bantam Doubleday Dell), which so far consists of three volumes; and *The Translator* (William Morrow). He teaches fiction writing at Yale.

ANDY DUNCAN is the winner of two World Fantasy Awards and a Sturgeon Award, and is the author of *Beluthahatchie and Other Stories* (Golden Gryphon). His "Daddy Mention and the Monday Skull" will appear in *Mojo: Conjure Stories*, edited by Nalo Hopkinson and forthcoming from Warner Aspect Books. Also forthcoming is an anthology he edited with F. Brett Cox, *Crossroads: Southern Stories of the Fantastic* (Tor Books). He lives in Northport, Alabama.

KAREN JOY FOWLER is the author of *Sarah Canary* (Ballantine), *Black Glass* (Henry Holt), and, most recently, *Sister Noon* (Plume), and this year was a nominee for the PEN/Faulkner Award.

NEIL GAIMAN's most recent book for adults is *American Gods* (William Morrow), which was awarded the 2002 Hugo Award for best novel, the 2002 Bram Stoker Award for best novel, and the 2002 UK SFX Award. His most recent book for all ages is *Coraline* (HarperChildrens), and his longest work is the *Sandman* (1988–1996), collected in ten graphic novels (DC Comics).

JOE HALDEMAN's books include *The Forever War* (Avon), *Forever Peace* (Berkley Publishing Group), and *Worlds* (Victor Gollancz). His new novel, *Guardian*, excerpted here, combines science fiction, historical fiction, and magic realism.

ELIZABETH HAND has written seven novels, including *The Affair of the Necklace* (Harper Entertainment) and *Walking on the Moon* (Harper Mass Market Paperbacks), as well as the forthcoming *Mortal Love* and a short story collection, *Last Summer at Mars Hill* (Harper Prism). She is a regular contributor to the *Washington Post Book World, VLS*, and *Fantasy and Science Fiction*, among other journals. Her fiction has received numerous awards, most recently an Individual Artist's Fellowship from the Maine Arts Commission/NEA. She lives on the coast of Maine.

M. JOHN HARRISON is the author of eight novels and four collections of short stories, including *Climbers, Travel Arrangements* (both from Victor Gollancz), and the forthcoming *Things That Never Happen* (Nightshade Books). His most recent novel is *Light* (Victor Gollancz). He lives in London and reviews fiction for the *Guardian* and the *Times Literary Supplement.*

NALO HOPKINSON, originally from the Caribbean, now lives in Canada. She is the author of the novels *Brown Girl in the Ring* (Warner Books), *Midnight Robber* (Aspect), and *Griffonne* (Warner Books), and of the short story collection *Skin Folk* (Warner Books). She recently edited an anthology of short fiction, *Mojo: Conjure Stories,* forthcoming next spring from Warner Aspect Books.

JOHN KESSEL's books include the novels *Good News from Outer Space* (St. Martin's Press) and *Corrupting Dr. Nice* (Tor Books), and the short story collection *The Pure Product* (Tor Books). He is the winner of the 1982 Nebula Award for his novella "Another Orphan," and is director of the creative writing program at North Carolina State University.

JONATHAN LETHEM is the author of *Gun, With Occasional Music* (Tor Books) and four other novels, including *Motherless Brooklyn* (Vintage), which won the National Book Critics Circle Award. He lives in Brooklyn.

KELLY LINK's collection, *Stranger Things Happen* (Small Beer Press), was a Salon Book of the Year and a *Village Voice* Favorite.

CHINA MIÉVILLE has written several short stories and the novels *King Rat* (Tor Books), *Perdido Street Station,* which won the Arthur C. Clarke Award and the British Fantasy Award, and *The Scar* (both by Del Rey). He lives and works in London.

JAMES MORROW's most recent series of novels, the Godhead Trilogy, comprises *Towing Jehovah,* winner of the World Fantasy Award, *Blameless in Abaddon,* a *New York Times* Notable Book of the Year, and *The Eternal Footman* (all published by Harvest Books), finalist for the Grand Prix de l'Imaginaire. His current project is *The Last Witchfinder,* a novel about the birth of the scientific world view.

PATRICK O'LEARY's first novel, *Door Number Three* (Tor Books), was chosen by *Publishers Weekly* as one of the best novels of the year, and his second novel, *The Gift,* also published by Tor Books, was a finalist for the World Fantasy Award and the Mythopoeic Award. His collection, *Other Voices, Other Doors,* was published by Fairwood Press, and his third novel, *The Impossible Bird,* appeared this year from Tor Books.

PAUL PARK's books include *Soldiers of Paradise* (Arbor House), *Sugar Rain, The Cult of Loving Kindness* (both from William Morrow), *Celestis* (Tor Books), *The Gospel of Corax* (Soho Press), *Three Marys* (Cosmos Press), and a collection of stories, *If Lions Could Speak* (also by Cosmos Press).

PETER STRAUB is the author of fourteen novels, among them *Ghost Story* (Pocket Books), *Koko, The Throat* (both from Signet), and *Mr. X* (Ballantine Books), and two collections of shorter fiction.

GAHAN WILSON's cartoons appear regularly in *Playboy* and the *New Yorker*, among other periodicals. His most recent books are *The Cleft and Other Odd Tales* (Tor Books) and *Gahan Wilson's Gravediggers' Party* (forthcoming from iBooks/Simon & Schuster). His cartoons are also featured in *Gahan Wilson's Year of Weird 2003 Block Calendar* (Andrews McMeel Publishing).

GARY K. WOLFE is the author of several books on science fiction and fantasy, most recently *Harlan Ellison: The Edge of Forever* (Ohio State University Press), with Ellen Weil. He is professor of humanities and English at Roosevelt University, and is a contributing editor of *Locus* magazine.

GENE WOLFE has written numerous short stories and books, most recently *On Blue's Waters, In Green's Jungles, Return to the Whorl,* and *Strange Travelers* (all Tor Books). He also has received many awards, including three World Fantasy Awards, one of them for Life Achievement; two Nebula Awards; and the Chicago Foundation for Literature Award.

Why we published two new books by Carol Emshwiller

Because she's one of our favorite writers and we kept buying her books to give to friends. Her novel *Carmen Dog* has found fans in extraordinary places, from *The New York Times,* ("an inspired feminist fable. . . . A wise and funny book") to *Entertainment Weekly* ("a first novel that combines the cruel humor of *Candide* with the allegorical panache of *Animal Farm*") to *Penthouse:* "Carol Emshwiller tells the truths of feminism circuitously, brilliantly and painlessly in *Carmen Dog*. . . . coated in the outrageous imagination and gentle hilarity of this book, the truths are already in the system and working before the reader knows they have been swallowed."

High praise. But who is Carol Emshwiller? A writer friend says, jokingly, "She's a writer's writer's writer." Carol is 81 years old. She grew up in Michigan and France, studied art and music, drove an ambulance during World War II, and toured Europe on a motorbike with her husband, the artist Emsh—Carol was the model for many of the pulp magazine and book covers he painted in the '50s. She started writing when her children were young—she once described climbing into their playpen in order to have a space of her own to write in. Between 1975 and 1991 she published three genre-defying collections: *Joy in Our Cause, Verging on the Pertinent,* and *The Start of the End of It All.* She wrote two Westerns: *Ledoyt,* which Ursula K. Le Guin called a "fierce and tender portrait of a girl growing up fierce and tender; a sorrowful, loving portrait of a man whose talent is for love and sorrow; a western, an unsentimental love story, an unidealized picture of the American past, a tough, sweet, painful, truthful novel," and *Leaping Man Hill.*

We jumped at the chance to publish Carol's new novel, *The Mount* (already in its second printing), and collection, *Report to the Men's Club and Other Stories* ("Elliptical, funny and stylish, they are for the most part profoundly unsettling,"said *Time Out New York*).

The Mount received a starred review in *Publishers Weekly:* ". . . this poetic, funny and above all humane novel deserves to be read and cherished as a fundamental fable for our material-minded times." Then Paul Ingram, of Prairie Lights Bookstore emailed us: "Nearly every sentence is simultaneously hilarious, prophetic, and disturbing. This person needs to be really, really famous." Lastly, *The Boston Globe* wrote about Carol, "She has been for more than a decade now one of the finest writers in the United States and one of the most original. That last word may be the tip-off. Her work is undefinable. She is a feminist writer who adores men, a literary artist who often prefers to work in (or at least springboard off) fantastic literature, an experimentalist anchored firmly to plot and character . . ."

Carol Emshwiller's books are available from all good bookstores, the usual online sources (including our website), and from 800-345-6665, fax 603-357-2073.

The Mount	1-931520-03-8	$16
Report to the Men's Club and Other Stories	1-931520-02-X	$16
Kelly Link, *Stranger Things Happen*	1-931520-00-3	$16
Ray Vukcevich, *Meet Me in the Moon Room*	1-931520-01-1	$16

Small Beer Press, 360 Atlantic Ave., PMB 132, Brooklyn, NY 11217 www.lcrw.net

U N D E R W O R D S

Perspectives on Don DeLillo's *Underworld*

EDITED BY JOSEPH DEWEY, STEVEN G. KELLMAN, AND IRVING MALIN

This collection of thirteen essays marks the first in-depth examination of one of the most acclaimed and highly anticipated works of American literature of the last twenty years. Don DeLillo's 1997 masterwork *Underworld* was immediately recognized as a landmark novel, not only in the long career of one of America's most distinguished novelists but as well in the ongoing evolution of the postmodern novel and in the achievement of fin-de-millennium American literature. Vast in scope, intricately organized, and densely allusive, the text is nothing less than a cultural biography of postwar America, touching as it does on themes as diverse as environmental politics, nuclear apocalypse, the deep influence of film and television, the cultural positioning of sports, the disturbing psychology of contemporary violence, the intricate patternings of language, and the cultural role of the artist. That it does so without sacrificing the traditional elements of narrative—an engrossing plot and nuanced characters—makes the text an extraordinary achievement.

This collection brings together lively readings from both new and established voices in critical and cultural studies. These essays are organized into a pattern of expanding investigation, beginning with a close reading of a single pattern of images within the text, then moving to essays that examine the novel within DeLillo's larger catalog of fiction, and then essays that suggest important parallels not only to works of authors contemporary with DeLillo but ties to canonical works and authors of American literature. Finally, the closing essays audaciously explore the novel's achievement using baseball, the films of Stanley Kubrick, and the tradition of comedy that dates back to Dante. Such diversity only begins to suggest the stunning levels of interpretative possibilities at which this mesmerizing text exists. These essays mark an important first step in engaging the full achievement of this remarkable work.

Hardcover, 6 x 9 inches, works cited, notes, index, 220 pages
ISBN 0-87413-785-3, Price $39.50 (University of Delaware Press)

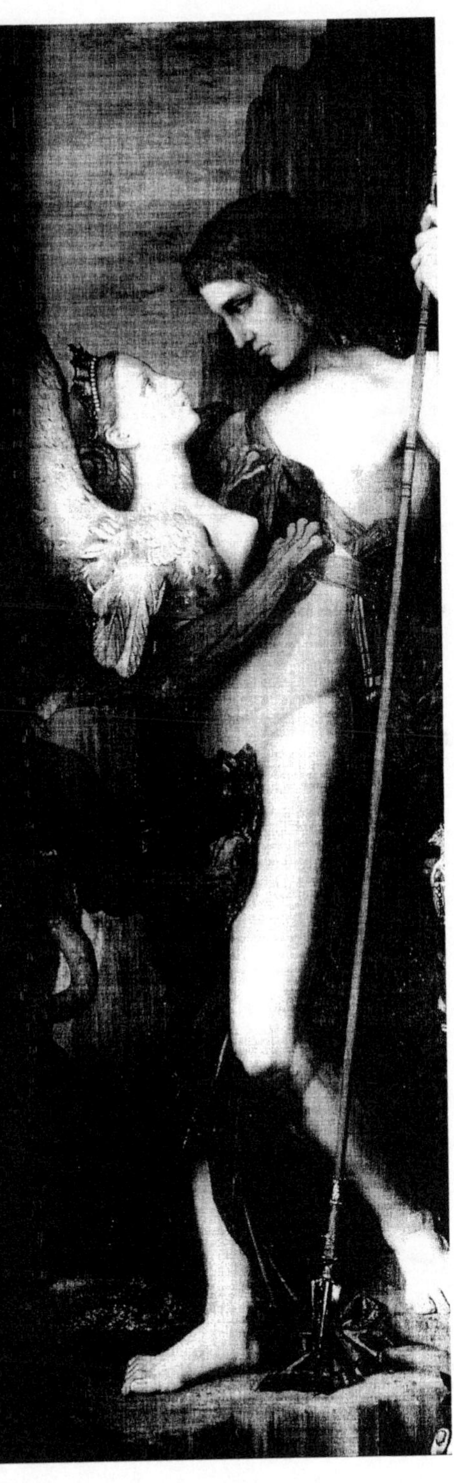